EPISTLE OF THE DAMNED

M. LEE MENDELSON

EPISTLE OF THE DAMNED

Cactus Moon Publications: Info@cactusmoonpublishing.com; http://www.cactusmoonpublishing.com

Book cover design: Cactus Moon Publications, LLC

ISBN: 978-0-9988932-9-7

This book is dedicated to my wonderful wife, Yvonne. Without your love, encouragement, and support this book would never have become a reality.

Acknowledgments

I would like to thank my wife, Yvonne, for all the inspiration and long nights sitting up with me and listening to all my ideas and giving your honest opinion. You steered me clear from some bad ideas. I would also like to thank all my family and friends who read my draft and encouraged me to move forward.

A huge shout out to Cactus Moon for accepting my work, and for believing in me. Big thanks go to Lily Woodmansee for her guidance and help throughout the process. And finally, I would like to thank my phenomenal editor, Andrea, for a job well done. She has an eagle eye, and her years of professional expertise were invaluable.

PROLOGUE

Predestined Recipient,

If you're reading this desperate correspondence, I implore you to take my words to heart. Please don't reject my story as mere fable without first granting me some considerations. If you think you've just happened upon this harrowing tale, be forewarned. It was by design.

You see, from the time I was a young man, I've been an advocate for true justice. I had always believed that if you did good, good would come back to you, trusting that what I did somehow mattered.

THE END

3:37 A.M., BOCA GRANDE SHORES, a peaceful upscale bedroom community on the West coast of Florida. It was a quiet night in the dispatch center of the Sheriff's Office when suddenly, "911, what is your emergency?"

A frail, desperate voice, clearly that of an elderly woman answered, "Yes, I can hear my neighbors screaming at each other. It sounds like they're having a terrible fight. I've never heard them fight like this before. I'm very worried. Can you please send someone right away?"

"What is your address, ma'am?"

"I live at 2700 Red Oak Circle."

"Is this a gated community?"

"Yes, it's the Mossy Hammock subdivision."

"Is there a gate code?"

"Yes, but there is a guard on duty at the main gate. In case he's not there, the code is star one-five-four-three-two. Please hurry! It sounds like it's getting worse."

"We have units en route to you at this time. Can you see anything?"

In an attempt to conceal her anxiety, the woman answered facetiously, "Honey, at my age I couldn't see anything even if it was light out. They sound like they're outside now. I'm too afraid to look."

"Yes ma'am, please stay inside. Will you stay on the line?"

"Yes, of course."

"What is your name, ma'am?"

"Beatrice Johansen."

"OK Mrs. Johansen, I'll stay on the line with you until the deputies arrive."

"Thank you."

"My pleasure."

Mike, a decorated deputy and ten-year veteran of the Sheriff's Office, was enjoying an unusually quiet night in Zone Four. Mike was conducting routine business checks when suddenly the radio crackled, "Four-thirteen and four-ninety-five respond to the area of 2700 Red Oak Circle for a possible domestic in progress, caller advised it appears to be intensifying, she's unsure if there are weapons involved, make contact with caller at 2700 Red Oak Circle."

Mike answered, "Four-thirteen en route from the Carson & Associates Law Firm."

Mike's backup, Steve Wilcox, a rookie with six months on his own since completing his field training, also responded, "Four-ninety-five en route from Tampa Trail and Palm Lane."

Mike recalled that Red Oak Circle was in Mossy Hammock. He was very familiar with this subdivision, since he had patrolled Zone Four for the previous three years. Mossy Hammock was an upscale community of high-end waterfront houses, home to executives and wealthy retirees. Mike thought, *I wonder if Old Joe's on duty.*

Joe McCallister, a night security guard at Mossy Hammock, was a retired New York City police officer. After losing his wife to cancer four years before, he had picked up the security job to keep from getting bored. Joe preferred the night shift and always had, even as a cop in the Big Apple.

When Mike arrived at the guard shack, he recognized that the guard on duty was Joe. On quiet nights, Mike would often visit Joe and swap cop stories. Joe was a tall, thin man in his sixties and it appeared that he had fallen asleep in his desk chair. Mike honked his horn, and Joe jumped up, rubbing his eyes. Mike smiled. He identified with how hard it was to stay awake on the graveyard shift, particularly when it was quiet. Joe lumbered to the door.

Mike, now chuckling to himself said, "Mornin', Joe. Didn't mean to wake you."

Joe countered in a gruff voice, "I wasn't sleeping, asshole. I was just checking my eyelids for leaks."

The two laughed briefly, and then Joe said, "What brings you around Mike—business, or just to screw with me?"

Mike replied, "We got a call from a Mrs. Johansen about a possible domestic."

"Old Lady Johansen . . . yeah, she's nice enough, kind of a busybody. She's always calling me about something she heard outside. To tell you the truth, I think she's trying to get me to come over. She lives alone in that big ol' house and she always wants me to come in for coffee."

Jokingly, Mike said, "Maybe you should court Ol' Lady Johansen."

"Don't think I haven't considered it, boy. But she might be a little *too* old, even for a geezer like me."

"Well, she called to say that she heard the neighbors screaming."

"Funny, she didn't call me tonight. Maybe it's legit. Watch your six. I haven't heard anything."

"How could you with all that snoring I heard pulling up?"

"Screw you! Get to work, ya prick!" Joe said as he opened the gate.

After a shorter than normal session of bantering, the two laughed, and Mike drove through.

Although he had been on hundreds of domestic-related calls in his tenure as a deputy, Mike knew that no two are ever alike. His training and experience had taught him to treat each one as a potentially deadly situation until proven otherwise. As he approached Red Oak Circle, Mike turned off the lights of his patrol car.

It was an uncharacteristically bright night. A three-quarter moon shone above in a clear, cloudless sky, creating a monochrome scene with a light blue hue, reminiscent of a black and white movie. Mike preferred patrolling on nights like this; stealthily driving, blacked out with the windows down, making use of all his senses. The November night air was remarkably cool and dry by Florida standards. An early cold front brought with it low humidity and temperatures in the low fifties.

Mike turned onto Red Oak Circle and reported "Four-thirteen arriving on scene," stopping his car four houses away from Mrs. Johansen's address. He knew this gave him a tactical advantage, allowing him to look and listen for danger as he drew closer to the scene. Before approaching the residence, Mike waited for his backup unit, knowing not to enter a potentially hazardous situation alone.

Shortly after his arrival, Mike heard over the radio, "Four-ninety-five on scene in the area."

Mike looked up to see the glow of Steve's headlights coming from around the corner, and with a brief radio transmission reminded him, "Four-ninety-five, kill your lights and park behind me." Steve complied and parked behind Mike's cruiser.

On the phone the dispatcher spoke, "Mrs. Johansen, the deputies are on scene, can you see them?"

"Let me look. I'll step outside. Oh yes, I see them."

"Okay, Mrs. Johansen. I'll let you speak to the deputies now.

Take care."

"Thank you, dear. Good night."

Mike and Steve exited their vehicles and closed the doors as quietly as possible. As the two walked toward Mrs. Johansen's house, Steve whispered, "What's up man? Been a quiet night so far, huh?"

Mike looked at him. "Rookie? Tell me you didn't just say the

"Q" word."

With an innocent grin, Steve said, "Oops, sorry."

"Damn F-N-G!"

As they approached, they could see Beatrice, a petite, 87-year-old, silver-haired woman wearing an elegant, flowing white robe. She was standing on her darkened front porch with a concerned look on her face.

When Mike and Steve got closer, she shouted in a shrill voice, "Over here, officers. I'm the one who called you!" Her voice cut through the crisp night air like a knife.

Afraid of losing his strategic edge, Mike took his right index finger and raised it to his now pursed lips, gesturing to Beatrice to speak softly.

Mike then approached Beatrice on her front porch. "Good morning, ma'am. Can you tell me what you heard?"

In a softer voice Beatrice said, "Well, I'm usually not a light sleeper, but tonight I woke up to the sound of a man and a woman screaming. It sounded like it was coming from that house." She pointed to the house across the street, 2701 Red Oak Circle. "They're usually such a nice, quiet couple. I

7

ordinarily wouldn't have heard anything, but I was sleeping with the windows cracked open. It sounded just awful. I was afraid they were going to get violent, but then it suddenly stopped just before you arrived. I've lived here for six years. After he retired, my late husband and I moved here from Long Island. He was the CEO of a brokerage firm. He was such a wonderful man, and generous. He always took good care of me . . ."

As Mrs. Johansen rambled on, Mike looked at Steve and rolled his eyes. Steve turned away to keep from laughing out loud.

" . . . miss him so much."

As she caught her breath, Mike quickly asked, "Have there been any other problems at that house that you know of?"

Beatrice replied, "Well, not since that nice couple moved in about a year ago. When my husband and I moved in, the house was vacant. About three months ago, late one night, I heard a siren and from my upstairs window I saw an ambulance in front of their house. Of course, I didn't know why they were there and I didn't see any police cars. A few weeks later, I was playing bridge with some of my girlfriends at the club house, and my friend Sophie told me that she heard that the wife had lost the baby. That was why the ambulance

took her away. But other than that, I can't recall."

Mike, seizing the opportunity to get away, said, "Okay Mrs. Johansen, thank you. We're going to get going now."

Beatrice began, "It's been quiet for several minutes now so maybe it was nothing."

Mike reassured her, saying, "I'm sure you're right, but we'll check it out just to make certain."

Relieved, Beatrice thanked Mike for his quick response and polite manner.

Mike, having avoided any major reports so far that night, was anxious to get back to his peaceful shift and write this off as another "bullshit" call.

Mike and Steve cautiously approached the house, a large, beautifully landscaped, two-story modern contemporary design home. There was what appeared to be a brand-new luxury SUV parked in the circular driveway, suggesting to Mike that someone should be home. The house was dark, with no glow of lights inside or out.

Mike told Steve to stand behind the left pillar on the porch as they neared the large double front doors.

"Watch that big window, and keep your eyes out for any movement." Mike was referring to what appeared to be the living room window, a large pane of plate glass to the right of the double doors. The curtains were drawn open, providing an unobstructed view inside the residence due to the exceptionally bright moonlight.

Mike rang the doorbell and took several steps back away from the door, standing behind the pillar on the right, shielding himself from any unexpected surprise at the door. From this vantage point, Mike could also see inside the living room. Neither Mike nor Steve saw anyone inside. After what seemed like several minutes, with no answer and no apparent activity inside, Mike rang the doorbell again. Again, no answer.

"What do you think, Stevie Boy?"

"I don't think they want to talk to us."

"I think you're right. Let's walk around the house and make sure we don't miss anything."

Mike and Steve walked around the outside of the residence, and neither of them found anything out of the ordinary.

"Four-thirteen to Dispatch, be advised that we are getting no answer at the door, nothing located. Make sure I'm primary, and show both units in service."

"Dispatch copy, four-thirteen."

"Well, Steve, I'll take care of the report. Thanks for the backup.

You got lucky this time with that "Q" word thing."

"I know, sorry."

Smiling, Mike said, "The night isn't over, though this better be it."

Steve laughed, "I hope so. Be safe, brother."

The two fist-bumped and Steve walked back toward his car.

Mike could see that Beatrice was still standing on her front porch. Hopeful he could avoid a lengthy dialogue, he reluctantly chose to make one last contact with her to reassure her that everything was fine.

Suddenly, out of the deafening silence, there erupted a bloodcurdling shriek from the quiet house which Mike had just walked away from, confident that all was well.

"I LOVE YOU! NO, DON'T! OH MY GOD! PLEASE NO!!!!"

Mike whirled around. As he did, he saw a bright flash looking like the strobe of a camera in a dark room, illuminating the large plate glass window of that beautiful house. With the flash came a single, thunderous "BOOM."

Mike's experience and training instantly took over. Instinctively, he drew his weapon and took cover behind the trunk of a large oak tree in Beatrice's front yard.

Taking a quick inventory of himself first, he then looked and saw Steve, who had almost made it to his car, standing in the middle of the road. He appeared to be paralyzed with uncertainty.

The senior, more experienced Mike called out, "STEVE, GET YOUR RIFLE AND TAKE COVER!" Mike then turned and cried out, "MRS. JOHANSEN, GET INSIDE YOUR HOUSE!"

Steve snapped to and reacted to Mike's commands. He ran to his trunk and retrieved his AR-15 rifle. He then took cover behind his patrol car.

"FOUR-THIRTEEN DISPATCH, SHOT FIRED, SHOT FIRED FROM 2701 RED OAK CIRCLE, REQUEST IMMEDIATE BACKUP, BE ADVISED WE HAVE A SINGLE SHOT INSIDE THE RESIDENCE!"

"Dispatch to four-thirteen, copy shot fired."

The once quiet radio now sparkled to life. "Dispatch to four-oh-three, four-oh-nine, four-twenty-two, four-thirty-seven, Supervisor six, Canine seven, respond to 2701 Red Oak Circle for a reported shot fired."

From the report, Mike could tell it had been a large caliber weapon that he'd heard, probably a shotgun or rifle. All units reported en route. Mike could now collect his thoughts.

He rapidly assessed. *Am I okay? Check. Is Steve okay? Check. Is Mrs. Johansen okay? Check. Help coming? Check.* In the distance, Mike could hear the sounds of sirens. *The cavalry is coming!*

In what seemed like an eternity, but in reality was only a span of a few seconds, Mike had run his checklist and was satisfied he was ready to continue.

11

His thoughts were suddenly interrupted by the sound of the same female voice piercing the silence.

Following the sound of her screams, Mike heard, "OH MY GOD! OH MY GOD, HE'S DEAD! HE'S DEAD! HELP ME, HELP ME!"

Mike took a deep breath and looked out from behind his sacred cover, seeing the silhouette of a woman running from the big double doors of the house. She appeared to be wearing only a sheer nightie and was still screaming.

Mike barked into his radio, "Steve, get up here and cover me!"

Steve swiftly moved up to the big oak tree and Mike instructed him to provide cover as he attempted to assist the woman.

Steve pointed his rifle at the house across the street, finger on the trigger, sweat seeping from his forehead. This was the real deal, what he had trained for. Adrenaline coursed through his young veins like a pyroclastic flow through the streets of Pompeii when Mt. Vesuvius erupted in AD 79.

Mike stepped out from the safety of his precious oak sanctuary to reveal himself to the panic-stricken woman.

"Ma'am, come over to me! Quickly!"

When she saw that Mike was a deputy, she ran hysterically toward him. He grabbed her, and pulled her behind the tree.

The woman was inconsolable. Mike tried to get information out of her, but to no avail.

"Is there anyone else in the house?"

"HE'S DEAD! HE'S DEAD! OH MY GOD, HE'S DEAD!" is all she kept repeating.

Mike could see that Steve was motionless, still in a perfect cover position.

"Steve, you good?"

"Yeah brother, I got this shit."

Mike and Steve held their position until the arrival of backup units.

Confident that Steve had his back, Mike continued to console the distraught woman. He didn't see any injuries on her, and in an act of compassion, took off his light jacket to provide her some cover in the unusually chilly Florida air.

The night rolled on. The scene had changed. It was now 6:30 a.m. and the sun was rising. Mike, now a half hour past the time when his shift was supposed to have ended, was still on the scene. The woman was at the police station being interviewed. The yellow police line tape was stretched across the street, and the scene was abuzz with activity. Half-dressed onlookers, the "uh oh" squad as Mike called them, stood in their yards in their robes, sipping cups of coffee and talking amongst themselves, speculating about what had occurred. Detectives were on the scene, interviewing neighbors. Crime scene technicians were photographing the area and the press was there to collect their dirty laundry.

The SWAT team had arrived on the scene to clear the house. In addition to his regular duties as a deputy, Mike was also a member of the SWAT team. From the information provided by the woman at the station, the command staff was confident that they were dealing with a suicide and that there were no other shooters. No one had yet entered the house. The SWAT team deployed a remote-control robot with a camera. The commanders watching the grainy video verified that the victim was deceased. Due to the limitations of the robot, the team was necessary to clear the rest of this large house to make sure there were no other victims.

The dawning light brought forth a new perspective, and as they approached the now open front double doors, Mike thought the house was even more beautiful than he had recalled. He had previously taken note of this house on his routine patrols at night, but never had cause to deal with the people inside.

As the team approached the house, Mike noted that the doors were beautiful carved mahogany that accented appealingly with the latte color of the rest of the house. By the light of day he could see the large plate glass window. What was once clear was now beclouded by a large smudge, clearly blood. Upon entering the residence, Mike was immediately overcome by a convoluted array of odors. His olfactory senses were nearly overwhelmed, and he had to swallow hard to keep from vomiting.

Since childhood, Mike had always had a weak stomach when it came to smells. The ghastly aroma of blood hung heavy in the air, with a thick, humid feel. It felt like a mid-July afternoon in town after a heavy rain, when the sun comes out immediately following. The smell reminded him of the summer he spent with his Uncle John in Tennessee. John was a butcher, and Mike worked with him in his shop. The odor of blood was always in the air, and Mike grew to hate the heavy, iron-like smell. Now, the stench of blood combined with that of gunpowder, cigarettes, alcohol and shit produced a nauseating bouquet.

"Shit? Why in God's name am I smelling shit?"

After entering through the vestibule of the grand home, the team turned the corner and entered the living room. Here the nightmarish scene unfolded and all the answers to Mike's questions were answered.

The first image that caught Mike's attention was the living room window. Resembling a work of abstract art, it was splattered with a bright red kaleidoscope of brain matter, hair, bone fragments and blood.

Sitting upright on the brown plush sofa in front of the window was the body of a man wearing nothing but a pair of boxer shorts. At his feet lay a beautiful, custom pistol gripped pump action shotgun. Proud that he had been able to identify the sound under stress, Mike thought to himself, *Yep, I was right, a shotgun.* Atop the undressed torso were the remains of what was once a human head. The scene called up images in Mike's mind from his time in college when his roommate threw a watermelon from the balcony of their apartment to the sidewalk below. Looking like a fleshy horseshoe with teeth was the only discernible part that remained, the lower jaw. The jaw hung low from the wanting neck, and was resting upon the hairy upper torso.

On the floor under the glass coffee table, he could see a half empty, open bottle of Scotch, accounting for the pungent smell of alcohol. There was also a single cigarette butt on the glass of the table top with a trail of ashes from where the lit cigarette had continued to burn itself out. But then he saw it… the shit. "Why in the hell did this guy shit himself?" Mike wondered if perhaps it was a natural occurrence as a result of such a violent demise. He could not recall having seen this on other death scenes before, but this one was exceptionally gruesome. Whatever the cause, Mike had to swallow hard after double clutching.

But this was no time to be weak; he had a job to do.

"Mike, you and Bill clear the upstairs."

Mike responded, "10-4, Sarge."

Other team members had been assigned to check the rest of the house.

Mike and Bill climbed the stairs with guns drawn and calling out, "Sheriff's Department," to elicit a response from anyone in need of help. At the top of the stairs, the hallway went in two directions.

Mike checked to the right and Bill checked to the left. Mike said "Bill, let's clear the left hall first."

"Roger that."

The two proceeded down the hall and checked each room.

Mike entered the first bedroom while Bill covered him from outside in the hall.

As Mike exited he called, "Clear!"

This continued until they had checked every room, under every bed and in every closet on the entire floor. Mike was absolutely certain that there was no one upstairs.

The two proceeded back down the stairs after Mike radioed, "Second floor clear. We're coming down."

Once downstairs, the whole team congregated in the vestibule, reporting all clear. The investigation could now continue. As the team prepared to exit the house and turn the scene over to the detectives, Mike abruptly froze.

He asked, "Hold on, did you guys hear that?"

Bill said, "Hear what? What did you hear?"

As Mike was explaining that he thought he heard a man's voice, the entire team was startled by the sound of a door slamming from upstairs.

"What the hell, Mike? I thought you said the upstairs was clear!"

Mike, visibly shaken, and baffled by the sound, responded, "It was, Sarge . . . I swear we cleared the entire floor. There's no way anyone could be up there."

"Well, genius, apparently you missed something! Get your ass upstairs and find out what the fuck is going on! You two go with them!" Mike, Bill and two other team members rushed upstairs to investigate.

SUMMER OF '85

JUNE 21ST, 3:29 P.M. One minute to go, thought Mike, staring at the clock on the wall of the dimly lit art class. This would be his last class before beginning the summer of 1985. That summer would mark the beginning of his high school years. He wondered if he would get through that last bus ride home without the usual torment, to which he had grown accustomed, but always hated. Middle school kids could be so cruel and immature. He was hopeful that high school would be an improvement over his current situation.

3:30 p.m. The silence was broken by the obnoxious sound of the tinny, clanking school bell that marked the end of the last day of school. Suddenly there was an outburst of noise throughout the school as young, enthusiastic teenagers took to the hallways, shouting with excitement because summer had finally arrived. It sounded to Mike like a football stadium after the home team scored a touchdown. Hundreds of young people flooded the hallways, hooting and hollering. Many were hugging, signing yearbooks, exchanging high fives, and saying farewell to friends they had made during the past three years at Lincoln Middle School.

Mike, a husky, brown-eyed, pimple-faced, fourteen-year-old teenager with blonde hair, was kind of a shy loner and he had always found it difficult to make friends. He cautiously maneuvered unnoticed through the minefield of excited bodies that filled the hallways. Beneath the sullen expression on his face lay a tenacious determination to emerge from this summer a new person. Ordinarily he was not an optimist, but he felt that high school could be a new beginning for him, a chance to re-invent himself, and he had already set in motion a plan to do just that.

About a month prior to the end of school, Mike had seen a plastic, cement-filled weight set at a neighbor's garage sale. Mike rushed home and pleaded with his mother.

"Nancy, can I please get a weight set? It won't take up much space in the garage. The McBrides are selling one at their yard sale and it's only ten bucks."

Mike's mother, Nancy, preferred to be called by her first name because she didn't like the stigma attached to being called "Mom." She had once been a beloved cheerleader in her high school and college years. She had always secretly desired for her son to be more popular, like she had been. Nancy felt the pain of her son's torments, but having been one of the "cool" kids herself, could see why Mike was such an easy target for them. She knew how much his school experience would improve if his status among his peers was to change for the better. But she loved her son and would not force him to do anything he didn't want to do.

"Now what in the world are you going to do with a weight set, Mikey?"

"I've decided I want to get myself in shape, and I want to get started as soon as I can. I'm tired of being pushed around and teased. I just want to be healthier . . . maybe the girls will finally notice me."

Nancy replied cynically, "Well, honey, remember it's not what you look like on the outside that matters, but who you are on the inside."

Mike laughed, "Yeah, right! When you were growing up maybe, but it ain't that way nowadays!"

Nancy thought to herself, *Wow, maybe there's still hope for him.* She knew that being popular and athletic would open many doors. She herself had always been very fit and was well liked. She was five feet two inches tall, with long blonde hair, and had always maintained her weight at never more than one hundred five pounds. Even when she was pregnant with Mike, she only gained ten pounds, and had refused to go out of the house the last month for fear of someone seeing her gigantic belly.

Nancy met Mike's father, Michael, as a junior in college. Michael, to whom they always referred as Big Mike to avoid confusion, was Captain of the football team, and Nancy was the Captain of the Cheerleading squad. They were a natural pair.

Big Mike graduated college, and eventually went on to law school. He was now a successful attorney in Louisville, Kentucky. Louisville had no shortage of criminal activity and was a fertile marketplace for a defense attorney.

"Good for you, sweetheart. Anything I can do to help, just let me know. If you're determined that's what you want, then here's ten dollars. You can set it up in the garage. Make sure you keep it out of the way, though. Your father will lose his mind if you come near the new Jag."

"I know. Thank you, Nancy."

Mike snatched the money from her hand and ran out the kitchen door to the McBride's house. He spent the rest of the day carrying the weight set home a few pieces at a time and setting it up as Nancy had instructed, in the far corner of the large three car garage, well away from where Big Mike had parked his new Jaguar.

Over the course of the next month, Mike used the weight set every night religiously, getting tips from the muscle magazines he collected. No one but him seemed to notice the changes, but he could feel that something was happening to him. Suddenly, the five-feet six-inch, two-hundred-twenty-five-pound kid was now two hundred ten pounds, and his once tight pants were now a bit looser.

3:40 p.m. The bus was still in line at the school. The kids around him were still carrying on and shouting with excitement. Mike thought to himself, *why haven't we left yet?* He was anxious to get home and start devoting himself full-time to his transformation. The last day was always hectic at the school and he figured there must still be kids coming. Mike looked around for his reviled nemesis, Frank "The Moose" Peterson. He realized that Frank was not on the bus yet. This made him happy. Maybe Moose got in trouble again and had to stay after school. Mike imagined it wouldn't be such a bad ride home after all.

Mike was peacefully gazing out his window when suddenly he heard, "WHAT'S UP, YOU DOUCHE BAGS?" as the bus driver yelled, "Peterson! Just find a seat and settle down!"

Filled with dread, Mike looked up at the sound of that all-too familiar voice to see the Moose clomping onto the bus like a Clydesdale. Frank had a deep and loud adult-like voice that carried over all the other noise on the bus. He was a freak of a boy, abnormally big for his age at six feet tall and almost three hundred pounds, with more facial hair than most men twice his age. Frank had been held back for failing the sixth grade, and had been the school bully since he was in the first grade. His clothes were always ragged, dirty and wet from sweat, and he smelled like stinky gym socks all the time because it seemed that he rarely showered. Mike figured The Moose had no concept of the word hygiene. No one ever really told Frank that he stunk, but why would they? He would just pound them into the ground.

Mike usually had a seat to himself because no one wanted to sit by him, but Frank was the last one on the bus and his was only one of a few seats left with an empty space next to it. Knowing it would only bring torture and pain if he put up any resistance if Frank sat by him, Mike sank a little lower in his seat, praying that the Moose wouldn't take this seat. To his relief, the Moose walked right past him to the back of the bus. As he passed, his rancid stench hung heavy in the air. The odor permeated the nares of Mike's nose and plastered itself like wallpaper glue. It reminded him of the boys' locker room at the end of the week before everyone was required to take their filthy shorts and t-shirts home to wash. Mike wanted to gag, but buried his face in his shirt instead.

Whew, he ignored me. This day is getting better by the moment, Mike thought.

4:05 p.m. *One more stop before I can put this year behind me.* The ride home had been uneventful until it was time for the Moose to get off at his stop. Mike was content; all had been going well, so he continued to gaze out the window, ignoring everyone else around him. Once again, Mike caught a whiff of that putrid Moose stench, letting him know that Frank had just passed by.

Mike looked up when he heard the Moose announce, "Oh yeah, fat boy, I bet you thought I forgot!" The Moose turned and walked back to Mike's seat, then sucker punched him in the right upper arm. It stung as usual, but for some reason not

23

as bad this time. Maybe he was getting used to it, or maybe the working out had been paying off. Either way, there wasn't much that could be done about it. Mike ignored it, said nothing, and turned his attention back to staring out the window. He knew it would only bring more pain if he reacted. "Hmmm, not as flabby as I remember. Are you tensing up on me or something, butterball?" Mike remained stoic.

"I'll see you next year, douche!"

The Moose walked away laughing, and Mike raged. In his most silent inner monologue he screamed out, *ONE OF THESE DAYS, YOU MOTHERFUCKER, YOU'RE GONNA PAY!*

Mike heard the snickers of other students around him, most just thankful that they themselves hadn't been the recipients of the Moose's personal attention that afternoon.

4:12 p.m. The bus arrived at Mike's bus stop. He composed himself and exited the bus with three other students, one younger boy, Tommy, and two girls, Sheila and Katie. The girls were both in Mike's class, but Tommy was two years younger. He had just moved here and had only started at their school a few months ago. All of them lived in the same neighborhood, but the other three kids never took the time to get to know Mike. Usually, they would just ignore him.

In a brief moment of self-confidence, Mike mustered up the courage to say to the girls, "Have a good summer, ladies. Maybe I'll see you around."

Sheila quickly turned around and after making a gagging gesture by sticking her right index finger in her mouth said, "Gag me with a spoon, Dweeb! I know you're not talking to me!"

Katie echoed the embarrassing assault, saying, "Like, in your dreams, scumbag. I'd rather eat shit and die!" The two girls walked away laughing aloud.

Tommy was laughing along with the girls.

Infuriated, Mike said to Tommy. "What are you laughing at, penis-breath? Who the hell are you? I'll make road pizza out of you!" Tommy was two years behind and was distinctly smaller than Mike. Mike was never known to be mean, but he had just suffered another humiliating episode and took this opportunity to lash out at a perceived weaker opponent.

Tommy was much smaller, but also much feistier. He ran up to Mike and punched him in the left eye. Mike was certainly not expecting this. Instantly, he felt the sting, then the sensation of swelling. "Oh great, a black eye for sure. This sucks."

It took all he had not to cry; both from the sting of the punch as well as the humiliating verbal assault from the girls, but that would be too embarrassing. He couldn't cry. Mike swallowed his pride and just turned around to walk home. All the fight had just been punched out of him by the lightning fast reaction of Tommy.

Tommy berated Mike as he sauntered away, "What a pussy! That's it? I expected a little more fight from someone with such a big

mouth. C'mon back when ya want some more!"

The girls laughed all the harder, and Katie said to Tommy, "That was awesome! You're kinda cute. You want to come over and hang out?"

Tommy replied, "Heck yeah! That would be totally radical!"

With that, the three new friends walked away, laughing at Mike.

The day that had started with such hope and promise turned out to be one of the worst days in Mike's adolescent experience. He walked the rest of the way home dejected and demoralized.

When Mike got home, he was thankful that there was no one there. Nancy was teaching her afternoon aerobics class at the gym, and Big Mike was at work, of course. He saw a note on the table in the foyer from Nancy that read, "Mikey, I'm meeting your father after work for a business dinner with his partners. I left you stuff for a salad and some chicken in the fridge. Don't make a mess. Call me if you need anything, Nance."

This did not seem unusual to Mike. He had been a latchkey kid for most of his life. Even though Nancy didn't work a normal nine-to-five-job, she was an active socialite and was rarely home. On the weekends, Nancy and Big Mike's days were filled with parties and short getaways. They rarely seemed to have any time for him, but then again, he didn't do much of anything to garner their attention. This was one of his primary motivations for turning his life around. *Maybe they'll want to spend more time with me*, he thought. But this was one of those times he was glad the house was empty.

Mike trudged up the stairs to his room. This was his sanctuary, where he could break down without fear of reprisal from his parents for being a crybaby, as he had so often heard.

His room was at the front of the house and was sparsely appointed. As is typical for most teenage boys it was messy, with dirty clothes strewn about and countless personal effects tossed randomly around.

Upon entering the room, his twin bed was against the wall on the right, with the headboard against the wall. Above the bed and pinned to the ceiling was a poster of a beautiful, voluptuous, red-haired model in a black string bikini. He called her Anna. Immediately to the right of the doorway was a brown wooden dresser that matched the headboard and nightstand. To the left was a TV stand which held a twenty-inch television, a VCR, a game system and a radio with a CD player. In the far-left corner of the room was a full-length, freestanding floor mirror. Directly across from the doorway was a large bay window that looked out across the front yard and across the street.

Mike walked in, collapsed onto his bed and cried himself to sleep.

5:37 p.m. After a short nap, Mike woke up feeling a bit restored. He stared up at Anna and thought, *At least I can always count on you, baby*. From his secret place under his bed where he would conceal the evidence, Mike grabbed a sock—his "crunchy" sock as he called it—and fantasized about Anna as any normal, testosterone-rich teenage boy would do.

5:38 p.m. Mike cleaned up and wondered what he was going to do for the rest of the evening. With the testosterone dump and an improved outlook on things, Mike got out of bed. He stood in front of his mirror, staring at himself and taking an inventory. "Black eye, great. How am I going to explain to Dad how I got my ass kicked by a smaller kid? But look, I can see the outline of some —abs—maybe not a six-pack, but hey, something is going on there." He thought he was looking better, but then he came to his senses and looked into the mirror and yelled, "But you're still a fat ass!" Now pumping himself up like a coach before the big game in a movie, Mike started to yell with more intensity. "C'MON fat ass . . . get with the program. You need to whip your marshmallow-y ass into shape, and round's not the shape to be! Let's go, fat boy! Come on, Chubs! Only YOU can make the change, Tubby!"

Now invigorated and feeling empowered, Mike grabbed a pair of his dirty shorts from the hamper. He sniffed them, and shuddered as the smell reminded him of the rancid Moose. He put them on anyway, along with a clean t-shirt and his high tops. He proceeded to the garage and put those plastic and cement weights to good use.

After the most intense workout of his life to date, he was drenched in sweat and sore in ways he never knew was possible. With his workout completed, he headed to the kitchen for dinner.

"Salad again? God, I hate salad," he said. But if Nancy knew anything, it was diet and nutrition. She knew what to eat and how much. "Look at her; she looks like a friggin' supermodel." Mike was always embarrassed when he would hear boys his age talk about her and say, "Man, your mom is way hot!"

He proceeded to eat the large bowlful of crisp Romaine lettuce, cucumbers, tomatoes, green peppers and spinach. *Why spinach?* He especially hated spinach. The salad was garnished with a splash of light dressing. Along with his salad, Nancy had prepared him a lightly seasoned chicken breast and some asparagus.

Mike felt that most of the time, Nancy was not much of a mom, usually distant and preoccupied, but since his decision to get in shape, she had taken more of an interest in him. She had been very supportive, and on more than one occasion over the past month, even complimented him on the effort he was putting into his workouts and eating. She encouraged and educated Mike on the importance of incorporating some cardio into his workouts as well.

One evening Mike determined, "Nancy's right. Tomorrow morning I'm going to go for a run."

Mike knew he was no runner, but he had been reading all the workout magazines, and with Nancy's encouragement he determined that he could do it if he applied himself. Besides, it would speed up his metabolism and help him achieve his goal sooner. He only had eleven weeks before school started, and he would need every advantage to achieve his goal.

After eating dinner, he watched a little TV on the large screen, rear projection television in the family room where Big Mike would religiously watch football games on Sundays, when Mike would usually sit up in his room. He never understood what his dad saw in football, or why he would get so intense, yelling at the TV all day long and into the evening.

10:42 p.m. Still alone, Mike was in bed and he looked up at Anna. He imagined Anna telling him how sexy he was, and how she wanted him. Mike thought, *I'm gonna give it to you good, baby.* Once again, he reached under his bed for "Old Crunchy."

10:43 p.m. Now spent, Mike smiled and turned off the light as he said to Anna, "I'll see you in the morning, good looking."

Saturday, 8:05 a.m. The alarm sounded. Mike sprang out of bed and checked his eye. *Shit, the eye looks worse than yesterday. That little shit has quite a punch.* Mike's eye had turned black and blue, though the swelling had gone down.

He could smell the coffee brewing downstairs. *I wonder if Nancy and Dad are both home.* This almost never happened. *What will I say if they ask me about my eye? I'll just tell them I ran into a door . . . again.*

29

Mike went downstairs to find Nancy in her old bathrobe, sipping coffee at the table in the breakfast nook. She still had the look of a beautiful model, even in an old, tattered bathrobe.

"Good morning, Nancy," He said as he gave her a kiss on the cheek. "Where's Dad?"

Nancy, never looking up from her paper said, "He had a 7:30 tee time at the country club. Where are you off to?"

"I'm going for a run."

With an astonished expression on her face, Nancy finally peeked over her paper and immediately saw the black eye. "Oh my God. What happened, Mikey? Don't tell me another door."

"Nothing. I don't want to talk about it."

"Okay, I won't press. So, you're going on a run, are ya? I'm very happy to hear that. I think you'll find it will help you achieve your goal much faster. Maybe one day we can run together."

"Really? You'd go with me?"

"Of course, honey. I just never thought I'd see the day that you'd be taking such an interest in fitness. I'm so proud of what you've accomplished so far. I'm starting to see the difference in you already.

Would you mind if I went with you this morning?"

"Sure. That would be great."

"Okay, give me five minutes to get dressed."

Mike was perplexed by Nancy's sudden interest in his life. He became filled with a feeling of satisfaction, and he smiled for the first time in a long time.

After thirty minutes of primping, Nancy came down the stairs in her bright yellow, spandex leotard that accentuated her toned abdomen, black spandex leg warmers that came to the top of her knees, and white running shoes with ankle socks.

The ripple of her toned thighs could be seen with every step she took. Of course, she had all her makeup on and her hair was perfect. To any other man, she was a goddess, but to Mike she was just Nancy, his mom.

This is pretty cool, he thought to himself as they stepped outside. Mike took the time to look around the still-quiet neighborhood. Across the street was the Miller's house that had been put on the market several months ago. They had moved to California after Mr. Miller got promoted to Vice President of his company. Mike noticed for the first time that the realtor's sign had been taken down.

He asked Nancy, "Did the Miller home sell?"

"I don't know, but the sign is gone. Maybe we're gonna get some new neighbors. Okay, let's get started. The first thing to do is stretch. Stretching is very important before and after your workouts," Nancy said, getting him to focus on the task at hand.

"Okay now, don't expect too much from the first day. It took me quite a while to get to where I could run comfortably. We'll just go until you get tired, okay?"

Mike responded, "Yep, sounds good."

The two headed down the sidewalk of their upper middle class, gated community that lay in the suburbs of the busy city. The sun was shining, the sky was clear and the air smelled clean. Mike never imagined himself running, but here he was, with Nancy coaching him all the way.

"Breathe in through your nose and out through your mouth. Purse your lips as you exhale. Heel to toe, shorten your stride, eyes ahead, and focus on an object in the distance."

Thinking Nancy sounded a bit like a drill instructor, Mike was getting frustrated and he thought to himself, *all right already, I get it!* But he remained silent; in the end he was grateful that she was there with him.

After the second lap around the big block, Mike was panting like a Saint Bernard in July. His clothes were so wet with sweat they were sticking to his body. He looked to his left, and there was Nancy, breathing normally, with not so much as a bead of sweat. It became immediately clear to Mike that she was holding back for his sake.

Mike pressed on, refusing to show weakness to his Olympian-like athlete of a mom. After about fifteen minutes, and the end of their third lap around the block, Nancy said, "Wow Mikey, do you realize you just ran a mile without stopping?"

"A . . . a . . . a mile?" Mike gasped. His lungs were on fire and his legs were shaky. Now hunched over, he said "I . . . I ser . . . seriously just ran a . . . a mile?"

"Ran? Well . . . we jogged a mile," Nancy explained with a smile on her face. "But still, I'm very impressed. I'm so proud of you. I could never have run, walked or jogged a mile without stopping when I first started way back in the day."

Mike had never heard such an uplifting discourse from Nancy before, and he was overcome with a feeling of accomplishment. Seeing the shape Nancy was in became an inspiration to him. *Maybe there's hope for me yet,* he thought. Mike knew this would be the start of a new chapter in his book of life. This was his time, and there was no way he would screw this up.

Mike and Nancy continued with their small talk as they went back in the house. "Great job today. I'm not doing anything tomorrow. Are you up for another run?"

Before he had a chance to think about how much pain he was in, Mike responded, "Yeah, I can't wait!"

Now with a lighter step, Mike bounded up the stairs to take a shower.

Nancy watched her son walk away. She saw him in a new way she never had before. She felt something that had escaped her as a mother—until then—pride. She thought to herself, *with a little tweaking, I bet I can transform this burly boy into a chiseled man. Maybe there's a little more of his father in him than I thought.*

9:43 a.m. Mike got out of the shower, wrapped himself in a towel, and stood in front of his full-length mirror to re-examine himself, this time with a fresh perspective. Now he could imagine himself in a different way. With the music blaring in the background from his Discman, he let his towel fall to the ground. Mike started to pose, like the guys in the muscle magazines he had been reading.

He envisioned himself with large biceps and ripped abs. Now naked in front of his mirror, he flexed and practiced the poses: the crab, the front double bicep, the front lat spread, the side chest, the side triceps, most muscular and several others. While he was distracted by his posing techniques, he didn't realize that his blinds and window were wide open.

Mike then heard a loud "PSSSSH." It was the sound of a truck's air brakes being set from across the street. He turned around and realized the window was open. To his horror, he saw a girl staring at him from the front yard of the old Miller house.

Oh my God, how long has she been there? he thought.

Mortified, he fell to the ground and grabbed his towel. He crawled to the window, reached up and closed the blinds. Now covered, Mike stood up and peered through the blinds. He stared at the girl. She was a redhead like his beloved Anna, kind of cute, not gorgeous, but not too bad at all. It was clear by the large moving van that she and her family were just moving into the Miller house.

"I thought yesterday was the worst day ever, but this might top it. I wonder if she saw me naked. Oh my God, I can never face her."

Mike could see that the girl was smiling, but not in a mean way. It seemed to be an innocent smile. The more he watched her, the prettier she became.

"Forget it, stupid. She'll never notice you, at least not yet."

***

Sunday morning, Mike awoke to Nancy badgering him. "C'mon sleepy head, it's nine o'clock. You promised me a morning run."

Mike begrudgingly woke up, feeling pains in places he didn't think were possible.

Nancy could see his anguish. "Did you remember to stretch like I told you?"

"No, I forgot."

"Now you know why we stretch. I'll see you downstairs. Hurry up, slowpoke," Nancy said in an unfamiliar loving tone.

Mike stared at the ceiling, admiring his Anna. "You get me, don't you?" Then he remembered the incident at the window the day before. "Oh man, I hope she's not outside." Mike knew he would have to hurry, and would have no time for intimacy with Anna. "Sorry sweetie, maybe later." He smiled and winked at the poster.

When Mike got downstairs, he was surprised to see his dad sipping on a cup of coffee. There was Nancy, standing behind

Big Mike, rubbing his neck. Of course, she looked like a Greek goddess as usual in her tight-fitting workout clothes, but what was more surprising to Mike was to see his father wearing gray running shorts, a blue tank top and running shoes.

Looking up from his paper, Big Mike said, "Hey! There he is. How ya doing, champ? Door again?" Big Mike said with a smile. "Your mother tells me you've been working out. She told me how good you did yesterday on your first run. I've been meaning to start running again. I hope you don't mind if I join you two."

Mike couldn't believe it. He hadn't done anything with his parents in such a long time. *If I knew this would happen, I would have done this a long time ago.* he thought to himself.

Mike responded, "No, sir. That would be awesome."

"Well then, let's hit the road, literally," Big Mike said in his best comical voice. Big Mike was always so serious, and it was odd for Mike to hear his dad trying to be jocular.

Mike did his best to smile at the lame attempt at humor.

The trio went outside to start their run.

Mike looked across the street. *Whew, she's not there. Thank you, God.*

They all stretched, and Nancy said, "Ready?"

Mike said, "I think so."

Nancy said to Big Mike, "How about you, big daddy?"

"As ready as I'm going to be. You know, I used to be quite an athlete back in my day."

"Yes, you were, daddy. That's why I fell in love with you."

Nancy gave his dad a kiss, and then she poked him in the belly with both index fingers, saying, "But that was a long time ago, chubby." The two laughed, then hugged and kissed again.

Mike was almost sickened by the public display of affection shared between his parents, but he saw them in a way he never had before. He liked it, and he smiled to himself.

"Let's go, you two. Geez, get a room."

They all laughed and started their journey through the familiar neighborhood. On their second lap around the block, Mike noticed the girl from yesterday.

Oh no, there she is. He started to sweat profusely, but not just because he was about to collapse from the running. Mike felt a wave of nausea come over him. *I'm gonna hurl, I know it.*

The three of them, jogging in unison, ran past the house with the girl in the front yard. She saw Mike and smiled at him. It was that same sweet smile he had seen the day before from his shameful perch, not the scornful sneers he had grown accustomed to from the other girls. She waved at Mike in a gentle way as he ran by. Distracted by the cute redhead, he stumbled over a crack in the sidewalk, but managed to keep from falling.

Mike's dad laughed, "She's kind of a cutie, huh son? Sort of reminds me of that hottie that stares down at you in your bed."

"She's all right, I guess," Mike said hesitantly, rolling his eyes.

"I guess someone finally moved into the Miller's house. Maybe later we'll go over and introduce ourselves." Mike panicked at the thought.

On their third lap, she was nowhere to be seen. Relieved, Mike said to Nancy, "Is that a mile?"

Nancy responded, "That's a mile."

"Can we go another lap?"

She smiled with pride and said, "If you're up for it. How about you, daddy?"

Big Mike, a once proud athlete, had become a middle-aged man, spending his days wearing a suit and moving only between a sedentary office and a courtroom. He realized that he had let himself go, but was now inspired by his son's enthusiasm. "I'm up if he's up. No way am I gonna let some young punk best me."

The three continued on, and Mike was the happiest he could remember.

***

The summer forged ahead, and it proved to be a busy one for Mike. He never wavered from the special diet that Nancy planned out for him, and he worked out every day. Mike's body transformed before his eyes. He would check his body fat, weigh himself, and eat everything in just the right proportions. Mike went through two complete wardrobe changes between June 21st when school let out, and September 3rd, the first day of high school.

He would spend most of his afternoons in his bedroom watching the girl across the street sunbathe. From his roost, he could see into her backyard and the area around her pool where she would lie in the sun. The cute redhead would often wear a black bikini, and when she did, she looked more like his beloved Anna. She, too, was transforming that summer. Her breasts had developed and filled out the bikini top now. More and more, he would think of her as he lay awake in bed, and Anna became less and less the object of his desire. On one occasion, he caught her sunbathing topless. *If only she knew I could see her and what I was doing now. Hello, Crunchy, my old friend.*

During that summer, Mike asked his father, a former college football hero and huge football fan, to explain the game to him. All too happy to oblige, Big Mike would take him into the back yard and throw the ball around. There, Big Mike taught him all about the game. Mike had been looking for some way to bond with his parents, and this summer proved to be the catalyst he was looking for; fitness and nutrition with his mom, and football with his dad. Mike found that he actually had learned to love the game and couldn't wait for football season to start so he could join his father in the family room and scream at the big TV with him. They could cheer for their favorite team, although he didn't know who his favorite team was yet.

Big Mike could sense his son's enthusiasm for the game growing.

"So, do you think you might try out for football this year?"

"I don't know Dad, you think I could?"

Having seen the dramatic change in his son's fitness level, his dad asked, "Son, have you seen yourself lately?"

Actually, Mike had seen himself. Every day, in fact, he would examine himself in front of his mirror, now careful to keep his window blinds drawn closed when doing so. Mike's confidence had skyrocketed throughout the summer. He felt his parents' pride growing. He had managed to transform his body and his life. He had experienced a huge growth spurt and now stood at five feet ten inches. He wondered if he would be as tall as his father, who was six feet three. This was the closest he had ever been with his parents, and he was truly happy for the first time in his young life.

Mike said, "Yes, sir, I feel great."

"You've easily picked up everything I've taught you about the game. I think you're a natural like your old man, and you have one hell of an arm. Yeah, I know you can do it son, if you want it bad enough."

Since the three often ran together as a family, his dad went on to say, "Now you can outrun your mother, which is no easy feat. Now she's the one who's tired when we finish our runs. Did you ever imagine you would see that day?"

Mike smiled and said, "No way, I still can't believe it."

"This just goes to show you something that I hope you'll carry with you for the rest of your life. With enough determination and perseverance, you can reach any of your goals, regardless of how unattainable they might seem. I bet three months ago you could have never dreamed you'd be at this level today. Your mother and I could not be prouder of you, son."

Mike reminisced about the last day of school, the day when he had truly made up his mind to change everything. But seeing himself now, he had far exceeded his own expectations.

MOVING UP IN THE WORLD

*S*ATURDAY, JUNE 22*ND*. It was a clear, bright summer morning. Sarah and her family were moving into the former home of the Millers. She and her parents arrived at the house ahead of the movers, who were supposed to be there between nine and ten. Sarah got out of the car and surveyed the new home.

This was her first time seeing the house, as they had just gotten into town late the night before and checked right into the hotel. She was awestruck by the impressive home in Oak Acres, a quiet, upper middle-class neighborhood in the sprawling suburbs of Louisville. *This place is so much nicer than our house back home,* she thought.

Back home was Memphis, Tennessee, where her father was a plant manager for a paper company. The family's move to Louisville, where the company was headquartered, was prompted by his promotion to Regional Vice President.

Since they had some time before the movers arrived, Sarah gave the house a walk-through.

"Mom, where is my room?"

Her mother replied, "It's upstairs . . . to the right, and it will be the first door on the right facing the front. You'll have your own bathroom."

"My own bathroom?"

Sarah dashed upstairs to find a freshly painted bedroom. Her parents had had the room painted in her favorite color, light pink. It was a much bigger room than she'd had back in Memphis, with two windows overlooking the big front yard.

And then she saw it, every teenage girl's dream come true—her own private bathroom. Sarah thought, *oh, my God, pinch me, I must be dreaming*. Just for fun, she gave herself a pinch on her forearm. She walked in and noticed she had her own shower, toilet and sink. This alone would have been enough for Sarah to want to move.

She surveyed the rest of the house, and became more amazed with every turn. "This house is amazing, Mom," she called out. Then she looked in the back yard and squealed with excitement. "Like, oh my God, a pool? WE HAVE A POOL?" Sarah pictured herself sunbathing during the warm summer days ahead.

9:42 a.m. Sarah heard her mom from the front yard yell, "Y'all get ready, I can see the moving truck coming down the street!" Sarah and her father ran out the front door in anticipation.

I think I'm going to like Louisville.

As the truck was approaching, Sarah heard some loud music coming from across the street. She looked, and through an open window in the house across the street, she saw a young man flexing in front of a mirror with music blaring, clearly oblivious that his window was wide open. Sarah stood there watching the young man through the window. From her angle, she could not see that he was naked, just shirtless. She thought he was kind of cute; a little on the chubby side, but cute. She thought it was funny the way he was moving around posing and flexing. It made her smile. *I hope I get to meet him soon.*

The truck pulled up. The brakes squealed when it came to a stop, then there was a loud "PSSSSH" sound from the air brake being set.

The boy in the window turned around and then suddenly vanished. A few seconds later, Sarah saw a hand reach from the bottom of the window then the blinds closed. But the window remained open and she could still hear the blaring music. Before turning her attention to the movers, Sarah thought she could see him staring at her through an open slit in the blinds. She giggled to herself and then turned her attention to the move-in process.

"Sarah honey, we asked the movers to start with your room first. You'll need to show them where you want your things."

"Okay, Mom!"

Sarah bolted upstairs with excitement. She hadn't forgotten about the cute boy in the window, but she had more important priorities at the moment. Sarah was now in full move-in mode, and would not be distracted while her furniture was moved in. She spent the next hour choreographing the movers, occasionally going downstairs to the truck to show them what furniture was hers. Every piece of furniture had to be meticulously placed to her exacting specifications.

The next morning, she was outside in the front yard getting some of her personal items from the minivan, and she was pleased to see the boy stretching on the front lawn with what must have been his parents. Sarah thought, *Wow, is that his mom or his sister? She's gorgeous. That must be his dad. What a big man he is. And there he is, my funny bodybuilder in the window.* She had a better view of him now that he was outside in the sun and thought, *He is cute.*

She sat on the front porch and waited for them to pass. After a while, she was walking around the front yard waiting for them to complete their next lap. Then she saw the boy and his parents running in her direction on the sidewalk across the street. She could see that the boy was looking at her. *Do I dare?* she thought. Then she mustered up the nerve to wave at him and smile. She saw the boy stumble and almost fall. She giggled to herself, but turned away so as not to embarrass him.

***

Monday morning. Sarah awoke to an empty house. Her father had gone to work and her mother had appointments all day with the utility companies transferring everything into their name. Sarah decided to try out the pool. Before getting dressed, she looked out her window and saw the funny boy across the street out running with his mom. Sarah wanted to meet him, but how? What would he see in her?

Sarah was considered pretty by most, but she was sort of gangly with red hair, and was often teased about her bright hair and pale skin. She was a late bloomer. All her friends back home started developing breasts over a year ago. Now, a few weeks before her fourteenth birthday, Sarah had finally started to develop, but still felt flat-chested.

Sarah donned her black bikini, stood in front of the mirror in her bathroom, and in a self-deprecating display laughed at herself, thinking, *this top is too big. My tits look like walnuts in a baseball glove.* "I hope I can fill these babies out soon," she said, staring at the top.

The summer progressed, and fill out she did. Within a few more weeks, Sarah filled out her B-cup size bikini. She would stand in front of her mirror, and was pleased that she actually had boobs. Her birthday came and went. She would regularly see the boy across the street, but still didn't have the nerve to introduce herself to him. She would always smile and wave, and he would always smile nervously back at her. Sarah wasn't sure who was more scared, him or her.

As she watched him develop through the summer, becoming more handsome with each passing day, she wondered if he ever noticed her and would often fantasize about their first encounter, dreaming that he would sweep her off her feet and they would fall instantly in love. One day, she caught him watching her in her black bikini by the pool, unaware he had a fetish for redheads, especially in black bikinis. Sarah could see that from his vantage point, he could see into a small portion of her patio around the pool. One day she looked up and saw him watching her, but he quickly walked away when he knew she saw him.

Sarah laughed. From that day on she would make it a point always to lie in that same spot so he could see her. She would always pretend she didn't notice him, though she always knew. "Maybe I can entice him to come and talk to me."

One afternoon, no one was home but Sarah. Her mother had gone out for the day and wouldn't be back until late that evening, and her father was at work. With no one to watch her but the boy across the street, Sarah suddenly got brave. "I think I'll give him a treat today."

Sarah had developed a routine, and would be at the pool the same time every day, barring any rainy weather. It was rare that she would not be able to see some sign of the boy watching her. The blinds would be rustling, or she would see a slight bend forming a slit in the blinds, her acknowledgement that he was peering through. She would stealthily gaze back through dark sunglasses so he would not know she knew of his presence. She never put lotion on until she was near the pool, and would apply the lotion as slowly and seductively as she knew how.

Sarah donned her bikini bottoms. She wrapped herself in a large towel and proceeded outside the way she always did. Surreptitiously, she looked through her dark glasses. "Yep, there you are, my peeping Tom." She let her towel fall to the ground and gave him a big surprise. She was not wearing her top, exposing her young, taut, developing breasts. They weren't big, but she was proud of them. Her enthusiasm was obvious as she applied an extra-heavy coat of lotion, being sure not to miss any part of her pale, young orbs.

She was careful not to be too obvious when she lay back in the deck chair. She could see through her dark spectacles that the slit in the blinds was wider than normal. Then she thought she saw something she had not ever seen before. There was movement at the lower part of the blinds, as though something was smacking against the blinds. Sarah could scarcely contain her joy at the thought of what he might be doing to himself. *This is for you, sweet prince. I hope you enjoy yourself.*

***

Summer drew to an end, and it was time for school to begin. Sarah told her mom she needed a new wardrobe; after all, it was a new school. Besides, it was high school and she had to look good. It was the mid-eighties, the height of terrible fashion and Sarah would not spare one penny of her parents' hard-earned money to get the proper "look".

With only one week to go, Sarah and her mother went to the local mall and spent a day acquiring all of the fashion hardware that she would need to make her preppy assault on John F. Kennedy Sr. High School. Spending well in excess of a thousand dollars, Sarah came home with an array of every 80's faux pas known to man. She had an assortment of acid-washed, pegged and pleated jeans with designer pockets. She clearly had to have the stirrup pants that she could wear with any of the four new pairs of pumps. To look good in the short shorts, every color of the rainbow including rainbow leg warmers was an absolute necessity. The ensemble wouldn't be complete without at least two pairs of lace fingerless gloves—one black and one white, a variety of shirts with fringe, and see-through blouses to accent the lingerie that would hug her recently acquired eye grabbers.

September 2, Labor Day. Sarah's family was having a barbeque at the house, and had invited most of the neighbors over to join them. This was their chance to get know some of them, including the family from across the street.

The house was abuzz with excitement as everyone started showing up. Everyone was so friendly. The last family to arrive, the guests of honor in Sarah's opinion, was the family from across the street. Now she would finally meet her mystery boy.

Sarah spent more than two hours locked up in her heavily armed war room, or bathroom to anyone else. It was well stocked with eyeliner, blush, and lipsticks of every color. She wanted to impress this young man and after an hour of applying her war paint like an Apache warrior, she was ready to impress. She exited her bedroom with her "big" red hair teased up. She was wearing a pair of short, white shorts with stockings and leg warmers and her new white sneakers. For her top, she chose a low-cut, tassel-fringed pink shirt that allowed her bra to show slightly. The pieces de resistance, the things that tied it all together, were the black lace gloves.

She performed a quick inventory before leaving the bathroom. "You look fabulous. He won't be able to resist you."

She blew herself a kiss and gave a quick wink as she bolted downstairs.

Sarah's mother saw her coming down the stairs. "Well, don't you look like a rock star?"

Sarah smiled and said, "What a good turnout."

"Yes, everyone showed up, including that nice boy from across the street."

Sarah's heart skipped a beat. Pretending not to be interested, she said, "Oh yeah?" Actually, she was more nervous than she thought she would've been. She went outside on the pool deck. Through the large crowd, she spotted the boy of her ever-increasing interest. He was standing alone by the fence with a diet soda in his hand. She collected her thoughts and walked over to him.

He looked taller up close. When she had first seen him, he would run with his shirt on. Now, he was looking very muscular and had been running with his shirt off lately. He was nicely bronzed as a result. His eyes were a light blue that stood out against his tan skin. He was wearing a pair of white pleated pants; a tight, yellow, collar-less shirt that accented his now tight stomach; and a white sport jacket with a pair of white sliders and no socks.

Timidly she approached and introduced herself. "Hi, I'm Sarah."

"I'm Mike." He looked away nervously, trying not to be obvious that he was attracted to her.

"You're very shy, aren't you, Mike?"

Trying to come off as cool, he said, "No, I'm just playing hard to get." Immediately he thought, *Hard to get? That was the lamest line ever. She's gonna think I'm such a douche bag.*

To his amazement, Sarah actually laughed at his one-liner, and in a demure way said, "Really? You don't look so hard to me."

Out of instinct, Mike looked down at his still-flaccid manhood. He silently instructed his one-eyed trouser trout, as he called it, *Okay, mister, you behave!*

The two wandered off and sat alone at the picnic table in the backyard. They spent the rest of the day getting to know each other until everyone left.

***

Later that evening, when the party was over and everyone, including Mike, had gone home, Sarah's mom asked her, "So, you guys spent a long time together. What was he like? He's awfully cute."

"Oh, Mom, he's the most amazing boy I've ever met! He's intelligent, cute and so sweet."

"Uh oh, sounds like someone's in love!"

"Oh my God, Mother! We just met!" Sarah smiled and said, "Well . . . maybe just a little."

Her father overheard the conversation. "Am I gonna have to oil up my shotgun?"

"DADDY!"

"I'm just saying, I have to watch out for my little girl. I can't have some young stud muscling in on my princess." "Oh, my goodness, you two are impossible!" Sarah ran upstairs and slammed her door.

Her mother said, "She's growing up."

Laughing, her father said, "Yeah, and way too fast for me." Then he somberly reminisced, "Remember the last boy back home in Memphis?"

"You mean Rupert? Oh, that was just puppy love. She was only nine."

"Maybe, but she became obsessed with him and she lost it."

"That was then. She's older now. She's been taking her meds and doing very well. The counselor said she should be fine, that it all related to her condition. Besides, she just met this boy today. He seems like a very nice young man. What harm can come from a little flirtation?"

"Hello? Did you ever date a teenage boy? Do I really need to express my concerns about a teenage boy and his hormones? Besides, it's not him I'm worried about."

Upstairs in her room, after taking her Haldol and Valium, Sarah felt very sleepy, as she always did. She never knew why, but the nice doctor with the beard in Memphis told her parents she should take them. Her parents used to make sure she took them, but now that she was older, she was trusted to take them on her own. She walked to the window that afforded her the best vantage point, and while she was lying on the built-in window seat, she stared across the street at the home of her new love interest. She thought to herself, *Michael Carson, Junior, my mom's right. I am in love with you. We will be together forever, I just know we will, I just know we will be together forev. . .*

***

Sarah finds herself with Michael walking along the shore of a large lake while holding hands and talking like they did at the party. They discuss their future—where they will live, what kind of job he will have, how many kids they want. Sarah is happy and content. She never imagined she could ever love someone the way she loves Mike.

Time moves forward and just as they discussed those long days before, they graduate from college and Mike is a successful architect with a big firm with Sarah is employed as an accountant.

While away for a long weekend to a cabin in the mountains, Mike proposes to her by putting her engagement ring inside the right front pocket of his jeans. While preparing to clean the fish he caught on the lake, he asks Sarah to grab his buck-knife in his right front pocket. Sarah obediently reaches into his pocket, digging around for a pocket knife. She pulled the ring-box out of his pocket and looks at him quizzically.

"Oh, maybe it is in my left pocket." He says, grinning at the look on Sarah's face. "Open it."

Sarah opens the box and immediately throws her arms around Mike's neck.

"Well, lady, should we get married?" He asks looking longingly into her eyes.

Sarah smiles broadly, "What do you think! YES!"

***

After the wedding, Sarah got her dream house with a white picket fence. This is truly the life she had always dreamed of and knew one day she would have.

Mike calls her on the phone regularly just to tell her how in love he is with her. "How are my girls?" he asks. Of course he is referring to Sarah as she is always "his" girl. But another lady was waiting to share Mike's time—Sarah was expecting a baby girl.

Sarah gave birth to their child on a stormy evening. Such a precious angel, so well behaved that everyone told them what a perfect little girl they had.

Sarah would not normally be willing to share her man with another woman, but this perfect baby was the sum of their love. What more could a girl want? Sarah spends her day cleaning and taking care of baby Alexis. Mike, being the model-man, insisted that the baby be named after Sarah's grandmother to honor her. What a man! Could there ever be a more perfect man?

Sarah swoons when Mike comes home. She has their dinner waiting on the table. She tells Mike of all the wonderful things that have happened that day. "Alexis said her first words. Guess what they were?"

Mike responds excitedly, "I don't know. Please tell me, honey."

"She said, 'Dada.'"

Mike, of course, being the perfect combination of sensitive and manly, gets choked up and tears of joy well up in his eyes.

"She misses you almost as much as I do, my darling."

"I miss the two of you, too. But what a joy to come home to you. I'm so in love with you. My life is perfect."

***

BLEEP, BLEEP, BLEEP, BLEEP, BLEEP!

Sarah was jolted awake by the obnoxious alarm clock that read six o'clock. She didn't remember how she got in bed, and woke up in a foul mood, not having had to get up this early in a long time.

Sarah stumbled to her bathroom to get ready for her first day of high school. She took a long, warm shower and began to feel alive finally. She spent the next hour getting herself primped and ready for school. Anxious, and in a rush to see her Mike, Sarah forgot to take her morning medication.

7:05 a.m. Sarah emerged from her bathroom looking like Madonna in her latest video on MTV. She was confident that Mike would go out of his way to be with her. Why wouldn't he? They were meant to be. This was going to be the best day ever.

Sarah ran out her front door and saw Mike come out of his house. She waved at him and cried out, "Hey, good looking!"

Mike smiled and waved back. They met in the middle of the road and walked together to the bus stop.

A FRESH START

Mike and Sarah walked the half-mile to the bus stop together, chitchatting. Sarah was happy as long as his focus was on her. Since meeting him the day before, all Sarah could think about was Mike. A whole summer of distant seduction and their flirtatious first meeting had left her with an irrational perception of their future together.

Mike now walked with a confidence that he'd never had before. This was going to be a great year. All he could think about was how he was going to show everyone who had put him down in the past.

His hair had grown out and was now shoulder-length, and lighter blonde due to his time in the summer sun. He also had a bronze tan from running shirtless. The workouts had given him definition. His arms were toned, and filled out the sleeves of his now taut t-shirt. And thanks to his growth spurt, he now stood at five feet ten, taller than most boys his age. His confidence had also improved, as he and Big Mike had started taking self-defense classes together and had been studying Judo.

At the bus stop there were two other people, Katie and Sheila. Sheila was a very pretty young lady, with long blonde hair much like Nancy's. She was green-eyed and athletic, too. In some ways she looked a lot like Nancy, but not in Mike's eyes. He always thought Sheila was the prettiest girl in his class and had secretly admired her from afar.

Sheila saw Mike first, and reacted in shock. "Oh... my... God! Dweeb?"

Immediately, Sarah hissed like an alley cat. "His name is Michael. You'd best watch yourself, bitch!"

Mike laughed and said, "Whoa, chill Sarah! Don't have a cow."

Sheila responded, "I didn't mean anything by it. God, it's just . . . you've changed so much. I mean . . . a lot! You look amazing." She was gawking at Mike, making her approval obvious.

Mike blushed. He was not expecting that from the prettiest girl he knew.

Sarah raged inside, *who is this whore putting the moves on my man?*

Katie, a slight brunette with brown eyes and braces, was pretty and popular also. She responded with the same astonishment,

"Wow, dork no more!"

The girls both asked, "So, your name is Michael?"

Suddenly, he was a hit. This was a far cry from the beginning of summer when he was getting hit by that little piss ant Tommy. Tommy was still in middle school and took the earlier bus. Mike secretly wished that Tommy was there so he could gauge his reaction to his physical change. *I don't think he'd try that again*, Mike thought to himself.

He smiled and said, "Yes, but you can call me Mike."

During the next ten minutes, as the four waited for the bus, it became clear that Katie and Sheila had taken quite an interest in Mike.

Sarah felt that she was being ignored as the other two chatterboxes wouldn't shut up, and she was growing impatient. "Um, Mike? Can I talk to you for a second? Alone?"

Mike, unaccustomed to all the attention, responded with a smirk, "Sure, Sarah."

Beaming at Sheila and Katie he said, "Be back in a sec, ladies."

As Mike and Sarah walked to the other side of the street, he overheard Sheila say to Katie, "Oh my God, he's gorgeous!"

Katie said, "Sure is! What a difference a few months can make.

Mmm, mmm, mmm! You should go for it, girl! I give you my approval." Sheila responded, "You think so?"

When Mike and Sarah got to the other side of the street, Sarah began berating Mike. "What the hell do you think you're doing?"

With a confused look on his face, Mike said, "Huh?"

"Talking to those two skanks! Did you screw them or something?"

Mike, remembering the incident in June, laughed, "You're kidding, right?"

Sarah felt her blood boil and a jealous rage built inside her. She screamed, "DOES IT LOOK LIKE I'M KIDDING? DO YOU SEE ME LAUGHING?"

Mike could see her face was now tomato-red, and beads of sweat were forming on her forehead. She had a disconnected gaze in her eyes. She began crying as she dropped her bag to the ground.

Mike tried to console her as he innocently picked up her bag. "Are you okay?"

"NO, YOU FUCKING JERK. I'M NOT OKAY! YOU'RE MY MAN! I GAVE MYSELF TO YOU AND THIS IS HOW YOU TREAT ME? WE WERE SUPPOSED TO BE

TOGETHER FOREVER!" She grabbed at the bag in his hands and it fell back to the ground.

With both hands in the air and a look of disbelief on his face, Mike stepped back. "Gave yourself to me? Together forever? We just met yesterday. Are you fucking nuts? Uh, I'm gonna let you be now." Mike turned around and walked away. Looking at the other two girls he mouthed, "WOW!"

Sheila and Katie started to laugh, only this time with him, not at him.

Sarah shouted, "DON'T THINK I DON'T KNOW WHAT YOU WERE DOING TWO WEEKS AGO WHEN YOU SAW ME BY THE POOL! YOU WANT ME, MICHAEL! I KNOW YOU DO!"

Mike had indeed fantasized about her that day, several times in fact, as well as many other days. But as far as that went, he had also fantasized about half the girls in his class, including, oddly enough, both Sheila and Katie.

Sarah looked up to see her love walking away from her, shaking his head.

She heard him saying, "What a crazy bitch!"

Mike returned to the other side of the street, where he started talking to Katie and Sheila again.

Sheila asked, "Girlfriend?"

Mike immediately responded, "No way, she just lives across the street from me. I think she's crazy."

Overhearing the exchange, Sarah was sobbing and grabbed her bag from the ground. "I . . . I'm not crazy, I'm not crazy . . . I'M NOT!!!"

As she skulked away toward her home, Sarah turned around and leered at Mike, Sheila and Katie. She then spitefully whispered to herself, "You cunts! You're gonna pay.

And you . . . you son of a bitch, you're gonna regret doing this to me. You will be mine, Michael. One day, we will be happy together, forever!"

Oblivious to the looming threat now walking away from them, Mike and the girls boarded the bus.

"Is that all of you?" the driver asked.

Mike responded as he looked back, "Well, there was one more, but I think she must have gone home." Sarah was nowhere to be seen.

"Whatever," the driver said apathetically as he closed the door.

Sheila found an empty seat, then asked Mike to sit with her. He was all too eager to oblige. Katie sat in the seat across the aisle. Katie winked at Sheila in approval, then silently mouthed, "Go for it." Sheila smiled and winked back.

First day of high school and things are really turning around for me, thought Mike as he now talked confidently with two of the most popular girls from his middle school.

But, it was inevitable--time for the Moose to get on the bus. As the bus came to a stop, the doors opened and Frank "The Moose" Peterson stepped on board. Mike swore he could feel the bus lean to his side. Then Mike heard the fifteen-year-old gargantuan man-boy with the baritone voice cry out his trademark, "What's up, you douche bags?"

Mike couldn't believe his eyes. As much as he had grown over the summer, this behemoth had taken on superhuman proportions. He thought, *Holy shit! This guy grew at least three more inches and probably gained another fifty pounds.*

In fact, Frank had grown another four inches and now stood at six feet four; however, he had only gained thirty pounds.

Mike couldn't help but think that the Moose looked different. *Did he actually shower? Were those clean clothes he had on? Had he actually shaved? What the hell is going on here?*

The Moose was still obnoxious and boisterous, and Mike grew secretly nervous as he approached. His palms grew sweaty and his pulse quickened a bit as he thought to himself, *this has been such a great start to the year. Please don't mess with me, Moose.*

To Mike's disbelief, the Moose walked right by him without as much as a snide comment. *Maybe he didn't recognize me.*

But what most surprised Mike — no trailing stench. *Maybe he had a good summer, too. He certainly cleaned up his act,* thought Mike.

With the Moose crisis averted, Mike could turn his attention back to the girls. He was surprised at how comfortable he felt talking to Sheila. He was thinking, *I can't believe this is the same girl who put me down so harshly just a few months ago.*

But here they were. He was hoping that the rest of the year would go as well. It certainly showed a lot of promise.

8:15 a.m. The bus arrived at John F. Kennedy High School, which was much bigger than Mike had imagined. He had only been to the school office with Nancy to pick his class schedule a few weeks prior, and had only seen the rest of the school from the outside.

Sheila never left Mike's side until after homeroom, which as good fortune would have it, they shared. Sheila asked, "What time do you have lunch?"

Mike answered, "11:15 to 11:55."

"Oh wow, so do I! Do you think we can sit together?"

Mike responded with a smile, "I think I can fit you into my busy schedule."

At lunchtime, Mike and Sheila met up outside the cafeteria and went in together. In a gentlemanly gesture he had learned from watching his father with friends when they would go out, Mike paid for Sheila's lunch.

Surprised by the gesture, she responded, "Thank you. That was very sweet." It was during lunch that he discovered they also had the same history class during fifth period.

Mike was pleasantly surprised that the rest of the day went so smoothly. He was making friends, and because this was a new school and most of these people didn't know him from last year, they had no preconceived notions about him. This would truly be his opportunity to complete his transformation from a chubby, shy geek to what he hoped to become, a cool jock.

After school, Mike and Sheila sat together on the bus again. The Moose never acknowledged him that day, and Mike was now more confident than ever that his transformation was well under way.

After getting off the bus, Mike offered to walk Sheila and Katie home. The girls eagerly agreed, and the three of them walked away laughing and carrying on.

In the empty lot across the street from the bus stop, Sarah was lurking, crouched down in some bushes. With her steely eyes fixated on the trio, Sarah watched and plotted.

She was dirty and sweaty. She had not been home at all that day. She had spent the day meandering alone in the unfamiliar woods that encompassed her new neighborhood. Her bright red hair was now unkempt, and her Madonna-cloned fashions were tattered and torn. She was covered in mud and looked as if she had fallen down on more than one occasion.

Neither Mike, Sheila nor Katie noticed Sarah when she emerged from her shaded sanctuary and stalked them from a distance. She stealthily darted from bush to bush and took great care not to be noticed.

As the three arrived at Sheila and Katie's houses, Sarah paused and thought, *So that's your house, bitch.* The two girls were next-door neighbors. They had grown up together and had been best friends from the moment they first met ten years earlier.

Mike said, "Here you go ladies, all safe and sound."

In unison, both girls said, "Thank you, Mike!"

Mike joyfully responded, "The pleasure was all mine."

Before leaving, Sheila gave Mike a hug, and as she slipped him her phone number she said, "You can call me later if you want."

Mike blushed and nervously responded, "If you want me to, I will."

Sheila said, "I wouldn't say it if I didn't want you to, silly."

Just within earshot, Sarah heard the happy exchange and seethed with rage. "You will never have him. I'll make sure of that!"

Mike then gave Katie a quick hug and walked away, grinning from ear to ear. As he walked, he thought he heard some rustling in the bushes.

Sarah held her breath, afraid she had been detected.

Mike stopped, looked briefly and said, "Eh, probably a cat." He continued on his way, unfettered by anything except joy.

Sheila and Katie stayed outside talking for a few minutes, discussing among other things, Mike of course. Being best friends, they never held back from each other.

Katie asked Sheila to tell her everything.

Sheila explained, "I'm really surprised. He is so sweet and gentle. He was so gallant and paid for my lunch."

Katie squealed, "Really? That's a pretty smooth move on his part."

"And it worked—I think he's wonderful. I never would have guessed that last year. He was quite the frog," Sheila exclaimed.

"I wouldn't have guessed it either, but that frog has sure turned into a prince," Katie responded.

Sarah could just make out their conversation from her stealthy vantage point. Simmering like a tea pot ready to scream forth a steamy shriek, she inaudibly responded, "He's my prince, not yours. He will never want you when I'm done. No one will!" Sarah had spent the entire day plotting her malicious revenge against all three. As she overheard the happy banter between these two that had caused her so much angst, her resolve to seek revenge was further strengthened.

After talking girl talk for a while, Sheila told Katie, "I better let

Benny out. I want to be available if Mike calls me."

"Okay, sweetie, call me as soon as you hear from him, love you!"

"Love you too."

The two girls parted after giving each other a best friend hug.

Sarah waited patiently. She watched as Sheila entered her house, and then she heard a small dog bark. She heard Sheila saying, "Hello Benny, who's my favorite little boy? You are . . . yes, you are!"

"Benny? Hmm, so Benny is your favorite little boy, huh? Well, whore, you'll soon find out what it's like being without your favorite little boy!"

After it was clear to vacate the safety of her leafy sanctuary, Sarah slipped out from under the bush and sauntered home, while still scheming about how to make Sheila pay for her interference. When she finally got home and walked through the door, her mother saw her all tattered and disheveled. "Oh my God, Sarah! What happened, baby?"

Sarah, oblivious to her mother's meddlesome inquiry, walked past as if she was in a trance.

"Sarah! Sarah! SARAH!"

Disconsolate, Sarah tramped up the stairs to her room and slammed the door.

Meanwhile, across the street, Mike was excitedly telling Nancy about his first day of high school.

" . . . and then she handed me her number. Can you believe it, Nancy? She gave me her number!"

Nancy was so happy to see her son finally enjoying his youth.

"Your father will want to hear about this, too."

"Oh, I can't wait to tell Dad."

When Big Mike got home, Mike rushed in and told him all about how great his first day of high school had gone. He especially bragged about getting the prettiest girl in school, Sheila's phone number. Big

Mike said, "That a boy! A chip off the old block."

"When should I call her, Dad?"

"Well, son, I always liked to keep 'em waiting for a bit. You don't want to come across too eager."

Eavesdropping from the other room, Nancy yelled, "DON'T LISTEN TO HIM, MIKEY. HE CALLED ME THE MINUTE HE GOT HOME AFTER WE MET!"

Big Mike winked and said, "Did I say always? Your mom was the exception, I knew it the minute we met. Just follow your heart, son."

Mike smiled at the thought of his parents' first meeting. Later that evening, the three went out for their family run, unaware that across the street Sarah was ominously surveying all their activity with icy vigilance from her unlit room.

Downstairs, Sarah's mother was talking to her father on the phone and crying.

"There's something wrong with Sarah. I think she's having another episode."

Her father said, "I think it must have been triggered by that boy."

"I don't know, but can you come home? I'm scared. She won't speak to me and has locked herself up in her room."

"Okay, hon, I'm leaving now. I'll be home in about twenty minutes."

Upstairs, Sarah's mother came in and found her in a catatonic state, staring out the window. She still would not respond to any of her mother's pleas.

When her father got home, he carried Sarah to bed. She lay in bed, still unresponsive. They had seen this before, but it did little to lessen their fears.

"What are we going to do? She's scaring me."

Her father answered, "I knew we should have found a new doctor as soon as we got here. Tomorrow, I'll call Dr. Greenberg in Memphis.

Maybe he can recommend someone in town. I'm sorry, honey. I've been so busy at work."

"Don't blame yourself. Dr. Greenberg did tell us she would have this the rest of her life. I was so hopeful that this fresh start would have helped her. She has been doing so well. I guess we just let our guard down."

***

After dinner, Mike made his way upstairs to his room, where he called Sheila. They spent three hours on the phone together. Nancy was walking by his room when she heard his voice. Being an expert eavesdropper and a nosy mom, she listened in.

"No, my parents are really cool. I think you'd like them. Maybe you can meet them one day. What do your parents do?"

Nancy then smiled and waltzed into their bedroom to tell Big Mike, "It sounds like this girl really likes him."

"Were you listening in again?"

"I am a mother, I'm entitled."

"I suppose. Well, with everything I taught him, she doesn't stand a chance."

"Yes, big daddy, he is your son. He looks more like you every day, and he's becoming quite a dapper young man, much like you were."

"Were?"

"I'm sorry, you are. I just hope his ego never gets as big as yours."

"Ego? You're my proof that the Michael school of charm works."

"Yes, dear, of course you're right," Nancy said in a patronizing tone. She leaned over and gave Big Mike a kiss before turning off the light.

***

Certain that Sarah was asleep, her parents also turned in for the night, optimistic that the next day would come with some resolution to their dilemma.

"We'll figure something out, sweetheart," her father said as he hugged her mother.

Still weeping, Sarah's mother responded, "I just want my little girl to be happy and healthy. Is that too much to ask?"

"I'll make that call first thing tomorrow. Did you get her to take her medication?"

"Yes. I watched her swallow them."

"Then she should sleep well tonight. I love you. Let's try and get some sleep."

Unbeknownst to Sarah's mom, she had been lucid the entire time. Sarah had put the pills in her mouth while her mother watched, but she hid the pills between her upper back teeth and cheek. She then proceeded to swallow the water. Her mother had verified that she took the pills. "Okay, open your mouth. Lift your tongue. Okay, sweetie, please try and get some rest. I love you."

Still unresponsive to her mother, Sarah lay back and pretended to go to sleep. Sarah knew how to play this game. Her mother never thought to check between her cheek and gum. As soon as her mother left the room, Sarah spit the pills out and put them under her pillow. She knew full well what the pills did to her, and she knew tonight would be no night for drugs to cloud her mind. She would have to be awake and alert to put her well-conceived, spiteful plan into action.

12:30 a.m. Sarah had not had her medication for well over twenty-four hours. A side effect of her condition was severe insomnia, particularly when unmedicated, so she remained wide awake and unable to sleep. With hours upon hours of brooding and plotting behind her, she quietly slipped out of bed ready to implement her destructive plan. She snuck out of her house and crept surreptitiously through the neighborhood toward her intended target, the home of Sheila.

It was a warm, humid evening. It had just stopped raining and the streets were aglow with the illumination of street lights reflecting off the wet asphalt. The neighborhood was quiet, with the exception of an occasional dog barking in the distance. A sporadic bolt of lightning would pierce the cloudy darkness like a strobe light, followed by the grumble of thunder.

In her light blue bathrobe, Sarah walked with resolute determination through the streets in her bare feet. She had a focused gaze on her sweaty face. She knew her destination and had plotted her course hours before.

"Say goodbye to Benny, bitch," Sarah mumbled through tightly clenched teeth.

As Sarah approached Sheila's house, she surveyed the two story Victorian style home. She noted that the front porch light was ablaze. "That's no good. Someone will see me." She then saw a dark route along the right side of the house that lead to the backyard. "Perfect."

With a cat burglar's precision, Sarah slithered along the darkened outside wall. When she got to the closed gate attached to a privacy fence, she stammered, "Damn it!" She was relieved to discover that the gate was unlocked. As she opened the gate it made a horrible groaning noise from the rusty hinges, much like the sound made by the proverbial creaking door in all the old horror movies that she watched as a little girl. She was sure the whole neighborhood was awake now, but all remained still. She opened the gate, just enough to slip in. In the backyard she was pleased to see it was pitch black with no lights on, and the large wooden privacy fence assured her that she would remain undetected by meddlesome neighbors.

Her mission now was to figure out how to get inside. She surveyed the entire back of the house, and to her delight, she discovered a small doggy door that led to the kitchen. Sarah was sure she could squeeze in through the tiny entrance.

"There's my ticket in. Here I come, Benny!"

Sarah checked the door handle to verify it was locked. Then, with unwavering determination, she managed to squeeze through that little door undetected.

Now standing in the kitchen, she looked around and grinned ominously as she saw the wooden knife block that was filled with a lovely assortment of specialty items perfect for carving up favorite little boys. She withdrew a large carving knife. She slid her left thumb along the razor-sharp edge, causing a slit which oozed forth thick, dark red liquid. "Perfect!"

The handle felt good in her hand and she whispered, "Here Benny, Benny! Come here Benny, you little bastard."

Benny was nowhere to be found. "I bet he's upstairs, probably in that whore's room. All the better if he is." Sarah had determined that she would filet Benny in front of Sheila so she could feel the pain of losing someone she loved. Then, Sheila could join her precious Benny by meeting the same fate at Sarah's hand.

Armed with her weapon of choice, she climbed the stairs like a ghost until halfway up, when she heard a *CREEEEAAAAKKK* from under her right foot as she stepped up. "Shit!" She whispered to herself. She froze, but suddenly there was a *Yip, yip, yip* from upstairs. That damn dog had heard her.

Sarah made a hasty retreat down the stairs, and for whatever reason, she bypassed the front door and returned to the kitchen. Panicking, Sarah decided to unlock the back door and run out into the dark yard. She opened the kitchen door, leaving behind a bloody thumb print from her fresh cut. As she exited, she could see a glow from behind her; the living room light had been turned on and Sheila's father was crying out, "WHO'S THERE? I HAVE A GUN! THE POLICE ARE ON THEIR WAY!"

A close-call. Sarah ran outside into the dark yard and out through the waiting open gate as it started raining again. Undaunted by the deluge, Sarah calmly strolled down the sidewalk humming love songs to herself. Her normally frizzy red hair now hung low and stuck to her face from the relentless downpour. She still had the knife, and Sarah conceived a new plan that would solve everything.

"We'll be together forever Michael, I promised you this. I know this is not your fault, I know you love me . . . I'm coming for you, my love. Everything will be all right soon."

The police had been dispatched to Sheila's house after Sheila's mother called 911. When they arrived, her father reported finding the back door open, and the door handle had blood on it. The only thing he discovered missing was the large carving knife from the wooden block. He told police it had just happened, and that he never saw or heard any cars leave the area. The police canvassed the neighborhood, anticipating that the perpetrator must have left on foot and could possibly still be in the area.

Ten minutes passed, and four houses down the street from Mike's house, Sarah was located by one of the police units canvassing the neighborhood. She was still wearing her now weighted down robe and was carrying a knife that matched the description given by Sheila's father.

With his gun drawn, the officer shouted out from behind the blinding spotlight, "DROP THE KNIFE AND PLACE YOUR HANDS ABOVE YOUR HEAD!"

Unfazed by the warning, Sarah continued walking and humming her love song, knife in hand.

Again, the officer shouted, "DROP THE KNIFE OR I WILL SHOOT YOU!"

Sarah remained resolute in her determination to get to her beloved. Nothing was going to deter her, especially the threat of death.

"Unit 17 requesting backup units to 56 Blue Jay Lane. I have the possible burglary suspect armed with a knife. I have her at gunpoint! White female, mid-teens, wearing a blue robe and is barefoot! She's not complying with my orders!"

With lights and sirens blaring, several more police units converged on the area.

Undaunted by the arrival of more officers, Sarah continued walking, humming and carrying the knife despite repeated orders to drop it.

Seeing that she was a young girl, the officers showed a great deal of restraint and were hesitant to use deadly force. She had not made any overt threatening moves toward them, and it was clear to them that she was not in a normal frame of mind. They wanted to bring this to a peaceful resolution and get her some much-needed psychiatric attention. The officers hatched a plan for one of them to come up from behind her and tackle her to the ground, while other officers would secure the knife and take her into custody.

The officers put their plan into motion.

As several of the officers distracted her from the front, another officer came up from behind her, grabbed her and simultaneously took control of the knife hand. Sarah's body went to the ground in a heap with the officer on top of her. Then, the others rushed in and secured the knife. Immediately, Sarah started kicking and shouting, "GET OFF OF ME! GET THE FUCK OFF ME! MICHAEL! MICHAEL! MICHAEL! I LOVE YOU, MICHAEL!"

The officers continued to wrestle her to get handcuffs on her. She calmed down briefly, just long enough for officers to move her arms around to her back and handcuff her. She continued to kick and scream all the way to the police station.

Meanwhile, four houses away, Mike and his family lay unaware of the deadly menace that had just eluded them. They slept peacefully, hypnotized by the soothing sound of the pounding rain and distant thunder.

Now in custody, Sarah remained in a focused trance and would not respond to any questions. Police had no idea who she was or where she lived. They placed Sarah in the back of a police car and drove her away to the station, while just a few doors down the street her parents still lay awake, sick with worry about their daughter's condition.

2:43 a.m. The phone rang and Sarah's father answered.

"Hello?"

"Yes, good morning sir. This is detective Franklin with the

Louisville Police Department. I apologize for the late hour."

"That's fine detective, I was already awake. How can I help you?"

"Sir, we have your daughter, Sarah, here at the station and we would like you to come down."

"I'm sorry sir, that's impossible. She's here in bed."

Sarah's father set the phone down, leapt out of bed and ran to Sarah's room, where he discovered that her bed was empty.

He got back on the phone. "I'm sorry, sir, it appears that she must have snuck out. What happened? Why is she at the police station?"

"Sir, I would rather not discuss it with you over the phone. Can you please just come down?"

"Is Sarah hurt? Is she okay?"

"Sir, I assure you she's physically unharmed. About how long before you can get here?"

"We'll be there in twenty minutes."

"That's fine. Oh, could you please bring her some dry clothes?

I'm afraid she's wet and is very cold."

"Yes, sir, we're leaving now."

Sarah's mother overheard the conversation, "Oh my God. What has she done?"

"He wouldn't say, but let's just hurry up and get down there."

Sarah's father and mother got dressed and drove to the police station as quickly as they could.

When they arrived, they met with Detective Franklin, who explained what had happened.

"Officers were called to the home of the Bannister family for a reported break in. Apparently, Sarah walked into the kitchen through an unlocked door and stole a knife. Responding officers found Sarah walking through the neighborhood, carrying the knife. It took an hour with one of our specially trained detectives to find out who she was and how to contact you. Otherwise, you would have been contacted sooner." Her father asked, "Can we see her?"

Detective Franklin explained, "She's fine. She's in an interview room with a female detective. We haven't questioned her yet. We wanted to get hold of you first. Can we get your permission to interview Sarah?"

"Can we be with her?"

Detective Franklin replied, "I can't stop you from being in there, but I'm requesting that you allow Detective Gilbert to interview your daughter alone. She is the special detective I told you about. We determined that Sarah must be suffering from some sort of mental break. Detective Gilbert has a degree in forensic psychology and has already built a rapport with Sarah. You can watch the interview from the other side of the one-way glass and still stop it at any time you wish."

"Can we have a minute to discuss it?"

"Of course, take a minute. I'll be outside." Detective Franklin stepped out of the room.

"What should we do?" Sarah's mother asked her father.

"I think we should tell them about her condition. Maybe they can help us get her into a program. She needs help, honey. Besides, we still don't know what happened."

A few minutes later, Sarah's father emerged. "You said we can watch from the other side of the glass, correct?"

"Absolutely, sir."

"And we can stop it at any time?"

"That's correct, sir."

"That will be fine. Can we please see that she's okay?"

"Yes, sir, come this way."

Sarah's mother had started crying. "I can't believe this is happening.

She's a good girl . . . she just has emotional issues!"

Detective Franklin asked, "What kind of issues? Can you elaborate?" Sarah's father explained, "Well, back home in Memphis, Sarah was diagnosed with schizophrenia and bipolar disorder. We were told by her doctor that hers was one of the youngest cases he had ever seen. She has been on anti-psychotic meds since she was ten. She had an episode with a boy in Memphis when she was nine, and that is when she was diagnosed. She attacked the boy because he was playing with another girl down the street from us. She imagined that she owned the boy, and he could not play with anyone else. Thankfully, the boy wasn't hurt, but her behavior was getting out of control. Her doctor placed her on meds, and she had been doing better for the past several years. We just moved here in June, and I've been so busy lately with my new job we haven't gotten her to a new doctor yet. She had been doing so well that we really didn't worry too much."

"Are you sure Sarah's been taking her medications?"

Her father answered, "We used to oversee her medication for the first few years, but then she would just take it on her own and I suppose we just trusted that she had been taking them. Last night, my wife oversaw her again because she had an episode yesterday afternoon. Normally when she takes her evening pills, she sleeps through the night."

Sarah's mom assured them, "I watched her take them. I even checked her mouth and saw no pills. I was sure she was asleep before I left her alone in bed."

Detective Franklin said, "It sounds like she hasn't been taking her pills, and pretended to swallow as you watched her. Unfortunately, I've seen this before when I used to work in the jail. People can get very creative when they don't want to take medication. She probably hid the pills somewhere in her mouth, and unless you probed her entire mouth it would appear that she had indeed swallowed the pills. This information will be very helpful to Detective Gilbert's investigation. I'll be right back. I'm going to pass this information and the dry clothes along to Detective Gilbert." He left the room and passed along the newly disclosed information.

When he returned, he assured them by saying, "Please know that with this new information, we're not likely to pursue criminal charges against Sarah. We want to get her the help she needs." "Thank you, Detective," said Sarah's mother.

He then ushered Sarah's parents into a dark room with a large window where he told them, "As you will notice, you can see Sarah, but she can't see you. Please have a seat. I'll be in here with you the entire time. I assure you that Detective Gilbert is excellent with people and will be gentle with your daughter. Are you ready?" In unison, her parents nodded yes.

Detective Franklin pushed a button which illuminated a red light in the corner behind Sarah. This was Detective Gilbert's signal to begin the interview.

"Okay, Sarah, as I told you before, my name is Connie. For the record, can you tell me your name and date of birth?"

Sarah nodded, and then in a soft-spoken voice answered the questions. The interview continued and Sarah's parents were relieved by the gentle nature of the questioning. They listened intently and were shocked by what was revealed.

"Sarah, do you remember having a knife?"

"I think so."

"Do you remember where you got the knife?"

Sarah's countenance changed, and through gnashed teeth, she responded, "From that bitch's house!"

Detective Gilbert could see that Sarah was getting agitated and quickly changed her line of questioning. "Sarah, can you tell me where you were going when we found you?"

Sarah smiled, and in a childlike, loving tone responded, "To Michael's."

In a whispered voice, Detective Franklin asked her parents, "Who is Michael?"

Her father replied, "Michael? I don't know a Michael."

Her mom whispered, "Yes you do, Michael is the boy across the street."

"Sarah, what were you going to do at Michael's?"

"We were going to be together, forever. He loves me. I was going to fix everything."

"Sarah, what about the knife? Can you tell me about the knife?"

Sarah was now fixated on her reflection in the mirror. A demonic grin appeared on her pretty young face. Her pupils were fully dilated, giving them a chilling appearance. She leaned forward with her fingers twirling her disheveled hair, and the tone of her voice dropped as she replied, "I was gonna make a way for us to be together forever."

After an hour, the interview ended, and Detective Gilbert met with Sarah's parents. "My concern is that she may have been en route to his location to cause Michael harm. Based on her condition and my interview, I'm afraid we will have no choice but to Baker Act her for now. Sarah will have to be institutionalized for the next seventy-two hours. During that time, she will be evaluated for further treatment."

Sarah's mother was sobbing and asked, "I can't bring my baby home?"

"I'm afraid she is a danger to herself and others at this time, possibly even you two. No criminal charges will be brought against her, considering the circumstances."

"Can we please see her?" begged her mother.

"Of course, ma'am."

Her parents entered into the room where Sarah was still sitting.

Sarah looked up. "Mommy?"

Detective Franklin told them, "We'll give you a few minutes alone."

Sarah's parents spent the next several minutes with her. Detective

Franklin entered the room and exclaimed, "Okay folks, it's that time." They stood by as officers escorted Sarah to the waiting transport van.

"Mommy!? I want to go home with you and Daddy! Mommy, MOMMY, MOMMY!"

Detective Gilbert told them, "The attending psychiatrist will be in touch with you after he evaluates her, I imagine probably sometime by the end of the day."

Her parents mourned as Sarah was driven away to the mental health center. She may as well have been going to prison for the rest of her life. Neither one said anything, but both knew in their hearts that the little girl they had loved and nurtured for fourteen years had been taken from them. Not by the Louisville Police department, but rather by the cruel fate that had stricken their precious daughter with this dreaded mental illness. All of their hopes and dreams of what she could grow up to be, of planning her wedding, spending time with their future grandchildren were all fading away as the police van blended into the horizon.

When they got home, it was nearly 9:00 a.m., and they saw police detectives across the street speaking with Nancy.

***

"Good morning, ma'am. We're Detectives Philips and Mendelson with the Louisville Police Department. May we have a moment of your time?"

"Of course, Detectives. How can I help you?"

"I understand that your son's name is Michael?"

Nancy said "Mikey? Yes, why? Is he in some sort of trouble?"

"No, ma'am, not at all."

"Thank goodness. He's a junior, named after his father, Big Mike.

I'm sorry where are my manners? Won't you please come inside?" "Thank you, ma'am." The two detectives entered the house.

"Is your son home?"

"No, he is in school. Why? Are you sure he isn't in some sort of trouble?"

"No, ma'am . . ." The detectives proceeded to tell Nancy the whole sordid incident that had played out just a few steps away from their house the night before.

". . . It is our belief that she meant to cause your son harm. She appears to be fixated on him."

Nancy replied, "They just met the other day. How is such a thing possible?"

"We believe that she may have a mental disorder. I can assure that she is in protective custody for now."

After approximately a half hour, the detectives left. Nancy was shocked at the news of the incident.

Nancy called Big Mike at work and explained everything that had happened. "The detectives said they think she will be locked up for some time and that Mike should be out of danger."

"Well, thank the good Lord for that."

Being a well-connected attorney, Big Mike used his influences to obtain some normally confidential information about Sarah. He felt at ease after finding out what he learned and called Nancy back.

"I made some calls and I think they were telling you the truth. I believe she won't be getting out for some time. She's a wreck from what I've been told. I think we should hold off on saying anything to Mike. I don't see any reason to worry him."

After talking to the detectives, Sheila's parents also decided not to tell her who it was that broke in, and decided to pass it off as just a random incident. After all, no one had been harmed and as far as anyone knew, Mike was the intended target of Sarah's rage.

Three months later, Sarah was in a bright room full of people her own age. Several of them were walking around holding entire conversations with themselves. Sitting in a chair, staring out a barred window, Sarah muttered, "Michael, I promise you, our time will come. I will find a way."

A FUTURE SO BRIGHT

T he next morning, Mike waited at the bus stop alone. *I wonder where Sheila and Katie are.* He heard the bus coming from around the corner.

As the bus pulled up, the door opened and he heard the two girls hollering from down the street, "Wait! Mike, tell him to wait!"

He turned and saw them running toward the bus so he got on and asked the driver to wait. "Two girls are coming."

The driver responded in the same monotone, apathetic voice, "Whatever!"

Mike saved Sheila a seat next to him, of course. When she and Katie finally got there, he said, "That was close. Did I keep you up too late last night?"

"Oh my God, you didn't hear what happened?"

With an alarmed look on his face Mike said, "No, I didn't hear anything. What happened?"

"Someone broke into my house last night."

Mike, now feeling foolish, responded, "Oh, I'm so sorry. Is everyone okay?"

With a coy smile, Sheila replied, "Well, I'm doing good, now that we're together."

Mike, oblivious to the menace he himself had faced the night before, listened to Sheila's account of what had transpired at her house.

"I woke up and Benny was barking. Then we heard a rustle downstairs. I got scared, but then I heard my dad telling us all to stay in bed. I guess my mom was on the phone with the police. My dad was yelling that he had a gun. I have never been more scared in my life."

She went on, "Next thing I know, the police are there. They took pictures and asked us all kinds of questions. My dad seemed upset with me, accusing me of leaving the back door unlocked when I let Benny out before I went to bed. But I swear I locked it. I always lock the doors. I've always been kind of paranoid about that."

Mike, in his bravest move ever, put his arm around Sheila to console her. He drew her close, and to his delight, she sank her cheek blissfully into his shoulder.

"I'm glad you're okay. I won't let anything happen to you," he said confidently.

Sheila seemed at ease and felt at peace as she nuzzled Mike. She continued her tale. "The crazy thing is that they didn't take anything but a kitchen knife. Isn't that scary?"

Mike whispered, "That is crazy. Thank you, Benny. I hope you give him a special treat when you get home."

"Oh, he was our furry little hero last night, that's for sure."

They arrived at school, and during homeroom were told that immediately following there would be a mandatory freshman assembly in the basketball gym and the next class would be cancelled. Mike and Sheila left, walking hand in hand to the gym. Once there, Katie flagged them down, she was already in the stands and saved two seats beside her.

Mike said, "I wonder what this is all about."

Suddenly, they heard a blaring squeal, followed by the voice of a soft-spoken woman, overpowered by hundreds of teenage voices excited to be out of class. "Test, test, test . . . can everyone hear me? I need everyone to find your seats, please."

They looked toward a makeshift stage in the middle of the basketball court. There stood a stout woman, a towering four feet ten inches and as round as she was tall, with horn-rimmed glasses, brown hair up in a bun, blue skirt with a matching jacket, a white silk shirt with buttons that strained from the pressure of her mammoth bulbous breasts, and two well-stuffed black flats with fleshy nylon-covered bulges protruding up and out from the strained leather uppers.

Mike laughed and said, "She looks just like Miss Piggy."

Sheila and Katie laughed hysterically at the all too accurate observation.

Sheila said, "You know what? She really does!"

The rest of the class was being unruly, ignoring the passive plea from the fat lady.

Then, without warning, the meek and portly announcer boldly asserted, "I NEED EVERYONE TO FIND A SEAT! SIT DOWN AND BE QUIET!" The once restrained voice erupted into a booming roar and immediately the entire class settled down.

"Thank you. Now that I have your attention, I would like to welcome the Class of '89 to their freshman year of high school." The crowd erupted into a raucous cheer.

The fat lady smiled and allowed the uproar to continue for a moment. "Okay, settle down, settle down." She said with an empathetic tone. The excitement was electric, and everyone, including Mike, was getting into it. The crowd eventually settled down and she continued, "I'm Mrs. Bertram. For those who don't know me, I'm the principal here at John F. Kennedy Senior High School. I've been teaching here for twenty years . . .," she went on for another thirty minutes, talking about the school rules and the discipline procedures. Finally she said, "And now I would like to introduce you to our faculty . . ."

Mike was oblivious and bored until he heard, " . . and this is Coach Peterson. He is our head football coach."

Mike looked up immediately. There stood an older man in his fifties with silver hair, a thick silver mustache and dark leathery skin from spending too much time in the sun. He was wearing gray polyester coaching shorts, white athletic shoes and white socks that came nearly up to his knees. He was wearing a dark blue, collared shirt with an eagle embroidered on the left side of his chest. And to complete the ensemble, he wore a blue and gold ball cap with the same eagle on it, and a shiny chrome whistle dangling from his thick neck.

From this giant man standing six feet six came an imposing, forceful voice. Mike could see this giant talking, but all he could hear was, "What's up, you douche bags?"

Mike thought, *No, it can't be. Peterson? Moose? Oh my God, is that Moose's father?*

The coach continued in his brusque manner, "For any one of you young men who thinks you have what it takes, there will be tryouts this Friday for the freshman team. I expect to see all you manly guys out there. The rest of you pansies can try out for band, or maybe you can be cheerleaders or something."

It seemed that all the boys in the crowd laughed at the slanderous quip, even the less than athletic types, not willing to come across as weak.

That voice, that build—he has to be Papa Moose.

Mike told Sheila, "I think I'm gonna try out for football."

Sheila said, "I bet you'll do great. Have you ever played?"

"Not officially, but my dad played in college and he spent all summer teaching me the fundamentals."

"You mind if we come out and cheer you on?" Katie asked.

Bashfully Mike answered, "No, I suppose that would be cool."

***

Friday afternoon, 3:45. Big Mike had come to watch his son's tryouts. He saw Mike on the sideline with the two cute girls.

"Oh, there's my dad."

Sheila smiled and said, "That's your dad? I can see where you get your good looks."

Katie also gave her approval, "Mmm, mmm, mmm."

Mike laughed while he shook his head and ran over to see his dad. Big Mike spent the next few minutes reviewing what they had gone over all summer. Then the whistle blew.

"OKAY LADIES, LINE UP!"

"Go get 'em son, make me proud."

"I will, Dad."

Mike lined up with ten other boys. An assistant coach announced, "Okay girls, this is the forty-yard dash. From a three-point stance on the twenty-yard line, you will run to the opposite forty-yard line where Coach Peterson will time you. You will go two at a time. Any questions?"

One kid raised his hand. "Where do we line up again?"

Screaming into the poor unfortunate soul's face, the coach yelled, "ARE YOU KIDDING ME? AM I SPEAKING SPANISH OR SOMETHING? YOU REALLY DIDN'T UNDERSTAND MY SIMPLE INSTRUCTIONS?

YOU MORON, GET THE HELL OFF MY FOOTBALL FIELD! YOU

HAVE NO BUSINESS BEING HERE."

Dejected and embarrassed, the boy slunk off the field.

"Any other questions?" asked the coach calmly.

Not a peep.

"First two, line up!"

The Moose was in the first group.

Mike couldn't help thinking, *Of course he'd be out here. Look at that animal.*

The Moose was surprisingly quick for a guy his size. Mike heard his time: "5.44."

"Wow, not bad for a Moose!" Mike said under his breath.

Mike was in the second group.

"Next two . . . ready?"

Mike crouched down into a three-point stance, just like his dad had taught him.

BEEEEP, the whistle blew.

Mike bounded forward, and with perfect sprinting form ran the hardest he had ever run. Mike got to the end, well in front of his competitor and heard, "4:42? HOLY CRAP!" Mike had set a new school record.

Coach Peterson said, "Damn son, you part jack rabbit or something?"

In disbelief, the other coaches congregated, thinking Peterson must have made an error. They let Mike rest a bit and made him run again by himself. This time there would be two stopwatches on the other end.

"Ready?" *BEEEEP!*

Again, running like his life depended on it, Mike got to the forty and waited to hear the times; they were even faster.

Coach Peterson. "4.39."

Coach Jackson. "4.41."

All the coaches were buzzing around this marvel like drone bees around a queen.

The rest of the day was spent running lineman drills, route drills, receiver drills and obstacle courses. At the end of the day, Coach Peterson came up to Mike. "Good job, son. I can use a man like you on my field. Is that your father?"

"Yes, sir. Coach, this is my dad, Big Mike. Dad, this is Coach Peterson."

"Pleasure to meet you, coach. I can see you're going to be tough on these guys."

"Well, football's not a soft sport, so I don't go soft on them here. Is that going to be a problem for ya?"

Big Mike adamantly denied any disapproval. "No sir, I played for Kentucky State back in college. I appreciate a tough approach. I expect nothing less for my boy. Besides, he can handle it."

"Football player, eh? Kentucky State you say? Good school. Sir, would you be interested in assisting us occasionally during practices?"

Mike looked at his dad and gave him a smile and a big "thumbs up."

"Well, sir, my schedule won't allow me to be here as often as I'd like, but I will be here every day I can."

Big Mike and Coach spent the next hour swapping war stories from their glory days as players.

Mike ran over to Sheila and gave her a hug. "I'm in."

"I'm so happy for you, baby! You were incredible."

In the locker room, the Moose walked up to Mike and said, "Hey douche bag, I remember you now. You're that pudgy little pussy from the bus. I didn't recognize you at first. You still a whiny little bitch? So now you think you're a football player, do ya? I don't think you have what it takes, PUSSY! Are you gonna cry now, pussy?"

A large crowd of boys had gathered around them in the locker room. Mike knew this could make or break his entire high school experience. He thought, *If I back down, I'll look weak. I have to stand up to the Moose. This is it, Mike, the big showdown.* He recalled the last run-in with the Moose on the bus. Now was his time to pay that fucker back.

The Moose pushed Mike into the lockers. "What are you gonna do, pussy? C'mon! Cry for me, speedy!"

Mike was filled with pent-up rage and rushed toward the Moose with that same blinding speed he had demonstrated on the field. Utilizing some of the martial arts skills he had learned over the summer, Mike let loose a volley of punches to the Moose's face, leaving behind a bloody nose, but to his horror a still standing Frank "The Moose" Peterson.

In a brash, animated and booming voice, the Moose laughed and said, "Fuck'n A! That was awesome. It didn't hurt, but damn man, you whaled on me pretty good. And look, you even gave me a bloody nose. No one but my old man has ever done that before!"

Puzzled, Mike stepped back, waiting for that unaffected mountain of flesh to bring the pain.

Instead, the Moose came up to Mike. "Good job man, you're all right!"

Still wet with sweat from the tryouts, he gave Mike a big bear hug.

Repulsed, Mike thought, *Yep, there's that old familiar Moose stench I remember.*

Smelly, but relieved, Mike gathered his stuff up and went to meet Sheila, Katie and his father outside.

Sheila came up to hug him and said, "Whew! You reek, sweetie!"

Mike laughed and told her, "I promise it's not from me." He went on to tell her all about his encounter with Frank in the locker room.

"You hit him? Oh, my word, you hit Frank? Frank the Moose? And you're still alive? I'm impressed."

Mike's confidence was at a new all-time high as he said, "Believe it or not, he's actually pretty cool."

Big Mike had just finished talking with the coach. He walked over to Mike and told him, "Congratulations son, you did it. The coach was really impressed by you. You're well on your way. Turning to Sheila and Katie, he asked, "Can we give you ladies a ride home?"

After Katie got out of the Jag, Big Mike asked Sheila if she would like to come over for dinner and help them celebrate Mike's football debut. "Nothing fancy, mind you, just some pizza."

Sheila excitedly answered, "Sure thing, but I better check with my dad."

"Of course. Why don't we all go up and ask him? I'd like to meet your father."

Two hours later, Sheila was at Mike's house. At dinner, Nancy said to Sheila, "So, are you a cheerleader?"

"No, ma'am."

"Just call me Nancy, dear."

Reservedly, Sheila answered, "Okay, Nancy. I never thought about cheerleading before."

"Well, honey, you are more than pretty enough and you look like you take good care of yourself. Let me tell you all about . . ."

Nancy stole Sheila away to the other room, where she shared all her tales of past glory being the high school Cheer

Captain and how she met Big Mike in college because she was a cheerleader.

"Well, they'll be a while," Big Mike kidded. "Once your mom gets started on the cheerleader talk, it's all over."

From the other room, "I HEARD THAT!"

"And yet she hears everything."

At the end of the evening, Mike walked Sheila home. When they got to her house, she told him, "Thank you for being a gentleman, and thank you for a wonderful evening."

Mike fumbled around for what to say. "You're welcome."

Sheila laughed. "Have you ever kissed a girl?"

Mike laughed nervously and said, "Of course!"

"Besides your mom, I mean."

Mike innocently looked down at the ground. Sheila had her answer. She told him, "You're adorable," as she pulled him down to her and kissed him good night. Mike was trembling, but was an eager student and quickly picked up the art of the French kiss. Sheila pulled away and said, "Wow, are you sure you've never done this before?"

Mike blushed. "You're my first."

"I'm hoping maybe I'll be your only soon. But I better get inside.

It's late. Good night, Mike."

The two kissed one more time before she skipped into the house. *This is going to be a great year*, he thought as he walked home.

***

Two months went by, and one Saturday evening when the family was on their run, Mike saw a for sale sign on the house across the street. He asked his parents, "So what ever happened with the people across the street? I see a realtor sign up again.

They didn't last too long. I was wondering what ever happened to their daughter . . . Sarah, I think it was? I haven't seen her around. She seemed a little off to me."

His dad answered, "I don't really know, but they must be gone. I haven't seen them around for a while either. That is strange."

Actually, Big Mike did know what happened. Shortly after Sarah was taken away, Sarah's father came to speak to Big Mike and Nancy to apologize for everything that had happened. Sarah's father told him that they would be leaving the area, going somewhere new where Sarah could get some good help. He told Big Mike that she wouldn't cause any further problems for them.

Big Mike never saw the point of telling Mike the truth about Sarah. He was safe now and living a good life. He was popular and had a beautiful girlfriend, everything a parent could ever want for their child.

The year progressed nicely, and Mike became an accomplished football player—one of his Coach's favorites. Nancy and Big Mike never missed a game and Nancy became the stereotypical football mom with a banner with his name on it, yelling and screaming, blowing an air horn for her son from the stands, driving all the other parents nuts.

Mike was so good, in fact, that he was moved up from the freshman team to the junior varsity squad. Mike progressed into the starting quarterback position with the Moose as his center. Mike and the Moose became very good friends that year and spent all their free time together. During the game, Mike could not have asked for a better center because Frank was bigger and tougher than any nose tackle in their division. The Moose never let Mike take one sack the entire season.

Nancy had talked Sheila and Katie into trying out for cheerleading and both girls were now junior varsity cheerleaders. Nancy became so involved that she volunteered at the school as a cheerleading coach.

Mike and his dad would watch Sunday football together on the big screen, cheering and screaming all Sunday afternoon and into the evening, while Nancy and Sheila would talk girl talk in the kitchen.

One day in the summer of 1986, Mike was at home and Sheila came over to spend some time with him. Mike's father was at work and Nancy would be teaching aerobics all afternoon. They had the house to themselves. Mike suggested they go up to his room and listen to some CD's, something they had done many times before.

Mike and Sheila had been going steady for almost a year. They had never really talked about sex before, but Sheila had been thinking about it, a lot. Mike was lying on his bed, staring at the now barren ceiling where Anna had once resided. Crunchy was still in the same hiding place, and got regular use, but he had a girlfriend to fantasize about now and didn't need a one-dimensional poster girl.

Sheila was lying in his arms when she asked him, "Don't you have anything more romantic we could listen to?"

Mike said, "Sure, babe."

He got out of bed and went over to his stereo. He sorted through his collection of over two hundred CD's and found Barry White. His father had always told him that Barry White was the mood man. He

placed the disc in the player then asked, "How's this?"

He heard a click, and then, "Mmm hmm, that's what I'm talking about."

Mike turned around to see Sheila standing by his now closed bedroom door, wearing only her lacy pink panties and bra.

Mike swallowed hard and began to sweat. "Wh . . . what are you doing?" he asked, apprehensively.

"Well, Mister, you had your birthday a few weeks ago and I figured it was time I gave you your gift."

"But you gave me that CD and took me to dinner."

"Oh, that was the decoy gift. I wanted to wait for the perfect time to give you your real present. Me."

Seeing that he was uneasy, Sheila said, "Relax, we don't have to."

Without hesitation, Mike countered, "No, no I want to. But, I've never . . . "

"Shhh, I know honey. I haven't, either. I love you and I want you to be my first."

Sheila summoned Mike to the bed. Like a moth to a street light, Mike was drawn in. They embraced, then Sheila told Mike, "Get my shorts from the floor and look in my pocket. I took something from my brother for us to use when I went to his apartment the other day.

Mike pulled from her pocket a condom. *A rubber?* Mike thought.

With trembling hands, Mike opened the foil package that concealed the purple ring. It was slippery. He said, "How do I . . ."

"Relax stud, Katie and I were practicing on a banana yesterday. Lie back and let me take care of it."

Mike and Sheila consummated their love for the first, but definitely not the last time that summer. Crunchy was discarded, and in the secret hiding place, Mike now maintained an ample supply of condoms. The two remained a hot item all the way through to the summer of their junior year when Mike and Frank went away to football camp for four weeks. This was the first time they had been apart in almost two years.

At first, Mike would call every night, but by week two, he was calling less often. He would tell Sheila that they were working out really hard and that he would fall asleep as soon as he got back to the hotel room. It wasn't long before Sheila realized that Mike had been going to parties, and then she found out from some of the other players' girlfriends that he had been with another girl.

When Mike returned home, Sheila confronted him about his activities. Her eyes were moist with pre-tears. "So, you want to be honest with me for once and tell me what you were really doing this past month?"

When Mike saw her, his heart sank. She really was his first true love, and he knew he had screwed up big time. Mike made the most mature decision he would ever have to make during his entire adolescence. He decided that it would be better to be honest with her than lie to her, even if it meant losing her.

Mike started crying, "I'm so sorry I hurt you, Sheila. I love you more than anything in the world. I don't know what got into me."

"I love you too, you jerk, but you know this changes everything. How can I ever trust you again?"

Mike told her, "I understand. I can't believe I did this to you."

"You'll always be my prince, but it is what it is. Who knows what the future will bring us? But I'll always be here for you. I will always love you."

Mike and Sheila broke up; however, they remained close friends throughout high school and she never harbored any resentment toward him. There were more than a few times that she thought they might even get back together again.

Mike dated many girls throughout the rest of his high school career, and became quite adept at the art of breaking a young lady's heart. However, the only heart he ever truly had any remorse over was Sheila's.

It was his senior year, and Mike was the starting varsity quarterback and the team Captain. Nancy was the most obnoxious mom on the sidelines with her posters that read "GO #6." She would scream so loudly that he could always pick her out of the crowd. At the Homecoming game, Mike led the Eagles to their final victory for the regular season. Playoff bound, Mike was the game hero.

Their team finished with a winning record of nine and one. They had made it to the playoffs and were playing a team that they had beaten decisively earlier in the season.

With twenty seconds on the clock, the game tied and with nothing to lose, the opposing team went for a field goal from the Eagles' forty-two-yard line.

Mike was confidently preparing to take the field. "No way can he make that, it's impossible. We're gonna have great field position, guys." They had heard that this kicker was good, and he hadn't missed a field goal or extra point all night. He had joined their team midway through the school year, after the two teams met the first time. Mike said to his teammates, "Don't sweat it guys. I mean, for fuck's sake, it's a 59-yard attempt! Get your asses ready to go out with me and win this thing! We're going to State, boys!"

Well, sometimes the most important life lessons sting the most, and that night the class of 1989 Fighting Eagles learned a stinging lesson they would never forget for the rest of their lives.

On that chilly fall evening of Friday, November 24th, 1988, on their own home field, The Fighting Eagles of John F. Kennedy High School watched history in the making. The ball was snapped. The whole play appeared to be going in slow motion. The quarterback placed the ball on the ground in perfect position. The kicker, with steely eyes fixated on his target, approached the ball.

Mike thought, *look at this douche bag in his unsullied, comical pale blue and orange uniform with "Carps" emblazoned across the jersey, topped off with a picture of an orange Carp proudly displayed on the appalling, pale-blue helmet. Who ever heard of a fighting Carp, anyway? Really?*

The thud was heard all throughout the stadium, and a hush fell over the crowd as the ball propelled from the freak of nature's foot like a missile from a silo. Straight was the ball's trajectory as it steadily climbed through the dry night air. The stadium lights were gleaming brightly, and the only sound was that of aggressive young linemen stretching out their bodies trying to get a hand on the ball, possibly the last chance in their lives to be a football hero. But there would be no last-minute heroes that night as the ball sailed through the tangled web of arms and hands as it emerged on its path to victory. The ball looked like it might be a little low as it barely made contact with the lower cross bar, then up and over. Two referees in unison raised their arms. It was good. A new state record. The crowd erupted in reckless abandon. Mike looked up and saw that it was the opposing side that was cheering.

They had lost. Harsh lesson learned.

Mike, with mouth agape, stood there motionless for several minutes. His teammates were sobbing, and even Mike, who had not shed a tear since he and Sheila had broken up, wept too. No State Championship. It was over. No more high school heroics.

The first one to come up to Mike was his now best friend, the Moose, whom he now referred to as Frankie. They hugged and reassured each other that they each had played a great game.

Then Sheila came up to Mike, and she had also been crying. "I'm so sorry, Michael. You were great. I love you." She gave him a kiss on the cheek.

He watched her walk away, realizing she really was the best thing that had ever happened to him.

In the locker room, Coach Peterson consoled the boys. Here, this giant, bigger than life man also had a tear in his eye. It was comforting for Mike to know that you can be tough and still have feelings. This too, was a lesson that Mike would carry with him for the rest of his life.

Coach's voice trembled as he prayed with the boys, then told them in a rare, soft-spoken speech that still managed to bellow like thunder, "Boys, you played a hell of a game. You had a near perfect season. You have no reason to walk out of here with your heads hung low. Remember this night for the rest of your lives. Remember, you're always in the game until you're not. Tonight, the other team fought till the end. You too, must never surrender. Always stay in the fight. We couldn't stop the clock, or maybe things would have been different. You will always be champions in my eyes. Now bring it in and huddle up . . . one, two, three . . . "

In unison, the forty-nine players and coaches shouted, *"FIGHTING EAGLES!"*

Mike had truly transformed himself over the past four years. He was now the most popular kid in school and was crowned Prom King in addition to Homecoming King. Sheila was crowned Homecoming Queen, but Maria Phillips edged her out for Prom Queen. Mike and Sheila went to the prom together. There, they managed to share a few dances, but his duties as King prevented him from spending as much time with her as they both wanted.

Mike and Frank had both received a college football scholarship to play for Florida Technical University in Jacksonville.

Friday, the day before he was to be leaving for Florida, Mike had one last thing he needed to take care of before he left. He first stopped by Katie's house and gave her a hug goodbye. They had become good friends through the years. She told him with a tear in her eye, "I'm gonna miss you, dork!"

"I'm gonna miss you, too. Thanks for giving me a chance."

"You're welcome, but you're still a dork. Have you been to Sheila's yet?"

"No, I'm going there now."

"You know she never got over you. She always loved you and still does."

"I know. I never got over her either. I was such an idiot."

"Yes, you were, but we all still love you. Take care of yourself, and Frank too."

Mike waved goodbye and walked next door to Sheila's house. Her parents weren't home and he rang the doorbell. He then heard the familiar *Yip, yip, yip* of Benny coming running to the door. Sheila opened the door and smiled despondently. "Hi, Dweeb."

The two embraced. He went in, and they talked for several hours. She told him all about the school in Ohio that she would be going to with Katie. He, of course, bragged about how great a football program Florida had. He shared with her his dream of turning pro one day, and as she always did, she encouraged him. "I know you will."

Then, in a moment of clarity, he apologized again for hurting her two years before. She told him that she had forgiven him a long time ago and that she would always love him. That day they made a pact. "In ten years, if neither one of us is married, we'll find each other and get married." They pinky swore and kissed each other goodbye with the same passionate kiss they had shared the first time in her front yard after he had walked her home.

Before getting through the door, he stopped and turned around. "Oh, I almost forgot. I got this for you." From the pocket of his blue jeans he revealed a gold chain, and on it was a gold heart medallion. Engraved were the words "Best Friend."

He gently placed it around her delicate neck, kissed her one last time, and then walked to his car. She had been his first true love and he would never forget her for the rest of his life.

Standing in the doorway, Sheila watched wistfully as Mike drove away. "Goodbye, my beautiful Dweeb," she whispered. Sheila would never see or hear from Mike again.

A DOSE OF REALITY

SATURDAY, JULY 29ᵀᴴ, 1989. Mike was having breakfast with his parents. Nancy said, "So this is it."

Mike begrudgingly responded, "Yep, this is it."

Big Mike, eyeballing Nancy said, "Well, son, I hope you know how proud your mother and I are of you. Are you as excited about college as we are for you?"

"Yes, sir, I'm really looking forward to getting started."

"Well, your mother and I hope this gets you a little more excited."

Mike looked up with a baffled expression.

Nancy grabbed Mike's hand and said, "That's right, sweetheart. Your father and I got you a little going away present for that long drive to Jacksonville."

"Really? What?"

"Well, son, you'll have to look outside to see for yourself."

Mike jumped up and ran to the kitchen door. He looked outside to see a shiny black 1987 Buick Grand National parked in front of the garage, but not just any Grand National—a GNX. Mike shouted, "NO WAY, ARE YOU KIDDING ME? OH MY GOD!"

With Mike still hollering in disbelief, Big Mike and Nancy smiled at each other. "I think he likes it," Big Mike said. Nancy nodded in agreement.

All Mike had ever dreamed of since his sixteenth birthday was getting a Grand National. The poster of Anna had been replaced with the only thing that could possibly distract a teenage boy more: a sports car. 1987 was the last year Buick produced the sporty beauty before changing the style of the Regal again. Mike fantasized about this car more than he ever fantasized about Anna. And here it was, right in front of him.

Laughing, Big Mike said, "Well, are you gonna stand there all day and stare at it, or are you going to check it out? The keys are in it."

Mike ran back and hugged his parents. "I don't know what to say. This is the most amazing thing ever. Thank you! I love you guys so much!"

Big Mike asked, "You gonna take me for a ride?"

Mike said, "Let's go!"

Nancy sarcastically hollered, "Be safe, you two! I'll clean up the mess—don't worry about it!"

"Now, I searched all over before finding this. It only has five thousand miles on it." Big Mike relayed.

"The GNX? I can't believe it . . . you are so awesome, Dad."

"Well, your mom convinced me. I was looking at a nice four-door economy car for you."

The two stared at each other in silence.

Then Big Mike laughed and said, "Just kidding! Your mom gave in and let me get this for you. She was worried you couldn't handle a

car like this, but I convinced her otherwise. So- start 'er up."

The shiny keys, begging for attention, dangled from the ignition, twinkling like icicles on the roof's edge in the morning sun in January. Mike trembled as he turned the key into the first position. The dashboard lit up; all systems check. With the next click, the 276-horsepower engine thundered to life. The exhaust rumbled with a unique sound that only a turbo-charged six-cylinder engine could produce. The instrument panel sprang to life. Oil pressure, engine temp and volts all checked out. With a rev of the engine, the coveted turbo gauge showed movement, accompanied by a whine from the turbo's ceramic intercooler.

Mike gripped the leather-wrapped steering wheel firmly with both hands. The bouquet of leather filled his nares and he thought to himself, *I'm in heaven.* He surveyed the interior. It was like showroom new. He stared up at the sky through the glass T-tops and envisioned himself driving down the highway with the wind in his hair from the open top.

A few last checks before he could unleash this beast on the wanting highway; a final adjustment of the seat to fit his now six feet three-inch frame. With mirrors in perfect position, Mike depressed the brake pedal and engaged the transmission. With an imposing clunk, the car was ready and begging for action.

Mike eased the gas pedal to get the four-footed monster rolling down the driveway. Mike thought to himself, *It's perfect.*

Big Mike was watching the glow on his son's face and said, "Let's take this out to old Highway 17 and open 'er up. What do you think?"

For the next hour, Mike and his father shared the most exciting hour they had ever spent together.

"I'm not sure who's having more fun—you or me, but we better get you home. You still gotta pack up the car and get Frank. I don't want you to get on the highway too late."

"Yes, sir, you're right." Not wanting this experience with his dad to be over, Mike reluctantly turned the car around to head home.

"Why don't you drive?"

Big Mike said, "I thought you'd never ask!"

***

Noon. Mike now had the car loaded and was standing in the driveway with his parents. He gave his dad a hug, reflecting on the past four years and how, because his parents took an interest in his transformation, he owed everything to them. "I love you, Dad. Thank you for everything you've done for me!"

Choked up and with a tear in his eye, Big Mike replied, "I love you too, son. I'm so proud of you. Call us when you stop for the night. Do you have enough money with you?"

"Yes, sir."

As restless as a six-year-old at Christmas waiting for a present to open, Nancy, now weeping, cried out, "Okay. Enough already, it's my turn now!" She grabbed Mike and squeezed him so tightly that he could hardly breathe. "My little Mikey, I can't believe how far you've come. I love you so much!"

Mike, now sobbing, remembered back to that summer when Nancy first ran with him, how she never let him falter and always encouraged him. "I love you, Nancy."

In a shaky voice, Nancy whispered in Mike's ear, "Call me Mom."

Stunned, Mike smiled and whispered, "I love you . . . Mom. I owe everything to you. Thank you for always being my number one fan."

"Okay, let the boy breathe. We'll see him in a few weeks. Get going boy, the Moose is waiting."

The two separated, and Mike got into his car. He waved as he backed out. In his rearview mirror, Mike could see Nancy and his dad standing together in the driveway, hugging as they watched him drive away. As they faded out of view, Mike's attention turned to getting to Frankie's house. "I know he's waiting. He's gonna freak when he sees this beauty."

As he pulled up to Frank's, Mike could see Frank pacing on the front porch.

When Frank saw the car pull into his driveway, he looked confused. Then he saw Mike step out.

Mike heard a thunderous, "What's up, douche bag? Holy shit! Is this your new ride? We're going to Florida in this?" Mike nodded.

"Oh my God, this awesome, just like the one in your room. I bet we get some pussy in this thing, huh?"

Mike and Frank loaded up and said their goodbyes to Frank's family.

Mike said to Frank's dad, "Thank you for everything, Coach." Mike recalled all the pep talks and wise lessons he had given all the players, especially to him and Frank.

"Just remember everything I taught you, son, and you'll do well. Keep my boy in line, will ya? Make sure he actually studies once in a while."

"Will do, sir."

Not a hugger, Coach Peterson extended his right hand and the two shook hands. Mike hugged Frank's mom, who was crying because her two favorite boys were leaving. Mike had become close to Frank's parents, and he called her Mama. After their final farewells, the two loaded up and hit the road.

The two drove several hours before stopping in Atlanta for the night. They made it to Jacksonville the next day. They drove straight to their apartment and unpacked.

The next day was Monday, and before the two pulled onto the campus of Florida Technical University they deemed it necessary to get the car washed. "Gotta look good for the chicks. I'll pay for the wash," said Frank.

It was still summer and the campus was not fully active yet, but the two drove around in awe looking at all the beautiful girls, buildings and beautiful girls. They arrived at the football practice field and spent a few minutes watching and dreaming.

They then journeyed to the big stadium. "This is it, Frankie! The Panther Den, home of the FTU Panthers. One day we'll be playing in front of fifty thousand screaming fans."

"Yep, at least I know I will be. You suck."

"Funny, Moose."

"Seriously though, here is where we're gonna leave our mark in history, Mikey. Think you can handle it, Pussy?" Frank said with a smirk.

"If I can handle your big dumb ass, I can handle anything," Mike replied.

"That's pretty funny, you little douche bag," said Frank as he grabbed Mike in a playful chokehold.

Off campus, the two got settled into their apartment. Their parents had rented them a luxury two-bedroom unit on the third floor that overlooked the huge Olympic sized pool. Frank went onto the balcony like a king surveying his kingdom, and to his astonishment saw the most beautiful sight he had ever seen—a pool full of skimpily clad young college girls in bikinis. Short ones, tall ones, thin ones, fat ones, small tits, big tits, brunette, blonde, and red hair; whatever your taste, they were all there.

"Mike, get over here and check this out!" Mike joined Frank on the balcony.

"Dude, are you seeing this? The girl to guy ratio must be four to one. I think we just settled in paradise!"

Between the buildings that surrounded the pool, Frank's thunderous roar reverberated like a yodeler in the Swiss Alps. "HELLO LADIES, WE ARE HERE NOW AND THE FUN CAN BEGIN!"

All the girls looked up to see this gargantuan man bellowing from the balcony. Standing next to him was his hunky companion. A large number of the girls started waving, whistling and yelling in approval. One even lifted her top, exposing herself.

Frank yelled to Mike, "Holy shit, dude! Check out those perfect pear-shaped titties—no tan lines, and her nipples are harder than my

pecker right now. She must want me!"

Mike said, "I think it may be because the water's cold!"

Frank and Mike started to laugh, and Frank sounded like a gray wolf on the prowl for a bitch in heat when he howled, "WOOOOO HOOOOO!"

Now that they were settled in, it was time to report for summer practice the next Monday. Mike and Frank reported to the practice field. Their first day of practice was tough. Mike thought the high school days were tough, but that paled in comparison to the demented torture these coaches put them through. In the scorching August Florida heat and humidity, Mike and Frank thought they would die.

"Fuck me, dude!" Frank told Mike. "This shit's killing me."

"I hear you, bro. Just hang in there. You're the toughest guy I know and I know you can make it."

Make it he did. Frank excelled and made it to starting center for the Panthers and he was the best center they ever had, probably the best any college had ever seen.

Mike, however, was the backup quarterback. Although he often practiced with Frank, he never saw any play time. In high school, Mike had grown accustomed to being the star and was having a tough time adjusting to being the number two guy.

Mike had acclimated to the college lifestyle. His grades were good and he never had any shortage of girlfriends. Occasionally, he thought about Sheila and thought maybe he'd look her up, but he never did. He was popular, but still lacked one thing in his life—no play time.

The starting quarterback, Scott Philips, was the big man on campus. This guy was good, though Mike thought he was better. Mike was a freshman and Scott was a junior. His coaches always told him to be patient.

Coach Brier, the quarterback coach, would encourage Mike. "Just wait, you'll get your shot. Scott had to put his time in. He put two years in the trenches. This is his first year starting."

Fourth quarter of game nine, and the Panthers were ahead three points. Victory was theirs for the taking. Philips was marching the offense down the field with their goal of one more touchdown to secure the win.

Third and two. Philips called a play that would have him keep the ball. They lined up. "HUT ONE! HUT TWO! HUT, HUT, HUT!" Frank flawlessly passed the ball between the two mammoth tree trunks he called legs to the sure-handed Philips. Like a bulldozer, the Moose plowed forward, creating a gap in the defense big enough to drive a tractor trailer through. Philips rushed forward for a five-yard gain and first down. The crowd went wild.

Up from the bottom of the tangled pile of sweaty padded bodies came a scream.

"AAAAAAHHH, MY KNEE, MY KNEE . . . OH SHIT, NOT MY KNEE!"

Frank pulled the bodies off the pile and tossed them aside like they were rag dolls, until he got to Scott. "Are you okay, brother?"

"MOOSE, IT'S MY KNEE! IT HURTS SO BAD!"

Frank looked down and saw that Scott's lower left leg was angulated to the left and his kneecap was offset to the right side of his leg. Frank thought it looked really bad, but all he could think to say was, "You'll be fine, brother."

The trainers rushed to the field. They called for the stretcher. Scott wasn't walking off this field. As Scott was rushed to the locker room for evaluation, Mike heard, "CARSON . . . CARSON! DID YOU FORGET YOUR FUCKING NAME!?"

It was the head coach, Coach Galliano.

"All right son, this is it. Are you ready?"

Mike confidently responded, "Yes, sir!"

After a reassuring, "Get your ass in there," and a smack on the butt from the coach, Mike donned his helmet and took to the field. "This is it, time to show what I can do."

Mike joined the huddle and Frank said, "Welcome to the big show, baby!"

"Thanks Moose," Mike winked and smiled.

Mike looked to the sideline for the offensive coordinator. "What? A deep pass?" They wanted to surprise the defense and go for the end zone now.

Because he was just a backup, Mike never wanted his parents at the games. But Big Mike and Nancy never missed a radio broadcast of FTU's games. That Saturday was no exception. Listening to the game on the radio at home, they heard the announcer say, "substituting for Philips, number 11, Michael Carson. He's just a freshman, but already getting some play time."

Mike's parents shrieked with excitement. The neighbors paid no attention to the noise, as they had grown accustomed to hearing hollering from the Carson household during football season.

The huddle broke, and Mike stepped up behind his roommate and best friend. Frank knew the play, and knew just how to release his gift to Mike on three.

"HUT ONE! HUT TWO! HUT THREE!"

Frank flawlessly released the ball into Mike's awaiting grasp. Frank stood up to defend his best friend from any attacking foe. Mike had all the time in the world to throw the ball. Frank and his line were knocking his opponents to the ground like bowling pins. No one was getting a sack today. Mike looked downfield and there was his target: number seventeen, Jonas Pickens. In practice, he had thrown to Jonas at least a thousand times. Jonas was an outstanding receiver and an easy target at six-two. All he had to do was get the ball anywhere within Jonas' long arms and it was caught.

Mike planted his feet, set himself, took a deep breath and released his projectile. It was a thing of beauty in flight. Soaring through the humid Florida air, the ball sailed upward toward its target in a picture-perfect spiral. During its inaugural flight, Mike briefly lost sight of the ball in the sun. It looked good, for a second or two. The ball then descended from its apex and was returning to the ground. Mike could see his target Jonas was nearly in the end zone. Jonas leapt up, his arms stretched out, making his already tall body looked like the Stretch Armstrong action figure that he had played with as a young boy. Jonas' right hand was out as far as it could go. The ball just touched his fingertips and bounced up.

The ball was caught. However, to Mike's dismay, it was caught by the opposing team's free safety.

An interception. Mike's initiation into the big game, and he threw an interception. Flashbacks to the days on the bus when Moose would whale on him for no reason, and the day Tommy gave him the black eye came rushing back. Mortified, Mike was expecting to hear the Moose attack him. Instead, Mike heard his best friend say, "Don't sweat it buddy, we got time. You were so close!"

Dejected, Mike returned to the bench and threw his helmet to the ground. Coach Brier saw and approached to encourage him. "Listen up, Mike. That was a great effort. Don't let it get to you. Get your head out of your ass and back in the game. We need you."

Mike collected his thoughts and apologized to Coach Brier.

The coach slapped him on the back. "It was a good throw, a lot of pressure for the first game."

The opposing team marched down the field and scored a touchdown, putting the Panthers behind four points.

Coach Brier was still counseling Mike, "Okay son, we have forty seconds. Get us down the field. Do what you do best. I've seen you in practice. You've got what it takes. Now get it done."

Reinvigorated, Mike ran onto the field. With the same determination he had shown that summer four years earlier to reinvent himself, Mike was resolute that he would not make the same mistake twice.

Coach Galliano asked Coach Brier, "What do you think, Ollie?" Ollie was short for Oliver, Brier's first name.

"I think he's ready, Bill. He's young, but he's hungry. I think I can make him a starter."

"Good. I just got word that Philips is out the rest of the season, maybe for good. Get him ready for next week."

"He'll be ready, Bill."

Though they lost, Mike finished the last forty seconds of the game confident that he had done his best. He completed eight passes with pinpoint accuracy. They ran out of time before finding the end zone, but he managed to impress his coaches.

The next day, Mike got a call from Coach Galliano. "I need to see you in my office tomorrow."

"Yes, Sir. I'll be there, coach."

Mike was positive he was going to hear about the interception.

Monday afternoon in Galliano's office. "Well, Mike, Philips is hurt real bad, torn ACL. Doesn't look like he'll be coming back. I'm moving you to the number one spot. You looked good Saturday. I know this is a lot of pressure for a freshman. Can you handle it? If not, I'll have to utilize Diaz."

Diaz was their punter and third string quarterback.

"I'm your man, Coach."

"That's what I want to hear, son. Now get with Coach Brier, and do whatever he tells you to do. Got it? I need you ready for Saturday!"

"Yes, sir!"

Mike was happy to be back at the top again, although he was sad he had to get there at the expense of Scott. He didn't think that Scott was a bad guy, but that was the way it went. This was going to be his time and he was going to take full advantage of it.

Mike called his dad that night. "Hey Dad, did you guys hear? I'm starting Saturday."

"Yes, we heard. You think we might be able to come watch your games now?"

Mike responded, "Of course! I can't wait to hear mom in the stands."

"She's been calling everyone to tell them. She has her banner and her air horn ready to go. We'll be driving down on Friday, but won't get in till late so we'll see you Saturday. Then maybe we can go to dinner that night after the game?"

Mike eagerly responded, "That sounds great. You mind if Frank comes along?"

Big Mike chuckled, "I'm not sure if I can afford to feed that gorilla, but yes, of course. We'd love to see Frankie again."

It was the last game of the season, and Mike played a good game. He threw only one interception, and thanks to Frank never saw the turf.

"Great game today, son," said Big Mike that night at dinner.

Coach Peterson had come to the last game also, and had joined them for dinner. Mrs. Peterson was ill and could not be there. "Yeah, you looked good out there, boy. Don't let the loss get you down. You looked good too, Frankie. The Dynamic Duo is back together."

Mike always liked that slogan, "Dynamic Duo." They had picked it up in high school, and after a local reporter wrote about them in the local paper, it stuck. With Frank as his front man, Mike didn't think anyone could stop them from achieving greatness.

Sophomore year. Mike was doing well in school and decided that he eventually wanted to go to law school. He chose to major in Philosophy, like his father had. He had researched and discovered that Philosophy majors often get accepted to law school above prelaw majors.

Mike also had dreams of playing football professionally, though his father kept him grounded and focused on his education. "You're great son, but remember to focus on your education. One injury and your football career can come to a screeching halt." Mike always remembered his father's advice.

Football and college continued, and Mike was now once again at the top of his game. He and Frank moved into the frat house, and Mike became Captain of the team. Mike always kept his promise to Coach Peterson and helped keep Frank up to date with his studies, as well.

Junior year. The Panthers were relishing their best season in ten years. With a record of eight wins and zero losses, they were looking at an invitation to their first bowl game in school history. Things were looking up, and Mike was feeling like the master of his own destiny.

Saturday, game nine. Mike looked in the mirror and repeated a mantra he had taught himself and would repeat before every game to psych himself out. "You are the man. You can do this. Nothing can stop you. No one can stop you. You are invincible and you are a football god." He raised his arms in a victory sign and then met up with the team in the locker room.

After a potent and inspiring speech from Coach Galliano, Mike was feeling empowered and invincible. They took the field. He was having an incredible first quarter, and they were up ten points. Second quarter, it was third down and three to go. A quick lateral to the outside should bring an easy first down. Mike lined up behind Frank. The ball was snapped, perfect as usual. Frank stepped up in defense of his Captain. However, the opposing line was prepared and double-teamed Frank.

In a dirty move, one player took him high, and the other took him low. They miraculously managed to topple the giant. Mike got mauled by the defense. A rare sack. Mike couldn't believe it. He got up ready to chew Frank's ass as he always did on those ever-so-rare occasions, when he saw Frank lying motionless. By some means, Frank took a blow to the head, and lay there unconscious.

Mike's heart sank. "Moose? MOOSE!"

Frank was out cold. The trainers came rushing out, and with a few minutes and a handful of ammonia pearls, the sleeping giant awoke. Frank stumbled off the field with Mike's assistance. The crowd cheered and Mike sighed with relief.

"You scared the shit out of me, you big oaf."

"I'm sorry I let you down, Mikey."

Looking up at Frank as they walked, Mike smiled and said, "Whatever,pussy!" The two laughed.

On the sideline, the trainers continued to evaluate Frank. "Sorry, big guy. You're out for the game."

"No way! I'm good—I can play!"

Coach Galliano came over to Frank. "Easy big boy, I need you healthy for next week. We got a bowl game to prepare for. Just take a rest."

Mike looked at Frank. "He's right, Big'n."

"But who's gonna watch out for your puny ass?"

"Don't worry, I can handle myself, Mother Moose."

Frank grabbed Mike's jersey and pulled him down to tell him, "Seriously Mikey, watch out. These motherfuckers are out for blood and they're playing some dirty ball. I won't be there to protect you."

Mike could see the seriousness in his eyes and said, "I hear you, brother. I'll watch myself."

Mike rubbed Frank's sweaty head, and Frank smiled.

Over the stadium loudspeakers, the announcer broadcasted, "And now coming in for the injured center number 50, Frank Peterson, is number 57 Miguel Menendez."

The team huddled up and Mike called the play. On the line, Mike would give the count. The play was designed to go on three. "HUT ONE! HUT TWO! WHAT THE FUCK?"

The ball was snapped early. Menendez, with whom he had never played in a real game, was totally off rhythm. It was most likely nerves from being in his first game.

Mike fumbled around with the ball, but managed not to drop it. He scrambled to correct the mistake, but the entire line was out of sync. Mike was looking for a way out. *Ground the ball? Go to the ground? No, I'll keep it and run.*

Before he could put his plan into motion, he felt the bus that hit him from behind. Mike thought he could hear in the distance a familiar bellowing voice calling out, "Mikey look ou-"

REALITY SUCKS

Tuesday morning, three days after the game, Mike woke up confused. He was in a dark room. He heard beeps and saw an IV in his arm. He called out, "Where am I? Hello?"

A petite, pretty woman in pink scrubs and with an ID tag hanging around her neck came into the room. "Oh good, you're awake!"

"What happened? Where am I?"

"You're in St. Bartholomew's Hospital in the ICU. You took quite a blow, young man. For now, you just need to rest up."

"How long have I been out?"

"This will be two and a half days."

"What time is it?"

She replied, "Around 2:30 in the morning."

"What happened?"

"All I can tell you is that you were in a coma. Your mother is in the waiting room. She refused to leave. Are you up to seeing her?"

"Yes, please, that would be nice."

"Ok, let me go get her."

A few minutes later, he heard a soft voice. "Mikey?" He looked up and saw Nancy.

Even now in her mid-forties, Mike thought she looked like she could be one of the cheerleaders at FTU. She approached him and touched his face with a soft, gentle stroke and her eyes were watery.

"Hi Mikey."

"Hi Mom. Where's Dad?"

"I made him go back to the hotel room. He's been here almost the entire time and needed some rest. I can sleep anywhere, so I just pushed some chairs together and the nurses were nice enough to bring me a pillow and blanket. He'll be here in the morning. He'll be upset he missed you coming to."

"What happened to me?"

"We can go over that with you in the morning. I want you to get some rest. I'll be in the other room if you need anything. I love you, sweetheart."

"I love you too, Mom."

Nancy leaned over and kissed him on the cheek.

In the morning, Mike woke up and his mom and dad were standing there with the doctor.

"Hi, Dad."

"Good morning, son. The doctor is going to go over everything with you."

The doctor was an older gentleman with unkempt gray hair, bushy eyebrows that pushed over the top of his thick, black-rimmed glasses and a white lab coat. He reminded Mike of a mad scientist in a sci-fi movie. "Hey there Mike, I'm Doctor Gerard. I'm the neurologist assigned to your case. I'm glad to see you're awake. Seeing that you're an adult now, I would like to discuss your situation with you. Do you mind if I speak with your parents present?"

"No, of course not. I want them here!"

Mike's mom and dad stood on either side of him. Nancy was holding his hand, and his dad kept a hand on his shoulder for reassurance.

"You suffered a significant subdural hematoma, essentially a brain bleed. There was a lot of pressure and we had to put a drain called a shunt in your head at the base of your skull to reduce the pressure. I must say, you are responding remarkably well."

"How long am I going to be in here?"

"Well, now that you're awake, I'm going to get you out of ICU later today and into another room. If you continue progressing like this, I can have you out of the hospital in a week, maybe less."

"But I have a game Saturday."

"This is what we call the proverbial reality check."

The tone of the doctor's voice changed, the kind that tells you that you're not going to like what comes next.

"Mr. and Mrs. Carson, you might want to sit. I'm afraid, son, that your football days are over. If you were to get hit a few more times like that, it could kill you. You're lucky that you survived this one. Repeated blows to the head could cause, at the very least, permanent brain damage. However, with the full recovery that I expect, you

should go on to live a full life without any restrictions."

Devastated by this life-altering news, Mike cried, much like he did in his room that day in June of 1985, only this time no amount of self-determination was going to change or improve his situation. His parents wept with him, knowing how important this was to him.

"Son, don't go thinking your life is over," his dad said. "Football was a great sport, and I'm so very proud of you. But it was always just a game. You will still go on to law school, you know that, and you will follow your dreams of being a lawyer. You know we'll make sure of that."

Mike remembered what his dad had told him about how one injury could be the end of his football career. Mike also looked back to Coach Peterson and how he had always emphasized education over football. But all the encouraging memories from the past could not bring him any solace. His dream of being a professional was over.

Mike thought to himself, *Reality sucks!*

Nancy told Mike, "I have someone in the other room who is anxious to see you. Are you up for another visitor?"

Mike sighed, and in a disheartened tone responded, "I guess so."

Nancy said, "We'll go for now and send them in."

Mike turned his head and stared dejectedly out the window. Frank tromped up to the doorway and saw his best friend lying pitifully in the dark room with IVs in his arm, patches on his chest and on the back of his head, where it had been shaved and a shunt had been placed.

Mike turned around when he heard the sound of large feet stomping up, and was surprised to see the colossal figure darkening the doorway. With a bold, audacious voice that Mike would recognize

anywhere, Frank shouted "WHAT'S UP, DOUCHE BAG?"

His boisterous announcement elicited an immediate angry response from the charge nurse, a small woman standing five feet nothing, scolding him in a thick, southern drawl. "Keep your voice down, young man! This is a hospital! You ain't got the good sense God gave a goose! Another outburst like that and I'll have you thrown out of here faster than a knife fight in a phone booth!"

Mike thought she looked like a child next to him, only coming up to the bottom of his chest.

After his scolding, Frank tiptoed into the room and whispered,

"I mean, what's up, douche bag?"

Mike couldn't help but laugh. It was the first time he had been happy all day.

In one of the most empathetic moves Mike had ever seen from the Moose, Frank came over and gave him a big hug. When he stood back up, Mike could see that he was crying. The biggest bully he had ever known, and the toughest man alive, was now weeping like a child who lost his favorite toy.

"I'm so sorry, Mikey. I let you down and this is all my fault! I should have been in there. I would have never let this happen to you!"

"Frank, you warned me, buddy. It just happened. Please don't blame yourself, brother."

Frank was inconsolable, and it took over a half hour to calm down the grief-stricken giant. Frank was finally comforted when Nancy came in and hugged him saying, "We love you, Frankie. We don't blame you.

You always took care of Mikey. We know you always had his back."

Frank immediately responded, "And I always will!"

Later that day, Mike was moved out of ICU to a private room. He could now receive visitors without restrictions, and there was always a steady stream of cheerleaders and other players coming in and out. His room was cluttered with flowers and get-well cards from people he had never even met.

The next night, Frank went to see Mike.

"So, you guys are flying out tomorrow?" "Yeah, we fly to Ohio. Big game," Frank said.

Ohio . . . for a brief second, Mike thought of Sheila and wondered how she was doing. Mike hadn't thought about her in a long time.

He was snapped back to the present when Frank said, "It's not gonna be the same without you there."

"I'll be there in spirit, buddy. I'll be watching you guys from the best seat in the house." Mike pointed to his hospital bed with the nine-inch television hanging from the articulating arm on the wall in his room.

"You gotta win this one for me, pal."

"The entire team is dedicating this game to you, Mikey. We're gonna kill these assholes."

Mike smiled a fake smile, pretending he was happy, but was still lamenting that he wouldn't be there.

"Go get 'em, buddy," he said in a shaky voice.

The two friends hugged and Frank left.

True to Frank's word, the Panthers won a decisive victory in Ohio. They finished the regular season nine and one, then went on to win their first bowl game ever.

The season was over and Mike had been released from the hospital. He returned to school and successfully got caught up with all of his class assignments.

Frank had already received some interest from the pros, and Mike had a full-time job keeping Moose in line and up to date with his studies.

That summer of 1992, Mike and Frank went home for a visit. Mike spent the weeks with his father, working an internship in his father's law practice. He was still close to his parents and was developing a real passion for the law. He would watch his father in trials and help him prepare for cases. Mike and his father were inseparable, and other than Frank, Mike considered Big Mike his best friend.

Summer drew to an end and it was time for Mike and Frank to return to school. Mike went to all of the practices, and actually assisted the coaches. He had lost his full ride scholarship since he could no longer play, but thanks to Big Mike, he continued on to his senior year.

The year was going well and Mike's grades were better than ever without the distraction of football.

Friday, November 20th, 1992. As Mike was packing for a flight home to spend Thanksgiving with his family, he heard Frank shout, "Hey Mikey, it's Nancy on the phone. She sounds upset."

Mike ran down the hall to the phone on the wall. Frank stood by his friend with a concerned look on his face.

"Mom? Is everything okay? What's wrong?"

Frank watched Mike's face suddenly go pale and expressionless, then tears filled his eyes.

Mike dropped the phone, and then collapsed to the ground. This confirmed to Frank that something terrible had happened. He picked up the receiver. "Nance, it's Frank again. Tell me what's going on." Nancy told Frank the tragic news.

It would seem that a former client, Peter Loomis, was disgruntled with the way Big Mike had represented him. Peter was sentenced to life in prison without the possibility of parole after killing his estranged wife. The day before, Peter had somehow escaped jail before being transferred to prison and went looking for the man he blamed. That evening, he found Big Mike outside his law firm while he was walking to his car.

He stabbed him twenty-seven times in the chest. Big Mike died on the spot.

"Don't worry Nance, I'll take care of him and get him home. We'll be there tomorrow. I love you too."

Frank looked down and saw his best friend weeping. He knelt down, picked his friend up, and like a mother carrying a newborn, he gently carried him to his room and laid him down in bed. Frank sat the rest of the night in a chair by Mike's side, refusing to let him grieve alone.

The next morning, Frank woke Mike and they went to the airport. Frank never left his side until he dropped Mike off at Nancy's house. Frank told Nancy, "He hasn't said much since yesterday. I'm gonna get going. Call me if you need anything."

"Thank you, Frankie. You're such a special man, and a good friend to Mike. I don't know how to thank you."

"You don't ever have to thank me. I love you guys. Just let me know if you guys need anything."

"I will, Frankie. Be careful driving home."

Nancy spent the next two days comforting and consoling Mike. Mike eventually came around and started to help Nancy with the funeral plans and preparing for the incoming guests.

Wednesday, the day before Thanksgiving. Mike was with Nancy by the graveside. Family and friends stood by and comforted them as best they knew how. Mike was silent and inexpressive as he stared at his father's casket. It had been a nice enough service, as funerals go. Father O'Brien presided over the service and was very reassuring to Nancy that Big Mike was in a better place now. Mike had a hard time believing that.

What was so wrong with the place he was at now? Mike angrily thought to himself.

Frank remained by his best friend's side throughout the holiday, but eventually Frank had to return to school and Mike would help him with his studies over the phone. Mike watched the last televised Panthers game in the family room on the big screen TV where he and Big Mike had watched the games.

Mike did not return to FTU that semester. He decided to help his mother through the holidays. Mike determined that he would not rely on his mother for money. Big Mike was the provider and always took care of her, but she did not have enough money to take care of him while he was in college and keep the same lifestyle to which she had grown accustomed. Mike decided that he would find a job and continue his studies part time.

After Christmas, Mike returned to Jacksonville. He enrolled in one class and started the arduous task of finding a job. He had been cleared medically from his head injuries, and was willing to do anything.

Jobs were tough to come by, and he worked a series of odd jobs from night clerk in a gas station, to a waiter. He made just enough money to move back into the apartments where he and Frank had stayed when they first came to Jacksonville.

This place held many happy memories for Mike, and the scenery wasn't bad. Frank would spend more time there than at the frat house, and howl from the balcony at the girls. Frank was quite the celebrity and would always liven things up for Mike.

June arrived, and Frank graduated with a business degree. The bigger news was that Frank had been drafted into the pros and was on his way to becoming a superstar. He received a considerable contract, being one of the highest paid centers in the history of the game. But why wouldn't he? He was by far the best the game had ever seen.

Mike said to Frank, "So much for the Dynamic Duo, eh?"

Frank looked at Mike and said, "Are you shittin' me man? I owe everything I am to you."

"What are you talking about?"

"I never told you, but you were my inspiration all throughout high school and I never would have made it through college without your help. You're the best friend I've ever had. I love you like a brother. We will always be the Dynamic Duo. You're gonna be a great lawyer, and who knows—without you to keep me in line, I'll probably require your services one day."

Grinning, Mike said, "You probably will Moose, you probably will."

Moose insisted, "Promise me Mikey, if you ever need anything, you'll call me first. You don't ever have any needs that I can't take care of, deal?"

"Deal."

"I wish you'd let me pay for your schooling."

"Moose, I love you pal, but I have to find my own way. I'll make it. Just knowing that you have my back is enough to keep me going."

"I will always be here for you, bro!"

The two hugged and Mike said, "You're all I got left. You better take care of yourself."

Frank said, "You're my boy, Mikey."

Mike and Frank remained best friends, and Mike watched Frank's career blossom. Mike never missed a game, and could always be heard cheering for Frank like Big Mike had for whatever team Frank played for. Several times every season,

Frank would fly Mike out to watch from the sidelines. Mike never had to pay for anything.

Now that Mike was struggling alone, working and trying to continue his education part time became more difficult. Mike could make the money to survive, but he was going deeper into debt. One day, there was a police recruiter on campus, explaining to students about a career in law enforcement. Mike listened intently, and discovered that most police agencies will help pay for continuing education.

Mike asked, "Excuse me, sir, does it pay well?" The recruiter told Mike what the average law enforcement officer earned, and it was two to three times what he was earning, on average.

Mike called Frank and asked him what he thought about him becoming a cop.

Frank said, "Bro, a cop? Holy shit, I'll have to be on my best behavior all the time now or you'll arrest me!"

Mike laughed and explained that it would be a means to an end; he would be able to finish his degree on someone else's dime.

"Sounds good man, I can totally see you in uniform. But remember, I won't be there to keep you safe. You better watch yourself. Are you sure I can't help you out? Money's not an issue between us, Mikey."

Mike snickered, "I appreciate it pal, but I think I can handle it. Besides, maybe I can get the satisfaction of putting some dirt bag away, like that piece of shit who whacked my dad!"

"Just be safe, my man."

"I will Frankie, thanks."

Even though no one seemed to be hiring, Mike still sent applications to agencies all across the state. In a few months, he read about a sheriff's department in Southwest Florida that was looking for deputies. Mike had never heard of Dolphin County, but decided to apply anyway. The city of Boca Grande Shores was the county seat. The testing would take place in January 1994.

The day came for the testing, and Mike arrived early. Of course, he was in peak physical condition and passed all the physical requirements with ease. His drug screen was clean, and even though he had a tough time talking about what happened to his father during the psychological exam, he managed to pass satisfactorily.

Mike spent some time exploring this town where he had never been. Boca Grande Shores seemed like a pleasant enough community. There were a lot of retirees in this part of Florida. He researched and discovered that the crime rate was reasonably low, which sounded good to him. He ultimately wanted to be a lawyer in a law firm, and working a low crime area didn't sound so bad to him.

Mike returned to Jacksonville while he waited for his background check to be completed. He continued taking his class and working part time. One evening he received a phone call.

"Yes . . . uh . . . good evening, Mr. Carson? This is Corporal Huffman with the Dolphin County Sheriff's Office. How are you today, sir?"

"Very good, thank you. How may I help you?"

"Say, you wouldn't be the same Michael Carson that played for

FTU two years ago, would you?"

Mike favorably responded, "Yes, sir, that's me."

"Wow, you were great. I'm an alumnus of FTU. I graduated in 1985. I was at that game when you got hurt. What a tough break. I still go to as many games as I can. You were the best quarterback

they had in years. I'm really sorry that you got hurt."

"Well, thank you, but that seems like a long time ago."

"The reason for my call is that I'm finishing up your background and I need to clear a few things up. Everything looks great so far, but there is the issue of your injury. Would you be willing to get cleared by our doctors?"

"If it would help me get the job, absolutely. I've been given full clearance and have all the documentation, if it will help."

"That shouldn't be necessary, sir. As long as you get cleared by our physician, I see no problem with forwarding your application.

How does next Tuesday work for you?"

"I'll be there, and thank you sir."

"No problem. We'll see you Tuesday."

Mike arrived in town the following Monday and checked into the Sand Dollar Motel, where he prepared to get a good night's rest. His appointment was at 9 a.m. the next morning with the department physician, Doctor Jansen.

3:00 a.m. Mike was startled to hear his phone ringing, and muttered, "Who the hell would be calling me at this hour? No one even knows I'm here."

Mike answered the phone, "Hello?"

All Mike heard was static. He said again, "Hello?"

Again, no answer. Mike hung up and called the front desk.

A man answered with a Hindi accent. "Front desk. This is Nandi. How may I help you?"

"Um, yes, I just got a phone call, and when I answered there was no one there."

"I do apologize, sir, let me see . . . I'm sorry, sir, I show no record of any calls to your room."

Mike, slightly agitated, said, "Look man, I have an appointment first thing in the morning and I really need a good night's sleep!"

"Please sir, do not take this tone with me. I'm telling you there is no record of any calls to your room."

"You're right Nandi, I apologize, but please . . . I really need to get some sleep. Is there anything you can do to make sure I don't get any more calls?"

"Of course, sir. I will be sure to put a block on your line."

"Thank you. Can you tell me if I'm still set for a 7:15 wakeup call?"

"No problem sir. It is taken care of."

3:45 a.m. The phone rang again. Perturbed, Mike answered. *"HELLO!"*

At first, the line was silent, but then Mike heard an unusual sound. He listened carefully and wondered, *is that the sound of cattle?* The sound was muted by static on the line, but he definitely heard the sound of cattle, like an entire herd. He immediately hung up and sat on the edge of his bed.

A cold chill flowed through his veins. He had an uneasy feeling. He assumed that someone must be playing a joke on him. Not feeling jovial, Mike once again called the front desk.

"Front desk. This is Nandi. How may I help you?" answered the same Hindi-accented man.

"Look, Nandi, what the hell kind of game are you playing? I explained to you that I needed to get some rest, and this shit keeps happening. I'm not amused, God damn it!"

The voice on the other end deepened and an unhallowed voice growled, "Sir . . . I . . . told . . . you . . . there . . . is . . . no . . . record . . .of . . . any . . . call!"

Overcome by a menacing sense, Mike hung up.

"What the fuck was that?"

It was now 4:00 a.m., and Mike was exhausted. He thought about an old black and white TV series he watched as a kid, and pictured himself in one of the episodes.

The phone rang again.

"This can't be happening!"

His anger conquered his trepidation, and Mike stormed out of the motel room with the phone still ringing. He marched to the front office and pounded on the door of the darkened room. A light came on from a back room, and Mike could see the silhouetted figure of the man who had checked him in earlier. As he drew closer, Mike could see that he was wearing a black bathrobe and brown slippers. He had dark olive skin and a large, bushy black mustache. His jet-black hair was disheveled. He had clearly just gotten out of bed.

The man shuffled to the door, opened it, and with a similar Hindi accent and a simultaneous yawn the man asked, "Yes, mister?

May I help you?"

Mike barked "NANDI!?"

The man looked perplexed and asked him, "Why would you call me that, sir?"

"Nandi. That's your name, right?"

"Sir, my name is Akbar. We have no one named Nandi here. Where did you hear that name?"

Mike enlightened Akbar about all that had transpired in his room, which included several phone calls with the strange sounds of cattle and a menacing voice on the other end identifying himself as Nandi.

Akbar took the time to explain to Mike that Nandi is the name of a divine, ancient Hindu bull and is not commonly worshipped in his culture anymore.

Not wanting to argue with the irate customer, Akbar said, "I apologize for your inconvenience, sir. This sort of thing has never happened before. Please let me get you another room, no charge."

4:30 a.m. Mike lay down. He had asked Akbar for a 7:45 wakeup, hoping to still get a little rest. Still uneasy about all that he had experienced, he lay awake in bed most of the remaining night, only managing about an hour's sleep. Mike thought, *Divine bull? Cattle sounds? Nandi? Man, this is fucked up! I'll be glad to get the hell out of here.*

7:45 a.m. The phone rang, and Mike bounded out of bed to get ready for the visit with the doctor.

As Mike was leaving the motel, he glanced back at the first room where he had experienced the unusual occurrences and thought he saw a dark-silhouetted figure standing in the window. It appeared to have the head of a bull and the body of a man. After a quick double take, he exclaimed, "What the . . .?" Suddenly, the figure was gone and the curtains hung motionless. "I must be losing my mind."

Mike dismissed all of the events as Akbar playing games with him, and continued on to his appointment.

A NEW BEGINNING

JULY 1994. Mike was getting ready to start the law enforcement academy. He had been hired by the Dolphin County Sheriff's Office and was excited at the prospect of actually getting paid to be in school.

For the next sixteen weeks, Mike would learn self-defense tactics, emergency driving, firearms, report writing, constitutional law and of course legal procedures. Physical fitness came easily to him, and he would often catch himself starting to laugh when other people struggled, but then he would flash back to the summer when Nancy encouraged him. Being a team player was in his nature, and instead of laughing, he would cheer on his classmates and encourage them to push a little harder.

Leadership and taking control came naturally to Mike, as was evident from his success on the football field. He was popular with the other recruits and they elected him as their class leader. He was in charge of forming the lines and marching the class to the flag pole every morning before class started, where they would recite the pledge of allegiance and take a moment of silence for the fallen officers who came before them. He exhibited a keen understanding of the legal material, and would spend hours helping others who struggled with the material.

The only area in which Mike did not excel and finish number one was marksmanship. Before the academy, he had never fired a gun in his life, unlike many of the other students who had grown up hunting with their fathers. Mike's only real connection to his parents didn't come until his summer transformation, when sports and fitness became their connection. Big Mike never owned a gun, and Mike would often say to himself, "If only you had a gun that day Dad, maybe you'd still be here with me." He read all the books and understood all the mechanics involved with shooting, but hitting the target proved to be more difficult than he had imagined. As he had helped so many of his fellow recruits, they, too, encouraged him at the gun range.

One fellow recruit, Saul Weismann, was a particular help to Mike. He and Saul became good friends, and Mike would often joke around with Saul that he was the one who should become a lawyer. "You got the perfect name for it!" Saul, in fact, was not Jewish himself, but his grandfather was Jewish and had immigrated to the United States after escaping Germany with his family during World War Two. Saul had been a competitive shooter since he was thirteen years old, when his father, who had been an Olympic competitive shooter, introduced him to the sport. On weekends, Mike and Saul would go to the range on their own time and Saul would work with Mike. By the end of the academy, with Saul's assistance, Mike had become one of the top ten shooters. Of course, Saul rightly finished number one.

To Mike's surprise, a career in law enforcement started out as a means to an end, but became something for which he developed a real passion. He grew eager as the time to graduate came closer. Soon he would be out on the streets, protecting and serving the public. By the time he completed the academy, Mike had finished number one in his class, a place he had grown accustomed to in all of his sports endeavors.

Lieutenant Albertson, Commandant of the law enforcement academy, had been with the Sheriff's Office for eighteen years, and had recently been put in charge of training new recruits. He called Mike into his office one day. "Congratulations Carson, you've surpassed everyone else in the course work and you will be receiving the top recruit honor at the graduation ceremony. Would you be willing to give a short—and I do mean short—speech after I present you the award?"

Mike replied, "I think I can come up with something, Sir."

"Very good. Just get me a draft by Friday so I can review it."

"Will do, sir."

Mike couldn't wait to tell his mom, who would be flying down to witness the graduation ceremony. To Mike, it seemed that it had been a long time since Nancy had anything to be proud of him for.

Since his father was murdered that tragic day before Thanksgiving, Nancy had become more distant. He hoped that this weekend might be a time for them to reconnect.

Mike also called Frank to let him know. "Hey Moose, can you be there at the graduation? It would mean a lot to me."

"When is it again, pal?"

"November 4th. It's a Friday."

"Yeah bro, that's our bye week. I'm so stoked how that worked out. Of course, I'll be there for ya, man! Is Nancy coming down?"

"Yeah, I believe so. She still hasn't given me a definite answer yet."

"How is she doing, man?"

"I'm not sure. She doesn't talk much. I hope things might turn around for us when she comes down."

"Has she been seeing anyone yet?"

"I don't think so, but I can't say for sure. She really misses my dad."

Frank playfully said, "Do you think she needs a little Moose meat? Maybe I can snap that beautiful lady out of it!"

Mike laughed, "Shut up, you asshole. That's my mom."

Frank laughed, "Just fuckin with ya, brother. You know I love Nance."

"I know, buddy. Thanks for the laugh, I needed it. It's been almost two years since my dad was killed. Knowing you're here means a lot to both of us."

"No sweat, you know I love you guys. See you in a couple weeks."

Nancy arrived the day before the ceremony. Mike had insisted that she stay at his apartment, but she insisted on staying in a hotel near the beach and he didn't want to push it. She still seemed fragile. Frank, on the other hand, insisted that he stay at Mike's. How could Mike say no? Mike picked up Frank at the airport, and instantly it felt like old times.

Mike, Frank and Nancy went out to dinner that night at a pricey restaurant called Taureau's. Frank insisted on paying for everything and Mike obliged him because he had learned long ago not argue with Frank. It was pointless.

Frank asked Nancy, "How are you, sweetheart?"

"I'm good, Frankie."

Frank looked at Mike in disbelief and shrugged.

Frank, playing on her ego said, "Well, you still look as beautiful as ever!"

Nancy perked up and smiled, "Thank you, Frank."

Mike jumped in and lightheartedly said, "Hey man, are you putting the moves on my mom? You want me to whip on you like that day in the locker room?"

Frank bellowed a raucous laugh, and then said, "Oh yeah, you mean the day of the infamous mosquito sting I got on my nose? No, no, please don't hurt me!"

Thanks to Frank's antics and lighthearted nature, the three were reminiscing and having a good time. After a few glasses of wine and Frank's witty humor, Nancy began loosening up and was laughing. It had been a long time; in fact, she couldn't remember the last time she'd had as much fun. It pleased Mike to see his mom smile again.

After dinner, Mike and Frank dropped Nancy off at her hotel.

"Love you Nance. Sleep well, gorgeous lady," Frank said.

Nancy blushed. "You are quite the charmer, Frankie," as she hugged him good night.

As Mike hugged Nancy, she said, "I'm sorry I've been so distant, sweetheart. This is the first time I've actually laughed since your father died. You know your father would have been very proud of you. I hope you know I am, too."

As she pulled back, he could see that she had tears in her eyes.

"I love you, Nancy."

She hugged him again, this time a little tighter, and implored him, "Please call me Mom. I love it when you call me Mom."

Mike hugged her tightly and said, "I love you, Mom!"

Nancy then piped up, "Okay, you two, get going. We have a big day tomorrow."

"Okay, Mom. We'll pick you up 10 a.m."

"10 a.m., got it."

Mike and Frank left her and returned to his apartment.

"I don't know how to thank you, Frankie. You are the man. Thank you for getting her to laugh tonight."

Frank bashfully said, "You never have to thank me for anything. I told you before, there's nothing I wouldn't do for you guys."

The two stayed up reminiscing for a few more hours, then went to bed sometime shortly after midnight.

3:00 a.m. Frank was asleep in the spare bedroom on the other side of the apartment when Mike was startled awake.

"What the hell was that?" Mike awoke to what he thought sounded like the snort of a bull. He listened intently in the darkness. All Mike could hear was the sound of Frank snoring from across the apartment. Assuming it must have been Frank that he'd heard, Mike

looked at the clock. 3:01. "Shit, I need to get some sleep."

As Mike was slowly drifting back to sleep, he was again startled by the same disturbing sound, and sprung up, now wide awake and with all his senses keenly focused on his surroundings. His heart was racing so hard and fast that he could hear his own heartbeat.

A grunt? That's not Frank. It's in the room! Petrified, Mike rapidly scanned the dark room that was illuminated only by the glow of his digital alarm clock. All of his senses were on high alert, including his sense of smell. *That smell, what the hell is that smell?* Mike thought. Instantly, he imagined he was back at his uncle's cattle farm. *Cow crap. Putrid, smelly cows!* He was examining the obscurity that surrounded him when he became fixated on a menacing silhouette standing in the doorway. Then he heard the ear-piercing roar of a bull, "MRRAAAWWW!"

"WAAAAAHHHHH!" Mike screamed as he fell out of bed.

Frank came running into his room and turned on the light. "What happened, Mikey? Are you okay, buddy?"

Mike, lying on the floor with a horrified expression on his face, was sweating and trembling. Frank walked over and said, "Bro, are you okay?"

With a disconnected gaze, Mike looked up at Frank looming over him, then screamed again.

"Whoa, whoa, Mikey. It's me . . . it's Frank."

"Frank? Oh my God!"

"What happened, chum?"

"I . . . I saw it again. It was right there!" Mike was pointing to his doorway. "It roared that terrifying roar! You didn't hear it?"

Frank snapped, "Hear what?"

"That roar, that dreadful roar. It sounded like an angry bull!"

"Bro, all I heard was you screaming, and I came running in here to find you lying on the floor. Look around, buddy. There's nothing in here." In an effort to make Mike smile, he said, "I know I'm ugly, but damn, man."

Mike was beginning to calm down. He looked up at Frank, smiled and said, "You are one ugly son of bitch."

Frank laughed and said, "I think you must have been having a nightmare."

"I guess so, but it seemed so real. Help me up, you bastard." Mike reached out to Frank the same way he used to when he was on his back in football, and like old times, Frank was there to pick him up.

The two best friends stayed awake for the next hour, talking on the couch. Mike told Frank about the incident at the motel earlier in the year, and the disturbing image he had seen in the window.

Frank reassured him, "So there you go, buddy. A nightmare. You just relived that night again. Shit man, after hearing that, I'd have nightmares too."

The two went back to bed.

8:30 a.m. The alarm went off and Mike stumbled to wake up Frank.

Mike called Nancy. "Are you up, Mom?"

Nancy, yawning, responded, "I am now."

"How'd you sleep?"

Nancy replied, "Not so well. At around 3:00 a.m., I woke up, and kept waking up every hour after that. But that's not unusual. I often don't sleep well since your father passed."

"I'm sorry. I had a rough night too. I had a nightmare. But anyway, can you be ready in forty-five minutes?"

"I'll be ready, hon. What time will you be here?"

"We'll be there at 9:15."

"I'll be ready by 9:10."

9:30 a.m. Mike knocked on Nancy's hotel room door again.

"C'mon mom, we're going to be late!"

"I'll be right out. Give me just one more minute!" Five minutes later, Nancy finally emerged.

Frank catcalled her and said, "Well, it was certainly worth the wait!"

Mike teased her. "Good thing we're just around the corner from the academy or we'd never make it."

Nancy playfully stuck her tongue out at Mike, then said, "Thank you,

Frank. At least someone appreciates the work I put into looking good."

Frank laughed and said to Mike, "Yeah, you jerk!"

At the ceremony, the three sat together in the front row. Nancy wore a slinky black dress that came to her knees with a slit up the right side that accentuated her still toned legs. Many people asked with sincerity if she was Mike's sister. Nancy relished all the accolades and perked up. She had not been social in quite some time, not since Big Mike's passing, and had forgotten how much she appreciated the attention of others. Frank was a hit, also. Many people recognized him as the superstar pro football center. Mike sat nervously as he went over his speech.

When he was finally called forward, Mike was presented with a plaque and several other awards.

Lieutenant Albertson announced, "And now a word from Deputy Carson."

Nancy beamed at her handsome son, a truly proud mother. Mike stood tall in his green, perfectly pressed uniform with crisp creases. His badge and brass items all glimmered in the light, and the black leather accessories were polished to a high gloss. Nancy held her head up with pride as she watched her son deliver his heartfelt speech.

"Thank you, Commandant. Fellow graduates, guests and loved ones, welcome to the graduating Class 66-6 of the Dolphin County Law Enforcement Academy. We started four months ago thirty strong, and we stand here today a stronger twenty-three. We regret the loss of seven comrades, but let us not forget, this is a higher calling, and not everyone is called. Ours is a noble profession. Let us take pride when we don our uniforms and go out to defend the helpless, and even, when called upon to do so, help the unworthy.

"Look around you. Take pride that you have received that calling and that you had the courage to answer that call. Always be accountable to yourself first, then your fellow officers, and last but not least, the public we protect. Serve with honor. Never soil the integrity of this honored profession. Train hard, be vigilant, and always remain compassionate.

"Thank you to the instructors for sharing their knowledge and experiences, and affording us a solid foundation for the challenges ahead. And finally, thank you to all the families and loved ones who supported their recruits and encouraged them over the past sixteen weeks. Take pride and continue to lift up and encourage your warrior, knowing that no matter how courageous their facade, at the end of the day they are only human, and as such, flourish with the support of those they hold dearest.

"To recruit Class 66-5, thank you for laying down the gauntlet and setting a high standard for our class to strive for. I pray we have made you proud. To recruit class 66-7, my hope is that we have left a legacy worthy of your admiration as the class before us did. Good luck to us all, and always watch your six."

The crowd applauded as Mike returned to his seat between Nancy and Frank.

"Nice speech, bro. You almost convinced me to become a cop," Frank whispered.

"They don't make a uniform big enough for you, Moose," Mike quietly retorted.

Frank chuckled to himself and said, "True dat."

After the ceremony, many people came up to Frank, wanting his autograph. Frank politely indulged them all until there was no one left clamoring for him. Mike sat back and watched his best friend revel in the attention, and rather than being jealous, was proud of him. Frank had come so far from being the school bully. He was now just a big teddy bear. But Frank still remained the fun and obnoxious oaf Mike had grown to love like a brother.

On Sunday, the three sat around watching football, hooting and hollering like old times. Frank spent half the time on the balcony looking out at the girls by the pool.

"Not quite as satisfying as our old apartment in Jacksonville my friend, but your pool still has quite a few good-looking ladies. Nice view!" Frank then howled out from the balcony at the unsuspecting girls in the pool. Several of them waved at the unfamiliar colossal character on the balcony.

Mike and Nancy sat and laughed at his childish antics.

"Just like old times, is it?" Nancy asked.

"He hasn't changed a bit, thank goodness."

Nancy smiled, "Yeah, there's something special about that big lug. He's a good friend to you. I'm glad you have him."

"I think I'd be lost without him, Mom."

"Well, we've all been through a lot the past couple of years, sweetheart." With moist eyes and a quivering voice, she remarked, "I miss your father so much."

Mike looked despondently into his mother's eyes as he held her hand. "Me too, Mom. Me too."

Monday morning, Frank and Nancy were getting ready to leave.

Nancy's flight left first, and Mike was hugging his mother goodbye. She whispered, "Please take care of yourself, Mikey. I'll worry about you every day. Please be safe. I can't lose you too, son."

"I'll be careful, Mom. I love you. Call me when you get home."

After seeing Nancy off safely, Mike and Frank had two hours before Frank's flight. They went to the lounge and had a few drinks.

"Well Mikey, I'm proud of you, bro."

"Why would you be proud of me? I'm just a cop, not a big football star like you, buddy."

"Don't ever let me hear you say that!" Frank barked. "You're my best bud, and you are so much more than just a cop. Just be safe, and promise me you'll get through law school one day."

"I promise you, brother."

"Are you sure you won't let me help you out with finances?"

"No Frankie, I need to do this on my own. But thank you."

"Well, you're doing it, my friend. I'll call you later. I gotta get on board soon."

A quick best friend hug, and Mike watched Frank meander through the security checkpoint. He laughed as Frank scarcely fit through the metal detector. He continued to watch until Frank vanished into the crowd, which took quite a while since he stood so tall above everyone else.

When he did finally lose sight of Frank, Mike turned to walk back to his car. He felt a heaviness in his heart watching his mom and best friend fly away. He was alone again.

Mike decided to spend the rest of the day getting to know his new hometown. He took mental note of the quiet community, and where the places were that people would congregate. He noted that there was an alarmingly large number of pubs and bars for such a small community. *They must be a very sociable lot around here,* Mike thought. Besides the number of bars, he noted that there was an unusually small number of churches. *I guess they like to drink without guilt,* Mike mused. Despite all that, the town still had a nice charm and very low crime rate, according to everyone he had spoken to.

Mike drove to the sheriff's station on the edge of town and introduced himself to several of the deputies who were present. Mike asked Deputy Hank Stubbard if he could recommend where a good place in town would be to get dinner.

Hank asked, "You like a good greasy spoon or something a little better?"

"It's just me, so something quick but good."

"All the single guys usually end up at Diablo's Pub after work.

You can get a few drinks, and the food is pretty decent."

"That sounds good, thanks. Hank, was it?" "Yeah, and you're Mike, right?" The two shook hands.

"I'll be going there after I go home and clean up."

"Sounds good, Hank. Maybe I'll see you there."

"Oh, I'll be there. Several of us will be. Come on out and join us."

When Mike arrived at the pub that evening, he met up with Hank, who introduced him to several of the other deputies and they all got along well.

Hank asked, "So, you're the new guy everyone's talking about. When do you start?"

"I start Wednesday."

"Don't be late. Sergeant Constantine hates it when you're late. You don't want to cross him. He's tough but fair. I worked for him my first year and I loved it. Just stay on his good side."

"I can handle that. How long you been on the department?"

Hank replied, "Four years as of last week. It's a good agency. I think you'll be happy."

The two chitchatted for several hours, then Hank said, "I gotta get going, Mike. I'm on duty in the morning. Take care of yourself."

4:30 a.m. Wednesday morning. Mike woke up to get ready for his first day. He got out of the shower and the bathroom was very steamy. As he was shaving in front of the steamed-up mirror, he felt the sensation of warm breath on his neck from behind him. He spun around, but nothing was there. When he jerked around to look behind him, he sliced his face with the razor.

Now he was distracted by the deep gash on his right cheek. Mike refocused, "Oh great, now I'll show up with red toilet paper stuck to my face. Holy cow, I really got myself good."

It took several minutes for Mike to stop the bleeding. "I really sliced the crap out of myself." He looked and saw it was now 5:30. "Oh shit, I gotta get going." He looked down. There was blood all over the vanity top, and bloody tissues in the sink. "I'll clean this up later. I'm going to be late."

Mike hurriedly dressed and ran out the door to get to work. At 5:47, he pulled into the parking lot of the station. Everyone else was already there. *Damn. This isn't going to look good,* he thought.

At 5:55, Mike walked into the roll call. Standing in the front of the room behind a podium was Sergeant Constantine. On top of the podium was a stack of paperwork for him to review with the squad. He was an average height man at about five feet nine, with a gray flat top. He had deep stress lines on his face, probably from so many years on the street, and a scowl that looked permanent. While still looking down, he peered over the top of his dime store readers and saw Mike entering the squad room. "You're late, new guy!"

In unison, ten other deputies exclaimed, "F-N-G!" Most laughed as Mike stumbled in and looked around for a seat.

Over the next several minutes, Sergeant Constantine berated Mike for being "almost" late. "Okay rookie, here's the deal. I don't know how you do it where you come from, but around here on my squad if you're on time, you're late. I expect your ass warming that seat no later than ten minutes before the shift starts. Got it?"

"Yes, sir, Sergeant."

"Well, why are you still standing? Do you have your notebook?"

Mike panicked as he thought, *oh, fuck, I left my notebook on the counter.* Nervously, he replied, "Um . . . no sir, I left it at home."

At this point, most of the guys were laughing at Mike. Memories of middle school came flashing back into his mind.

"For Christ's sake, what kind of an idiot did they hire? Can someone help Princess out?"

Now sitting nervously in the back of the room, Mike noticed the deputy next to him lean over. "Here ya go. I have an extra. Got a pen?"

"Dear Lord, I forgot my pen too. SHIT!"

Smiling as he handed Mike the pen, the deputy said, "Got you covered, bro. Here ya go, F-N-G."

Mike whispered, "Thanks. I'm sorry . . . F-N-G?" "Fucking New Guy. Get used to that for a while." Mike slid a little lower into his seat.

"He's good, Sarge! He found his stuff."

"Well, thank God for small miracles! Can we begin, F-N-G? I'm talking to you, new guy!"

Mike nodded affirmatively.

"Thank you very much!"

At the end of roll call, Sergeant Constantine once again turned his attention to Mike. "Okay sweet lips, you got a name, or do you prefer F-N-G?"

Again, the scornful laugh from others that he had despised as a kid echoed through the room.

Nervously, Mike responded, "Michael, sir."

"Michael what? Are you the damn archangel or something? You got a last name?"

Mike was feeling a bit humiliated by this point, but dared not express it. "Carson, sir. Michael Carson."

"Michael Carson, huh? Okay boys and girls, everyone say hello to Michael Carson." In unison, the whole group responded, "Hello Michael Carson, F-N-G."

"Okay, which one you unfortunate souls gets to ride with this dumb ass?"

Everyone in the room looked around as if there was a big surprise about to be revealed.

Finally, from the front of the room, the corporal, Corporal Oren said, "Don't everyone jump up at once." Corporal Oren was a tall, lanky man in his late thirties. His uniform was too baggy on him. He was balding with a horseshoe hair ring that circled his shiny dome.

Feeling like he did in elementary school as the last kid picked on the kickball team in the school yard, Mike thought, *this is not starting out like I had hoped. These guys are assholes.*

"All right, ladies. Gather around. We're going to have to draw straws to see who gets the F-N-G."

A groan of disgust resonated throughout the room, as all the other deputies lined up to get their straws.

Mike sat passively in his chair. For some reason, everyone made it a point to walk past him and he heard, "This is bullshit!" "Fucking new guy!" "God, please don't let it be me!"

Mike, for a moment, wanted to run back to his empty latchkey kid house, fly up to his room, hide under his sheets and cry. But he remained stoic. He told himself, *Relax, you've endured worse. Don't show any weakness.* He recalled the days when The Moose would whale on him for no reason, and how helpless he had felt. "Okay. Everyone got their straws?" It was time for the big reveal.

Corporal Oren shouted, "Okay! Hold up your straws!"

From across the room, "This is bullshit, Sarge! Not again! No fucking way! C'mon, can't we do best two out of three?"

"Okay, and the loser . . . er . . . I mean, the lucky winner is Deputy

Barber. Everyone give Paul a big hand."

Everyone began clapping and whistling for Deputy Paul Barber.

"C'mon Sarge, I got stuck with the last idiot."

Sergeant Constantine replied, "Sorry Paul, that's the luck of the draw."

"SHIT!"

Mike looked back to see it was the same deputy that had given him the notebook and pen.

Everyone in the room looked at Mike, who was sitting motionless. The pen in his large hand was trembling and his grip was straining the limits of the pen, then "snap", and the pen broke.

Paul then walked up to Mike laughing, "Take it easy rook, we're fucking with you."

The whole group, including some of the command staff that had entered the back of the room to watch the fun, laughed out loud.

Mike was relieved and smiled.

"How ya doing, buddy? I'm Paul. I'll be your Field Training Officer. Congrats, we can usually break people long before you. Good job! Were you told your radio number yet?"

"No, I haven't been told much yet."

"Your radio ID number is four-forty-two. As you move up in seniority, your radio number will lower. My number is four-sixteen.

Got it?"

"Yeah. Thanks Paul."

One by one, the rest of the squad came up to Mike to shake his hand and introduce themselves. Some remembered him from his college days, and told him how great he was and what a tough break he got.

Lastly, Sergeant Constantine approached and shook his hand. "Welcome to the agency, Mike. Sorry—I couldn't resist setting you up a little. I hear a lot of good things, and I'm going to expect a lot from you. But, seriously, don't be late again," he said with a smile.

Mike's first day of field training was fairly uneventful, mostly traffic-related calls and a burglary. When Mike got home, he remembered the bloody mess he had to clean up in the bathroom. When he went in to clean it up, he noticed a set of smudged, bloody fingerprints on the mirror while he was wiping out the sink. He could not recall touching the mirror, but then concluded he must have done so at some point that morning while he was rushing around bleeding like a stuck pig.

He finished cleaning up the bloody mess, and relaxed the first evening at home. He called Frank and Nancy to share about his first day, then went to bed early. He would make sure he was not late again.

Over the course of sixteen weeks, Mike worked with a total of five different Field Training Officers. He excelled at the job and was well-regarded by his peers and supervisors.

By special request, Mike was assigned to Sergeant Constantine's squad. Constantine was the most senior sergeant in the department and pretty much got what he wanted. Mike enjoyed working for Sergeant Constantine, and was grateful to work and learn from someone he respected as much as Constantine.

FORGING AHEAD

*D*ECEMBER 1998. Mike finally graduated from FTU with his Bachelor's degree in Philosophy. Because of his work schedule, he did not attend the graduation ceremony. There was little fanfare with his graduation because he didn't think it to be that big of a deal. He was only half the way to achieving his goal of graduating law school.

FTU had a renowned law school, one of the best in Florida. Mike immediately applied and was accepted based on his academic achievements as an undergraduate. He could continue his studies part time; however, he was required to drive to Jacksonville periodically for mandatory lectures and proctored exams. Though the distance proved to be a hardship, he was on his way to completing his objective. It would take longer than he had originally hoped, but at least he was able to work in a career that he enjoyed, and it allowed him to reach his ambition without relying on the help of anyone else.

Mike worked hard and was now one of the top-performing deputies in the Sheriff's Office. His supervisors asked him to become a Field Training Officer. He accepted the responsibility and was well liked and respected by the junior deputies he trained. Mike enjoyed training the younger deputies and molding them.

By early 2001, he had been decorated multiple times. He was awarded Deputy of the Year in 2000 and Deputy of the Quarter on three separate occasions. He became antsy and was eager to try something new. He was looking for a challenge.

Mike had developed a reputation as a perfectionist and became quite adept at testifying in criminal cases. There was an opening in Major Crimes, a special detective unit that handled the most serious of crimes, from rape to murder. This position was usually reserved for people who already had experience as a detective, but Mike was asked to apply for the position. After serious consideration, Mike applied for the opening, as he believed it was just the challenge he was looking for.

Lieutenant Robert Peterson, in charge of Major Crimes, called Mike on the phone one Sunday afternoon. "So, Mike, you think you'd like to be a detective?"

"Yes, sir. I know I don't have experience, but I'll work hard for you if selected, and I am definitely looking for a challenge."

"Challenges are what we specialize in, Mike. We have no shortages of those around here. I know your reputation and have no doubt that you'd be an asset to our team. Your success in trial is enviable, and your education level is higher than anyone else applying for the position.

That reminds me, aren't you working toward your law degree?"

"Yes, sir."

"How much longer do you have to go before you finish?"

"Well, sir, I'm going part time, so it's going a little slower than I had hoped. But I should be done in another three to four years."

"Well, nothing official mind you, but I think it's safe to say that you can expect to receive a call from me next week sometime. Of course, we still have to complete the selection process, but I believe it's just a formality. How do you think you'll feel about wearing a suit instead of a uniform?"

"I do love the uniform, sir, but the idea of wearing a suit and tie kind of appeals to me, also. It might help with the transition to the courtroom in the future."

"I agree. Okay, then. I'm sorry to have called you on your day off, but I just wanted to touch base with you. We'll know by Friday."

"Sounds great. Thank you for the call, sir."

It was time for the next shift rotation from days to nights. At 5:51 p.m., Mike reported for work. During the Friday evening roll call, Sergeant Constantine, looking over the same now scratched and smudged dime store readers said, "Damn it, Carson! You're late again. It's nine minutes till!"

"Sorry Sarge, my watch is slow."

"Well, apparently you won't be my problem much longer. Listen up, everyone. It seems that Deputy Carson will be leaving us. He wants to be a dick."

The squad all laughed in unison.

"He's leaving us to become a Major Crimes Detective."

Deputy Lou Praft called out, "Won't that make him a Major Dick, sir?"

Deputy Melissa Glanz continued, "So what you're saying is he's making a lateral transfer then?"

"Yeah. Once a dick, always a dick," said Lou.

Mike laughed along with everyone else. He was going to miss the squad. He had become close to all of them, and loved the camaraderie and banter.

After roll call, Sergeant Constantine called Mike into the office. "Congratulations, Mike. I remember six years ago when you walked through the doors of the squad room."

Mike interrupted and said, "Oh yeah, me too!"

"Anyway, I told you not to let me down, and you haven't. I'm gonna miss having you around. I was hoping you'd see me into my retirement in two more years, but you gotta spread your wings. I'm proud of you, son."

"I appreciate that, Sarge. I can't thank you enough for sharing all your knowledge and experience with me. You've been a big part of why I'm getting this opportunity."

"You can thank me by being as good a detective as you are a deputy. I worked as a detective way back. Always wanted Major

Crimes, but I got promoted instead."

"Well, I'm glad you did, sir."

"All right, that's enough of that. Get the hell out of my office. My ass can only handle so much kissing! Jesus, do you want me to propose to you now, or what?"

The two shook hands and with mixed emotions. Mike continued on to work his final shift on the road, his last shift in uniform. He was hoping to slide to the finish line with an uneventful day.

There's an old saying... wish in one hand and shit in another, see which fills up first. It became readily apparent that Mike's day would be full of . . . well, not wishes.

His first call of the day was a burglary. He had worked so many burglaries before that day that he had lost count. Two hours later, he completed his first call. Immediately afterward, he was dispatched to a domestic in progress. Mike arrested the husband, who was drunk and had smacked his wife because she didn't have dinner on the table for him when he got home late from work. Mike had no sympathy for wife beaters, and always got a particular pleasure when he incarcerated a wife-beating dirt bag.

After leaving the jail, he made a traffic stop. It was intended to be a simple stop, a warning for having a driver's side headlight out. He called into dispatch and advised that he was pulling over a red 1978 Camaro at the corner of St. Mary's Ave and Fruitland Road. He illuminated the driver's mirror with his spotlight. As he got out of his patrol car, the hair stood up on the back of Mike's neck. Something was off. Something was wrong.

Mike hesitated for a moment and said, "Dispatch, four-twenty-two, send me a backup unit. Everything is 10-4 for now."

"10-4, sending backup."

Something about the demeanor of the driver sent red flags up for Mike. He could see through the back window that the driver was nervous and fidgeting around. Mike approached from the passenger side window. As he drew near the open window, he was horrified to hear what sounded like a child crying in the trunk of the car.

"Help me . . . help me."

What the fuck!? Mike thought.

Immediately, he drew his gun and pointed it at the driver. From the vantage point on the passenger's side of the Camaro behind the door, Mike yelled, "DRIVER! TURN OFF YOUR ENGINE AND SHOW ME YOUR HANDS! DO IT NOW!"

Rather than complying, the driver quickly pulled a large caliber, chrome revolver from his lap and managed to get one round off simultaneously as he depressed the gas pedal. Mike immediately started firing his nine-millimeter semi auto at the driver. The tires spun and smoked as they made a horrific squeal. The rear of the car slid to the right. Mike tried to jump out the way, but got hit by the back end as it sped away.

He wasn't hurt. "Holy shit, I'm alive. I'm not shot . . . oh my God, a kid!"

He sprang up and ran back to his car, shouting into his radio, "FOUR-TWENTY-TWO DISPATCH, SHOTS FIRED, SHOTS FIRED!

I'M IN PURSUIT! BE ADVISED IT SOUNDED LIKE THERE WAS A CHILD CRYING IN THE TRUNK OF THE CAR!"

Calmly, the dispatcher replied, "10-4, four-twenty-two, all available units respond to assist four-twenty-two in pursuit of suspect with a firearm, shots fired, possible victim in the trunk of the vehicle."

Anxiously, he continued on the radio, "DISPATCH, WE'RE NORTHBOUND ON FRUITLAND ROAD! SPEEDS IN EXCESS OF

100 MILES PER HOUR!"

"10-4, four-twenty-two, northbound Fruitland, 100 miles per hour."

Then in the kind of calmness only age and experience can afford, Sergeant Constantine called on the radio, "Four-hundred to four-twenty-two, are you hurt?"

Now bringing himself under control, Mike replied, "Negative, Sarge. I'm not hit, but I think he has a kid in the trunk!"

Suddenly, he cried out over the radio, "FOUR-TWENTY-TWO, DISPATCH, THE SUSPECT JUST CRASHED INTO A TREE! SEND EMS!"

"Four-twenty-two, what is your location?"

"FRUITLAND AND MAIN! FRUITLAND AND MAIN!!!"

Mike jumped from his patrol car with his gun drawn. At the same time, the suspect exited the Camaro with his gun drawn. The driver was a skinny white male in his early twenties, with long black hair in a ponytail. He was covered with tattoos. He wore a bloodstained white t-shirt and blue jeans. The suspect raised the shiny tool of death to take aim at Mike. Mike immediately opened fire, striking the suspect four times in the chest and once in the head. The driver collapsed into a heap next to his smashed-up car.

"FOUR-TWENTY-TWO, DISPATCH, SHOTS FIRED. SUSPECT DOWN, NOT MOVING!"

Mike could hear the other units approaching. His attention immediately turned to the child he had heard in the trunk. He darted to the suspect, secured the suspect's weapon, and checked his carotid artery. "No pulse. Good, you piece of shit!"

"Four-twenty-two Dispatch, suspect is signal seven!"

"Dispatch copy, suspect signal seven."

Mike grabbed the keys from the ignition and dashed back to the trunk. His hands were trembling, fearing what lay in wait for him inside. It was not normal procedure to go any further without a backup unit, but if this was a child, there was no time to waste. Mike opened the trunk and his heart sank. Before him lay the motionless, crumpled up body of a small, blonde-haired little girl. She appeared to have been slammed up against the back seat, apparently as a result of the violent crash. Her tiny body was tangled up among the spare tire, jumper cables, some tools and other trash. She was bleeding profusely from her head and appeared to be unconscious. She looked as if she was only three or four years old and was wearing a pink nightgown with the word "Princess" in silver glittery letters emblazoned across the chest. Her hands and feet were bound with duct tape, and a single piece of tape had been placed across her mouth to keep her silent, but looked as if it had come loose.

Mike straightaway checked her carotid pulse. "A pulse! Thank you, God! It's weak, though. She needs an ambulance right now!"

"FOUR-TWENTY-TWO, DISPATCH, I HAVE AN APPROXIMATELY FOUR-YEAR-OLD GIRL, UNCONSCIOUS WITH SHALLOW BREATHS AND THREADY PULSE, ADVISE

EMS TO EXPEDITE!"

"Dispatch copy . . . EMS is three minutes out."

While waiting, Mike continued to monitor the girl. As he watched her, she stopped breathing. Mike carefully pulled her from the trunk to start rescue breathing. His emotions were on overload. He didn't bother to get his CPR mask. Who cared? This was an innocent little girl.

Mike was so focused on the task at hand that he didn't even notice other units arrive on scene. The next deputy on scene, Lou Praft, came running over to Mike, seeing he was doing CPR.

"Four-thirty dispatch, four-twenty-two is performing CPR on the child."

"Dispatch copy, CPR in progress."

Within a few more seconds, there were multiple units on scene. Melissa Glanz ran over to help, "Oh my God, Mike, you're bleeding!"

He was bleeding from his right thigh where a round had struck him. "We got this, Mike. Go sit down!"

"Four-thirty-one dispatch, we need another rescue to respond to the scene, we have an injured officer. Four-twenty-two was hit." Mike sat down and watched in silence as his comrades attended to the little girl. He broke down and cried, not from pain where he had been hit, he never felt that; but from the sight of that beautiful, innocent child lying there motionless.

As his fellow deputies attended to him until the arrival of the ambulance, Mike thought, *what could I have done differently? I should have done more! Please be okay, sweetheart. Please God, let her live!*

The first ambulance arrived, and the crew declared that the girl had a good pulse and that she was now breathing. Mike breathed a sigh of relief as they rushed her from the scene via medical helicopter.

The paramedic attending to Mike told him, "You're lucky, brother. It looks like it just nicked your thigh. It may not even need stitches, but you should let the ER doc check it."

Mike said, "I don't want to go anywhere right now."

The medic told him, "Okay then, let me just clean it up and wrap it for you. Just get it checked out later. I'm glad you're okay, brother."

In all the activity and the adrenaline rush, Mike never realized that he had been hit. He thanked the medic and turned his attention back to the suspect.

He thought, *What kind of monster was this asshole?*

Sergeant Constantine came up to him. "You okay, son?"

With a distant gaze Mike responded, "10-4, Sarge."

"Funny, you don't look okay."

"It's just a nick, sir. I'll get it checked out when we finish up here."

"You did a hell of a job tonight, Mike. Paramedics said if you hadn't gotten her out of the trunk when you did, she wouldn't have made it."

"Thank you, sir. I just can't imagine what she must have been going through."

"I'm glad you're physically okay. I guess that's one way to spend your last shift with us on the road. You certainly finished with flair, didn't you?"

Still with a blank, expressionless gaze, Mike nodded and said "Uh-huh."

After about half an hour, Mike had calmed down. Word had gotten back that the girl was going to make it.

By this time, he had collected his thoughts and his new colleagues from Major Crimes were now on scene.

Lieutenant Peterson walked up to Mike. "How are you?"

Trying not to show emotion, Mike said, "I'm better now, sir, thank you."

"Good. Of course, after this you're gonna enjoy a little well-deserved vacation. I suggest you take that time to relax. Listen, this is tough, I've never been in your position, and I can only imagine it must be very surreal."

"So, what do you think this was all about, Lieutenant?"

"The little girl's name is Suzy Shinner. She was abducted earlier tonight from her house in Brandon."

"You mean this was the girl in the BOLO from earlier?" Mike asked.

"That's her. Great catch. It appears that this guy broke in and took her from her bedroom while the parents were asleep in the next room. Thanks to you, she's going to be okay. Come with me, I want to show you something."

The two walked over to the suspect. "This scumbag's name is Jeremy Pickford."

Mike could now see some of the tattoos on Jeremy. Across his upper chest was tattooed 'S A T A N' in fancy script. He had tattoos of pentagrams and demons on both of his arms.

"It appears that this guy was part of some sort of local satanic cult. Did you look around inside the trunk?"

"No, I just grabbed the girl after she stopped breathing."

"Come look at this."

They walked over, and inside the trunk were several objects that sent a cold chill up Mike's spine. Among the trash and other debris in the truck was a dagger. The dagger's handle appeared to be made from a bull's horn. Inscribed on the horn was the picture of a Minotaur-like creature. It had a man's body with a bull's head. There was a jar that had a thick red liquid in it, marked "bull's blood" on the label. There were five black candles strewn around the trunk as well as a black shroud with a red pentagram sewn onto it.

Lieutenant Peterson explained that this had all the makings of a ritual sacrifice. There was one candle for each point of a pentagram.

On the cover of a pamphlet in the bottom of the trunk was a picture of a demon, a Minotaur-like creature. Across the top of the pamphlet it read "The Moloch Society."

Mike's mind flashed back to the motel room and the image of that dark figure in the window. He broke out into a cold sweat.

"Are you okay?" asked the Lieutenant.

"Huh? Oh yes, sir. This is just some creepy shit."

"Yeah, we've recently been having a wave of occult-related crimes. They've become more prevalent over the last five years, and getting worse. But this is the first time that I know of where a child may have been the target of a sacrifice.

Usually they have been sacrificing cats, and some dogs, but until now no humans, at least not that we're aware of. They're becoming a big part of what we're dealing with in Major Crimes. I have researched other communities in the state who don't seem to be having these same issues. I'm afraid we may be dealing with a major cell of some type of secret cult, apparently devil worshippers. Think you'll be able to handle this shit?"

Mike said, "Wow, that is some creepy stuff. Against my better judgment, I'm in. Anything I can do to prevent this kind of thing from happening again, I'll be more than happy to do."

"Good, I'm glad to have you on board. You'll get probably two weeks paid administrative leave, and meanwhile the shooting review board will do what it has to do. I'm not worried. Looks like a clean shoot to me. You just take this time to rest up. If you need anything at all, you call me."

"Will do, sir. Thank you."

As was the policy, Mike was required to turn in his handgun that he had used in the shooting. He was issued a loaner, however, until the review board completed its investigation.

Mike talked with a counselor for a few days, then took some time to go and visit Nancy.

"Oh honey, I was so afraid when I heard what had happened. But I'm so proud that you could save that sweet little girl."

Mike was in a safe place now, away from his peers. Home with his mom, he could allow himself to show his emotions. Nancy held her tough young man in her arms as he sobbed. She could feel the intensity of his emotions, and was proud that he could be such a brave man with such a sweet heart.

"Let it go sweetheart, you're safe now. Let it all out."

Let it out he did. He laid his head in Nancy's lap and fell asleep after a good long cry.

When Mike awoke, he was lying alone on the couch. Nancy was cooking in the kitchen. He went in and said, "Smells good, Mom."

"Well, I hope you brought your appetite. It's your favorite, lasagna."

Mike always loved the way Nancy made her famous vegetable lasagna. It was the tastiest indulgence with a healthy twist. She would always make it for him on special occasions.

At dinner, they talked and Nancy asked, "So when are you going to find that someone special, Mikey?"

"Why? Are you anxious to be a grandma?"

"Lord, no," Nancy replied. "I just worry about you being alone, that's all. And if I happen to become a grandma in the process, I guess that wouldn't be so bad."

"Between work and school, I don't have time to date anyone seriously right now."

"I worry about you working so hard, honey. And this whole shooting thing really troubles me. I lost your father. I can't stand the

thought of something happening to you."

"I know, Mom. That whole scene did a number on me, too. But now that I'm moving up to detective, I shouldn't have to be exposed to as many threats on the street."

"I'm grateful for that. I'm also so very proud of what you did for that little girl. All the articles are calling you a hero, and saying that she would have died if it weren't for you."

"I was just doing my job," Mike said humbly.

That night, Frank called Mike. "Hey there, my heroic little douche bag."

"Hey there Frankie, it's good to hear from you."

"You're all over the news up here, bro. I'm pretty damn proud of you, man. But remember, you promised me you'd be safe."

"It's all good, Moose. I'll be wearing a suit here soon. The most dangerous thing I'll face is my leg falling asleep from sitting at a desk too long."

"I'm glad to hear that."

The two old friends talked for a couple hours and reminisced before Mike turned in for his best night's sleep in almost two weeks.

At the end of the week-long, invigorating visit home, it was time for Mike to get back to Florida so he could return to work and school.

When he returned, Mike learned that he had been exonerated in the shooting. He was notified that he was going to receive the Sheriff's Gold Star, the highest award given to deputies for bravery above and beyond the call of duty.

He had been cleared by the department shrinks to return to duty, and was set to report for his first day as a Major Crimes Detective.

Mike reported to headquarters, where the Major Crimes Unit was located. He was greeted by Lieutenant Peterson. "Everyone, you know Mike Carson. He'll be working with us from now on. I'm gonna have you shadow Robert for a while. Rob, I want you to bring him up to speed. You can start with the Pickford case. Are you okay working that case, Mike?"

"Yes sir, Lieutenant. I was hoping I would get to work on that."

"I figured you would. Rob will get you going. Good luck, you two. Let's get these freaks."

"Hey there Mike, Robert McDougal," Robert said while holding out his hand. "Glad to have you on board, buddy. Great job with that Pickford character."

"Thanks, Rob." The two shook hands.

After roll call, Robert was going through their procedures when Sergeant Smith called out, "Okay ladies, I need all hands on deck for this one. We just got a report of a homicide. Rob, you and the new guy will take the lead. Everyone else, get out there and assist. Welcome to MCU, kid."

"Wow, a homicide right out of the gates. It took me six months before I got a homicide. You don't mess around, do you? Let's hit the road," Rob said.

They arrived at the home of the murdered subject. By first appearance, it appeared to be a drug related incident, but only a thorough investigation could prove or disprove that theory.

They walked into the bloody scene. The victim, a white male in his twenties, had been gutted. His intestines lay strewn about on the floor from the lower half of his shirtless abdomen. On the coffee table there was a scale, and an empty plastic bag with white residue that would later test positive for cocaine. Cash was scattered about on the table and floor.

"The victim—you recognize him?"

Mike did recognize him. He had arrested him for possession of narcotics two years ago during a traffic stop.

"Yep, Phillip Lugowski. He was a real piece of work. I busted him a while back for possession with intent to distribute."

Philip was a well-known local drug dealer who had a rap sheet a mile long.

Mike said, "This doesn't surprise me."

"Me either, partner. I dealt with him when I worked narcotics. I'm actually surprised he lasted as long as he did. He hung around some unsavory characters."

The rest of the day was spent interviewing neighbors while crime scene technicians processed the house for evidence. The neighbor interviews produced a lead on a vehicle. One neighbor reported seeing a black, four-door vehicle speeding away from the scene around five o'clock in the morning while she was letting her dog out. She reported that this was nothing unusual because there were always cars coming and going from that house all hours of the day and night. "I think he was dealing drugs," she commented.

"Did you hear anything prior to that? Any fighting or screaming?"

"No, I didn't hear anything. I'm sorry."

Rob replied, "That's okay, ma'am. You've been very helpful. Thank you."

When they finished their interviews with the neighbors, they went back inside to investigate further. In the house, Mike saw something that alarmed him: a shrine in the closet of the master bedroom. It was an altar to worship Moloch, with a picture of the same bull-headed demon from the pamphlet in Pickford's trunk above the altar. Mike was troubled, but kept his cool. The altar was a black, shroud-covered table with a single black candle centered inside a red pentagram, and a dish with what appeared to be bones of some small animal. It looked like cat bones.

"What is it, Mike?"

"It's this Moloch thing. This is the second time I've seen a reference to this thing since Pickford. I wonder if there's some kind of connection."

"Who knows? Take a lot of notes. We'll look into it."

Over the next several months and on his own time, Mike searched in vain for leads on the Moloch Society. They were apparently very well organized and secretive; no one would talk about the group.

THE DARKEST HOUR

*A*fter a month, all the Major Crimes Unit detectives and supervisors came to the same conclusion, that the Lugowski murder was in fact a drug deal that had gone bad. It was determined that the rest of the case would be turned over to Narcotics. Their investigators would spearhead the investigation to develop leads on suspects. Major Crimes would take back over once suspects were identified. Mike never could make a Moloch connection, even though his instincts told him otherwise. Eventually, due to a heavy caseload, he would have to write it off as a coincidence, even though he didn't believe in coincidences.

Mike worked side by side with Robert for six months. He was eventually cleared to take the primary role on cases by the Lieutenant. His first big case was a nightmarish child abduction that would haunt him for the rest of his life.

January 28th, 2002, 4:03 a.m. Mike received a call from Sergeant Smith. "Carson, I need you to respond to 27 Eagle Circle for a kidnapping. It appears that someone broke into the house and abducted a little girl. Her parents are Paul and Melinda Rollins. Crime Scene should already be there. You're going to be lead. I'm gonna send you a couple more guys to assist you."

"Got it, Sarge. I'll be there in 30 minutes."

"Okay, get there ASAP. The clock is ticking. I'll be out there shortly as well. Call me if you need anything."

"Will do, Sarge."

Mike quickly got dressed and left the apartment. While driving to the scene, he recalled the little girl in the trunk, Suzy Shinner, who was abducted from her house in the middle of the night as well. He shuddered as he recalled the cult connection that case had. Knowing that the Pickford case most likely would not have ended well, he silently prayed that this was not another cult abduction. Mike could handle just about any type of crime scene, but he struggled with the ones that dealt with kids. He accelerated to get there as quickly as he could.

4:29 a.m. Mike arrived on scene. The scene was illuminated by the bright strobe lights of the half dozen patrol cars parked in front of the residence. He exited his unmarked vehicle and was greeted by a familiar face, Sergeant Constantine.

"Mornin' Mike. I'm afraid this isn't looking very good."

"What happened, Sarge?"

"Around 3:15, we received a call from the mother, who was hysterical, saying that her daughter was not in her crib and was nowhere to be found. She believed that her daughter had been abducted. The first unit on scene was Miller. I arrived shortly after. The first thing we did was check every inch of the house. During our search, we found a rear window opened in the family room and footprints in the carpet. I backed everyone out and that's when I called for you."

"Was a bloodhound called out?"

"Yes, the hound tracked from here to just around the corner and stopped. We believe that a car was used to get away."

"This is starting to sound all too familiar, Sarge."

"I was thinking the same thing."

"Which one is Miller?"

"Miller! Detective Carson wants to ask you some questions." Miller was a newer deputy with one and a half years on the job.

"How are you doing, Miller?" asked Mike.

"Good, sir."

"Tell me what you have so far."

"The girl's name is Amanda Rollins. She's a four-year-old Caucasian with blonde hair and blue eyes, approximately three feet tall. Last seen wearing white pajamas with pink teddy bears on them. Her date of birth is 12/16/1997."

"Have you already issued a BOLO?"

"Yes, sir. She's been entered into NCIC."

"Have you been able to canvass the neighborhood and interview neighbors yet?"

"No sir, I haven't had the opportunity yet."

"Okay, I have more detectives coming out. We'll interview the neighbors. Do me a favor and just keep the onlookers away."

"Will do, sir."

"Oh, by the way, good job Miller. Thank you."

Mike asked Sergeant Constantine, "So has Crime Scene found anything yet?"

"No, they're still inside."

"Okay. Thank you, Sarge. I'm going inside to get a layout." Mike entered the residence and spoke with the Crime Scene Tech.

"Any prints?"

"No fingerprints. It looks like they wore gloves. We have a partial shoe print on the tile floor by the front door, and I have several shoe impressions in the carpet that don't match anyone on scene. Looks like a size twelve shoe, but that's all we have so far."

Mike sighed, "Well, that's something, at least. Thanks."

"There's one more thing, Detective. I found a strand of hair in the crib. It doesn't match the parents or the girl."

"Let's hope that will give us a lead."

Mike then met with Amanda's parents at the dining room table. "Do you folks mind if I record this?" "No, that's fine," said Paul Rollins.

"Mrs. Rollins, have you received any threats from anyone recently?"

"No, of course not."

"Have you had any problems with anyone lately? Any enemies?"

"No, we have no enemies."

"Any unusual people around the neighborhood that you've noticed? Any strangers?"

"None that we've noticed."

"That's fine, sir. What was the last time you saw her?"

"My wife put her down around nine, then I went in and read her a bedtime story. I kissed her and left the room about twenty minutes later. She was fast asleep when I left. We stayed up till about eleven, then went to bed. I never fall asleep right away, and I was awake until eleven-thirty at least. I never heard anything until I heard my wife screaming."

"Mrs. Rollins, can you tell me what happened? What caused you to get out of bed? Did you hear anything that woke you up?"

Mrs. Rollins said, "We were sleeping, and I woke up and thought I heard. . ."

Understandably grief-stricken, Mrs. Rollins broke down and was unable to continue answering questions.

"That's fine, Mrs. Rollins. We'll take a break for now and we'll talk some more later. We'll be around for quite a while. Let me know if you need anything."

"Thank you, Detective," said Mr. Rollins.

Mike excused himself.

After the Crime Scene Technician was done taking pictures, Mike walked through the house to get a better understanding of the layout. He started in the back room. The window was open and the screen was pulled out. This had to be where the suspect made entry. Mike walked down the hallway toward the bedroom, trying to imagine what it must have been like with all the lights out. He stopped and stood just outside the doorway of Amanda's room. He scanned the room before entering, looking for anything out of the ordinary.

Mike saw that there was something in the carpet in the corner of the room—an impression? It was only visible at certain angles when the light was just right. He looked closely and thought, *A pentagram?*

As he stood there looking at the pentagram, he felt an eerie presence in the room, then a familiar sensation like warm breath on his neck. He then heard an echoing voice whisper from behind him, *"Mmmmiiichaellll."*

Petrified, his blood curdled as he whirled about. He exclaimed, "This can't be happening."

Behind him in the room stood the technician who asked, "What's that, Detective?"

"Huh? Oh, nothing I guess. I thought I heard something."

There was no one else there. The room was empty except for the two of them.

Michael started to review all the strange occurrences he had experienced to this point. From the motel, his first day on the job, the Moloch Society, the altar and now this. He had never believed in spiritual matters, but this was all too much to ignore. Maybe all these odd experiences were getting to him.

I need a vacation, Mike thought.

Mike then asked the technician to photograph the corner of the room. He had to point the pattern out to her. "If you hold a flashlight at a low angle, I think the pattern will stand out better for the picture. Do you see it now?"

She replied, "Oh yes, I can see it now. I can't believe you saw that. Good eye, Detective."

Mike went back to Mr. Rollins and asked him, "Sir, have you ever had any dealings with a group called the Moloch Society?"

"No, why do you ask?"

Mike explained that it was just a theory he was working on.

Mr. Rollins, who had tried to stay strong for his wife, broke down and said, "This is all my fault. I must have forgotten to set the alarm last night."

"You forgot, sir?"

"Yes. We just had the alarm installed last month, and I catch myself forgetting to set it all the time. How stupid am I? A lot of good that did us. I've been doing better lately though, but that's the only explanation I have. I was so sure I set it last night before I went to bed."

After an extensive neighborhood canvass, talking to as many neighbors as he could find, Mike cleared the scene and returned to the office.

Later that morning, Robert came up to him and asked, "How you doing, buddy? Any luck with your canvass?"

"No, I came up empty."

"Well, I had a little better luck. I was talking to one of the neighbors, a Mrs. Crenshaw, and she said she heard a car with a loud exhaust driving through the neighborhood and thought it was the newspaper delivery guy. Get this—I then spoke to Mr. Jackson. He said he was on his way to work around three a.m. and saw a black four-door car parked around the corner of the house, right where the hound tracked too. He had never seen it before, but he didn't see anyone with the car, so he continued on to work."

"Could he tell what kind of car?"

"No, but are you sitting down?"

Mike had been sitting in his desk chair all along.

"You're gonna love me. You owe me big for this one, pal. A fancy dinner at Taureau's will do. A Mrs. Barbara Benderson said she heard a car speeding through the neighborhood. She was in the front yard around 3:15 walking her poodle, Curly, and could hear it coming closer. She picked Curly up as the car drove past, and said she was pissed at the way he was driving. She stepped out to get the license plate and was going to report it, but didn't bother once she was inside. Guess what kind of car?"

"A black four-door?"

"A BLACK FRIGGIN FOUR-DOOR WITH TINTED WINDOWS AND A LOUD EXHAUST!"

"For this I have to buy you dinner at Taureau's? That'll barely get you lunch at Taco Hut."

"Hang on my friend, hang on, there's more… a lot more. So, she gave me the Florida tag. Ready for this? A custom plate, 'DVLINME,' and it comes back to 1989 black Ford Taurus." "Devil in me?" asked Mike.

"Yeah, so I ran the plate, got a name and an address. Mark Kearcy at 22062 Abaddon Lane. So, you ready to go pay Mr. Kearcy a visit?"

Mike said, "Looks like dinner's on me. Taureau's it is, but only if this pans out."

Robert laughed.

Mike then asked Robert if he could go with someone else to see if the car was at the house. "If it's there, call me, and I'll push a search warrant through. I want to find this kid fast!"

From the house, Robert called Mike, "Sorry bud, the car's not here. It looks like someone's inside, though."

"I'll be right there."

8:36 p.m. Mike arrived and the three detectives approached the house. The house was a run-down old wooden "Cracker Style" house. The neighborhood was known as a high crime area, and a lot of drug activity was known to take place there. Robert and Mike went to the front door, and Detective Will Mowry went around the side to keep an eye on the rear of the house.

B-R-R-R-I-I-NGGGG!!! Mike heard the clanging of the old-style doorbell as he pushed the button and waited. He could hear some movement inside the residence. The door creaked open and a skinny, young man in his late teens answered the door. He was not wearing a shirt and had black jeans on. He had a tattoo on his left forearm of a pentagram with the letters M and S in the center. Mike quickly realized that it stood for the Moloch Society.

Mike said, "Good evening, sir. I'm Detective Carson and this is my partner, Detective McDougal. We're investigating an incident that occurred earlier this morning. May we ask you some questions?" The subject seemed uneasy, but reluctantly agreed to talk.

"May we come inside and talk?"

The subject blocked the entrance and closed the door behind him, saying, "No man, I know my rights. You pigs can't come in without a search warrant."

"Of course, sir. I just thought you'd be more comfortable inside."

"Look man, we can just talk right here."

"Can I get your name?"

"Gordon."

"Do you have a last name, Gordon?"

"Preacher."

Mike laughed inside at the parody between his last name and the tattoo on his arm.

"Mr. Preacher, can you tell us where you were this morning between the hours of two and four?"

"Yeah man, I was here sleeping, why?"

"Do you own a black Ford Taurus?"

"No, my roommate does."

"Is your roommate home?"

"No. I haven't seen him for two days. Hey man, what's this all about?"

"Is there anyone else in the house with you? I thought I heard someone else inside."

"No man, I'm alone, why?"

"May we come inside and look around?"

"You got a warrant, Pig?"

"Not yet. Do we need one?"

Mike turned to his fellow officer. "What do you think, Rob? You think he wants to come downtown and talk?"

Rob replied, "I think that's what he's saying."

"Hey, look man, I didn't do anything, and you can't make me go anywhere!"

"Actually, sir, the truth is you're a material witness in a capital kidnapping case, and I think you're withholding information. So yeah, I can take you down. Unless, of course, you'd be more comfortable talking inside your own home. Oh, and don't worry about the weed I smelled. I'm not here for that. I don't really care about a little weed.

You get a free pass if the dope is all you're worried about." With a heavy sigh, Gordon agreed to let them inside.

Mike called out to Mowry, "Hey Will, we're going inside. Watch the back for me."

"You got it, Mikey."

The three entered the dark house. The smell of burnt hemp hung heavy in the air. It was clear that Gordon had just been smoking prior to their arrival.

"Like I said, Mr. Preacher, I don't care about the weed. Tell me about your roommate. What's his name?"

"Mark."

"Mark what?"

Another heavy sigh. "This is bullshit. Kearcy, Mark Kearcy! Shit man, he's gonna kill me if he finds out I talked to you guys."

"What are you trying to hide?'

"Me? I'm not trying to hide anything, man."

"We have reason to believe that your roommate may have been involved in the abduction of a little girl."

"Look man, I didn't have anything to do with that."

"Okay, listen to me very carefully. This girl's life may be in your hands. The next few minutes can make the difference between you staying a free man or going away for the rest of your life as an accessory in a capital crime. Do you understand what I'm saying here?"

"I hear ya."

"Do you have any objections if my partner looks around while we talk?"

"Whatever, man!"

"Is that a yes or a no?"

"Yes man, go ahead and take a look around! There ain't no kid here!"

Rob looked around the house while Mike talked with Gordon.

"What do you know about this Moloch Society?"

"Those freaks? Yeah man, I got caught up with them at one time, but they were way too extreme for me. I got out of there when they started hatching a plan to sacrifice a young kid. I really didn't think they would do it man, I just didn't even like the talk of it. They worship some demon called Moloch."

"Do you know who started the cult?"

"I don't know all that much about it. I was only involved with it for about six months. I just got into because the chicks are smoking hot and are into anything, and the parties are off the charts. But

when they started getting into the weird shit, I bailed."

"What about Mark?"

"Yeah man, he really got into it, still is. I overheard him talking with someone on the phone the other night about how he knew where to find a kid. Again, I didn't really think they would do anything. That's just crazy."

"Well, it would seem they followed through with their plan." Rob called out, "Hey Mike, come here and check this out!" Mike went to the back bedroom where Robert had found an altar. This was similar to the one Mike had found in the closet in the Lugowski murder. It had a black shroud over the table with several black candles and a red pentagram. A picture of a Minotaur demon was placed prominently above the altar.

"Look at this, Mike."

On the dresser was a stack of photos that showed the Rollins' home. There was a drawing of the layout of the interior of the home, highlighting Amanda's room. Next to the papers was a photo ID that showed Mark. It read Superior Alarm Corporation, Technician Mark Kearcy, five years.

Mike recalled seeing a Superior Security sign near the front walk of the Rollins' house.

Mike returned to the living room and spoke to Gordon, who appeared nervous and was smoking a cigarette.

"Gordon, do you have any idea where Mark is?"

"I . . . I don't know, man."

It took all that Mike had not to lose his cool. "Gordon, do you know where Mark is!?"

"Look man, I'm scared. You don't know what these people are like." Mike stood up, towering over Gordon, and he started to yell,

"GORDON, YOU DON'T WANT TO KNOW WHAT I'M LIKE! TELL ME WHERE TO FIND MARK!"

"All right, all right, but I'm just guessing. There's an old shanty the group uses for rituals and parties. It's out in the woods off of

Highway 27 in the swamp."

"Can you show me on a map?"

"Yeah man, but look, you gotta protect me, please!"

"Gordon, I promise you, help me find this girl and no one will hurt you."

Mike went out and called to Will, "Will, can you get a map from the car and bring it in here?"

Gordon then proceeded to show exactly where the shanty was and how to get there. "I haven't been there in months, but here is where I know it to be. They do everything out there. Man, you gotta protect me!"

"We will, you have my word. I need you to go to the station with Detective Mowry. We can keep you safe there. Will, can you take him back and sit on him after you get a marked unit to come and sit on the house?"

"Can do, Mike. Go find the girl."

10:09 p.m. Mike and Robert ran to the car and headed out toward the swamp. While they were responding, Mike got on the radio. "MC 17 to Dispatch, I need any available units to respond to the intersection of Highway 27 and Old Camptown Road. We are responding emergency to that location. Request the SWAT team to respond as well. This will be a possible location for our kidnap victim."

"10-4, MC-17."

The watch commander, Lieutenant Eberle, stated on the radio, "L-9, MC-17, I'll be responding as well."

"I copy L-9, we're about twenty minutes out. We'll need all units to stage out on the highway before going back. We have reliable intel that the girl may possibly be out there."

10:47 p.m. When Mike and Robert arrived, four marked units were already on scene. There were no highway lights out that far, and it was dark.

"MC-17, Dispatch, do we have an ETA for SWAT?"

"10-4, SWAT ETA fifteen minutes."

Mike met with the deputies on scene. "Okay guys, this is a long road. Did anyone see any cars heading back into town on their way out here?"

Deputy Ferrindale spoke up, "I was the first one on the scene, Detective. I saw a caravan of about fifteen to twenty cars on my way out here, but I didn't think much about it at the time."

"Shit! I pray we're not too late."

The shanty sat back off the highway approximately two miles down a long dirt road. Mike looked, and because of all the mud on the paved highway coming from the dirt road, it appeared that all the fresh tire tracks were leaving the scene. There were multiple tracks.

"We don't have time to wait. We gotta get back there, Rob!" Mike said impatiently.

Rob replied, "I agree, brother. Let's do it."

"Okay, I need two of you to come back with us and two of you stay here and watch the highway. Grab your rifles. This might get messy. Two of you jump in my backseat. We're gonna head back there."

"MC 17, Dispatch, we don't have time to wait. Advise SWAT to come back quietly upon arrival."

Mike and Rob donned their vests, and the four officers drove down the long, dark road blacked out. It was a dark night and it had recently rained. The road was nearly impassable, especially in a large four-door sedan, but somehow Mike managed. Ten minutes later, they neared what looked like the entrance to a camp. Mike parked off the road behind some bushes to stay out of sight.

The four exited, and Mike whispered, "We'll walk back. Keep your eyes and ears open. But be quiet. According to the witness, the shack should be down that road about five hundred yards."

As they got closer to the camp, Mike could smell the smoke of a fire. The smoke had an unusual odor, not the typical oak and pine wood smell, but a distinct odor that he had never smelled before. They got around the curve in the road, and there it was, the shanty. It was dark, and in a large clearing in front of the cabin were the remains of a large bonfire. There were no cars, but they found dozens of fresh tire tracks. Clearly, whoever had been there was gone.

Mike took out his flashlight and illuminated the dilapidated structure. He could see a freshly painted red pentagram on the door. *Painted with what?*

The closer he got, the more it looked like blood. His heart was pounding. "Oh my God, please no! You two, go around the back!"

"C'mon Rob." Mike and Robert approached the front door. It was blood and it was still dripping wet. Mike cried out, "AMANDA!?" No response.

Mike's heart sank.

Rob said, "Ready, partner?"

Mike took a deep breath and moaned, "Ready."

They opened the door, and inside was a large, makeshift altar. It looked like the others they had seen. It had a large black shroud covering the table. The shroud was saturated with fresh blood. On the ground in front of the altar was the massive carcass of a young bull that had had its throat cut. The bull was laid gingerly on a bed of red roses, soaked with blood. The table sat in the middle of a large red pentagram painted on the floor. At each point of the star was a tall candlestick with the melted remains of black candles.

Mike searched all over the room. No Amanda.

"Oh God, maybe she's still alive," he said to Rob.

"Maybe, pal. Don't give up yet."

As other units arrived, Mike searched the surrounding property. When he walked over to the bonfire pit, he looked down. He was horrified by what he saw.

Mike screamed, "NO, NO, NO, NO, NOOOOOOO!!!" as he fell to his knees. "DAMN YOU, GOD DAMN YOU!!!"

Everyone on the scene jumped at the sound of his screams as they echoed through the swamp, drowning out the sound of the frogs and crickets.

Rob and several others ran over to the fire. "Mike? What is it, pal?"

Robert was astonished to see what had made Mike cry out. At the edge of the fire ring was a partially burned piece of bloodstained white cloth with pink teddy bears. In the ashes of the fire were the sooty, charred bones of an approximately three-foot-tall child. Through the now empty eye sockets that had once cradled two beautiful, blue eyes, Rob could now see inside the pitifully little skull containing the remains of sizzling, fleshy material. The jaw, with two missing front baby teeth, was stuck open, positioned in a perpetual scream of terror, but no sound emanated from the desecrated remains. In fact, the only sound that could be heard was Mike's muttering through tightly clenched teeth, "I'm gonna get this motherfucker. He's gonna pay!"

An all-points bulletin was immediately issued to be on the lookout for a black four-door Ford Taurus bearing Florida tag DVLINME. Within the hour, the radio crackled with a barely audible, "Dis--t-h, 317, I h-ve a visu--l on th-- -lac- -ord Tau--

s." Because they were so far out of town, Mike could barely make out the scratchy radio transmission.

"Did I hear someone just call out they have the car? Listen up!"

Several minutes passed and they heard, "3--, --spat--, we hav- the dr--er in cus-ody. En rout- to the di--ict off--e."

Mike called on his cell phone and spoke to the dispatcher, "Dispatch, this is Detective Carson. We have terrible radio reception out here. Did I just hear someone say that they stopped that car?"

The dispatcher responded, "That's 10-4, Detective. They are en route to the office with the driver at this time."

"Tell them to put him in interview room two." Two was Mike's favorite room. He'd had good luck interviewing people in that room and would take no chances tonight.

"Rob, we gotta roll. They got that son of a bitch!"

"Let's do it!"

Mike told Lieutenant Eberle, "We've got to go, sir, we got the guy."

"Go get 'em. We'll hold down the scene. Crime Scene is on their way out. We'll keep you up to date."

12:51 a.m. Mike and Robert arrived at the station. "Where is this asshole, Sarge?"

"He's in your room Mike, just the way you like."

Mike went to the observation room on the other side of the one-way mirror. He spent almost twenty minutes sizing his guy up before going in to interview him. The suspect, Mark Kearcy, had no prior criminal arrests. In fact, he was a model citizen by all accounts.

Yet, there he was, in handcuffs, all six feet, one hundred ninety pounds of him. He had a sinister countenance, black hair that came to his shoulders, and a long, black beard. He appeared to have all of his teeth. His hazel eyes stared at his reflection in the mirror with a distant gaze, as if looking across a great plain at a far-off mountain range. He had an upsetting grin on his face. He wore a black t-shirt with black jeans. His black leather boots still had a coat of mud that looked like the mud from the swamp.

Mike thought to himself, *so there you are, you baby killing psycho. I'm gonna burn your ass, just like you burned that precious little angel.*

Suddenly Mark's countenance changed. His hazel eyes became a solid, shiny jet-black. His grin changed to a wide, smug smile that showed off his bright ivory teeth, and said in an eerily deep voice like a demon out of a horror movie, "I don't think so, Michael, but you can try!"

THE ONE

Mike nearly fell from his stool. "Did you hear that?"

Rob responded, "Hear what?"

"What he just said!"

"What are you talking about, Mike? He didn't say anything. He's just been sitting there with that same eerie ass grin. I think you must be exhausted, buddy. It's been a long, emotional night."

"Yeah, and it's not over yet."

Rob replied, "Are you ready for this?"

Mike said, "I'm ready. Let's get him."

After checking all the recording equipment to make sure it was operational, Mike and Rob entered the interview room. Mark seemed disinterested that the two detectives had entered the room. He continued to stare blankly at his reflection in the mirror.

Mike started off, "Good morning, Mr. Kearcy. I'm Detective Carson and this is Detective McDougal. Are you comfortable? Would you like some water?" Mike seethed inside, convinced about what this scum of the earth had done, but knew it was necessary to make the suspect comfortable.

"Mr. Kearcy, do you hear me?"

Void of any emotion, Mark responded, "I hear you, and no, thank you. I don't want any water."

"Well, if you change your mind, just let one of us know."

"Actually, come to think of it, a cup of water would be nice."

Rob replied, "No problem, I'll be right back."

As Rob left to get him a cup of ice water, Mike sat in the room alone with Mark. He continued, "Mr. Kearcy, do you know why we're here this morning?"

Mark's gaze now turned to Mike, and it appeared that his eyes once again changed to a glossy black. He seemed to see right through to Mike's soul and his voice changed, sounding like a multitude of voices speaking in unison. "Of course, we know why we're here,

Michael. Do *you* know why we're here?"

"How did you know my name?"

The voices replied, "We know everything, Michael. Soon you, too, will understand. All will be revealed. Your time is closer than you think."

Unnerved, Mike quickly got up and left the room.

Rob was coming back and saw Mike standing in the hallway, sweating and looking on edge. "Hey man, are you okay?"

"This case is really getting to me. This guy is creeping me out something awful."

"Why? What happened while I was gone?"

"He called me by my first name. Did we ever mention our first names?"

"Not so far as I can recall. He called you by your first name?"

"Yeah. He looked right at me and called me Michael. How could he have known that?"

"Let's go review the video. I gotta see this for myself."

Mike and Rob went into the media room and rewound the tape. "Here's where I got up to get his water. There you two are, and he's still staring into the mirror." The two watched the video for the next sixty seconds. "And here you are getting up and going outside. He never said anything, Mike."

"How is that possible? Rob, am I losing my mind?"

"No way, my friend. Look, this is turning into a nightmarish case. In my seven years in Major Crimes, I've never dealt with anything like this before. Do you want me to take over the interview?"

"No, just give me a few minutes to collect my thoughts."

"Take your time, bud. I'll stay by your side from now on. I don't think either of us should be alone with this asshole. Maybe he's using some mind fuck technique on you. Just hang in there, pal.

We'll stick together."

Mike and Rob re-entered the room and started the interrogation. Rob stated, "Here's your water, Mark."

After picking up the foam cup with the ice chips and water, Mark said, "Thank you, Detective McDougal."

Mike said, "Okay, let's begin again. I'm going to start by reading you your rights." He read his Miranda warning from a sheet of paper, and Mark acknowledged that he understood his rights and was willing to answer questions.

"Okay, if you could just sign here for me acknowledging that you understand your rights."

"My pleasure, Detective. There's no need to bother with any lawyers."

Mark signed the paper, and then sat back, expressionless once again. "For the record Mr. Kearcy, could you please state your name?"

Mark responded appropriately, providing all information as requested. Now with all the legal formalities out of the way, the interview could begin.

"Mr. Kearcy."

Mark interrupted, "Please, call me Mark."

"Okay, Mark, if that makes you more comfortable."

"It does, thank you."

"Mark, can you tell me where you were last evening?"

"Oh yes, I was out at the camp."

"The camp?"

In the same placid voice Mark replied, "Yes, our camp. My friends and I get together there, occasionally."

"Where is this camp?"

"It's in the Everglades out off Highway 27. I believe you know the place."

"Yesterday morning between the hours of 2 a.m. and 4 a.m., can you tell me where you were?"

With a smile and a heavy sigh, Kearcy answered, "I think you know that too, Detective, but I'll play your game with you. I was in my car around the corner, waiting for the Rollins' to go to sleep. Do you know they are real night owls? I had to wait for several hours before all the lights were out. Then I had to wait to be sure they were asleep so I could enter without being noticed."

"Explain to me how you got in without tripping the alarm?" Conceitedly, Mark replied, "Detective, didn't you find my ID on the dresser? You know I installed the alarm. I never activated the sensor on that window. After I removed the screen, I checked to see if the window was still unlocked the way I had left it. To my delight, they, like most people, never check their window locks. Why would they if they never open the windows? Of course, once I was inside, I knew how to override the system."

Mike looked at Rob in disbelief. Was this guy really confessing this easily?

"But, why Amanda?"

"For years we've been searching for the perfect girl. I found one last year in Brandon and my associate—I believe you know him, Jeremy— retrieved her. But someone, Detective Carson, spoiled those plans. But as you know, everything happens for a reason, and I believe my master was truly waiting for little Amanda."

Mike proudly responded, "Yes, I do seem to recall a little something about that incident last year. But why Amanda?"

"Because Detective, she was exactly what He wanted. Perfect in every way. I can imagine how proud she must be now."

When he heard that, Mike had to restrain his emotions to keep himself from reaching across the table and beating the hell out of this sicko.

"Why would she be proud?"

"Because Detective, Amanda was chosen from among millions of other girls, but she was to be the one to fulfill the prophecy."

"What prophecy would that be, Mark?"

"The one foretold by our High Priestess, Priestess Sable, before she was ushered into the netherworld."

"Priestess Sable? Who was Priestess Sable?"

"She was the one chosen to summon the powerful Moloch from beyond. He now roams freely in this realm. He protects us, and in return, we serve Him."

"So how does Amanda fit in?"

"Since ancient times, select children were honored and chosen to be a sacrifice to Moloch. This was always a great honor for the children and their families. In return for their loyalty, Moloch would provide their culture with bountiful crops and peace. He has always required the sacrifice of an innocent child. Amanda was the child chosen, and was required for him to fulfill his vow to our Priestess. In return for bringing him forth and freeing him from the bonds of his unearthly realm, he would grant her the desire of her heart. Amanda is her gift to Him, and now it's complete. She has fulfilled her promise and now he will honor his oath to her."

"How was she sacrificed, and why?"

"Her innocent blood was required to be co-mingled with that of the consecrated bull. Their throats could only be slit with a Sacred Horn Blade, and their blood would be sprinkled together upon the altar to signify their eternal union."

"Then why was she burned?"

"The burning of the innocent's flesh has always been required to release the soul from the bondage of this world. The young one is now free to wander the realm of her beloved. Can you see now why she would be so proud? Forever abiding with our Lord Moloch. And

now, the Priestess awaits her betrothed."

"But you said she's dead?"

"No, Detective. Her physical form is no more, but her spiritual body is alive and in waiting, serving alongside Moloch."

The interview continued for over two hours. Mark confessed willingly to abducting and killing Amanda.

Mike finished the interview by asking, "You understand what you have confessed to Mark, correct?"

"Oh yes, Detective. I fully understand. And it doesn't matter what happens to me in this life. I was chosen and I will receive my reward in the next. I will walk beside my Holy Master."

As Mark was escorted to a holding cell, Mike and Robert talked about what had just happened.

Robert said, "That was one of the easiest confessions I ever witnessed. Usually, easy confessions are given out of guilt. But I saw no guilt and no remorse in this guy at all. He seemed pleased with himself."

Mike said, "I think the guy's a sociopath. I hope he doesn't get off with an insanity defense."

"Me either."

The next day in court, Mark was arraigned on first degree murder charges. Mike was present and anxious to witness the initial court hearing. As expected, the defense attorney pled not guilty by reason of insanity.

The prosecuting attorney was a beautiful, auburn-haired woman. She wore a skirt that came to about her knees, and Mike could clearly see that she worked out. Her calves were toned, and she did not wear stockings. The skin of her legs was silky smooth and shiny. She didn't need hose. When she stood up, she stood at just over five feet, but just barely with low heels on. Mike had always been attracted to shorter women. Her hair was long, and she wore glasses to read, which accentuated her green eyes. She was the most beautiful woman he had ever seen. Mike was smitten.

Twenty-seven-year-old Meredith Porter was an exceptional lawyer with the District Attorney's Office. She had been working in the misdemeanor crime division for the previous two years. She had recently been promoted to the felony division, specifically high-profile cases. This was her first big case. After she presented her case to the judge, and easily convinced him that Mark should be held with no bond for the heinous nature of his crime, she turned around to exit the courtroom.

Standing before her was Mike, all six feet three, two hundred twenty-five pounds of him. Mike's white dress shirt was form-fitted and accentuated the V-shape of his muscular frame. His blonde hair was neatly parted and combed to the right, and his pale blue eyes stood out against his bronze tan.

Their eyes met and they were fixated on each other for a few seconds. Mike wondered if she felt the same attraction that he did. He smiled, as he hoped that her blushing was a sign that she was struggling to hide her attraction to him. He held the courtroom door for her as she exited. Mike, too, was trying to maintain a professional composure.

As she exited through the door, Mike asked, "So, do you think we'll put him away for good?"

Meredith responded, "I'm sorry, who are you again?"

"I'm Detective Carson."

"Oh, you're the famous Detective Carson." Unknown to Mike was the fact that all the ladies at the District Attorney's Office spoke very highly about him. Every time he would go there for a deposition, they would secretly gather to drool over him.

"Nice to meet you, Detective. I think we have a pretty good chance of putting him away for a very long time. Actually, I'm going to be seeking the death penalty. You did an incredible job catching him. I'm so sorry about the girl. I read your report and cried. It still horrifies me."

"Thank you. Yeah, it was bad."

"I'm sorry, but I have to get going. I have a deposition in an hour. I'll be in touch."

Beaming, Mike said, "I look forward to it."

As she walked away, Mike caught her looking back, and then she quickly turned away in embarrassment. He thought she was blushing. Mike watched her all the way until she got into the elevator. Before the doors closed, they once again made eye contact and they both smiled.

Mike returned to the office and spoke to Rob. "Man, have you seen that new Assistant D.A?"

"You mean Meredith Porter? Yeah, I've seen her. She's not new, though. She's new to the felony division. Good luck on that one. I hear she doesn't date, especially cops."

"Oh yeah? Sounds like a challenge."

"Well, if anyone can do it, rock star, it's you." Rob quipped.

Three weeks passed, and Mike received a subpoena for a deposition about the Kearcy trial. Kearcy was still in jail, and the Grand Jury was set to review the case in another week. Meredith needed statements from Mike about the case.

"I'm going to meet with my future bride on Friday!" Mike told Robert.

Robert laughed, "Man, you're really hung up on her, aren't you?"

"I gotta tell you Rob, she's the most beautiful woman I've ever laid eyes on."

"Ten bucks says you don't get her number."

Mike smiled, "You're on, pal."

Mike arrived for the deposition a half hour early, hoping he might see Meredith and get a chance to talk to her. Mike's appointment was for 1:45 p.m. When he arrived at the District Attorney's Office, the receptionist advised him that they were running about twenty minutes behind schedule. This gave Mike time to review his notes. He was oblivious to all the ladies who had suddenly congregated around the receptionist, ogling him.

At 2:10 he heard, "Detective Carson?"

Mike looked up and there she was, Meredith Porter, looking prettier than the first time they had met.

"I'm sorry to keep you waiting, Detective. We're running way behind schedule. This is a big case, a lot of people to interview."

"No worries, I've been going over my notes, not that I need them. I've been reliving that nightmare nearly every night since."

"Oh, my goodness, I can't even imagine. Just reading your report has been difficult. And the pictures are beyond words. I am so sorry for everyone that was there. This must be hard on you."

They entered a windowless room. In the room was a team of defense attorneys for Kearcy, three in all; a stenographer and two Assistant D.A.'s, including Meredith.

After being sworn in, Mike was asked a series of questions about his involvement in the case. He would occasionally make eye contact with Meredith, and he could feel that same weird connection with her. Her voice was calming and reassuring, and he felt easy answering her questions. When questioned by the defense attorneys, Mike was purposefully evasive in his responses. He was not willing to give them any more ammunition to use against him in a trial situation.

Meredith spoke, "Okay, Detective Carson. I'm going to ask you to recount the events at the camp. Please review what you did and what you saw when you arrived."

Mike grew cold as he began to recount the images of the altar and the blood, knowing now it was Amanda's blood mixed with that of the bull. He became uneasy and his voice started to crack. It was clear that he was becoming agitated. Then he recounted finding the fire pit where the bonfire had taken place.

"And then I looked down and saw the remnants of the pajamas at the edge of the fire pit. White cloth with pink teddy bears, soaked in blood . . . " Mike's voice was starting to break. His eyes welled up with tears. " . . . And then the bones . . . the bones . . . the burnt bones of that little baby . . . "

Mike suddenly went silent, as if he had fallen into a trance. Images of the hellish scene, and then the interview with Kearcy were racing through his mind.

Meredith called out, "Detective? Detective Carson? Are you okay?"

Mike felt uncomfortable breaking down before this beautiful woman, with tears rolling down his chiseled jaw line. Since that first summer of his transformation, he had grown uneasy with showing his emotions, choosing rather a tough guy facade. *I feel so stupid,* he thought to himself. Meredith, however, appeared moved by the sincerity of his emotions.

Mike was frozen, paralyzed with a look of fear. He could see Kearcy's eyes, black as coal, and heard the sea of voices crying out, "Michael . . . your time is closer than you think!"

"Detective? Detective Carson?" Meredith touched his arm and Mike recoiled with a jerk.

"Huh?"

"Detective Carson? Would you like to take a break?"

"Um, ye—yes, please."

"Let's take five minutes." Everyone in the room agreed.

Mike stepped out of the room, and Meredith followed him. "Are you okay, Detective Carson?"

Mike answered, "Yeah, I just need to collect my thoughts. I'm sorry for losing it in there. I'm usually not like this."

"Don't be sorry, I think it's attractive. Oh my God, I can't believe I just said that. I'm so sorry, that was very unprofessional of me."

Mike looked into her eyes. Now he knew there was a connection. Meredith made him feel things he hadn't felt since his time with Sheila. He never thought he could feel that way again about anyone, but there he was. He was almost giddy, a nice change from the terror he had just relived moments before. Her perfume was light, refreshing, and calming to him.

He smiled and said, "I'm not sorry. I just need a few minutes."

Meredith said, "No, please, take your time. I'll leave you alone."

As she got up to leave, Mike mustered the nerve to say, "You don't have to."

Blushing, Meredith looked back at him and smiled, just like that day from the elevator. She returned and sat in the chair next to him.

"Just let me know when you're ready to continue, and I'll let them know."

After a few minutes of small talk, Mike was calm enough to go back and continue.

"Okay, I'll let them know. Stay here and I'll come back for you in a minute."

Mike felt butterflies in his stomach as he watched her walk away.

When they returned to the meeting room, he composed himself and managed to get through the rest of the deposition, though he had to stop and collect himself on more than one occasion as he relived the nightmare.

At the end of the deposition, Meredith walked Mike out of the office. The deposition had taken several hours, and all the other ladies in the office were gone for the day, disappointed they didn't get one more opportunity to see Mike in his form-fitted shirt and snug slacks.

Meredith said, "I don't normally do this, mind you, but I'm going to write my personal cell phone number on the back of my business card. This is a big case. If you can think of anything that might help me, call me. Anytime, day or night."

Mike simpered, "What if I called just to talk? I might need a counselor after today."

Coyly, Meredith whispered, "If you need some counseling Detective Carson, the number is on the back of the card."

Mike asked, "Day or night, huh?"

Meredith smiled and winked, and then walked away. Again, as she had in the courthouse, she looked back at Mike, who was watching her walk away.

It was after six o'clock, and Mike knew Robert had gone home for the day. Mike called him on the phone.

"You owe me ten bucks, dude!"

"No way, you sly son of a bitch."

"It's not like that man, there's something about her. She seems really special."

"Well, we'll catch up tomorrow, bud. I'm getting ready to sit down for dinner."

The next morning at the station, Robert walked in and asked, "Well?"

"Well what?"

"Did you call her yet?"

"No way, man. I don't want to come across as desperate."

"But you are, brother. Those blue balls of yours must be ready to burst by now. You haven't been on a date in months."

"Funny, very funny!"

"Look, she sure didn't give me the time of day when I went for my depo earlier in the day."

"Well, it could be because of that shiny gold band around your finger there."

"You mean the ol' hand anchor here?"

Mike laughed, "Helen's a good woman. I don't know how you ended up with her or why she puts up with you."

Smiling, Robert agreed. "That she is buddy, that she is," and the two went to roll call.

Late that night, Mike had fallen asleep in front of the television. The lights were on and the TV was blaring when he fell into a deep sleep.

In his dream, he heard the sounds of cattle. Suddenly he was standing on his uncle's cattle farm when he heard, "Michael, your time is near. All will be revealed." Terrified, he found himself now running through the woods. It seemed that he had been running forever, then abruptly he was standing in front of an old, broken down cabin. He thought, *Where the hell am I?* There was no one around the cabin. It was foggy and dark. Then through the deafening silence, the terrified shriek of a little girl crying, "MOMMY? MOMMY? DADDY, IM SCARED! WHERE ARE YOU, MOMMY!? DADDY,

DON'T LET HIM HUR- NO! NO! NOOOO!!! M-O-MMM-E-E-EEEE!!!" In a blink, he was then standing in a field surrounded by hundreds of grunting, snarling bulls, all with their throats cut. Then he screamed, "AMANDA-A-A-A!!!! NOOOOOO!!!!"

Mike screamed aloud as he woke up. He was saturated with sweat and had somehow ended up on the floor. Trembling, he began whimpering, "I'm so sorry, Amanda. I'm so sorry I couldn't save you, baby! God, why did you let this happen?"

After several minutes, he was able to regain his composure. His thoughts switched from Amanda to Meredith.

Still traumatized by the dream, Mike determined that he could really use the sound of a friendly voice. For as long as he could recall, Frank was always the first person that he would call when he needed someone to confide in when his soul was vexed. But this time, he could think of no other voice than Meredith's.

Mike retrieved her business card from his wallet. He flipped the card over, and the handwritten number stared back at him. "She did say anytime, day or night." He looked up at the clock. "9:07. It's not too late."

After a few more minutes, he got up the nerve and placed the call.

"Hello?" The friendly voice he longed for said on the other end.

"Hello, Meredith?"

"This is she."

"It's Mike."

"I know, Detective. I recognized your baritone voice. Is this business or pleasure?"

Mike hesitantly answered, "Well, pleasure is much more fun than business, and business was the last thing on my mind."

"I couldn't agree more. I was hoping that was the case. I was beginning to think you didn't take the hint the other day and was getting worried I wasn't going to hear from you."

"To be honest with you, counselor, I was afraid I had misread your intentions and I was a little nervous about calling."

"Oh, Detective Carson, you have no reason to be nervous with me. I don't bite . . . hard." Meredith giggled on the other end.

This was going better than Mike had hoped. "Do you think you can call me Mike?" "I will if you quit calling me counselor." Mike snickered and agreed.

The two talked for the next two hours. Mike told her all about the nightmare that had prompted him to call.

She reassured him by saying, "That's terrible. You can always call me. I would love to be your comforting voice."

"You've done that already. I'm glad I got up the nerve to call you."

Meredith replied, "Me too. I did say if you needed any counseling I was here for you. Seriously though, if that's what it took for you to call, I'm not sorry you had the bad dream."

"I'm not sorry either, at least not anymore."

"I'm glad you feel comfortable sharing your inner thoughts with me. I know a man of your caliber must not be very comfortable sharing his feelings with many people."

"That's true. In fact, you're only the second person in my life I have really opened up to."

"I'm honored."

"For some reason, I feel very comfortable talking to you."

They continued to talk for several hours. Mike explained that he was still in law school at FTU and was hoping to graduate in the next few years. He told her how his father had been murdered outside of his law firm. He shared his dream of following in his father's footsteps and becoming an attorney.

Meredith told him that she also had attended FTU. "Now I remember why you looked so familiar to me! You and I sort of met once in school."

Mike asked, "When did we ever meet? I would have remembered you for sure!"

"We didn't officially meet. You pulled this huge lummox off of my hood one night after a football game."

"Oh, my goodness, that was you? Are you kidding me? I remember that night. That lummox is actually my best friend, Frank. We call him 'The Moose'. He and I grew up playing football together in high school, then college, up until I got injured the year before. He is still my best friend today."

"That's your best friend, huh? What does that say about you, I wonder?"

"I promise you he's every bit as obnoxious as he seemed that night, but he's really a giant teddy bear. He's been the rock for both my mom and me since my dad was killed. He would do anything for a friend. Maybe one day you'll meet him and get to know him for the real cool guy that he is."

"Hmmm, we'll see about that."

Mike found himself thinking how he had never before been able to communicate so easily with any other woman. He felt that he could tell Meredith anything.

He then found the courage to ask, "So maybe we can go out sometime?"

"Why Detective, are you asking me out on a date?"

"I believe that I am, Ms. Porter."

"Why, sir, this is so sudden . . . not! We've been talking for over what—two hours now. I've been dying for you to ask me out, you knucklehead! How many signals did I have to throw out?"

Mike was surprised and relieved at her wit and sense of humor. He smiled and then said, "So, Friday night at Taureau's? I'll pick you up at seven?"

"Oooh, Taureau's. It's a date. I can't wait. I'm so glad you called."

"Thank you for answering your phone and quelling my nightmares."

"The pleasure was all mine. Call me again should those dreams haunt you anymore. Good night, Mike."

"Good night, Meredith."

It worked. The nightmares had subsided and Mike fell into a deep, peaceful sleep, the best sleep he'd had in a very long time. He woke up the next morning refreshed and in a joyful mood. He hadn't smiled in weeks since Kearcy had injected himself into his life.

When Mike got to work, he found a card on his desk. There was no name on it, just a blank envelope. Inside was a white card with the outline of lips from bright red lipstick and a note. "For the nightmares." A heavenly scent wafted up from the card. It had been sprayed with the same sweet-smelling fragrance that Meredith wore.

Mike's face radiated in a way that his partner and friend had never seen.

"What's up? You get laid or something?" Rob asked.

Then he saw the card and grabbed it out of Mike's hand.

"WHOA, what's this, lover boy?"

Smiling Mike said, "Give it back, you moron!"

"Wait now, I'm a detective. Mmm, that scent. I recognize those lips. Could this be that sweet little ADA we were talking about the other day?"

"Maybe. Oh, that reminds me—where's my ten bucks?"

"Haha, here you go my friend, you've earned it." Rob pulled a ten-dollar bill out of his pocket and threw it down on Mike's desk. "Truth is, I was here earlier when she came in and asked which desk was yours. I think she likes you, bud."

"She's pretty amazing, isn't she?"

Robert looked at him and gave two thumbs up in approval. "I'm happy for you, Mike. It's nice to see you smile. So, fill me in, give me the dirt."

"There's no dirt. I'm taking her out on Friday." He went on to explain how he got up the nerve to call her the night before and how they had seemed to hit it off.

During roll call, Sergeant Smith asked, "Does anyone else have anything to add before we hit it?"

Robert called out, "Yeah, I got something. I want to inform everyone that our own football legend here has fallen in love with the beautiful ADA, Ms. Porter. They have a date Friday night!"

Every guy in the room moaned, "Oh yeah! Ms. Porter, she's fine!" "Thanks a lot, you idiot. Why would you do that?" Mike asked. Robert laughed, "I love ya, man. It's pure jealousy, that's all." Mike smiled and shrugged it off.

Robert pulled a piece of paper with a number on it from his pocket. "Here you go, partner."

"What's this?"

"The number of my florist. I use them to send my sweet Helen flowers. Plus, they give us a cop discount."

"You must use them a lot."

Rob laughed and said, "Yeah, I got 'em on speed dial. I have to, I'm always in trouble! Seriously, take it from a happily married man. Send her some flowers, bro. You can't go wrong."

Mike did make the call and asked the florist what color he should send. The florist explained that pink roses symbolized admiration and gratitude, and that red roses traditionally symbolized love. Mike believed that the red might be a little presumptuous for now and sent Meredith a dozen pink long-stemmed roses.

Meredith received the flowers at her office. They caused quite a stir among the ladies. She smiled when she read the attached note. "Nightmares gone, thanks to you."

Meredith was heard unintentionally humming as she meandered her way through the office the rest of the day.

The catty office hens gathered around the break room. "She's got it bad!"

Another lady said, "Can you blame her? Mmm, mmm, mmm!" They all cackled in unison.

Friday afternoon, two hours before their date, Mike was getting ready. He received a phone call. Thinking it was Meredith, he eagerly answered, "Hello there!"

The line was silent. "Hello? Hello-o-o-o?" He hung up. A few minutes later the phone rang again, "Hello?" Nothing.

Curious, Mike thought to himself, *I hope the line's not having problems. What if she's trying to call me? I'll call her back in a few minutes.*

Mike went back into the bathroom. As he was brushing his teeth, the phone rang again and he thought, *that must be her.* Without thinking, he ran out to grab the phone. With a mouth full of toothpaste, he answered, "Hewo-o-o?"

That familiar legion of voices cried out, "M-m-m-i-c-h-a-e-l-l-lllll, we are waiting!"

Horrified, Mike dropped the phone and stepped back. He was instantly transported back to the interview room with Kearcy. "What the hell?"

He snapped to and heard a heavenly voice calling out from the receiver on the floor. "Mike? Mike, are you okay?"

His hands trembled as he picked up the phone and said, "H-He-

Hello?"

"Michael? Is everything okay? I heard the phone drop. You sound nervous."

"Huh? Oh. Oh, yeah—yeah. Sorry, my hands were wet."

"Are you sure? You sound unsettled."

"Yeah, I'm sure. I'm just rushing around, running behind."

"Well, that's what I was calling about. . . "

"Uh-oh. You can't make it, right?"

"You are a terrible sleuth. You couldn't be more wrong, Detective Carson. I just wanted to let you know I'm running behind, too. I had to work a little late tonight. Can you pick me up at 7:30 instead of 7:00?"

Relieved, Mike said, "Whew, I thought you were gonna cancel on me. Of course, I can. That's no problem at all."

"We've been talking all week. You really thought I'd do that?"

"I suppose not. I'm glad. I can't wait to see you. I'll be there at 7:30."

"Thank you, sweetie, see you soon."

For the next half hour, Mike was confronted by every possible obstacle imaginable. First, there was no hot water and he had to take a cold shower. Then he ran out of shaving cream and had to shave with soap and water. His face was on fire, but he managed. His favorite shirt that he was sure he had washed and pressed was found on the bottom of the hamper, all balled up and stinky. He went through three pairs of socks before finding ones with no holes in them. He went to apply his best cologne, and dropped the bottle, smashing it into oblivion. He had to settle for the cheap stuff. His blow dryer stopped working, and as he was walking out the door, he ran into the corner of the table, causing his shin to bleed all over his tan trousers. "Great, now I have to change my pants. What the heck is going on?" To add insult to injury, his car battery was dead, and he had to get a jump start from a neighbor.

Mike thought for a moment that someone or something must be trying to prevent him from going on this date. But his will was stronger than any outside force. He was not going to be deterred.

Success. Mike pulled up in front of Meredith's condo. "Only ten minutes late. Not bad, considering."

He went to the door, and Meredith was waiting. She reached up to hug him. "You look very nice."

"Thank you. You're more breathtaking than ever!"

Blushing, Meredith said, "Thank you."

They went to Taureau's, the finest restaurant in Boca Grande Shores. The two instantly hit it off. They took their time; they were in no rush. After three hours, neither one was ready for the date to end.

The conversation seemed effortless for both of them.

Mike suggested, "Would you like to take a walk on the beach?"

"That would be wonderful. It's so beautiful out tonight," Meredith said.

They drove to the beach. The surf was gentle, and the moon was full, creating a beautiful backdrop of glimmering moonlight reflecting off the water. The sand was soft and cool on their bare feet. They held hands as they walked and talked. After they walked for what seemed like hours, Mike looked down and saw that it was almost midnight.

"Look at the time."

"You gonna turn back into a pumpkin or something?" Meredith said.

Mike chuckled and said, "No, I just didn't want to keep you out too late."

"I promise I won't turn into a pumpkin either."

They stared longingly into each other's eyes. Mike couldn't remember being this nervous with any other woman. He thought to himself, *should I kiss her or what?*

As if she could read his mind, Meredith said, "Oh, for goodness sakes, I can see I'm going to have to break the ice." She pulled down on his shirt collar, beckoning him to bend down and kiss her.

The two parted after a long, passionate kiss. Mike responded with, "Wow!"

"Wow, indeed. You're an amazing kisser."

"So are you," said Mike.

The two walked back to Mike's car. He held her hand as if his life depended on it. He sensed that she felt secure in his strong, yet gentle, grasp.

When they got to her condo, he walked her to her front door.

"Well, Meredith. This was by far the best date I've ever been on."

"Are you psychic? Are you reading my mind? I swear to you I was going to say the same thing."

The two kissed goodnight, and Mike politely opened the door for her as he had done all night long. They kissed one last time.

"Can I call you when I get home?"

"You better!"

Meredith stood with her door slightly ajar, watching Mike walk back to his car. When he was gone, she closed the door and leaned against the wall. "Wow. Wow, wow, wow," was all she said to herself.

Of course, Mike did call her as soon as he got home. The two talked on the phone until they both fell asleep. The last thing Mike remembered hearing was Meredith yawn and say, "I really, really had a nice time tonight. . ." Mike couldn't remember later if she fell asleep first, or if he did.

A LIFE WORTH LIVING

Mike awoke the next morning with the phone receiver still lying on the bed. He picked it up and listened closely, as the line was still open. He could hear Meredith breathing softly on the other end. Apparently, she was still sleeping. He hung up the phone and lay in bed, invigorated with a new perspective on things.

What an amazing woman, he thought.

Mike felt like he had to call someone. At first, he thought about calling Frankie, but he was in California, and it was three hours earlier. Frank would kill him if he woke him up this early.

Mike decided to call Nancy. It was nine o'clock. Surely, she'd be awake.

Nancy answered, "Hello?"

"Good morning, Mom."

"Mikey? Is everything okay?"

"Yeah Mom, everything is amazing."

"Oh really? What's going on?"

"Well, I met someone. She's so great. I think you'd really like her." Mike went on to tell her all about Meredith and their first date.

"That sounds wonderful, honey. I've never seen you this excited about a girl before. She must be very special."

"She is Mom, she really is. I know we just went out for the first time last night, but she is so much more than I ever imagined."

"So, tell me how you two met."

"It's funny you should ask. We actually first sort of met in college. I was with Frank, and he left quite an impression on her."

Nancy laughed, "As he does with everyone."

Mike went on to explain to Nancy how they had met while working together on the Kearcy case.

Nancy asked, "So how are you doing with all those horrific images?" She knew how hard Mike took the case.

Mike got quiet for a minute, and then said, "I'm doing okay."

"Mikey? Are you still having those nightmares?"

"I was, but not in the past few days since Meredith and I have been getting to know each other."

"Then I like her already. If she can help you get past this God-awful grisly murder, then she must be quite a lady."

"I don't want to sound premature or anything, and I feel so silly saying this, but I have a strong feeling she may be the one."

"I would love to see you finally settle down, sweetheart. By the way, how is school going?"

"I'm still on track. It's going pretty well, actually. A lot of driving back and forth. It's a long drive to Jacksonville, but I'm sure if things work out with Meredith, she'll help me out a lot. She's supposed to be an amazing attorney."

"Well, you've done it all on your own so far. Your father would be so proud of you. I know I am."

"Thank you, Mom. Wow, it's ten o'clock. I can't waste this Saturday. I have a paper to write and I want to check on Meredith." "Thank you for the update, Mikey. I love you. Keep me informed."

"I will. I love you too, Mom."

Mike immediately called Meredith.

She answered and said, "There you are. I was so sad to wake up and discover you were no longer on the line. You fell asleep on me while I was talking last night."

"I'm sorry. I woke up this morning and couldn't remember who fell asleep first. I feel bad about that."

"Don't feel bad. I loved falling asleep to the sound of you breathing on the other end."

Mike replied, "That's funny, because I woke up and I listened to you breathing for a while, too. I didn't want to wake you, so I hung up."

"Oh no, you did not listen to me! Was I snoring?"

"No, it was nice."

"So, Mister, what did you have planned for today?"

"I have a paper due Monday on civil procedures, so I figured I should knock it out."

"That shouldn't be too bad. If you can use a tutor, I happen to know a brilliant lawyer."

"Oh really? Does she do house calls?"

"Who said anything about a she? Besides, it depends on the house she's calling on."

Within the hour, Meredith arrived. Mike didn't manage to get his paper written that day. But the next day, Meredith helped him. It turned out that she really was a brilliant lawyer. Mike turned in the paper and got a perfect grade.

For the next six months, Mike and Meredith dated exclusively. Things were going so well for them. They never disagreed about anything. For the first time, Mike was truly happy.

***

The Kearcy trial was fast approaching. Multiple psychological exams proved that Mark Kearcy was competent to stand trial. Even with his confession on tape, his lawyers were still fighting for his life. Meredith was convinced that the trial would be quick and more of a formality.

Meredith helped Mike prepare for his testimony. She told Mike that her co-counsel, Shawn Banks, would be asking him questions during the trial. She would be careful not to mix their personal life with business.

Monday, November 18th, 2002. It was the day of the trial and Mike was nervous. *I hope I can keep it together up there.* He would still occasionally struggle with the images of that night, but had overall come to terms with the incident, largely due to the distraction of Meredith. When recounting the night Amanda was murdered, he teared up and his voice broke several times when describing the pictures. This drew a sympathetic response from the jury, and the defense tried to object to his testimony. The judge, of course, denied their motion.

The trial went quickly, as expected. On Thursday, the jury returned a guilty verdict and they recommended the death sentence. Mark never admitted to any accomplices and faced the entire trial alone.

Mark sat still, apathetic to the reading of the verdict. In one month, all parties returned for the sentencing hearing.

On the day of the hearing, the judge re-read the verdict aloud. "Mark Stephen Kearcy, you have been found guilty by a jury of your peers of the abduction and murder of four-year-old Amanda Rollins. Before sentencing, do you have any words you wish to share with the court?"

Mark stood and made a brief and dreadful monotone statement. "I have no regrets for what I've done. The child is in the hands of the Master."

Amanda's father, Paul, cried out, "YOU EVIL MONSTER! YOU SON OF A BITCH! I HOPE YOU BURN IN HELL! DEATH IS TOO

GOOD FOR YOU!" Paul had to be restrained by the bailiffs, and they escorted him from the courtroom. Amanda's mother wept inconsolably.

After a short recess, Paul and Melinda had calmed down, and the hearing continued.

The judge read the sentence. "Mark Stephen Kearcy, for the first count of child abduction in the first degree, it is the ruling of this court that you spend the remainder of your days in prison with no possibility of parole. For the second count of murder in the first degree, it is the ruling of this court that you shall be sentenced to death by lethal injection." A sigh of relief echoed through the courtroom.

Mark remained stoic throughout the reading of the sentence, and at the end, he smiled malevolently.

He turned to Meredith and they smiled at each other. The monster had been defeated.

As Mark was being handcuffed to be returned to jail, he called out to Mike in the voice of a thousand lost souls, eyes black as coal. "Michael, your time is near!"

When Mike turned around to look back in horror, he tripped and fell, hitting his head on the ground.

When Mike awoke, Meredith, several bailiffs and Mr. & Mrs. Rollins were standing over him. Meredith asked, "Are you okay, my love? You were out cold."

"Yeah, yeah, I'm fine." Mike countered. Then he asked, "Did you guys hear that?"

Meredith asked, "Hear what?"

"Kearcy!" Mike exclaimed. "No one heard what he said?"

Everyone looked at him curiously before they looked at each other and shrugged their shoulders.

Meredith told him, "Honey, Kearcy never said a word. He did laugh when he saw you fall, though."

Frustrated, Mike sighed, "Never mind!"

As he struggled to his feet, Meredith asked, "Are you sure you're okay, baby? Here, let me help you."

"Thank you, hon. I'm fine, I promise. This case has really messed with my head."

As she was touching the now large bump on his head, Meredith said, "It literally has."

As usual, she was able to make Mike laugh during a bad time. He smiled and said, "Let's get out of here."

The night of the sentencing, Mike and Meredith went out to celebrate with their friends and co-workers.

Robert spoke up first. "I'd like to propose a toast to my partner, for a job well done, and to his beautiful lady friend who successfully prosecuted the evilest human being I have ever had the displeasure of encountering. You two make not only a lovely couple, but a force to be reckoned with in the courtroom."

After the celebratory meal, Mike and Meredith were at his apartment. Mike said, "Hey babe, there's something I've been meaning to ask you for a while now."

"Yes, my love?"

"What would you think about us moving in together?"

Meredith shrieked in excitement. "There you go, reading my mind again!" She hugged and kissed him. "I'm so in love with you!"

Mike looked deep into her eyes and he knew she meant it. He responded, "I love you like no other. I have never felt like this about anyone else before."

Over the next two weeks, Mike and Meredith searched for a place and finally found a nice luxury condo to rent in a good part of town.

It was their first night together in their new condo, and all was going well. Mike got home early and cooked dinner for Meredith to surprise her.

"This is a nice surprise," Meredith said when she got home.

They had no cable TV installed yet, so they each sipped wine and talked the whole evening.

"I can get used to this," Mike said to her.

"Mmmm, me too," she responded.

3:00 a.m. "YOU DIRTY WHORE, YOU'RE GONNA PAY!"

Meredith woke up, startled. "Mike, did you hear that?"

"Hear what?"

"That girl screaming."

Mike sat up in bed, "I don't hear anything. What did you hear?"

"I heard a girl scream out, 'Whore, you're gonna pay!' You really slept through that? You're a heavy sleeper, aren't you?"

"Not normally. Usually, I wake at the drop of a pin."

Meredith continued, "Well, I'm glad it was no one trying to get me. You'd have slept right through it."

Mike laughed and held her in his arms. "I would never let anyone harm you."

"I thought this was a good neighborhood," she said.

"It is, honey. It was probably just a couple arguing. It can happen anywhere, even good neighborhoods. I don't hear anything now. Let's try and get back to sleep."

"You better keep me safe, Michael Carson, or I'll come back and haunt you if you don't."

"No one will ever hurt you, I promise! Scout's honor."

"You were never a scout, you idiot!"

"True, but I dressed up like a girl scout at a college Halloween party once."

Meredith giggled, "Idiot!"

Over the next year, Mike seemed to catch all the bad cases. Mike had two other cult-related homicides. Each case took a heavy toll on Mike's psyche. There were so many similarities to the Moloch murders, but luckily, none involved children.

*   *   *

At roll call, Lieutenant Peterson came in to talk with the detectives. "Gentlemen, and lady. We have seen a marked increase in these cult-related crimes. Some of you have worked many of these cases. As of now, we have no idea who these people are. They are very secretive. I was approached by the Sheriff and he asked me to form a cult task force. We'll be working alongside the District Attorney's Office. I expect everyone to be actively involved. We'll be working late, with a lot of undercover work. I have selected the two best people to be lead on our side, though we will all be working together. Mike and Robert, you two have the most experience with these crimes. Mike, I know this isn't easy for you, and I won't make it mandatory, but I really need you on this."

Mike was uneasy, but he was always a team player. "I'm yours.

Whatever you need, Lieutenant."

"Good man. Robert, are you on board?"

Robert replied, "I'm with him, boss."

"Okay. The rest of us will be working very closely with you both. Anything you need, you just ask. We need to focus our efforts on finding this group, The Moloch Society. We believe that they are very well organized, and they're going to be tough to infiltrate. Their crimes are extremely violent and they must be stopped."

Mike and Robert took the lead, and they worked together closely with the District Attorney's Office. Meredith was assigned to be the lead counsel on any cases that Mike and Robert would make. Mike and Meredith made a pact not to discuss anything related to work while they were home. It would be their sanctuary from the madness.

From Mike's research and from what he had learned during the previous investigations, he discovered that Moloch was a god worshipped by the ancient Phoenicians and Canaanites. A major part of their worship included the burning sacrifice of their children.

Sunday, May 11th, 2003. It was Mother's Day. At 3:00 a.m., Mike got a call from Sergeant Smith. "I hate to do this to you, Mike. This is a bad one."

"What do you have, Sarge?"

He heard a heavy sigh on the other end of the line. "Well, it seems that a mother has murdered her child, and on Mother's Day of all days, of course."

"Oh my God, are you kidding me?"

"No. We need you on this one. Let Meredith come out if she wants to. I don't want any mistakes made on this one. She can make sure every I is dotted and T crossed."

"We're on our way."

He hung up and turned toward his girlfriend. "Meredith, honey, we gotta go."

Half asleep, Meredith asked, "What? Why am I going?"

"C'mon babe, I'll explain on the way."

In the car, Mike explained what little he knew of the case. Meredith was horrified at what he had told her.

When they arrived on the scene, Sergeant Smith met with them.

"The father came home just a little after midnight. He assumed the family was asleep, but then he heard a strange noise coming from the nursery and went to investigate. When he entered the room, he found his wife standing in the middle of a large red pentagram and holding their baby. As he ran toward her, she said 'This is for my Mistress.' The father said she then plunged a bull's horn dagger into the child's chest. He tackled his wife, but it was too late. He's been transported by EMS. He had to be sedated."

Mike was dismayed, and stood with a blank expression on his face.

"Now Meredith, I don't expect you to go inside. I just wanted you on scene to review everything we do, to make sure there aren't any mistakes made. I don't want this psycho walking on a technicality," Smith told her.

"Of course, anything I can do to help," she answered. "Are you gonna be okay, honey?"

Mike replied, "I should be okay. I'm glad you're here with me. I don't want you to come inside. I expect it's a pretty awful scene."

"Just be safe. If you need a break, come out here with me. I'm worried about you."

"I'll be okay sweetheart, knowing you're here with me."

"I am here, honey. Now get going. Let's put this woman away." They kissed and Mike went inside.

Inside, Crime Scene technicians were snapping photos, and Mike spoke to Sergeant Smith on the front porch. "Where's the wife?"

"Mrs. Carmen Lopez, 27-year-old Hispanic female. She's at the station. She hasn't said a word. No one has interviewed her yet. I'll leave that to you."

"Thank you, Sarge. I wish Robert wasn't on vacation. I could use him on this one."

"Anything you need, I'm here for you."

"And the father?"

"Rafael Lopez, 31-year-old Hispanic male. He's at Merciful Heart Hospital. I understand he had to be sedated and can't be questioned for a while."

"And the child?"

"Six-month-old Miguel Lopez. He's still on the floor in his room. He hasn't been moved or touched yet. EMS never touched him because there were obvious signs of death. Mike, I gotta warn you,

it's bad in there. I'll be right here if you need me."

"Thank you, Sarge."

Mike took a deep breath and stepped into the single story ranch- style home. It was simply appointed with what looked like rental furniture. He saw one of the crime scene technicians exit the nursery, and she was visibly shaken.

Mike asked her, "Are you okay, Samantha?"

She approached Mike and said with tears in her eyes, "It's a mess in there."

With great trepidation, Mike walked down the long, narrow hallway. It was quiet, and grew quieter as he distanced himself from the outside commotion. He entered the nursery. What was once a peaceful, happy place with eggshell-colored walls and a decorative border with fire trucks under a chair rail that wrapped around the room was now a dreadful scene. Red blood saturated the once light blue carpet around the baby's tiny body. The two colors mixed looked dark purple. The baby's tiny corpse lay motionless, crusted in dried blood, face up. The garish ritual blade was still plunged into the miniature cadaver. Mike had become all too familiar with this sort of blade—the tool of choice in the cult murders. Then there was the equally familiar red pentagram that had been crudely painted with red spray paint on the carpet. The empty can sat on the floor in the corner of the room. Mike took a step back. His eyes watered. There was no way he could go any further. He had seen enough.

Mike quickly exited the residence. He was pale and sobbed out of control. Meredith rushed over to him. "Honey, are you okay?"

Tearfully, Mike said, "I'll be fine. I just need a minute."

After several minutes, Sergeant Smith approached him. "Are you ready to go interview the mother?"

"As ready as I'm going to be, I suppose."

Mike, Meredith and Sergeant Smith went to the station.

"She's in the room, Mike," said Sergeant Smith.

"Give me a few minutes alone. I need to prepare myself for this."

Mike stood on the other side of the one-way mirror, staring at his adversary. He thought, *Your baby . . . how could you murder your innocent baby? What kind of a monster kills her baby, and on Mother's Day?* Suddenly, the Legion of voices thundered forth from the woman. "Welcome back, Michael. We've been waiting for you. Your time is close!"

Mike stumbled backwards and fell against the opposite wall.

Rattled, he ran out of the dark room.

"Mike?" Sergeant Smith asked.

Mike responded with tears streaming down his face, "I'm sorry, Sarge. I can't do it. I just can't. I've seen too much. I'm done."

Meredith came over and hugged him. "Shhh, it's okay, baby. It's okay."

Sergeant Smith responded, "I can't blame you, son. You have seen a lot of shit lately. I'm going to reassign this case to someone else."

Meredith said, "Thank you, Sergeant. I'm going to get him home now."

"You do that, hon. Take good care of him."

Mike would never again return to Major Crimes. He met with Lieutenant Peterson and Sergeant Smith. He had seen too much over the past year and a half. It had finally broken him.

"I'm sorry. I can't keep doing this."

Lieutenant Peterson said, "Mike, don't be ashamed for making this choice. You saw more in the fifteen months you were here than most of us will ever see in a whole career. You are one hell of a detective. I hate to lose you, but I'd rather see you happy again."

"Thank you, sir." Mike shook both of their hands and walked out to start his vacation.

Mike spent a month in counseling. The department put him on administrative leave with pay. Once Mike was cleared to return to duty, he was reassigned back to road patrol.

He enjoyed being back on the road again. He and Meredith were still doing great. He was finally putting the nightmares behind him. Occasionally, he would be involved in a case that would bring back some of the nightmares, but he had learned some techniques to deal with the stress.

Mike continued his studies over the next year, and with Meredith's assistance he finished law school.

***

Friday, December 3rd, 2004. "C'mon babe, we're gonna be late!"

This was the big day. He was finally graduating law school. Unlike his graduation with his bachelor's, Mike allowed this to be a big deal. He would celebrate his accomplishment with those closest to him.

Meredith said, "Your mom called. She and Frank are already downstairs in the lobby. They checked in late this morning and rushed to get ready."

Mike came out of the bathroom and Meredith said, "Don't you look nice? You better get used to wearing a suit more often. And you certainly do that suit justice. Do you have your cap and gown?"

"Right here."

" Let's go then," Meredith said. "We need to get Cynthia and my parents before we go downstairs."

Mike and Meredith collected her parents and Cynthia, Meredith's best friend. The five took the elevator downstairs. When they exited the elevator, there stood Nancy and Frank. Due to a recurring knee injury, Frank had had to retire from professional football and was now a sports consultant. He had played for ten years, a long time for a center. He had put on about sixty pounds since he stopped playing ball, and was bigger than ever. But he was still the same old Frank.

When the five exited the elevator, a bellowing howl echoed throughout the hotel lobby. "WHAT'S UP, DOUCHE BAG?" The big man came running up to them.

Mike laughed, and the two old friends hugged. Then Frank picked Meredith up off the floor and hugged her as she screamed, "Don't crush me, Moose!" Frank laughed.

Nancy then hugged Mike and Meredith. Meredith's parents had never had the occasion to meet Frank, and were taken aback at first.

Frank announced to her parents, "Hi, how you folks doin'? I'm Frank, but you can call me Moose!"

Frank went up and hugged Rebecca, Meredith's mom. "I can see where Merry gets her hotness from!" Frank would often refer to Meredith as Merry, a coined name she became fond of in time.

When Frank shook Henry's hand, Meredith's father, his destructive bear paws swallowed the surgeon's delicate instruments of healing and he said, "What's up, Doc?"

Then Frank's attention turned to Cynthia. "And who's this vision of loveliness?"

Cynthia blushed and Meredith said, "Frank, this is my best friend, Cynthia."

Frank was mesmerized. In an uncharacteristically gentle manner, Frank took Cynthia's hand and kissed it.

"It's so nice to finally meet you, Frank. I've heard a lot about you. I had forgotten how adorable you are, though."

Mike couldn't believe it when he saw his giant blush.

Frank asked Cynthia, "Have we met before?"

Cynthia and Meredith looked at each other and laughed, recalling the night Frank assaulted Meredith's hood.

"We have never met in person, but I saw you around the campus once or twice back in college."

Frank was smitten by Meredith's best friend and seemed almost speechless at times. But within short order, he was back in his form. Cynthia thought he was charming.

While Frank entertained the Porters and Cynthia with his antics, Nancy said to Mike, "I'm so proud of you, sweetie. Your father would be so impressed by you right now. You have accomplished so much."

"Thanks, Mom. I'd like to think he has been my inspiration."

Then she whispered to Mike, "So what about you two? When are you going to make her an honest woman?"

Mike shrugged and said, "Oh, Mom, not that again. One of these days I might surprise you."

"Well, just don't let this one get away. I like her a lot. She's good for you, honey."

"I couldn't agree more, Mom. I love her more than you can imagine. But don't worry, things are good between us. We're doing great."

Nancy then got the opportunity to finally meet Rebecca, Henry and Cynthia. She could see the look of repulsion on Rebecca's and Henry's faces regarding Frank. She smiled and told them, "Don't worry, he'll grow on you. You'll find he's truly a sweet man."

After the graduation ceremony, they all went out to dinner. While at dinner, Mike got up to excuse himself. "I gotta go to the bathroom. You need to go too, Frank?"

Distracted by Cynthia, Frank said, "No, I'm good."

Mike punched Frank in the arm. "You need to go, too?!" Mike raised his eyebrows and Frank said, "Oh yeah! Yeah, I really need to piss!"

Meredith, Cynthia, Nancy, Rebecca and Henry sat together, looking at each other suspiciously. Nancy said, "I wonder what those two are up to?"

Meredith quipped, "If Frank's involved, I don't want to know."

Cynthia laughed like a school girl. Meredith could see that she was intrigued by Frank.

Walking away and laughing, Mike said to him, "Dumbass, did you forget the plan?"

"No buddy, I got your back. Just a brain fart, that's all."

"Must be because you're all google-eyed over Cynthia. Just don't blow this, knucklehead! Did you remember the ring?"

"Right here, shithead." Frank pulled a black velvet hinged box from his pocket.

Mike opened it to examine the simple solitaire diamond ring that held a brilliant one carat round stone. Meredith had, in a roundabout way, implied several times that she preferred a simple solitaire ring over an ornate, gaudy setting.

"It's beautiful, bro. Just like your lady."

"You think?"

"Yeah! She's hot, dude!"

"I mean the ring, you asshole!" Mike laughed. "You'll never change, Frankie."

"Hell no. Change is something that gets thrown on the floor and walked on. And no one is walking on me!"

"Geez, no one could even step over you if they wanted to, big boy." "I ams what I ams." Frank laughed in his best Popeye impression.

"Let's go, Popeye," said Mike.

Mike signaled the maître d'. It was show time.

Mike returned to the table with Frank. They both sat down when a single violin player waltzed by them, quietly playing Mendelssohn's Wedding March. Meredith looked at the violinist, bewildered, thinking that it was a strange song to play in a restaurant.

When she turned back around, Mike had gotten on one knee and held the box open. Meredith was shocked and the violinist stopped playing. Mike asked, "Meredith, it's been two and a half years since we met, and you have seen me through some of the worst times of my life. Through it all, though, you've always reassured me with your love. I couldn't have made it the past few years without you, and I don't want to waste another day without you being my wife. Meredith Porter, will you do me the honor of being my bride and sharing my life with me?"

With tear-filled eyes, Meredith responded, "Yes! Yes, a million times yes!"

Frank howled, "WOO HOO! She said yes!"

Nancy, Rebecca and Cynthia all cried with joy, and Henry congratulated them both, hugging Mike.

Frank, of course, stepped in and hugged Henry. "We're gonna be family, Doc!"

Henry had been standoffish all night, but finally relented and smiled at Frank's boyish charm.

The entire restaurant erupted in applause.

Mike winked at Nancy. "I told you one day I'd surprise you. How does today work for you?"

"Oh Mikey, I can't wait to help her plan the wedding. I'm so excited! I love you two so much."

Nancy then hugged Meredith and they cried tears of joy together. There was a small dance floor, where Mike and Meredith danced. Nancy said to Frank, "How is it you knew about this and I didn't?"

"He swore me to secrecy, Nance. I couldn't tell you anything or he'd kill me."

She smiled and said, "You're a good friend to him, Frankie. Thank you for being in his life. I love ya, big guy." Nancy reached up and kissed him on the cheek.

Frank blushed. "I love you too, Nance. Since Momma passed, you're like a second mom to me and I love that guy like a brother. Now it looks like I'm gonna have a little sister to watch out for."

Nancy watched her son and new daughter celebrating. She joyfully reflected on the night Big Mike had proposed to her, and she smiled contentedly, recounting their happy life together and how he would have loved to be here. At one point, she became a bit melancholy, wishing her man was there to enjoy this special night with her.

Henry and Rebecca swelled with pride that their beautiful daughter had found such a wonderful man. They were not so sure about their loyal protector, Frank, though. Henry looked at Rebecca and smiled.

"Honey, I think this could be a good thing for our little girl."

Rebecca smiled and nodded in agreement. "But *the* Moose?"

"Yes, dear. Look at him, he's a gentle giant. I think our little girl's in good hands with these two." They knew their little girl would be well cared for and loved.

And lastly, due to all the excitement about the engagement, two people sat relatively unnoticed. What everyone failed to notice was that Frank, "The Moose," Peterson and Cynthia Sanders sat alone in the corner of the room, staring longingly into each other's eyes. Frank was being unusually reserved and well-behaved, which went unnoticed to all but Mike. Even through all his excitement, he was watching his best friend and thought to himself, *I can't believe it. The Moose is falling in love. I never thought I'd see the day.*

The seven of them celebrated long into the night. It was a happy time. Mike seemed to have everything falling into place, better than he could have hoped for.

Later that night while Meredith lay in his arms, Mike reflected on his life and was confident that all was going to be okay now. Things were a far cry from his days as the pathetic, shy, chubby teenager getting beat up in middle school. Life was good; he was happy.

The nightmares would finally be over.

MEREDITH

*A*UGUST 1992, THE FLORIDA TECHNICAL UNIVERSITY. An ambitious young woman was starting her first day as a new student. Meredith Porter was a year younger and two years ahead of her fellow students. Due to her advanced intellect, she was allowed to test and skip a grade in high school. Due to a special program that her school offered gifted students, Meredith also graduated high school with a two-year degree from the local community college. She earned her high school diploma and degree concurrently while attending high school. Meredith entered FTU as a seventeen-year-old junior.

Meredith, a beautiful young woman with long, auburn-colored hair and green eyes, always had plenty of suitors, but never experienced a serious relationship. She was too goal-oriented to waste time on dating boys in high school. College would prove no different for her, and while she was ogled by many men, she would pay no attention to their advances. She gave many the impression of being unapproachable. She was not necessarily a prude, but just extremely ambitious and determined to achieve her goals before ever considering a relationship.

Meredith was the only child of Dr. and Mrs. Henry Porter. Her father, Henry, was an accomplished orthopedic surgeon in her hometown. Her mother, Rebecca, was an astute and feared local attorney. For as long as she could remember, Meredith had wanted to follow in her mother's footsteps and become a lawyer. She had worked with her mother after school and during the summers at her law firm, and had developed a love and respect for the law. Currently, her immediate goal was to become the youngest female to pass the bar exam in the state of Florida. This would require her to remain focused on her studies.

There were, however, no shortage of distractions on campus. Parties nearly every night, good looking guys hitting on her constantly and a myriad of extracurricular groups and societies wanting her to join. But she remained steadfast and resolute in her objective. She would be too busy taking classes for her double majors in philosophy and economics to allow any disruptions.

Meredith's social activities were limited to seeing movies in town with her girlfriends on the weekends, working out five days a week, study groups and being President of the Legal Society. The Legal Society was a student group that she helped start and was the only school-related extracurricular indulgence she would allow herself. She started it with several other students who shared a similar interest in the law. They would conduct mock trials and attend actual court hearings at the local courthouse, then critique the cases afterwards.

One Saturday night, after seeing a movie, Meredith and her best friend Cynthia Sanders were driving back onto campus. Their route took them by the football stadium, where the Panthers had just relished in another victory. Although Meredith was very athletic, she took no interest in football or any other sport as a spectator; she just had no time for it. While she was driving, the campus police stopped them at an intersection to allow a large group of players and fans to cross the street.

They were a large, raucous bunch. There was one, in particular, a mammoth, boisterous beast wearing a number fifty football jersey who stopped in front of her car, leaned over onto her hood with both hands, then tapped on the hood like he was playing bongo drums. The brute proceeded to shout, "WOO HOO BABY, PANTHERS KICK ASS! WOOOOOH! WE'RE NUMBER ONE! FUCK YEAH!!!"

Another man, maybe a player, but instead of wearing a jersey wore a tight-fitting Panthers Football t-shirt that accentuated his rippling arms and chest, grabbed the behemoth and cried out, "C'mon Moose, leave the pretty ladies alone!"

The gorgeous blonde-haired Adonis made eye contact with Meredith and mouthed, "I'm sorry," then shrugged his broad shoulders. The two animated figures continued on their way as the bigger one continued hooting and hollering.

Meredith said, "Why are football players so crass?"

Cynthia giggled and said, "I don't know. I think he was kind of funny."

Meredith smiled. "I suppose so. His friend was gorgeous, don't you think?"

"Uh, yeah, they both were."

"Ew, gross! The big one he called Moose?"

"What? I thought he was adorable! He seemed funny to me. I like a big man."

"Whatever sicko, but his friend was definitely cute."

Cynthia was two years older than Meredith and a freshman; however, Meredith and Cynthia shared similar ambitions and remained lifelong friends.

June 1994. Meredith graduated with her double major degree in philosophy and economics. Because of her outstanding academic endeavors, she graduated summa cum laude and was class valedictorian. She, of course, presented the valedictory speech. In attendance were her parents and her best friend, Cynthia.

"And lastly, let us remember those who have encouraged and supported us through the years. Whether they be outside mentors or family, give thanks. Most of us would not be in this room were it not for their encouragement and support. To my mom and dad, from the bottom of my heart, thank you. To my fellow graduates, go forth with the knowledge that this fine institution has imparted on you and use it to better your world.

"When I look around this auditorium, I see an incomplete puzzle; thousands of individual pieces all thrown together into a box in random chaotic order. Individually, I am just one piece of this puzzle. Alone, I can't finish the picture. But like a puzzle, if I am connected with another piece and we then are joined with other pieces, eventually when we are all connected the way we were meant to be, we can create a lovely image. I challenge us all, as individual pieces with limited influence, to unite with the other pieces in this great hall to complete that image. Let the positive influence we have on this world be our beautiful finished picture. Citizens of the world, be forewarned that the graduating class of 1994 is coming and we will not be overlooked. Go forth, my fellow graduates, and be excellent. Thank you."

"That was quite a speech, don't you think honey?" Meredith's mother, Rebecca, asked her father.

Her father, Henry, pretending to be asleep, opened his eyes and said, "Huh? What? Oh—oh yeah, great speech, and short, too."

"Oh Henry, honestly!" Rebecca said as she slapped his arm.

Henry laughed.

Rebecca asked, "So Cynthia, this will be you soon I hope?" "Unfortunately, not for two more years. I'm so proud of Meredith. She is amazing. I wish I had half her ability."

"You're a brilliant young lady, Cynthia. You'll do great things. I just know you will."

"Thank you, Mrs. Porter."

During her senior year, Meredith had applied to, and of course was eagerly accepted, into law school. She spent that summer at home working with her mother as an assistant and helping her in preparing cases for trial. She would observe her mother in court, studying her every move. She would try dreaming up ways she could beat her. Of course, she never let her mother know what she was up to. Meredith would often ponder, "If I ever have to face this woman in court, how could I defeat her?" She could not have envisioned how handy this training would be to her in the future.

August 1994. Meredith started law school at FTU. She and Cynthia had moved in together again and shared an apartment off campus. One Friday evening as she was trying to study, she heard a howling from outside. It sounded like a wolf howling at the moon, "WOO HOO! C'MON UP LADIES, IT'S PARTY TIME!"

Frustrated, she went to the living room and told Cynthia, "I can't concentrate with all that racket outside. Do you want to go out for a while?" She couldn't help but think to herself, *that voice sounds so familiar. I just can't place it, but it sure is aggravating.*

Cynthia laughed, "Maybe we should go find the party; it could be fun."

Meredith stared at her in disbelief and said, "Ugh, I'm in no mood. I really want to get this paper done. Besides, it sounds a little too rowdy for me."

Unbeknownst to Meredith, the gorgeous Adonis was staying in his old apartment in the building across from hers, and "The Moose" had come over to party, as he often would.

Cynthia laughed and said, "I knew you would say that. Come on, girl. Let's go de-stress at The Chablis Cabaret." This was a quiet jazz club, with a soft atmosphere where many upscale residents would go to unwind. Cynthia and Meredith would often go just to relax from their intense studies, and it was a place where no self-respecting college football player would be found dead. Being too young to drink, Meredith would sip on a ginger ale, while Cynthia would have a glass of wine.

By the time the girls had returned that night, the cops had already been there and broken up the party. Meredith could once again concentrate. She worked long into the night and completed her paper, which freed her up for the rest of the weekend to unwind.

June 1996. Cynthia graduated with her degree in engineering. Meredith and her parents went out with Cynthia and her parents to celebrate. That evening at home, Meredith said to Cynthia, "I can't believe you'll be moving out. My best friend is abandoning me."

Cynthia told her, "Well, maybe not. I have an opportunity to work with an engineering firm here in town. Do you think you can stand having me around another year or so?"

Meredith squealed with excitement. "Oh my God, that's so awesome! I thought you were going to work at your cousin's firm in Philadelphia."

Cynthia said, "I was, but the man I was going to replace decided to stay on for one more year. They offered to let me start at another position, but then I heard about this opportunity here in town. I wanted to stay around here a little longer. The job in Philly is mine when he leaves, so here I am and we get at least one more year

together. Now I can watch you graduate law school."

Cynthia stayed, and during that year their friendship grew even stronger. Each of them was an only child and they had become as close as sisters.

June 1997. Meredith graduated law school with honors, of no surprise to anyone who had ever met her. That night after the ceremony,

Rebecca asked, "So honey, are you still planning on moving home?"

Meredith said, "That's the plan, as long as I'm still welcome."

Rebecca asked, "Can I count on your expertise in the office?"

"Of course, Mom. Where else would I be?"

"Then of course you're still welcome. What are your long-term thoughts?"

"Well, I would like to try something different. I was thinking that after I pass the bar, I'd like to be a prosecutor, at least for a while. Maybe I could get hired by the District Attorney."

"I think that's a wonderful idea. You know I'm good friends with Allen. I could put in a good word for you. You really could develop a deeper appreciation of the law by experiencing it from the other side for a while." Laughing, she said, "I suppose I've always been too much of a bleeding-heart liberal to be a prosecutor."

"Yes, but if I ever needed a lawyer, Mom, you'd be the one I want in my corner."

Henry chattered, "Hear, hear!" as he raised a glass of wine to toast. "To the three beautiful ladies in my life."

On the last night in their apartment together, the two best friends were discussing their futures.

"So, now it looks like you're the one abandoning me," Cynthia said.

"You're leaving this Saturday. Don't make me feel bad, girlfriend."

Cynthia giggled, "I'm just kidding. Say, are you up for one last drink at the Cabaret?"

"Sounds great."

The ladies, now both of legal drinking age, would regularly go to their favorite spot to unwind. With their glasses full of a delightful Pinot, Meredith proposed a toast.

"To our futures!"

Cynthia echoed the sentiment, "To our futures. I'm gonna miss you, girlfriend."

"I'm gonna miss you, too. Thank you for all your encouragement."

"Thank you for getting me through advanced calculus. I never would have made it without you!" Cynthia replied.

The two girls laughed and enjoyed their last night of college life together in their favorite watering hole.

Meredith and Cynthia would stay in touch and remain best friends for the rest of their lives. They would regularly visit each other, and rarely a day would pass when they didn't talk at least once.

Meredith returned home and was working for Rebecca. She was set to challenge the bar exam the following month, at the end of July.

Every evening after work, Rebecca would help her prepare for the exam.

One afternoon while eating lunch, Rebecca told Meredith, "I hope you don't mind, but I invited a friend to join us. He should be here in a few minutes."

"Oh really? Who is it? Are you cheating on Daddy?"

"Oh Meredith, stop. Here he is now . . . Allen, over here! Meredith, this is Allen Markowitz. Allen, this is Meredith, my daughter."

Meredith stood up and nervously shook Allen's hand. "Mr. Markowitz, it's a pleasure to meet you."

"Please Meredith, outside the office call me Allen. And the pleasure is all mine. Rebecca, it's always a pleasure." The two old friends hugged and the three sat down to lunch.

"So, your mother tells me you want to try the other side for a while?" "Yes sir, Mr. Markow —."

"Allen." He interrupted.

Smiling, Meredith said, "I mean Allen. I would work tirelessly for you."

"Of that I have no doubt, young lady. I've been following you for some time. I have many friends up at FTU. Not sure if you knew this, but I'm also an FTU alumnus. 'Go Panthers!'"

The three laughed, and Meredith said, "No, I never knew you went to FTU."

"Absolutely, and I stay in touch with the staff. I'm always looking to recruit bright new talent. Throughout your time there, your name constantly came up as a top candidate. Your mother informed me that you were hoping to come to work with me, so I figured recruitment wouldn't be necessary. Frankly, I'm a bit surprised. You know I can't pay you much. Working with your

mother, you could definitely make much more money."

"Mr. Ma- I mean Allen, I'm not as concerned about the money as I am about the process of law. I want to experience all aspects of the law. I love the legal process, and I want to get a taste for it all."

"That's a good plan. As I'm sure you know, I'll have to start you out in misdemeanor crimes, and you can work your way into felony after you prove yourself. As soon as you get the results of that bar exam, I expect to see you in my office, young lady."

"Oh Mr. Markowitz, thank you! I mean Allen! Thank you so much!" Laughing, Allen said, "Thank you. I look forward to you working with us. We can use a bright young talent like yourself. I do expect results, though. Just because your mother and I are old friends doesn't mean I'll go easy on you. You'll start at the bottom and move up if you can show me you've got what it takes. What are your long term goals?"

"One day, I want to sit on the bench."

"Well, well. A judge, eh? That's very ambitious. I raise a glass to Judge Porter."

Rebecca responded, "That's my girl. I told you she's an ambitious one."

"Well, from everything I've learned about you from the school and what your mother tells me, I have no doubt that one day you will be a Supreme Court Justice."

With a confident smile, Meredith said, "Thank you, sir."

"Now, enough business. Let's get back to lunch. I'm starving."

After ordering their meals, Allen continued, "You know, your mother and I met when I was a young, wet-behind-the-ears prosecutor and she was a ruthless public defender. She embarrassed me on more than one occasion. If you're half the lawyer she is, I'm getting quite a catch."

Rebecca smiled and said, "Ah yes, those were the good old days."

"Sure, good for you. I'm glad I'm a politician now. I don't have to face you in court."

Meredith joked, "That's my Mama, The Queen of the Courtroom."

Allen laughed and said, "Young lady, you have no idea how accurate a statement that is."

October 1997. Meredith finally got her results from the state bar. At dinner, she revealed to her parents the big news.

In a solemn voice, Meredith spoke. "Mom, Dad? I have something to tell you."

Henry and Rebecca looked at each other with concern. They asked in unison, "What is it, sweetheart?"

Suddenly, Meredith's countenance changed and she screamed, "I PASSED! I PASSED, I PASSED! I GOT THE RESULTS THIS AFTERNOON WHEN WE GOT HOME FROM THE OFFICE!"

Henry cheered, "Hey! That's my girl! I never had a doubt!"

Rebecca replied, "So, you're a lawyer now. Congratulations, darling. I guess this means I won't be seeing you around the office as much."

"Maybe not, but you might see me in court."

Two weeks later, Meredith was starting her first day as an Assistant District Attorney.

In Allen's office, Meredith stood quivering with excitement, anxious to get started.

Allen asked, "Are you nervous?"

"No sir, Allen. Oops, I mean Mr. Markowitz."

Allen winked and smiled at the beautiful young prosecutor and said, "That's good. I'm going to have you shadow Jill here for a few weeks until you get your feet wet. Jill, this is Meredith Porter. She'll be starting with us today."

"Jillian Strowesky, but call me Jill. Nice to meet you, Meredith."

"Nice to meet you, Jill."

"Okay, you two. Get the hell out of my office and put some bad guys in jail for me, will ya? I have an upcoming election. I need these clowns off the street!"

Laughing, Jill said, "C'mon, let me show you to your office."

After two weeks, Meredith was released on her own. She worked zealously for the next six months and enjoyed an astonishing ninety-one percent conviction rate, while her counterparts averaged about sixty percent. Meredith had quickly earned quite a name for herself in the court system. Allen had taken notice, as well.

One afternoon, Allen called her on the intercom. "Meredith, can

I see you in my office?"

Meredith rushed to his office. "Mr. Markowitz?"

"I just wanted to say thank you. I asked you not to let me down, and you have not disappointed me yet. Keep this up, and you'll be a judge by the time you're thirty. I see great things in your future."

"Thank you, sir."

"Okay, that's it. Go put some more bad guys away for me."

Smiling, Meredith walked away saying, "That's what I do, sir."

Her next case was seemingly simple, open and shut. A nineteen-year-old was caught shoplifting, on camera, with a clear shot of his face as he exited the store. Meredith received notice that he would be represented by the most powerful defense attorney in the tri-county area, Rebecca Porter.

Meredith was a bit unnerved as she realized that her dream of facing her mother in court could become a reality.

That night, at her condo, Meredith received a phone call. "Well, counselor, seems like you are trying to put away my poor, innocent client. I hope you don't expect me to go easy because you're my

darling daughter. Just so you know, I don't like to lose."

"Oh, I know Mom, but I don't like to lose either, just to let you know."

"Oh, I know. You're quite the talk among my peers. Maybe I'm the one who should be worried."

They laughed, and Meredith ended, "I'll see you in court. Love you, Mom."

Rebecca would not normally take on such a menial case, but the accused was the son of a wealthy family, and they had very high hopes for his future. They were willing to pay any price to keep him out of trouble, with a clean record.

A month passed, and Rebecca refused the plea deal that Meredith had placed on the table. Meredith offered him no time in jail. In return, he would plead guilty and perform one hundred hours of community service.

Another month passed and it was time for the long-awaited mother-daughter courtroom showdown. Meredith went first.

She presented her case before the jury in a clear, concise and professional manner. Rebecca then presented her case with her typical flair, utilizing every tactic of her well-seasoned profession. Meredith secretly felt that her mother had pulled the proverbial rabbit out of the hat. She thought, *that was amazing. I believe he's going to walk a free man for sure.*

The jury deliberated for approximately one hour, then reported back to the courtroom. The verdict was read aloud, "Guilty!"

Meredith's knees nearly buckled, but she maintained her composure. Not only did she just do the seemingly impossible, beat her mother, but she beat her decisively. The young man got six months in the county jail with one-year probation to follow.

"I guess I should have taken the deal," Rebecca said.

Meredith smiled, "I told you I was tough, Mom."

"So, it would seem." Rebecca winked and said, "Congratulations counselor. Don't get too comfortable, though. See you at dinner?" "I'll be there at six." Meredith said.

Meredith walked out of the courtroom on cloud nine. When she returned to the office, she saw three ladies from the office huddled together, talking amongst themselves. Meredith was convinced that they were abuzz about her victory over her mother in court. But as she got closer, she heard, "Can you believe how gorgeous he is?" "I know, every time he comes here for a depo, I can't ever get anything done." "I wish I could depose him. Depose--that means to undress, right?" "Why yes, officer, I will consent to strip search!" "He could read me my rights, 'You have the right to remain silent, I will hold things against you!'" The three women laughed out loud.

They sounded like cackling hens to Meredith. She stormed past them thinking, *Really? Some hot cop? Who cares?*

As she walked by Allen's office, he called out, "Good job today, Ms. Porter."

Meredith immediately forgot the hens and smiled. "At least someone noticed."

Another six months went by and Meredith faced her mother two more times in court, losing the next case but winning the last.

January 1999. Meredith's phone rang. "Ms. Porter, can I see you in my office?" It was Allen.

She assumed it was to discuss the latest case she was getting ready to take to trial. She arrived at Allen's office.

"Ms. Porter, please have a seat."

Cheryl Patterson, the new attorney, was in the room also. "Meredith, I want you to bring Cheryl here up to speed on the Barberson case. She'll be taking it over as lead counsel."

"What? Wait . . . why? Mr. Markowitz, I'm ready to go to trial next week."

"Then I suppose you better get her up to speed ASAP, don't you think?"

"This isn't right, Allen. Why are you pulling me from this case?"

"I'm sorry, who's the District Attorney here? Who do you work for, Ms. Porter?"

"You are sir, but . . . "

"And I think I'm within my rights to assign and reassign attorneys as I see fit, don't you?"

"Y-yes, sir. I'm sorry, sir."

"And I have a damn good reason for doing what I'm doing. Do you think I owe you some sort of explanation or something?"

"No sir. I'm very sorry for questioning you, Mr. Markowitz."

"The reason I'm doing this is because I'm reassigning you to felonies. I certainly hope that is okay with you, Ms. Porter?"

"WHAT? Are you serious, Mr. Markowitz? Please don't pull my leg."

Smiling, Allen said, "Mrs. Patterson, can we have a minute? Close the door on your way out, please. I am serious, Meredith. You were the youngest attorney ever hired by this office. When I brought you in here, I asked you to prove yourself. You have surpassed my expectations in every way. I should have promoted you six months ago, the first time you beat your mother. But I waited for Burton to retire. You've been my choice for his replacement all along."

"Thank you, sir. I won't let you down. I'm sorry for getting so upset earlier."

"Okay, okay. Enough groveling," he said with a smile. "Bring her up to speed quickly, I have some real bad guys I need you to put in prison for me. Ready for a new challenge?"

"Yes sir."

"Well then, go get 'em Meredith. I know you'll make me proud."

For the next two and a half years, Meredith was indeed a force to be reckoned with. She was considered by all the defense attorneys, including her mother, to be a ruthless prosecutor. In two and a half years, she did not lose a case that went to trial. Despite her young age of only twenty-six, she displayed a tenacity and experience well beyond her years. The many years of observing her mother in court had paid off decisively.

November 2001. Meredith was once again summoned into Allen's office. When she came in, George was sitting on the sofa in Allen's office. The two long time colleagues were laughing and joking around. They had worked together for over fifteen years and had become close friends.

"Ms. Porter, come on in. Please have a seat. George here has just announced to me that he is retiring from public service and going into private practice. It seems that the lure of easy money beckons him."

She said, "Congratulations, George. You will be missed."

"Thank you, Meredith, but I believe we've already found my perfect replacement."

George had been the dedicated attorney who handled all the capital cases, such as rape and murder.

Allen spoke, "I believe we have, too. George and I have been talking, and we think that only someone special could take his place. So we started our search by each putting a name on a piece of paper. We then handed each other our folded papers. We opened them at the same time, and lo and behold, we discovered we had both written the same name. Meredith Porter. So, it would seem that our search for George's replacement was over before it began."

George said, "Congratulations, Meredith."

Meredith's eyes welled with tears. She could not believe it. She believed that capital cases would have gone to a more experienced attorney. "Why me? There are so many others who have put more time in than I have."

Allen answered, "That may be true, but these cases are the worst of the worst, the most significant cases we handle. I need only the best and brightest for these. George and I both agree—that's you."

George chimed in, "I have no doubt that you can handle it. I've been watching your career over the past few years and I can think of no one better."

Allen replied, "I absolutely agree. George has graciously agreed to stay on board for the next few months to work with you until you're comfortable. Now, I won't force you to take this position. If you're uncomfortable with these types of cases, I can reassign the job to someone else."

"I can handle it, sir, I promise."

Smiling, Allen said, "Congratulations, young lady. Don't let me down. There will be a lot of people who are upset about your promotion, but they haven't proven themselves the way you have.

Go get 'em, girl."

After Meredith left the room, Allen asked, "So, do you really think she's ready, George?"

"I've never been more certain of anything, Al. She's a brilliant young woman and one of the most astute criminal attorneys I have ever seen."

January 18th, 2002. George invited Meredith and Allen to lunch. When they arrived, Rebecca was there, too. "Well, Meredith. This will be my last day. You're ready now; besides, I booked tickets for the Mrs. and me to take a nice long cruise before starting the new practice. What do you think of your little girl, Rebecca?"

Rebecca answered, "I've never been prouder. I feel sorry for you if you ever have to face her, George. In fact, I feel sorry for me as well."

"Not as sorry as I'll be, I'm sure."

They all laughed while Meredith blushed reservedly, masking her pride.

Allen told her, "This is it, kiddo, the big show, center stage. You ready?"

"Yes sir, Mr. Markowitz."

"I think we're past all that, Meredith. It's Allen, anywhere we are from now on, except on camera of course. You're now my number two. You'll be receiving a lot of exposure. Anything you need, ever, you come straight to me. You don't answer to anyone but me from now on, agreed?"

"Agreed. Thank you for believing in me, Allen."

"I should be thanking you for helping me to stay in office," he jested.

January 29th. Allen gestured for Meredith to come into his office. She was now in George's old office directly across from Allen's.

Meredith came in and sat in the chair in front of his desk.

"What's going on, Allen?"

"Have you seen the news?"

"No, I haven't been watching anything lately. Why?"

"Well, it's all over the news and I just got the file. It's a bad one. It would seem that this piece of trash abducted a little girl from her house and murdered her in a grisly manner. Detectives were able to locate and catch the guy in record time. Here's the file. I gotta warn you though, it's a real stomach turner. If you need someone to talk to later as you're reviewing it, I'm here for you, okay? Just call me."

"I'm sure I'll be fine."

"I'm sure you will. You have the arraignment tomorrow morning at nine, so you have a lot to get ready by then."

"Thank you, Allen . . .I think. Big file! It looks like I'll be up late."

Meredith worked long into the night, reviewing the file and preparing herself for court the next day. True to Allen's word, she was sickened by the forensic photos and the graphic report from the detectives. Meredith had to compose herself on more than one occasion while reviewing the case and looking through the dreadful photographs. She actually contemplated calling Allen, but she reluctantly gritted it out.

The next day in court, Meredith had no problem convincing the judge that the killer, Mark Stephen Kearcy, should be held without bond to face charges of first degree murder.

Immediately following the judge's ruling, Meredith turned around to exit the courtroom. At the back of the courtroom stood a man in black slacks, with a white, tailored shirt that accentuated his bulging shoulders, a dark blue tie and a Sheriff's Office detective badge. When he stood, he towered over the people around him. He was gorgeous, with blue eyes. His perfectly parted blonde hair shimmered like strands of gold thread in the morning sunlight that shone through the courtroom window. Meredith had the strange feeling she had seen him before, but she could not place him.

She composed herself and proceeded to exit the court. As she approached the doors, this perfect specimen of a man politely held the door for her. When she walked through he asked, "So, do you think we'll put him away?"

Startled by his baritone voice that sounded like Zeus himself beckoning down to her from Mount Olympus, Meredith asked, "Who are you again?"

"I'm Detective Carson."

"Oh, so you're the famous Detective Carson. It's nice to finally meet you. I think we have a pretty good chance of putting him away for a very long time, though I'm actually going to be seeking the death penalty. You did an incredible job catching him. I'm so sorry about the little girl. I read your report and I cried. It still horrifies me." Meredith struggled to maintain her composure talking to this wildly attractive man. She tried to hide her flushed face, feeling silly, like a giddy little school girl. She made up an excuse to leave quickly and said, "I'm sorry, Detective. I have to get going. I have a deposition in an hour, but I'll be in touch."

When Mike said, "I look forward to it," Meredith nearly swooned.

She had never acted this way over any guy before. *What was so special about him?* She wondered to herself as she quickly walked away. She had been hit on by the most desirable men her entire life, but this guy . . . what was it?

As she walked toward the elevator, she glanced back quickly to see Mike still watching her. She instantly blushed and turned back around.

Oh my God, that was embarrassing! She thought to herself.

She entered the elevator, looked up and thought, *He's still watching me.* Their eyes met, and she bashfully smiled. Mike returned her smile.

A month passed, and it was time for a deposition with all the officers involved in the case. Meredith not only had to prepare for the deposition with all her notes, but she had to mentally prepare to see this gorgeous man again. She had not stopped thinking about him since they met in the courtroom. She was hoping to avoid another embarrassing encounter. Maybe the last time was just a fluke. She wondered if he had been thinking about her the whole time the same way she had been thinking about him.

Meredith never openly expressed it, but she had purposefully avoided dating cops because she felt they were a little beneath her. She had worked herself tirelessly through college and law school. She knew now that this man was an exception to all that she had believed. He was articulate, smart, educated and of course gorgeous. For a moment, Meredith imagined herself falling for this guy.

The day of the deposition arrived and in the room were three defense attorneys, a court reporter, Mike, Meredith and her co-counsel. Halfway through Mike's deposition, he broke down while recounting the terrible murder scene and the tragic sight of Amanda in the fire pit. Meredith requested that they take a recess for Mike to compose himself. Mike was allowed to go and sit in another room alone. After several minutes, Meredith went in to check on him. Her heart skipped a beat when he made it clear that he did not want her to leave the room.

It soon became painfully obvious that they both shared a mutual attraction for each other. Before her sat this beautiful, sensitive man, weeping openly; not in any way he should ever be ashamed of, but in a caring, loving and compassionate way over the loss of an innocent child. The guilt he felt for not being able to save her was evident.

Looking back on that moment, Meredith would recall how this was the time she really started to fall for Mike. She never could have dreamed how that moment would change her life forever.

At the end of the deposition, Meredith escorted Mike out of the office. They nervously exchanged small talk when she got up the nerve to give him her business card with a little something extra written on the back, her personal number. Mike appeared eager and happy to get the number.

Meredith anxiously hoped he would call her that night, but he didn't. He did call her, however, the next night. Mike had had a bad dream, reliving the nightmarish events of the case. They talked for a few hours, and he revealed to her that he was in law school at FTU, and that his father had been an attorney. He told Meredith how his father had been murdered, and that was why he was so determined to make it on his own.

Meredith told him that she also had attended FTU, and said, "I have to admit that I now remember you from school."

Mike asked her, "Really? When did we ever meet? I would have remembered you for sure!"

"We didn't meet in person. You pulled this huge lummox off of my hood one night after a football game."

Meredith teased Mike when he revealed that the aforementioned lummox was his best friend, The Moose, recalling the incident the night after the game. Mike laughed after explaining about that night and how he remembered that incident.

Meredith was relieved, and readily accepted when Mike finally asked her out on a date.

For the next several months, they dated, and Meredith clearly had it bad for Mike. The cackling hens at the office would talk scornfully behind her back, jealous that she had landed the big prize they had all sought.

November. The Kearcy trial was about to start. Meredith and Mike were as ready as they could be to finally send the devil back to hell, as Mike would assert.

The trial lasted two weeks. There were two extended recesses after several members of the jury vomited when subjected to the images of that night. The judge ordered that the courtroom be cleared of nonessential people to prevent any unnecessary interruptions from the gallery when the most graphic of photo evidence was presented. The jury was instructed to keep bags to contain their vomit to prevent unnecessary clean up and disruption. Even the judge squirmed uncomfortably in his large leather chair during the presentation of photo evidence. All the while, Kearcy sat quietly, never expressing any more emotion than a devilish grin.

It was no surprise to anyone in attendance when the jury returned a guilty verdict. After the sentencing a month later, the monster had been sentenced to eternal damnation. He was finally defeated.

The night after the sentencing, Mike, Meredith and all their coworkers from the District Attorney's and the Sheriff's Office went out to celebrate. It was a good night for Meredith, especially after Mike suggested that they move in together, to which she enthusiastically agreed. They found a beautiful luxury condo uptown and moved in together. Life was good for them, and they were happy.

Meredith's parents took an instant liking to Mike. On weekends, they would go to Henry and Rebecca's house. Mike and Henry would watch football together like he would with Big Mike. Meredith and Rebecca would visit in the other room, usually the kitchen, making the boys football snacks. Neither one had a particular interest in sports, but they both loved their sports nuts and would laugh at them behind their backs, listening to them yell and scream. Mike missed his father and really looked up to Henry. Likewise, Henry grew fond of Mike, and Mike became the son Henry never had.

Meredith had gotten to know Frank during the many visits when he would come to see Mike. It took a while, but Frank grew on her with his boyish charm and playful antics. She realized that Mike was right. He really was a big teddy bear. She grew to love Frank as much as Mike did. When she met Nancy, the two became instant friends. Nancy and Meredith would constantly stay in touch. Nancy told Meredith how grateful she was that Meredith was in Mike's life, and how happy she was that Meredith would keep her informed with all that Mike was going through. They were very happy and content in their lives together.

It was finally time for Mike to graduate from law school. Cynthia, Frank and Nancy had joined Mike, Meredith and her parents to celebrate. Not only was this a special day because Mike had finally achieved his goal of graduating from law school, but this would prove to be the night that Meredith had been dreaming of since she first fell for Mike on that fateful day of their courtroom encounter.

After the graduation ceremony at the restaurant, Mike and Frank had concocted a scheme to surprise everyone with a proposal of marriage. All of the important people in both of their lives were present. The setting was romantic, and with attention paid to all the special details. Meredith wholeheartedly accepted. Everyone was so excited. Love was in the air that night.

Mike and Meredith beamed with joy. They danced and celebrated for hours. People they never met came up and congratulated them.

Meredith could have never dreamt of a more perfect night.

BACHELOR NO MORE

The evening drew to a close and it was late when they all returned to the hotel. Mike and Frank sat in the lobby and talked while everyone else went upstairs to get ready for bed.

"Man, I can't believe you're getting married, brother! I'm so happy for you. She's a special lady."

"Thank you, brother. Having you there tonight meant a lot to me. This has been the best day I can remember."

"I'm proud of you, Mikey. We've been through a lot together. I hope you know I'll always be there for you."

"I know Frankie. I love you, man."

"Aw, you know I love you too, little bro. And I really love that Merry. She's a great gal . . . you're lucky. You better take good care of her or I'll kick your ass!"

Mike laughed and said, "Yeah? You and what army?"

Frank laughed, "I'm the only army you need to worry about."

"She is a good woman, and I know I'm lucky. But I don't think I'm the only lucky one. So, um, what was that thing that I saw between you and Cynthia?"

Defensively, Frank said, "What do you mean?"

"Don't bullshit me, Moose. I'm not blind. Lucky for you, though, outside of Cynthia I think I'm the only one that noticed."

Frank uncharacteristically turned beet red. "Shut up, dickhead!"

Mike laughed, "Frank Peterson, I do believe you might be in love. Don't be so embarrassed, pal. It happens to the best of us. She's a good lady. If she's interested in you, I say go for it. You're my best friend. I wouldn't steer you wrong."

Meanwhile, upstairs in Mike and Meredith's room, the other two best friends who shared everything were lying on the king size bed. Cynthia was ogling Meredith's beautiful ring and said, "You're so lucky. I wonder if that will ever happen for me."

Meredith answered, "You know it will."

"Frank is quite charming, don't you think?" asked Cynthia.

Remembering the night in her car when they first encountered

The Moose, Meredith blurted, "Uh-oh!"

"What? I still think he's adorable."

"This time honey, I would have to say I agree with you. That first encounter I wanted to slap you, but he's grown on me. He's the sweetest guy I know, with the exception of my Mikey."

"You really like him?"

"Honey, I would never let you be interested in anyone I didn't approve of."

The two snorted with joy, and Meredith asked, "You think he might be interested?"

"Oh Mer, we talked for hours tonight. He is so gentle and sweet. His gruff exterior hides a gentleness underneath. When we danced, I don't think I've ever felt safer in my entire life."

"Hmmm, I think you've been smitten by the love bug. Just don't get too distracted. You have to help me plan this wedding."

"You know I'll do everything I can. It'll be challenging from Philly, but thanks to my frequent flyer miles, I'll be here whenever you need me."

"It goes without saying—you're my maid of honor."

"I better be!" Cynthia exclaimed.

Mike and Frank finished talking downstairs and were walking toward the elevator. Mike said, "Crap, I dropped my room key back at the sofa. Go ahead on up, buddy. I'll see you in the morning."

Before Frank got onto the elevator, he gave Mike a big bear hug.

"I love you, buddy. I'll see you in the morning."

"Okay Moose, you're crushing my spine. I love you too, big guy." Frank laughed then continued up the elevator to the tenth floor. Mike went back to look for the key card to his room. He located it under the sofa. When he stood up from the floor, he was overcome by a sudden chill. There was a whisper from behind him and he felt warm breath across the back of his neck. Mike spun around as his heart pounded. This was not his first encounter with this type of inexplicable event. The lobby was empty. Even the front desk clerk was nowhere to be found. It was eerily quiet. Mike collected his thoughts and walked briskly back to the elevator. His heart was still racing as the elevator doors closed.

Mike breathed a deep sigh. "Okay, settle down Mike. Just push the button and get yourself upstairs."

Mike pushed the button for the tenth floor. Beginning to calm down, *you're just having early wedding jitters*, he scolded himself. *There haven't been any dark encounters in a while, not since the nightmarish cases stopped. It must be jitters.*

When the elevator reached the fifth floor, it suddenly jarred to a stop and the lights went out. A legion of voices from a thousand tortured souls enveloped him as if in surround sound—*they're back.*

The voices shrieked, "MICHAEL, WE ARE WAITING. YOUR TIME IS NEAR! DON'T RESIST HER, MICHAEL, SHE AWAITS!"

Then, in the reflection of the mirrored doors, Mike could see glowing red eyes behind him. He could smell the wretched stench of the bulls at his uncle's farm and he heard a terrifying *MRRAAAWWW!*

Mike screamed in horror and collapsed, landing in a crumpled heap against the rear wall of the elevator.

Frank heard the scream from his room two doors down from the elevator. Frank recognized the voice as his best friend's. "Mikey? MIKEY!"

Frank bolted out of his room to the now open elevator doors. There lay Mike, in a state of shock, unresponsive, his eyes stuck in a fixed gaze staring off into eternity. He was sweating profusely and would not answer Frank. In the same gentle manner with which he had done before, the Goliath man stooped down and picked up his closest friend and carried him to his room. Other people had come out to see what caused the commotion. Frank went into cop-mode, assuring the curious onlookers, "He's okay, everybody. Sorry about all the noise. He just had a little too much to drink, that's all."

When Frank got to Mike's room, Meredith and Cynthia were still awake. There was a knock on the door and Meredith said, "Mike must have forgotten his key." When she opened the door, she was horrified at the sight of Frank carrying Mike like he was a helpless infant. Mike had been crying and was shaking, still not responding to anyone's prompts.

"Oh my God. What happened, Frank?"

Frank laid Mike down in bed and said, "I don't know, Merry. I went up ahead of him because he dropped his key in the lobby. A few minutes after I got back to my room, I heard a scream from the elevator. I ran and found him curled up in a fetal position on the floor of the elevator."

Twenty minutes later, Mike came back around, surrounded by EMS personnel and all of his loved ones.

"What happened?" he asked.

Meredith said, "I don't know, sweetheart. We were hoping you could tell us. Let the paramedics check you out first, though."

The paramedic examined Mike thoroughly and said, "Well, all your vitals check out fine, but I recommend you let us take you down to the hospital. Having an unexplained blackout could be something

serious. You really should be seen by a doctor."

Mike said, "No, thank you. I don't want to go anywhere. I feel fine now. I can get checked out when I get home."

"Okay, sir. I can't make you go, but you sure put a scare into everyone. I hope you feel better soon. I just need you to sign here saying you refuse to go to the hospital with us."

Mike signed the form, then sat up in bed. He was surrounded by all the people he loved.

Meredith asked, "Do you remember anything, baby?"

"No. I remember getting my key, then something spooked me and I got into the elevator. Next thing I knew, I woke up here in bed."

"Frank found you unresponsive in the elevator and he carried you here."

Frank was lingering over Mike, as concerned as a mother attending a sick baby. "Are you sure you're okay, buddy?"

"Yeah, thanks pal. Seems like you're always there to pick me up."

"That's my job, Little Mikey."

Mike smiled up at him. No one else in the world could ever get away with calling him Little Mikey except Frank.

The incident passed and the wedding plans ensued.

Back home in Boca Grande Shores, the wedding plans moved forward. Nancy came down to assist with the plans, and had practically moved in with Henry and Rebecca. After Meredith moved out, they had plenty of room and they all got along very well. All Meredith had to do was suggest an idea, and before she could change her mind, Nancy and Rebecca would have it taken care of.

Mike still enjoyed being on road patrol and had actually joined the SWAT team. This afforded him the opportunity to get a little excitement without having to deal with things all alone, like in Major Crimes. Everything would be a team event, and like always, he enjoyed being part of a team.

Frank and Cynthia were always coming and going, always having a part in all the planning. Unbeknownst to everyone else, they too were getting closer. Frank would fly to Philadelphia at least twice a month to spend time with Cynthia. Other times, they would mysteriously show up in Florida at the same time. Everyone was so busy with all the planning that they never took notice.

February 2005. Mike had just passed the bar exam and was trying to decide what to do now that he was a lawyer. He still enjoyed the Sheriff's Office and wasn't in a particular hurry to leave. He was vested in his pension and was in no danger of losing anything, but his passion to be a trial lawyer was still heavy in his heart. Then an unexpected opportunity presented itself.

Colonel Talbot, second in command of the Sheriff's Office, was also an attorney and had been the legal counsel for the Sheriff's Office for many years. When Talbot announced his retirement and that he would be leaving in two months, a vital hole for the agency would need to be filled.

Sheriff Ron Hill was concerned because he didn't have anyone else in his command staff that could do Colonel Talbot's job. The Sheriff knew that Mike was in law school, but was unaware that he had finished. Talbot advised the Sheriff that Mike had indeed finished and had passed the bar. Sheriff Hill knew all about Mike's reputation, and had followed his career for many years. One evening, he called Mike at home.

"Deputy Carson? Sheriff Hill."

"Sheriff Hill? Yes sir, this is an unexpected surprise. How are you this evening?"

"Very good, thank you for asking. Listen, Mike, I want to have a meeting with you. Can you be in my office tomorrow afternoon at three?"

"Yes sir, I'll be there. May I inquire as to what this is about?"

"Let's just say I have a proposal for you that I think you may be interested in."

"I'm intrigued, sir. I'll see you tomorrow at three."

The next day at three o'clock, Mike was waiting outside Sheriff Hill's office. His secretary, Amy Billings told him,

"I'm sorry, Deputy, the Sheriff is running a bit late. He got held up in a Commission

meeting, but he just called and he should be here in about ten minutes."

"No problem. Thank you, ma'am."

The Sheriff arrived. "Mike, sorry to keep you waiting. That damn commission meeting lasted forever. The new budget is going to be tight."

"No problem, sir."

"Okay then, come on in and have a seat."

Mike entered the Sheriff's Office and sat in front of the desk.

"I appreciate you meeting with me such short notice, Mike."

"No problem at all, sir."

"I was just informed yesterday that Colonel Talbot is throwing in the towel and retiring. My problem is, no one in the command staff has his credentials. My term ends in a little more than two years, and I'm not seeking re-election. His departure leaves me without an in-house legal counsel for the agency. I understand that you just passed the bar, and that you're getting married to that hot shot —DA—Ms. Porter, isn't it?"

"Yes sir, true on all accounts."

"Well, son, I was hoping you might be interested in being my legal counsel. I can't rightly put you into the Colonel's title because you have no command experience. But I will be making some command adjustments, and have it within my means to promote you to Captain. I'll be moving Captain Rodgers up to Colonel, leaving his spot open. Would you be interested?"

"Well, sir, as you said, I have no command experience, — but yes— I would be very interested."

"Understand, you will be a Captain, but your primary responsibility will be to perform legal counsel duties. Some of these duties may not be pleasant and can come in the form of discipline issues. You'll also be reviewing all of our policies to make sure they are all legal. Captain Rodgers' current duties will be divided among the other command staff."

Mike said, "I was undecided as to what I wanted to do, so this is an incredible opportunity, Sheriff. Thank you!"

"And I thank you, Mike. This helps me out of a jam. Your promotion will be effective as of next Monday. I want you to work with Colonel Talbot for the next week. He'll be your FTO," Sheriff Hill joked.

Mike laughed and asked, "Sir, will I be able to remain part of the SWAT team? I really enjoy my duties there."

"You're a Captain now Mike, aren't you? So, you tell me."

Mike knew where he was coming from and smiled. "Thank you again, sir."

A promotion, a pay increase and an upcoming wedding. Mike was excited. He now had almost two years to decide which direction he wanted to go with his legal career. Meredith could assist him along the way. Now, having this job he actually had time to attend some of her trials and learn from the master.

That night, Mike told Meredith the good news. She was excited for him, and the extra money would come in handy. Though her parents were picking up a lot of the expenses of the wedding, Meredith didn't want to depend solely on them. She wanted Mike and herself to be more independent.

June 4, a week before the wedding, Frank flew into town for the traditional bachelor party, and Frank had big plans. He had gathered all of Mike's buddies from the Sheriff's Office, as well as some old teammates from college who lived in the area. They were going to paint the town red. Frank had rented a limo bus and planned a tour of only the best strip clubs in the Central Florida area between Tampa and Orlando. On board the bus would be a fully stocked bar and big screen televisions that would play only the finest midget pornography Frank could find.

Frank had even employed the services of two call girls to be the onboard entertainment between the clubs while on the road.

Cynthia arrived in town at about the same time for Meredith's bachelorette party, but her plans were not quite as extensive as Frank's.

3:00 p.m. "I don't even want to know what Frank has planned for you guys, but promise you'll be a good boy."

Mike laughed, "Honey, I'm not sure I want to know what he has planned, but I'm sure it will be memorable and filled with depravity. One thing you can be sure of though, is that you have no need to worry. There is only one woman that I will be looking forward to coming home to at the end of the night."

From downstairs, Mike and Meredith heard a loud air horn honking to the tune of *Dixie's Land*.

They looked at each other and burst into laughter, saying simultaneously, "Frank!"

They hugged and Mike ran downstairs, where he was greeted by Frank exiting a large, blacked-out party bus. He was smoking a large cigar and wearing shorts, sunglasses and a brightly colored Hawaiian shirt. "WHAT'S UP, CAPTAIN DOUCHE BAG!?"

All of the other friends disembarked as well, and Mike couldn't believe how many guys had shown up.

"Wow, you put all this together, Frankie?"

"Oh, you ain't seen nothing yet, pal."

Mike looked up, and Meredith was shaking her head and laughing. Frank looked up and waved excitedly at Meredith. She opened the window and shouted down, "You take care of him, Frank!"

"I got it, Merry. He's my boy. He's in good hands. I'll keep him safe," Frank hollered back with a roguish grin.

"Oh, dear Lord, keep him out of trouble," Meredith said as she closed the window.

When Mike entered the bus, there were two ladies in various stages of undress on top of each other on a mattress in the middle of the bus. There was midget porn playing on the two big screens, and several empty beer bottles strewn about the bus cabin already. He shouted, "God help me!"

Frank got on board. "Hey, hey, hey there ladies, you can't start that yet! Man, they're frisky. Let the guest of honor get a few drinks on board first, geez! Mike, this is Bunny and this is Sunshine. Girls, say hi to Mike." In unison, the two girls said, "Hi Mike." Frank was laughing aloud with his typical animated, boisterous laugh.

Mike's friend and old partner, Robert McDougal, came up and patted him on the shoulder. "Buckle up, pal. Looks like it's gonna be a bumpy ride tonight."

Now, it's common knowledge that cops know how to party. And it's also common knowledge that football players know how to party. But when you combine the partying talents of cops with football players, things of epic legends are created. That bachelor party would go down in the annals of bachelor party history as being the crown jewel of all bachelor parties.

The debauchery was legendary, and the alcohol flowed like the mighty Mississippi. The last strip club of the night, "The Pig Pen," was a dive so dirty and foul that the name could not be more fitting. Frank put this on his list as a joke, a way to wrap up the strip club tour. The girls were raunchy and willing to do anything for a buck. Frank had a lot of bucks and lots of ideas.

Frank put Mike up on stage and bought him a lap dance from Jasmine. Frank tied Mike's hands up behind the chair with a silk feather boa from one of the girls. Mike was so intoxicated after having an untold number of kamikazes, his favorite drink, that he couldn't see straight.

Jasmine was a tall skinny girl with long black hair, black fingernails and pasty-white skin with a large upside-down pentacle tattoo on her upper left-. She had nearly every body-part pierced and wore a spiked collar on her neck. Mike sat helplessly in the chair as she approached. She removed her top, exposing her tattoo-covered breasts.

As she neared Mike, he was in disbelief as he saw her eyes mutate to a solid black, which stood out in stark contrast against the pale white skin of her face. She straddled Mike's hips and grabbed his head with both her hands. As she stared into his eyes, Mike could see through to her soul and found himself enveloped in total darkness, a place of utter despair.

Over the loud, blaring music and the cheers of Frank and the others, he heard a distinct sound that stood out from among the weeping, wailing, and gnashing of teeth from a sea of countless tormented souls. It was the sound of the tortured screams of a helpless little baby. He was instantaneously transported back to the bedroom of little Miguel Lopez. Standing over the dead baby boy, his heart was filled with dread when Jasmine breathed into his ear, "The body was yours, but his soul belongs to us forever!"

Terror swept over Mike. His muscles strained as he ripped the boa apart. He grabbed Jasmine by the shoulders and pushed her off of him onto the stage yelling, "NO, NO, NOOOO! LET HIM GO, YOU EVIL BITCH! LET HIM GO!"

When she fell to the floor, the music abruptly stopped. Jasmine cried out, "What the fuck is your problem, you freak? What an asshole!"

The bouncer, who was half the size of Frank, wisely approached him and said, "I think you might want to get your friend home now." Frank cordially agreed and gave Jasmine another twenty for her trouble.

Picking Mike up and throwing him over his shoulders, Frank said, "Okay buddy, party's over. Let's get you home."

Frank and all his buddies loaded Mike onto the bus for the two-hour ride home. It was 3:00 a.m. and they had been going at it for nearly twelve hours.

Rob said to Frank, "What do you think got to him?"

"I don't know, buddy. He occasionally has these outbursts. I think some of those cases you guys worked together must have really gotten to him."

Rob replied, "I can understand why. I got out shortly after he did. He saw more than me for some reason. I just assisted him on a lot his cases. It's crazy. I worked Major Crimes a lot longer, but he seemed to get all the truly horrific cases. I know he saw a counselor for a while and it seemed to help, but I think it might be PTSD."

"Well, he's been through a lot. I always worry about him. But I think Meredith is good for him. He seems so at peace when he's with her." Rob agreed, "Yeah, he really seems happy. You guys are close. Thanks for doing this for him. I know I had a blast."

Frank looked at Robert and said, "My pleasure, pal. I'm glad everyone had fun. Looks like we're the only ones still awake." Everyone, including the call girls, had passed out.

Frank and Robert talked the whole way home, and Frank told Robert, "I'm glad he's got friends like you to help me keep an eye out for him. You guys are all right in my book, for a bunch of cops."

"It's my pleasure, Frank. You're a good man for a football player. A little wild, but a good man," said Robert.

Frank laughed as they continued down the road.

They had dropped everyone off and Mike was the last one left. Frank had arranged with Meredith to sleep at their place when they got home. It was now 6:00 a.m. and Mike was still passed out. After paying the driver and giving him a healthy tip for the enormous mess left in the back, Frank picked up a still passed out Mike, again threw him over his shoulders, then hauled him up the stairs.

Meredith could hear the two come in. Relieved that Mike was home safe, she rolled over and tried to go back to sleep.

Frank threw Mike on the couch and covered him with a throw. He then grabbed a pillow from the love seat and fell asleep on the floor. Meredith had to bury her head between two pillows to block Frank's snoring.

TILL DEATH DO US PART

Later that morning, Meredith awoke to find Mike was still asleep on the couch and Frank was sleeping on the floor, blocking the hallway.

"I guess I'm gonna have to scale Mount Moose to get to the kitchen," Meredith laughed to herself. "Clearly, these two are going to need several pots of coffee."

As she attempted to traverse the massive, intoxicated corpse that lay in her path, the sleeping giant awoke, and staring up at her in her robe said, "Nice panties!"

Meredith shouted, "OH MY GOD, YOU PIG!" and she stomped on his belly.

Frank bellowed with laughter and said, "Don't worry, I'm not offended by a pretty pair of pink lacy G-strings."

"Pervert!" Meredith said, smiling back at him.

Groaning as he struggled up from the floor like a grizzly awakening from a long winter nap, Frank said, "I really need to piss!"

Meredith shouted, "Try to hit the toilet this time, you animal!"

"Shhhhh! Oh my God, woman. Why are you screaming? My

head feels like it's going to split in half!"

"I'm gonna make some coffee. Why don't you go take a shower? I laid a towel out for you. I also found a pair of shorts you left here the last time, and a pair of your underwear."

"How do you know they're my underwear?"

"Because I pulled them from the linen closet. They were mixed in with our king size sheets!"

"Funny girl, funny girl!" Frank chuckled. As he was closing the bathroom door, she heard him exclaim, "One of these days Merry, bang, zoom, to the moon!"

Meredith giggled to herself. He was really the big brother she'd never had. How could she not adore him?

After he emerged from the bathroom, the two sat on the balcony, sipped coffee and ate toast while Mike still slumbered away on the couch.

Meredith asked, "So did you guys have fun?"

"From what I can remember? Yes!"

"Was Mikey a good boy?"

"Now Merry, do you really think I can tell you all the details?"

"I know you better start talking before you're wearing that coffee!"

Frank laughed, "Sweetheart, let me tell you something. That guy in there is so in love with you, you have nothing to worry about from last night or any other night. There's not enough alcohol to make that guy do anything to hurt you. Besides that, he knows I'd

kick his ass if he ever did anything to hurt you."

Meredith smiled as she sat back in her seat and sneered, "Hmmm, I don't know about you two, but good answer. You're sweet, Frankie. I love you."

Franks suddenly got serious. "I love you too, Merry, but I have to tell you something. Mike had another episode last night. I'm

worried about him. Robert thinks it's part of his PTSD."

"What happened, Frank?"

"Well, it was at the end of the night. He flipped out and threw that stripper off of him onto the floor."

"Stripper? On top of him? Go on!"

"Merry, seriously, it was all in fun. He did nothing, I promise you."

"Okay, okay, I see no problem yet. He threw the skank off of him . . . so far so good!"

"MERRY!" Frank growled. Meredith could tell the gentle giant was extremely concerned about Mike.

"I'm serious. I'm really worried about Mike. He blacked out again. I don't know if it was from the copious amount of alcohol or something more sinister. He was screaming 'let him go!' You need to promise to keep me up to date. If he needs help, you need to let me know. Anything he needs, I'll take care of it. He doesn't come to me with personal stuff like you and Cynthia do. It's a guy thing. But I'm really worried about him. I need you to keep me up to date with everything. That goes for both of you, for whatever you guys need. But promise to look out for him."

"You are truly full of surprises, my sweet hulk. I'm so grateful he has you in his life. What more could he ask for? I love you. I promise, you'll be the first person I call for anything." She stood up on her tip toes to kiss him on the forehead while he sat on the patio chair.

Frank smiled, reassured by her kind words. "I'm glad he found you, Merry. He's a lucky man. Thank you for being so good to him. Please take care of my buddy. I wouldn't bring up last night. I don't think he'll remember much. I got him pretty drunk. Probably better to leave it be. I just wanted to make you aware."

From inside, they could hear Mike stirring. "Oh, good Lord. My head!"

Frank perked up, ran inside and shouted at the top of his lungs,

"GOOD MORNING, YOU HUNGOVER DOUCHE BAG!"

"AAAAAAH, you asshole! I'm gonna kick your ass!"

Meredith laughed as the two bickered back and forth like brothers.

The following week was a whirlwind of activity. All the preparations had been made, but the last-minute details were a typical nightmare. The florist called to say that they could not get the flowers Meredith wanted, and the caterer had a death in the family and had to cancel. Frank was the rock that kept the whole plan on track. Frank used his celebrity influence to get the best caterer in town, and after a brief visit to the florist from Frank, they were miraculously able to produce the desired flowers.

All was going as expected until the day before the wedding. Meredith went to pick up her dress from the seamstress with her mother. She tried it on and it was flawless. They went to lunch, and while they were inside the restaurant, someone smashed her car window and stole her stereo, leaving her dress in the backseat. A sudden thunderstorm blew through, getting the inside of her vehicle soaking wet, including her delicate wedding dress, ruining the pressed seams in the fabric and leaving streaks of mud from the dirt that had blown in and gotten inside the garment cover that she had accidentally left unzipped.

Meredith was obviously heartbroken, but a quick call to Frank would prove to be the answer to all of her problems.

Frank was the only one who could do it; Mike couldn't see the dress.

Sobbing, Meredith called Frank on the phone, who was also at lunch across town with Mike. "Oh, Frank, it's ruined. My wedding dress is ruined! What am I going to do, Frankie? My beautiful dress is ruined!"

Frank was moved to tears hearing the wails of painful anguish from this woman he loved like a little sister.

"Don't cry, Merry. You leave it to me. I'll take care of everything. I'm on my way to you now."

He put the phone down and turned to Mike. "I gotta go, brother. You got lunch?"

"Yeah, sure. I can take out a small loan to pay for your meal. Is everything okay?"

"Don't worry, just call me if you need anything," Frank told him as he dashed out of the restaurant. Frank rushed to Meredith's location.

When he arrived, the deputies were still on scene taking the report. Frank rushed up. "You okay, Merry? Rebecca darlin', you okay?"

Meredith blubbered, "Oh Frank, it's ruined!" She ran up and hugged him around his waist.

Frank asked, "Where's the dress?"

In the car, Frank found the dress dripping wet and soiled with dirt that had blown in from the wicked summer storm.

Rebecca was consoling Meredith when Frank snatched the dress up and said, "Don't worry, ladies. I'm on the case! Will you guys be okay getting home?"

Rebecca told him, "I'll get her home, sweetie. Thank you for trying to help."

Frank bolted out of there in search of the closest dry cleaner. "Oh, Mom, my dress! What am I going to do?"

"When we leave here, we're going to find you something. It won't be your dress, but you'll be beautiful."

"What about Frank?"

"Sweetie, he has a big heart, but it's three o'clock on a Friday.

Tomorrow is the wedding— what can he possibly do?" Meredith wept inconsolably.

3:12 p.m. A speeding rented Lincoln Town car screeched to a stop in front of Mr. Woo's dry-cleaning store. Frank ran inside and spoke to a small, oriental man. "Are you Mr. Woo?"

The small shop owner said, "Noooo, my name is Rilliam Chang. The business name is Mista Roo. You assumed I Mista Roo just because I Chinee!?"

Frank innocently said, "Well, yeah!"

The infuriated Lilliputian of a man was now yelling at the proportionally gargantuan Gulliver, "What you rant big man? You come in here harass me? You get out or I call porice!"

Normally, Frank would find the whole exchange amusing, but he was on a life or death mission. He had never let a friend down yet and was not going to start now. He swallowed his pride and submissively pleaded his case with Mr. Chang.

"No, no Mr. Chang, please, I'm sorry. I didn't mean anything by it. I'm just in a terrible rush. It's an emergency. Please, you have to help!"

"Rhy I help you? You come in shop and make fun of Rilliam!"

Frank continued to uncharacteristically grovel, explaining all about the wedding and what had happened to Meredith's dress. He pulled the dress out of the saturated plastic. Mr.

Chang was still angry, but moved with compassion when he heard the story. When Frank pulled out a wad of hundreds, Mr. Chang's anger instantly subsided.

"So how much to have it done tonight?"

Mr. Chang smiled and said, "Rhat's it rorth to you ju wu ba?"

Translated from Chinese, this means "jumbo."

Frank started by placing a one hundred dollar bill on the counter.

Mr. Chang rolled his eyes and said, "Rell, it's a big job. Could take days to get ready!"

Frank continued to pile hundred upon hundred. With each hundred Frank looked up at Mr. Chang, who just stood there smiling and raising his eyebrows with each hundred placed on the counter. When he got to five hundred dollars, Mr. Chang said, "Okay, okay yuan, you stop. I have ready by nine o'crock. You here no rater than nine-fifteen or I go home!" Yuan is the Chinese word for ape, but Frank was oblivious.

"Thank you, Mr. Chang. You're the best!"

At nine o'clock, Frank was pounding on the front door of Mr.

Woo's dry cleaner.

From inside, Mr. Chang was screaming, "Hord on, hord on! I coming, mee!" Mee, the Chinese word for moose, was a more appropriate slur than Mr. Chang could have imagined.

Frank examined the dress. His face lit up with excitement. "That's incredible, Mr. Chang. How did you get it so clean? Ancient Chinese secret?"

Mr. Chang, now re-infuriated, started yelling, "Oh you funny man! You rike jokes? I give you joke!"

Frank started to howl with laughter and said, "I'm sorry, Mr. Chang, I couldn't resist." He then pulled another hundred out of his pocket, and Mr. Chang suddenly calmed down. He said, "It ras a preasure dowee busiress rith you! Come aga."

"Really, thank you Mr. Chang."

Chang smiled as he watched the enormous elf prance out of his store. Plus, he had just made six hundred dollars, which he placed in his pocket as he walked out.

At ten o'clock, Frank showed up at Henry and Rebecca's house where Meredith was staying the night before the wedding. Frank rang the doorbell and Henry answered the door dismally. He sighed,

"Oh, hello, Frank."

Frank whispered, "What's up, Doc? Where's Merry?"

"She's upstairs with her mother, Nancy, her aunts and Cynthia. She's trying on different dresses. She hasn't stopped crying all night.

What are you doing out so late?"

Frank said, "I have a surprise. I'll be right back."

Frank scurried to his car and retrieved the now restored fairytale gown. As he returned and Henry asked, "What is that you have there?"

Frank answered in a soft voice, "It's her dress. I got it fixed."

Henry's eyes welled up with tears. "But how? Frank, what did you do? You did this for my little girl? Frank, I can't tell you how much that means to me."

"Okay, okay, go upstairs and get the girls. I'll stand in the living room and model the dress. Well, sort of."

Henry gave Frank a hug. "Thank you, son. You saved the day. She will be so happy."

Henry went upstairs to get the girls, and Frank stood in the living room with his back to the stairwell.

Henry knocked on the door where all the ladies were clamoring as to what to do. Rebecca came to the door and Henry asked, "How's it going in here?"

"Oh Henry, it's just terrible. Nothing is working. She's still so beautiful, but her heart was so set on that dress. She just can't settle on anything."

Henry demanded, "OKAY LADIES, I THINK IT'S TIME YOU COME DOWNSTAIRS AND TAKE FIVE!"

Meredith looked at him and cried, "But Daddy!"

"No buts. Everyone downstairs, take a break. You can think more clearly after a few minutes and a cup of joe to clear your heads."

Reluctantly, the six women were corralled down the stairs. When they entered the living room, they saw a menacing figure with his back turned toward them.

They then heard a thundering voice proclaim, "Well I have tried and tried, but I just don't think it's gonna fit me. Always a bridesmaid, never a bride!"

Frank pirouetted around with the seemingly tiny dress pressed up against his enormous chest.

Meredith screamed with excitement. "Oh, my God! Frank! Aaaaaaah, my dress, my DRESS! Oh, Frank, I love you sooo much! You're the best!" She ran and jumped up to hang from Frank's hearty neck, bawling and kissing him on the cheek. Frank had to hold the dress out to one side to keep her from crushing the delicate prize.

The girls, including her aunts, were crying and hugging on Frank as he blushed with embarrassment.

Nancy looked up at Frank and said, "You're a good boy. I love you, Frankie."

Frank blushed, "Aw, thanks Nance."

Henry and Rebecca were hugging each other, and Henry was brimming with joy. "What do you think about 'The Moose' now, darling?"

Rebecca sighed, "I think our little girl's in good hands with these two."

Henry smiled, "I couldn't have said it better myself."

As Meredith bolted up the stairs with her mother and aunts, Cynthia whispered into Frank's ear, "Sir, you are my hero. I would like a moment alone with you outside."

The two disappeared unnoticed for the next half hour in the back yard. Frank returned to Mike's a much happier man than when he left. He had received all the reward he could ever want from the girl he had blissfully fallen in love with.

When Frank walked in, Mike asked, "Where have you been?

You disappeared at lunch and I haven't seen you till now."

"Well, you know, I've been busy saving the day, that's all." Mike looked puzzled and Frank said, "Never mind, I need a beer!" Mike brought him a beer as the two sat in the living room talking.

Frank started, "Well, pal, this is it. No turning back after tomorrow. Getting cold feet yet?"

Mike countered, "No way, I've never been more certain of anything in my life. She's the one, I know it."

"That's good, Mikey. She's a good girl. You're a lucky man."

"What about you, Frank? When are you gonna settle down?"

Frank scoffed, "Me? Settle down? You must be kidding!"

Mike smiled, "What about Cynthia? Don't think I haven't noticed you two sneaking around all the time, a-whisperin' an' agigglin' like little kids."

Frank sat quietly while grinning, gulped down his beer, then burst out, "Shut up, douche, and get me another beer!"

"Haha, I knew it!"

As Mike went to get his buddy another beer, he walked away singing, "Frank and Cynthia sitting in a tree, K-I-S-S-I-N-G . . . "

Frank smiled and yelled out, "Shut up, dickhead!"

The next morning Mike woke up and shouted, "SHIT! TEN O'CLOCK? MOOSE! MOOSE, WAKE UP! WE'RE GONNA BE LATE!"

He had forgotten to set his alarm, and the two of them had stayed up late gabbing like old ladies. Mike had to throw a pillow at Frank to wake him up as he lay blissfully asleep in the guest room. "Get up, Moose. We gotta go!"

The wedding was scheduled to start at noon at St. Mary's Cathedral, twenty minutes away. They had to shower, shave, don their tuxedos and be waiting at the altar exactly at noon. The two managed to get out of the condo by 11:15, and Frank sped the whole way, saying, "You better get me out of any tickets, 'Captain!'"

Mike chortled, "I got you covered, pal. Just get me there on time and in one piece!"

11:40 a.m. Traffic was heavier than they had anticipated for a Saturday. Frank pulled up in front of the church. Mike exclaimed, "You did it. Thanks, brother. Go park and get inside. The limo's pulling up." Mike ran inside so as not to accidentally see the bride in her dress.

When Mike got inside, the guests were all already seated. Henry was waiting by the front door, and as he looked at his watch he said, "Cutting it little close, boy. Thought you might have gotten cold feet."

"Pop," Mike said, using the term of endearment he had given Henry since they had become so close and he had become a father figure to Mike, "I wouldn't miss this for anything. You're not getting rid of me that easy!"

Henry smiled and said, "Good answer, son. I was wiping down the shotgun, just in case."

Mike and Frank escorted Nancy and Rebecca to their seats in the front row, and then they took their positions up at the altar. They took notice of the sound of distant thunder. Mike whispered, "The

weather report said it would be clear and sunny."

Frank smirked, "Well, what did you expect?"

Then suddenly the organ erupted in Wagner's Bridal Chorus. The music filled the church with a beautiful tapestry of sweet sounding notes. After a life filled with horrific images and tragic events, Mike looked up to see the most beautiful image he had ever seen. Meredith was walking down the aisle, her right arm firmly locked with Henry's left. Her long train flowed behind her as the beautiful sequins on her white gown glistened in the light. Mike could not hold back the tears as he watched his beautiful bride advance. He heard Frank exclaim, "Wow!"

Reverend Mory was presiding over the service. Mike looked up at him and The Reverend smiled with approval.

Henry, with a tear of joy, placed Meredith's hand in Mike's, whispering, "Take good care of my little girl. Love you, son!"

"I will, Pop."

The service began, and the storm seemed to grow stronger and draw closer. The lightning struck and the thunder boomed relentlessly, yet Reverend Mory never missed a beat. The thunder was so loud that many of the guests often jumped in their seats. Reverend Mory pressed on, not allowing himself to get rattled.

The time to exchange vows was at hand. Mike was oblivious to the storm outside, mesmerized by his beautiful bride. As Mike was speaking his vows, " . . . to be my wife, to have and to hold from this day forward, for better or for worse . . . ," immediately the wind amped up and howled furiously outside, creating a sound reminiscent to that of a woman's scream of anguish. Suddenly the front doors blew open, causing many attendees to shriek from the surprising incident. Several men rushed up and secured the doors.

Reverend Mory, never missing an opportunity for an interesting anecdote, changed course for a moment and declared, "Well, before we have Meredith deliver her vows, let me say to the two of you that in every marriage there will be storms, but if you continue to look toward each other with the same love in your eyes as you have on this day, you will surely endure those storms just like we will endure this one."

The crowd breathed a sigh of relief and smiled at the Reverend's reassuring manner.

Meredith recited her vows without incident.

When it was time to exchange the rings, Mike recited his well studied lines. "With this ring, I seal my oath, to be a faithful and loving husband, before God and these witnesses."

As he slipped the shiny, diamond-encrusted gold band onto Meredith's delicate finger, there was a sudden eruption of thunder that rattled the building, and all the lights went out except for the candles.

Reverend Mory, in his typical calm manner declared, "It would seem we will continue with a more intimate candlelight service."

The crowd chuckled at his lighthearted response to the peculiar events.

By the end of the service, the storm subsided and they now exited the building, running through a new storm—only rice instead of rain. The thunder had been replaced with the cheers from loved ones, and not angry skies.

The remainder of the day was beautiful and special. The reception was successful, except when Mike and Meredith danced their first dance. The DJ apologized when the song curiously stopped playing on two occasions. But after the third attempt, he was able to correct the problem. By now, nothing could faze the two as they continued to dance through the starts and stops. They never took their eyes off each other. Oblivious to the world around them, nothing could ruin their day. With their resolute determination readily apparent, it seemed as though whatever malevolent force causing the disruptions just gave up and the rest of the day went smoothly.

Now it was time for Frank, the best man, to offer a toast. He stood and walked over to the podium.

An uncharacteristically serious Frank began, "I met Mike back in high school. He was the first guy who ever stood up to me, and after that we quickly became friends. He has been my best friend for twenty years now. He is my brother in every sense. Our families are one family. And when he introduced me to Meredith, I knew he had found his soul mate. Merry, I have never seen him happier, and I thank you for being such an incredible woman. Now our family has grown with the addition of Meredith and her family. To my new sister Meredith and her fortunate husband, and our now larger family, I raise a glass. I thank you for being part of my life. I love you all." Everyone raised a glass and cheered the toast.

They danced and celebrated late into the evening. Mike and Meredith spent their first night as man and wife at the nicest hotel in town, overlooking the harbor. Frank had booked them a surprise honeymoon cruise out of Miami that left the next Thursday on the newest and most luxurious cruise ship.

The next day, Sunday, the newlyweds were on their way to South Beach in Miami where they would spend the next few days relaxing until they left on the cruise. Mike and Meredith checked in to the hotel—the honeymoon suite, a penthouse that overlooked a beautiful beach with glowing sand and waves gently pushing into the shoreline.

TWO EQUALS ONE

The next morning Mike surprised Meredith by ordering room service and pampering her with breakfast in bed. He had also arranged a facial and a massage in the hotel spa for later.

Mike told her, "Go ahead and enjoy the morning at the spa. I'm going to the gym to work out. I'll meet you back at the room when you're finished."

"Oh, thank you, baby. You're so good to me. I love you."

"I love you too," Mike said. "Afterwards, we'll go down to the beach to relax and have a few drinks."

"Mmm, that sounds wonderful."

At noon, they headed downstairs and ate lunch at the Tiki Hut Grill. Then they secured two loungers on the beach and ordered some drinks.

Mike said, "I think I'm gonna take a little dip, sweetie. Join me?"

Meredith said, "Sure, why not?"

Three days prior, Tropical Storm Arlene had stirred things up in the Gulf of Mexico. Even though it was so far off the coast, Mike was convinced that Arlene was the cause of the bizarre weather during the wedding service. It was actually several hundred miles off the west coast and had made landfall in the panhandle of Florida the day of the wedding. The storm was still causing quite a mess along the east coast, with strong currents and high tides.

On the beach, Mike and Meredith could see red flag warnings posted, which indicated dangerous surf conditions related to the storm. They saw hundreds of other people, including children, swimming in the water and the lifeguards standing dutifully at their posts.

Mike said, "It can't be too bad or they wouldn't let people in the water. The waves don't look too rough."

The two entered the water and were frolicking the way newlyweds should. The surf felt strong, but the waves seemed moderate. Meredith wanted to play a little Marco Polo with Mike. "Winner gets their choice of extra special attention tonight!"

Mike felt silly, but obliged, saying, "I have a feeling that even if I lose, I'll win."

Meredith smiled and winked. "We'll both win, I promise you that!"

Eagerly, he closed his eyes and called out, "Marco!"

Of course, Meredith was swimming around and responded, "Polo!"

This continued on for several minutes. Meredith would move stealthily to reposition herself before responding, "Polo."

Mike was never a cheater, and kept his eyes closed, until he heard Meredith's voice cry out for help.

"HELP! MIKE, HELP ME!"

Mike opened his eyes, and to his horror, Meredith was now twenty yards farther out to sea than she had been just moments before. Her voice was growing fainter, and he could see that she appeared to be getting pulled away from the shore at a rapid speed.

Mike screamed, "HANG ON, HONEY!" He swam toward her as fast as he could. Meredith was screaming and waving her arms frantically. To the lifeguards on the shore, she appeared to be caught in a rip current. The harder she fought to swim against the current, the more fatigued she grew.

In the growing distance, Mike could hear the lifeguards' whistles blowing as he continued to swim faster towards her. As he drew near, he himself was becoming exhausted, and Meredith was in full panic mode. Suddenly, he saw Meredith disappear below the water. Mike dove down in an effort to find her. He saw her approximately five feet below the surface and was able to grab her. She was still flailing around when he surfaced with her.

Meredith was out of her mind with panic. As he struggled to maintain control, she screamed and clawed at him, trying to climb on top of him, pushing his head under the water. On several of these occurrences, Mike inhaled small amounts of salt water into his lungs as he tried to control her, coughing when he would surface.

Out of nowhere, four lifeguards made it to their location. They were on two jet skis. Two of the guards jumped into the water and secured Mike and Meredith with safety harnesses. Once the two calmed down, the lifeguards pulled them back to shore.

Lifeguard Supervisor, Manuel Rodriguez then asked, "Are you two okay?"

Coughing and sputtering, Mike answered, "I'm fine! Honey, are you okay?"

Meredith responded, "I—I think so. Oh my God, I was so scared."

Manuel advised that they may have been caught in a rip current.

The lifeguards evaluated their vital signs but Mike and Meredith refused any further treatment.

Meredith said, "It felt like someone grabbed me by my ankles and was pulling me out to sea."

Manuel described that a rip current can sometimes feel like you are being pulled from under the water when in reality, you are simply floating in one spot, unable to swim forward despite all efforts He expounded that the current is horizontal and tends to pull you out along the surface of the water.

Meredith said, "No, you don't understand. It felt like someone's hands grabbed my ankles and pulled me under."

Manuel stated, "During panic situations, the mind can play tricks on you."

Meredith became incensed and said, "Then why did I go under so quickly?"

He explained it was most likely due to her becoming exhausted from fighting against the current. While Manuel patiently enlightened Meredith with his extensive knowledge and experience with rip currents, Mike started coughing more frequently and more forcefully.

Manuel asked, "Are you sure you're okay, sir?" Coughing, Mike nodded that he was okay.

"I really think you should get checked out. You may have aspirated some water into your lungs. This can be very dangerous." Mike insisted that he just wanted to go back to the room and rest.

Manuel said, "Okay sir, but if you find it difficult to breathe, please call 911 immediately."

Meredith answered, "Our room is right over there. I'll keep an eye on him."

The two got up and started to walk to their room. About half way to the room, Meredith could hear that Mike was struggling for breath.

"Honey, are you sure you're okay?"

Coughing harder, Mike said, "I'm fine. I just need to lie down."

By the time they got back to the room, Meredith was helping him stand and his breathing was extremely labored. When she helped him lie down in bed, she could see that his face was turning blue.

"Oh my God! I'm calling 911! You need a doctor!"

By the time the paramedics arrived, Mike was sitting upright, leaning forward and struggling to breathe. With each breath, Meredith could hear wheezing and gurgling. It sounded like he was drowning.

Mike was rushed to the hospital, where the doctor explained that he suffered what's known as a near drowning, and that his lungs were struggling to move oxygen because of the fluid building up in his alveoli. Mike once again was placed into intensive care and on a ventilator to force the oxygen in.

Meredith, now alone on her honeymoon in a strange city, watched as her husband was placed into a dark room in the intensive care unit of St. Matthew's Hospital.

She called her parents and explained what had happened. Henry took the time to explain to her in more detail what to expect in the next few days, and reassured her that Mike would be in good hands. "St. Matthew's is a fine hospital, honey. They deal with this kind of thing all the time."

"Oh Daddy, I was so scared."

"I know, sweetheart. Just sit tight. We'll be there in a few hours. I love you."

"I love you too, Daddy. Thank you. You and mom drive carefully, please."

Remembering her promise to keep him informed, she called Frank next.

"Frankie?"

"Hey there, Merry. I knew you couldn't resist me! But on your honeymoon!?" Frank then heard Meredith crying and asked, "Merry, what's wrong!?"

Sobbing, she explained what had happened.

Frank and Cynthia had not left town yet and Frank said, "I'll be right there!"

"Frank, you don't have to. I know you have to get home."

"MERRY, I'LL BE RIGHT THERE!"

Several hours later, Frank and Cynthia arrived.

Running in, Frank asked, "How is he?"

Meredith answered, "He's on life support."

"Does Nancy know yet?"

"Oh my God, no! I've been so preoccupied that I just forgot to call her. How did you get here so fast?"

Cynthia answered, "You don't want to know."

Meredith looked at the two and asked Cynthia, "Wait, how did you find out? I thought you left already. That's why I didn't call you."

Frank and Cynthia looked at each other, then Henry and Rebecca came rushing into the waiting area.

Frank hastily said, "Um, I'll call Nancy for you. You guys talk."

Later that night after catching the red eye out of Louisville, Nancy arrived in Miami.

When she got to the hospital, she saw Meredith and everyone else in the waiting area. Nancy told everyone to go get cleaned up and get some rest, and that she would stay there that night. She promised to call immediately if anything changed. Meredith was still in her bikini, but did not want to leave.

Nancy reassured her, "Honey, you go get some rest. Get yourself dressed. I'll be here. Call me if you can't sleep. You can come first thing in the morning and relieve me."

Weeping, Meredith confessed to Nancy, "I'm so sorry, Nancy. This is all my fault."

Nancy scolded her saying, "Nonsense! This is not your fault. If he didn't come after you, you might not be here and I couldn't stand the idea of losing my precious daughter-in-law. Now, go on sweetie, go get some rest and put some clothes on. You're driving the men crazy around here."

Meredith left, and got dressed at the hotel. Within the hour, she returned and stayed up with Nancy for the rest of the night.

During the next three days, everyone took rotating shifts standing by, but Meredith refused to leave the hospital again. The staff, knowing she was on her honeymoon, took pity on her and allowed her to shower in the nurse's lounge after her parents would bring fresh clothes. Frank also stayed the whole time in the waiting room with Meredith, but the staff did not have the same compassion for him. He would sneak out only for a quick shower at his hotel, then return immediately.

Three days later, Mike woke up. Meredith was, of course, by his side. She called everyone to tell them. Frank was still in the waiting room and the nurse went in to tell him.

"Hey, Merry. Well, douche bag, thanks for scaring the shit out of me again! I'm glad to see you're back among the living."

Mike smiled, raised his right hand and shot Frank a bird. He was having a hard time talking since having the tube removed from his trachea. He was breathing on his own now, but had developed a respiratory infection and would have to remain in ICU for another week.

When Mike was finally transferred to a private room on the fourth floor, Frank came by to see him.

"Hey, douche bag. This is getting kind of old, you know what I mean? I don't want to be visiting you in the hospital again, you got it?"

Smiling, Mike said, "Got it!"

"I love you, bro. I'm heading home today. I got a big meeting tomorrow in Des Moines. I'll call you later."

In a rare solemn moment between the two, Mike said, "Thank you for everything, Frank. Thank you for being there for Meredith and Nancy. She told me how fast you got here."

"I'd do anything for you, ya prick. You know that."

"Ditto, pal. So best friend, now that I know you drove Cynthia to the airport yesterday, are you gonna tell me what's going on between you two or what?"

Frank, with a mysterious grin said, "Well, buddy, I gotta be going."

Mike said, "Frank?"

Frank sauntered over to Mike and the lumbering giant bent down and gave Mike a hug saying, "Love ya, pal."

"Frank? Frank! Don't you leave here without telling me something, anything? FRANK!?"

Frank stopped at the doorway, looked back, smiled and winked, then shrugged his shoulders and walked away whistling down the hallway.

"Frank! Frank!!" Frank didn't come back. From down the hallway, he heard, "See ya later, douche!"

Mike sat in his bed laughing to himself. "That big goon has fallen hard for her."

Meredith came by to visit a couple hours after Frank left.

Mike said, "I'm so sorry about all of this, sweetheart. I sure made a mess of things."

Meredith gently put her delicate fingers on his lips and said, "Shhh . . . stop it. I panicked out there and caused all this. This is completely my fault. I'm so sorry, my darling. I grew up here in Florida and have spent countless hours in the ocean. I knew about rip currents and how to get out of them, but I never experienced it before and I just panicked. It really felt like someone was pulling me under though, and that was the most terrifying thing of all. I'm just glad you're okay. You saved my life. You're my hero! I cherish you."

Mike looked at her lovingly and told her, "We'll just agree to disagree. It was no one's fault, just bad luck. It was that damn rip current. I'm just glad you're okay, baby. I can't stand the thought of something happening to you, and I would have died trying to save you. I love you so much."

Meredith said, "And I love you. We'll go on our honeymoon another time. Frank got his money back and said he'll reschedule the trip when we're ready."

"Yeah, he came by to see me this morning before his flight left. Some honeymoon, huh?"

"Someday when we're telling our grandkids about this, we'll look back and laugh, I'm sure."

Mike said, "Grandkids? Whoa, there little lady. Don't you think we should start our family first?"

"Michael Carson, I plan on living a very long and happy life together, provided you don't go drowning on me."

Mike agreed, "Okay boss, deal!"

After two weeks in the hospital, Mike was discharged.

Mike and Meredith returned to Boca Grande Shores, along with Henry and Rebecca. When the four pulled into town, Henry suggested that they go out to dinner. Henry said, "Let's go to Taureau's, my treat. We can celebrate your recovery and a safe return home."

At dinner, Henry proposed a toast. "To the newlyweds. For better or worse, may the worse part be behind you."

Mike, Meredith and Rebecca all raised their glasses in agreement.

"Thank you, Pop," Mike said, "for everything."

Henry pulled Mike aside to talk to him privately. "Son, I can never repay you for saving my little girl. The emergency room doctor told me what you did and how you ended up there. I know you're going to take good care of her."

He hugged Mike and told him, "The worst is past you now, I'm sure of it. I foresee nothing but good things from here on out for you two."

A week after returning home, Mike went back to work, confident the worst really was behind them.

THE END OF THE BEGINNING

On the scene of a grisly suicide, Mike and his SWAT team partner, Bill, had just finished clearing the second floor of the residence when Mike thought he heard a sound.

As Mike explained to everyone that he thought he'd heard a man's voice, the entire team was startled by the unexpected sound of a door slamming from upstairs.

"What the hell, Mike? I thought you said the upstairs was clear!"

Mike, visibly shaken, and baffled by the sound, responded, "It was, Sarge . . . I swear we cleared the entire floor. There's no way anyone could be up there."

"Well, genius, apparently you missed something! Get your ass upstairs and find out what the fuck is going on! Pete and Steve, go up there with them!"

Mike, Bill and the other two team members hurried up the stairs to investigate.

As the four heavily armed and intently focused deputies ascended the stairs, Mike took the lead. He clamored, "SHERIFF'S OFFICE! ANYONE UPSTAIRS IDENTIFY YOURSELF. COME OUT

WITH YOUR HANDS UP!"

No response.

At the top of the stairs, Mike said, "Pete, you and Steve stand by here and watch that end of the hall. Bill and I will sweep the other end again."

Mike and Bill proceeded to the opposite end of the hall first.

"Bill, we'll go in together, check?"

"Roger that, brother."

Mike shouted through the closed door, "ANYONE IN THE ROOM, COME OUT OR WE'RE COMING IN!"

Again, he didn't hear a sound. They entered the master bedroom. Both men searched every crevice of the room, under the bed, in the closets, in the shower—anywhere that someone could be hiding. They repeated this in the next three rooms. All was clear. The two men contacted Pete and Steve, who were still holding their positions at the top of the stairs.

Mike said, "Okay, we got nothing on this end. You guys want to check the other side?"

Pete readily accepted, "That's a big ten four. We got it!"

Mike replied, "Watch your ass. We had nothing on this end."

Pete and Steve searched the remaining three rooms on the opposite end of the hall. When they returned, Pete said, "We got nothing, Mike. What the hell was that?"

"Maybe the wind blew the door shut?"

"I didn't feel no wind, Mike."

Mike said, "I know, brother, but I ain't got no other explanation."

Suddenly, Mike thought he heard a voice coming from the attic.

It sounded like a man's voice lamenting in terror.

"SHHHH! Did you guys hear that?"

None of the other three had heard anything.

"It sounded like it came from the attic." At the end of the hallway was a pull-down attic ladder.

"C'mon, let's check the attic."

As Mike grabbed the cord to pull down the ladder, the other three were pointing their automatic machine guns toward the opening. Mike opened the attic and hollered, "ANYONE IN THE ATTIC, IDENTIFY YOURSELF. COME OUT NOW, OR WE'RE

COMING IN AFTER YOU!"

No response.

The ladder was now extended, and Mike flipped the switch on the wall which illuminated the once dark attic. Mike climbed the ladder halfway and stopped. From his pocket, he pulled out a mirror on an extendable stick. From his vantage point he could safely scan the attic to look for anyone hiding up there. "It looks clear. I'm going up."

"Careful, Mike!" Pete warned.

Once in the attic, Mike could stand upright. His pulse was racing and he quickly scanned the attic with the flashlight attached to his machine gun. He checked all the dark areas that the attic lights could not penetrate. He saw a stack of boxes at the north end of the attic. His senses were on high alert. He listened intently for any unusual noises. It was quiet though, except for the sound of his own heartbeat that thundered like the distant drums of a warrior tribe preparing for battle.

Maybe someone is hiding behind those boxes, he thought.

Mike approached the boxes cautiously.

"ANYONE BEHIND THE BOXES, IDENTIFY YOURSELF!"

Again, no response.

Mike walked around the boxes and lit up the dark space. No one was there but he did find collection of what appeared to be occult ritual items. There were golden candlesticks with black candles melted from the attic heat, a black shroud crumpled up in the corner with a shiny object reflecting his rifle light back to him from underneath. He lifted up the shroud, revealing a bull's horn blade. He had seen this before. A creepy feeling swept over Mike and he quickly dropped the shroud and immediately exited the attic.

Bill asked, "Well?" as Mike scurried down the ladder.

"Huh? Oh, it was clear," he answered, trying to sound nonchalant.

"Why do you seem so spooked?"

"I'm good, buddy. Just some strange shit up there, but no people. Let's get out of here."

Mike took up the rear as the three others descended the stairs. As Mike was starting his descent, his blood chilled when he thought he once again heard the sound of a distant scream of a man in anguish.

He thought to himself, *you're hearing things, Mike. This shit's creeping you out.* Then he swiftly ran down the stairs.

Downstairs he reported, "Sarge, we searched the entire second floor, including the attic. There was no one upstairs. I can only guess that the wind must have slammed the door. Maybe it happened when we opened the front door."

The Sergeant said, "Whatever. As long as it's clear. C'mon boys, let's get out of here. This place stinks."

The team exited the house and Mike returned to his patrol car to dress down from his heavy SWAT gear. He could see Mrs. Johansen standing on her front porch. She was visibly shaken. Against his better judgment, knowing he would be there for a while, he decided to go and speak to Beatrice to reassure her.

"Good morning, Beatrice," Mike said in a reassuring voice. "How are you doing, hon?"

In a shaky voice, Beatrice responded, "I've never been so afraid. That poor girl. I feel so bad for her."

Mike told her, "I know what you mean, ma'am. It was a very frightening event, indeed. She'll be okay. We have her in a safe place now. How are you doing, though?"

"I'm good now. I've seen a lot of things through the years, but never anything like this. I've heard stories about that house, but never paid much attention to them."

Mike was curious and asked her, "What do you mean? What kind of things have you heard?"

Beatrice started telling about her girlfriend who told her, "You know, she's the one I play bridge with at the clubhouse? Well, she told me that after she and her husband Fred—he was an engineer from Detroit—moved in, they were home and heard a similar commotion in the neighborhood. It seems that a young woman who lived there disappeared and no one ever heard from her again. This was all after her parents were tragically killed in a freak accident. But that was so long ago. . ."

Mike knew that this would take a long time, and he still had a mountain of paperwork to finish before he could ever think about going home.

"Well Mrs. Johansen, I'm glad you're okay. I really have to be going. Just so you know, there will be a lot of activity around here for quite some time."

"Thank you, officer. You know, I never got your name, dear."

***

303

In a quiet office at the Sheriff's station, a terrified woman sat, still wrapped in the deputy's jacket, and also wore a pair of jail scrubs that were kept on hand for just such occasions. The woman was curled up on the sofa in the Lieutenant's office with her knees drawn up to her chest, still in a state of shock. Deputies had gotten her a cup of coffee and were awaiting the arrival of a counselor. They had not determined her identity as of yet.

When Yvonne Stark, an on-call psychiatrist used by the Sheriff's Office for Major Crime investigations, arrived, she asked if she could speak to the woman alone. The detectives agreed, and brought her up to speed on what had transpired. They then led her into the office. They informed her that they would be just outside if she needed anything.

Yvonne entered the room and saw the woman on the couch. In a quiet, reassuring voice, Yvonne spoke to her. "Good morning, ma'am. My name is Yvonne. I understand you have had quite a scary experience this morning. I just want to let you know that what you're feeling is completely normal and it's okay to be scared. . ."

After an hour, Yvonne exited the office and spoke to Detective Corporal Bobby Pell.

"She's in a state of shock, Bobby. But I've managed to get her name out of her. Her name is Meredith Carson."

Detective Pell exclaimed, "That's right! Now I remember her from when she was a prosecutor. I was just a rookie cop then. Say

Brad, isn't she married to that guy who used to work here?"

"You mean Mike Carson?"

"Yeah, that's the guy. He was a hell of a cop."

"If that's her, then yes."

"I wonder if they ID'd the guy out there yet. Do you think it might have been Carson who offed himself?"

"Man, I hope not. He was a great guy."

Yvonne said, "I'm going back in and speak to her a little more."

Bobby said, "Let us know if she'll be up for a few questions."

"I'll let you know. But don't expect a lot. She's very distraught. It may be some time before she'll talk."

Detective Pell made a phone call to the detectives on the scene.

"Roger? Hey, it's Bobby. Say, do you have an ID on that guy out there yet?"

"Not yet. We just got the house cleared. We're going in now.

Any luck with the woman?"

"Yeah. Ready for this? Meredith Carson. Isn't that Mike Carson's wife?"

"I believe it is."

"Is there a vehicle parked outside?"

"Yeah, there's an SUV."

Bobby said, "Read me the tag and I'll run it on the computer." Roger read Bobby the tag and Bobby ran it.

When he got the name return he said in disbelief, "Oh shit. It's not looking good, Roger. It's registered to Michael Carson."

"I pray that's not him. I can't see him doing something like that. All right, Bobby, thanks for the heads up. I'll let you know as soon as we find out anything. But from what I understand, there isn't much left to make a positive visual ID.

Maybe she'll open up and let us know a little more. We may have to wait on the M.E."

"Okay Roger, I'll keep you up to date."

In the other room, Yvonne had developed a rapport with Meredith.

"Meredith, would you like some coffee?"

Meredith quietly answered, "No thank you. But could I have some water?"

Seeing this as a breakthrough, Yvonne responded, "Yes, yes of course. I'll be right back."

Yvonne exited and told Detective Pell that she was making some headway with Meredith. "Can I get a bottle of water for her?"

"Of course. Say Doc, you don't think she could be faking any of this do you?"

"Bobby, this is a classic case of an acute stress reaction. This poor girl has seen something traumatic and is terrified beyond belief. I'm actually surprised she's said anything at all. Sometimes it takes much longer for people to open up at all after something like this."

"Huh! Well, you're the expert, Doc. I'll be right back with that water." Bobby returned and gave her the bottle. "Just let me know if you need anything else."

Yvonne reentered the room and Meredith was sitting up now.

"Here's your water, Meredith. Is there anything else I can get for you?"

"I have a terrible headache. Do you have any aspirin?"

"I do have some in my purse . . . here you go, dear."

"Thank you, you've been very kind."

After several hours, Yvonne again exited the room. "I haven't made any more headway with her. I'm afraid she'll shut down further if we push her more today. The only thing she's been asking for is her parents, Dr. and Mrs. Henry and Rebecca Porter."

"Rebecca Porter? That's her mother? Oh man, I know Rebecca very well. I'll contact them immediately," Bobby said.

Half an hour later, Henry and Rebecca rushed into the station.

Rebecca shouted, "WHERE'S MY DAUGHTER?"

"Mrs. Porter, I'm Detective Pell. Please calm down and have a seat."

"Oh yes, of course Detective. Bobby, isn't it?"

"Yes, ma'am."

"I remember you from that aggravated battery case last year. What about my daughter?"

"Of course, ma'am. Meredith is safe and secure. She's with Dr. Stark and is relaxing right now in the office."

"Oh good, Yvonne is with her? That makes me feel better. She is really good."

Bobby proceeded to explain what they knew so far.

Yvonne came out and spoke to Henry and Rebecca. "Hello, Rebecca. I'm sorry we're meeting again under these circumstances. I think it's a good idea if she goes home with you tonight. We aren't going to question her anymore. I believe she's suffering from an acute stress reaction. I've prescribed her some sedatives to help her relax. I'll check in throughout the day tomorrow to see how she's doing."

Henry asked, "Where's Michael?"

Bobby explained what he could. "At this time, we have not identified the subject in the house, but we have reason to believe that it is her husband, Michael Carson. We'll know more when the Medical Examiner finishes the autopsy. Meanwhile, if you can, keep an eye on Meredith for us. When the doctor says she's ready, we'll want to talk to her."

Rebecca broke down in tears. "No, not Mike! NO, NO, NO, NO, NO! HENRY, NO!"

Henry held her tightly and the two took several minutes to gather themselves. Yvonne spoke to them before she let them in to see Meredith.

When Henry and Rebecca had regained their composure, Yvonne went into the office with them. Meredith looked up, broke into tears and ran to her parents. "Mom? Dad?"

Yvonne and Bobby escorted them out of the office to their car.

Henry spoke to Yvonne. "Doctor, thank you. My wife said you are highly regarded. I hope you will be willing to help Meredith through this."

"It will be my pleasure, Dr. Porter. I've worked many cases with your wife; she is very highly regarded herself. Like I said, I'll check in on Meredith throughout the day tomorrow. She's traumatized right now. Here is my private number. Call me if she has any outbursts. Don't question her about anything that happened right now. We risk shutting her down further if she's pushed. She needs time to sort all of this out in her mind. We actually made more headway than I thought this afternoon. It normally takes several

days for people in this state to come around."

"Thank you again. We'll keep an eye on her."

When they got home, Henry escorted Meredith to her old bedroom. Rebecca made sure she took her medication and stayed with her until she finally fell asleep.

When Rebecca climbed into bed, Henry was watching the news. The news was broadcasting about the event that had taken place at Mike and Meredith's house earlier that morning.

". . . Officials aren't releasing many details about the incident that has the normally quiet upscale community of Mossy Hammock quite upset. At this time, officials aren't able to tell us much more than one person is dead and his identity has not been released, pending notification of family. We'll continue watching this story. More details to follow as we get them."

Henry declared, "I can't believe it! This can't be happening."

Rebecca broke down again. "Oh Henry, what could have possibly gone wrong? Everything seemed to be going so well! They were so happy . . . he was so good to her. He did love her, didn't he? We weren't fooled, were we?"

Henry replied, "He loved her, no doubt in my mind. There's something much more to this than we may ever know, honey." The two held each other tightly until they fell asleep.

3:00 a.m. Henry and Rebecca were awakened to the sound of Meredith screaming, "NO, MICHAEL! PLEASE DON'T! I LOVE YOU. NO, NO, NO, NOOOOOO!"

They both ran into Meredith's room and held her, mindful not to ask any questions.

The next morning, Dr. Stark called and spoke to Henry. Henry explained about the outburst at three o'clock.

Dr. Stark asked, "Would it be okay if I came by and spent some time with her this afternoon?"

Henry said, "That would be good. Yes, please do."

On day two, Henry received the disturbing phone call from Detective Pell. The Medical Examiner had made a positive ID on the body from the scene. It was the body of Michael Carson. It was confirmed by fingerprints and DNA.

Henry asked, "Detective, what about his mother, Nancy? I don't have the heart to tell her. She'll be so distraught."

Bobby responded, "I understand, sir. I will take care of that. It's part of what I need to do anyway. How is Meredith holding up, sir?"

"She's the same as far as we can tell. Dr. Stark is coming over this afternoon to spend some more time with her. Please— when you

talk to Nancy, can you have her call us?"

"I will pass on the message, Dr. Porter."

"Thank you, Detective."

After hanging up, Henry told Rebecca and they both wept bitterly, but dared not tell Meredith, not yet.

After four days of Dr. Stark visiting Meredith at her parents' home, she asked, "Meredith? I think the time has come for you to

talk about what happened that night. Are you up for it?"

Meredith responded, "I'll try."

"Okay then, tomorrow I will meet with you in my office. Are you okay with that?"

"That will be fine, Doctor."

"Detective Pell will be there, too. He's going to want to speak with you. I'll be there the whole time, okay?"

Meredith gently responded, "Yes, that will be fine."

The next day in Dr. Stark's office, Meredith, Detective Pell and Dr. Stark were all sitting in the conference room adjacent to her office.

Before starting the meeting, Yvonne spoke privately to Bobby. "It's imperative that you don't push her. Let her speak at her own pace. I have no idea where she'll begin, but you must just let her go."

"Luckily, things are sort of quiet in Major Crimes lately, so I'm in no rush."

Detective Pell had placed a tape recorder in the middle of the table. "Good afternoon, Meredith. I'm Detective Pell with the Dolphin County Sheriff's Office. I want to thank you for taking the time to meet with us today. I know you've been through a lot, and I just want to let you know that we're in no hurry. We need to talk about the incident that occurred at your house. Begin wherever you feel comfortable."

After several moments of silence, Meredith began by saying, "He was so beautiful. The perfect gentleman, the best husband anyone could ever ask for."

"Who's that, ma'am?"

"Mike, my Michael."

"Tell me a little about Mike."

Smiling, Meredith sighed and said, "I saw him the first time in college. He was with Frank."

Bobby asked, "Frank?"

"Frank was the biggest, most obnoxious human being with the sweetest heart you could ever meet. A gentle giant. He was Mike's best friend. We had the best marriage. Everything was going so well, until . . ."

Meredith stopped and stared blankly at the wall. Bobby looked at Yvonne. Yvonne indicated for him to be patient. She asked, "Meredith, would you like to take a break?"

Meredith, as abruptly as she had stopped, began again. "Those two were inseparable." She began to laugh as she recalled the many antics that Frank and Mike would get into.

311

After a couple of hours, Yvonne stated that she believed that was enough for the day.

"Detective, can I speak to you?"

In the other room, Yvonne explained, "She's actually doing quite well. But I know you want answers about that night. I propose you let me meet alone with her. I'll video tape our sessions with her permission.

She's not crazy by any stretch of the imagination and is willing to cooperate, but she needs to sort out the events on her own. She is salvageable. I don't want to lose her."

"Doc, do you believe she is in any way responsible for her husband's death?"

"Unequivocally, no. Her state of mind is not a result of guilt. This is someone who has lost everything in the world. She is every bit the victim, more so than her husband, I believe. Whatever pain caused him to kill himself is over for him, but hers will last long into her future. She'll require a lot of therapy to move past this trauma."

"Okay Doc, I trust your judgment. You've never been wrong before. I'll let you do your thing. Just let me know what you can."

"I will, but remember, Detective, I can only let you know what is relevant to your investigation. Please don't ask me to compromise my doctor-patient confidentiality."

"Wouldn't think of it, Doc. Okay, I will say my farewell to Mrs. Carson and leave her in your capable hands." He moved back into the room, to Meredith.

"Mrs. Carson, I want to thank you for coming in today. I will leave you my card. Should you have any questions, please feel free to call me."

Meredith said, "Thank you, Detective."

Dr. Stark said to Meredith, "Well, I think you did very well today. Can we meet again on Friday?"

"Okay, Dr. Stark," Meredith said. "I'll be here."

Yvonne briefly met with Henry and Rebecca. "I just want to say that I think she's making some good progress. She's in a very fragile state still, but I think with enough time, we can get her back to the woman you knew before. Just be patient. We'll get her there."

Henry replied, "Well, Doctor, your reputation precedes you. I just want to see my little girl smile again."

"You will, sir, I'm certain of it. But be forewarned, I sense some dark times ahead in the weeks and months to come. We'll give her a few days off, and then I want to see her on Friday."

Rebecca said, "I'll have her here, Yvonne. Thank you."

"Very good. Of course, you understand I can only reveal to you what she wants you to know."

Henry and Rebecca simultaneously affirmed that they understood.

After Nancy was notified about what had happened, she spoke to Henry and Rebecca on the phone. Devastated, Nancy asked, "Why did this happen? My baby boy! What is happening? I can't go on. . .

Rebecca snapped at her, "Nancy, pull yourself together. We love you. We'll take care of everything at this end. You just fly down. We'll put you up in a hotel. We'll get through this as a family."

Ashamedly, Nancy said, "Oh, I'm so sorry, Rebecca. How is Meredith? I'm so sorry this happened."

"She's traumatized. We don't even want her to know that we're having a service for Mike."

"I certainly understand. Thank you for all you're doing. I don't think I could get through this alone."

"Just get here safely, dear. We'll pick you up and figure this all out together."

After hanging up, Rebecca turned to her husband. "Oh Henry, that poor woman. How much tragedy can she endure? First her husband, and now Mike."

"She's stronger than she looks, sweetheart. Yes, she has endured too much. But she's family now, and we'll look out for her as best we can."

"You're a good man, Henry Porter. I love you so much."

"And I love you, my dear."

OPENING OLD WOUNDS

*F*RIDAY, 12:00 P.M. Rebecca met with Dr. Stark first. She advised her that Meredith had been waking up screaming throughout the night. She would then get out of bed and wander the house till the wee hours of the morning. Rebecca noted that during the daytime hours, Meredith would just sit in her room and refuse to interact with her family or friends.

Rebecca revealed they were having Mike's service that afternoon. Dr. Stark had advised Rebecca days before that she believed it would be detrimental for Meredith to attend the service since she was still in denial about Mike's death. In the future, when she is ready, they could have a separate, private memorial for him so Meredith could have closure. Dr. Stark cleared the afternoon so she could spend it with Meredith, and the family could attend the funeral. She hoped the extra time would help them make positive headway.

"Good afternoon, Meredith. How are you feeling?"

"Much better, thank you," she responded.

"Have you been able to sleep?"

"Oh yes, I'm sleeping much better."

"Really, Meredith? Are you telling me the truth?"

Meredith's head sunk low. "No, Dr. Stark, things have not been so good."

"Meredith, if you want to get through this, and I believe you do, I need for you to just be open with me. I'm here to help you, dear."

"Okay, Doctor."

"Okay, I would like to try some relaxation techniques first."

After about twenty minutes, Meredith was feeling quite relaxed and comfortable. Yvonne asked if she would like to start off by talking about Mike.

Meredith smiled wistfully and said, "Oh yes, I love talking about Mike. He's so wonderful. I love him so much."

"Meredith, I know when you two got married you had something awful happen to Mike on your honeymoon. He had an accident and was sick for a while, is that correct?"

Meredith's countenance changed and she became distraught as she recalled the events that happened in Miami when Mike saved her from drowning and almost died himself as a result. "It was terrible. He almost died and it was all my fault. He saved me, but almost died trying."

Yvonne could see that these were very painful memories and that she would need to employ a less traditional method to achieve her goal for Meredith. Yvonne would sparingly use hypnosis in her practice as a means to help people relive painful events from their past. She preferred her patients face their realities head on, but in certain cases like this one, she would employ hypnosis as an aid. Yvonne understood the controversies over the use of hypnosis, but felt there was minimal risk to her patients.

"Okay Meredith, I want to start by having you focus on the sound of my voice. I want you to relax and . . ."

After several minutes, Meredith was relaxed and calm. Yvonne asked her to go back to the time of their honeymoon in Miami. Meredith relived the tragic event that almost took Mike's life at the beach. Yvonne noted that Meredith was still struggling with guilt from the near-drowning incident, and she knew she would have to address this before she could help her deal with the suicide.

"Okay Meredith, now I want you to go forward to the time after the honeymoon. You and Mike are home now."

Meredith became tranquil. She smiled as she was transported back to a happy time after their wedding.

In March of 2006, Meredith came home exhilarated and told Mike some exciting news. "Honey, I'm leaving the District Attorney's

Office and going to work with my mama."

Mike laughed, "Going to the dark side, are ya? Good for you, sweetheart. What finally prompted that decision?"

"Well, Allen is stepping down and retiring. He almost had me convinced to run for office. He would have endorsed my candidacy, but politics is not for me. Besides, you might be working there soon, and I would absolutely be guilty of nepotism if my sweet man came to work with me."

Mike smiled and said, "I think it's a great idea and I support anything you want to do. I just want you to be happy."

"This was always my plan anyway," she said. "I knew I would eventually go into private practice."

"Then I say go for it, my love. You deserve it."

Then Meredith fast forwarded to January 2008. Sheriff Hill did not run for office again, and Mike was leaving the Sheriff's Department after nearly fourteen years of service. The timing was good and he was ready to pursue his goal of becoming a trial lawyer. Mike was hired by the new District Attorney, Ruben Greenberg. Ruben was a no-nonsense attorney and Mike enjoyed working for him. Mike was successful as a prosecutor, though never quite at the same level as Meredith.

One night after serving in the District Attorney's Office for two years, Mike and Meredith were talking at home.

Meredith started out, "I think it's time we take our marriage to the next level."

"You do, huh? And what level would that be?"

"I want us to start our family."

"Really? I thought I was the only one thinking that. I couldn't agree with you more. I've also been thinking about something else, as well."

"Really? What's that?"

"Well Mrs. Carson, I've been thinking that I might be ready to go into private practice. What would you say that we finally make that move we've been talking about for so long and go into practice together?"

"The Carson and Carson Law Firm?"

"The very same."

Meredith radiated with excitement when she realized that once again, she and Mike were on the same page. "Are you really ready for that?"

"I want nothing more than for us to start our family together," said Mike. "And as for having you as my business partner as well as my life partner—what more could a man ask for?"

"You, my dear, are a prince among men. Did you know that?"

Mike smugly replied, "Well, of course I am."

Meredith laughed and said, "Brat!"

The next day, Mike gave a month's notice to Ruben Greenberg.

After searching for weeks, Mike found a perfect office location less than a mile from the courthouse. They started their practice, Carson & Associates Law Firm. Things were going very well for them.

One evening, Mike told Meredith, "I think we should start looking for a home. What do you think? We don't want our baby growing up in an apartment, do we? I think we can afford one now that we're both high power hotshot attorneys."

"Seriously, baby?"

"Sure, why not? The practice is going well. I think it's time for us to take the next step in our family's evolution." Mike laughed.

They dreamed and planned their future long into the night. Meredith wore a big smile on her face as she recalled those memories.

By the next week, they were searching for a house. They began by looking for a modest first home. They found a three-bedroom ranch located in a good community. It was perfect for them. They both agreed it would be a perfect starter home. Meredith was excited about the prospect of their first house. Mike had secretly put a deposit on the house, and that night took Meredith out to dinner to break the big news to her.

"So, you know that three-bedroom house we both loved?"

"Yeah, do you think we might go for it?"

"I think we already have. I put a down payment on it. I wanted it to be a surprise."

Meredith screeched with excitement.

"We'll need to go to the bank and fill out the paperwork. How does Thursday work for you?"

"That works out well as long as we go in the morning. I have a new client coming in at one."

Mike said, "Great, I'll set it up for Thursday morning at nine."

On Thursday, they went to the bank and everything went smoothly. With a few signatures, they were closer to becoming homeowners.

A month passed, and Mike received a rejection letter from the bank. Dejected, he called Meredith about the bad news and read her the letter over the phone. "We regret to inform you that your mortgage application has been denied based on the following criteria: the value of the home fell below the bank's requirement."

Meredith was obviously disappointed, but as always, Mike was able to lift her spirits. He told her to cheer up, that it was probably for the best. "Something better will come along for us."

Over the next six months they found three different houses, and each one seemed better than the one before it. For one reason or another, each deal mysteriously fell through.

Meredith recalled becoming disenchanted with the whole house hunting process. That was until one Saturday when she was working in the office to get caught up on some paperwork. Mike stayed home to sleep in. She called Mike to tell him that she was on her way home and should be there soon. She left her office around noon.

On her way home, Meredith drove by a beautiful waterfront community called Mossy Hammock. She had passed by this neighborhood every day, and always dreamed of living in a gated waterfront community like this one. There was an open house sign and the normally closed guard gate was wide open.

Meredith decided to go in and take a quick look. She thought to herself, "What harm could come from a quick look, right?" Meredith knew it was a pipe dream to live in such a place, at least for now, but maybe one day they could if the practice continued doing well.

It was only about 12:30 when Meredith pulled up to the house at 2701 Red Oak Circle. Her breath was taken away by the magnificent home. She could not have dreamed of a more perfect house. As she approached the large, custom double-carved doors of the beautiful contemporary castle, she was mesmerized by the large bay window that provided her a view of the luxurious interior. When she entered the house, there was one other couple in the house looking around, but she overheard them saying, "We could never afford this. Let's just go."

Meredith was then greeted by the realtor, a short, portly man, balding with white horseshoe hair pulled back in a long pony tail.

He was sweaty, unshaven and wore an undersized brown plaid jacket, open collared shirt with gold chains and matching plaid pants. "Good afternoon, ma'am. Sam Haines, nice to meet you, Mrs. . .?"

He extended his hand and Meredith noted that he wore a silver ring on each of his fat fingers. She had to hold back a snicker as she shook his pudgy, well-dressed nubs. He had a pungent odor about him that reminded her of the cattle stockade at the county fair. To say he looked seedy would have been an understatement, but Meredith cordially responded with a smile, "Mrs. Carson."

"Well, Mrs. Carson. What do you think of our lovely little home so far?"

"I think it's a dream home, Mr. Haines, but I'm sure my husband and I could never afford such opulence."

"Now don't you go being so hasty there, Mrs. Carson. I think you might be in for quite a surprise. Come on, let me show you around."

Meredith was awestruck as the winded Mr. Haines took her on a tour of the lavish house.

"And here is your vanishing edge pool that overlooks the deep-water canal. Over there's your boat lift, and here you have a well-appointed outdoor kitchen. Can't you just imagine yourself socializing with family and friends on a beautiful day like today out here on this patio?"

Meredith was dumbfounded as she muttered, "Uh-huh!"

When they completed their tour, Sam studied Meredith and said, "I can see that you really like this house."

"Oh, I do, Mr. Haines. This house is perfect. But I have to be realistic. We could never afford this. I'm sorry if I've wasted your time."

Sam looked at her and said, "Little lady, what exactly do you think this house would cost you?"

"Mr. Haines, my husband and I are on a tight budget. Maybe one day we could live in a home like this, but not now."

"Go ahead, throw me a number. What kind of budget are you working with?"

"Honestly, I'm embarrassed to say. We only have a two hundred and fifty-thousand-dollar budget."

Mr. Haines looked at Meredith, smiled a greasy smile and told her, "What if I told you that on that kind of budget you could buy this place and would have money to spare? I'm here to tell you I think I can get you into this home for well under two hundred thousand."

Flabbergasted, Meredith retorted, "Mr. Haines, that isn't funny. I really don't appreciate being made fun of. I think I need to leave now. Good day, sir."

Laughing creepily, Sam said, "No, no, please Mrs. Carson, I'm being serious. This house can be yours for well under two hundred thousand."

"Sir, I know I may look like a ditz to you, but I'm not a fool.

Good day!"

"Mrs. Carson, please don't run off. Have a seat and let me explain."

Sam escorted her to the sofa in the living room by the large bay window and proceeded to explain. "You see, the previous owner was sort of a recluse. After her unfortunate early demise, discovered in her will were very specific instructions that the house would have to remain vacant until this year. No one understands why she specified this year, but the executor of the estate hired me to find a buyer who would appreciate this extraordinary home. I was told the house was to be sold to that individual, regardless of the price offered. There were no remaining survivors to the estate, so funds from the sale are to be allocated to a charitable organization. Beyond that, only the executor knows for sure. So, you see, when you walked in and I saw the look on your face, I knew you were the person I was waiting for."

"Mr. Haines, I have to tell you that I'm an attorney and I can easily verify all that you have told me. I'm sure my husband, who is also an attorney, would not take kindly to my being played."

"Mrs. Carson, I assure you that this is one hundred percent legit. After you do verify everything I've told you, you *will agree that this is a once in a lifetime opportunity to live in a neighborhood like this at this price. I hope that after you conduct your research you'll consider making this your new home. I'm confident that you're the one the benefactor was hoping I would find. She wanted someone who would cherish this home as much as she did. Your reaction when you walked in said it all. I know you'll love this home."*

"This is the perfect home in every way I can imagine, Mr. Haines. I will do my research and get back to you. If indeed this is as legitimate as you claim, I'm sure I can convince my husband to consider making an offer."

"I promise you Mrs. Carson, this is everything I said it is, or my name ain't Sam Haines. You won't be disappointed. Your benefactor will rest easy knowing her wishes have been fulfilled. Please do your research and get back to me as soon as possible. I would hate for you and your husband to miss out on this unbelievable opportunity. Here is the executor's business card. You can contact him if you have any more questions."

Sam handed Meredith a crinkled business card. On the front of the card was the name Mammon Abaddonus, Attorney at Law. When she flipped the card over, she saw a picture of a locust. How odd! she thought.

As Meredith was leaving, it felt to her as if she had been in the company of Mr. Haines for at least two to three hours. Thinking Mike would be worried about where she was, she hurried to her car. As Meredith was pulling out of the driveway, she waved at Mr. Haines, who was standing in the doorway smiling at her and waving back.

As she backed out and quickly drove away, she looked at the clock which read only 12:45. "Fifteen minutes? That's impossible. I was in there for hours. Wasn't I?" She assumed the clock must be wrong so she looked for her cell phone to check the time and discovered it was not in her purse. "Crap, I must have left my phone at the house."

Meredith quickly turned the car around and returned to the house. As she pulled up, she noticed the Open House *sign was gone and it looked like no one was inside. When she got to the front door, she found her cell phone on the threshold. She knocked on the door—no answer.*

She picked up the phone and thought, That's bizarre. How did he get out of here so fast? I was only gone a few seconds. Oh well, at least he left my phone out for me. That was nice.

As Meredith exited the development, she was stopped at the guard shack. An older, surly man in a guard's uniform with a thick New York accent asked her, "Ma'am, how did you get in here?"

Meredith looked at his uniform and saw that his name tag read "Joe." She thought he must have been kidding with her, and she said, "I came for the open house and the gate was wide open earlier."

Joe brusquely responded, "Are you trying to be funny? I've been here all afternoon. The gate was never left open and I don't recall any open houses scheduled for today."

Meredith said, "But there's the sign posted right over there . . ." No sign. Confused, she said, "I met the realtor, Sam Haines, at the house."

Joe looked at her like she was loony and said, "I guess you slipped in after one of the residents. Okay lady, get going. Have a nice day."

Mystified, Meredith drove away from the guard shack sure that the old guard must be senile. As she drove, she began daydreaming about the home. She restlessly drove home, eager to start her research on the house and the mysterious benefactor.

Normally a level-headed and practical woman, Meredith had allowed herself to get excited about this home even though she promised herself she wouldn't do that again. She had always been a firm believer that if something seemed too good to be true, it probably was. But still, people win lotteries every day. Why couldn't something good come along for them? Besides, creepy Mr. Haines had given her all the info. She would research and confirm everything before saying anything to Mike about it. "I don't want to get his hopes up unnecessarily."

When she got home, Mike asked her, "How was your morning, babe? I wasn't expecting you home for another couple hours. I was just heading out to the gym."

"I finished up a little earlier than I expected. But you go on ahead sweetheart. I have some research I want to do without your sexy distraction."

Mike replied, "Okay, you sure you don't mind? I could always just get naked and parade around the place for a while."

"Tempting indeed, but no, my hunky Adonis. Go get your workout in. I've got a few things I want to work on. Can I take a rain check for later?"

Mike could see she was anxious about something and told her, "Okay, double-O-seven, your loss. I'll leave you to your research. By the way, you might be cashing that rain check in very soon. Looks like a storm is brewing."

"I don't see a cloud in the sky."

With a suggestive and erotic grin, Mike said, "I'm talking about the storm that's brewing in my shorts."

"Hmmm, that sounds good. I'll fill you in about my research when you get home. Go on now! Be safe, I love you."

Mike laughed and said, "I love you too," as he left for the gym.

Meredith immediately jumped on the computer and began her research. She discovered that the home was indeed being held in trust for a private, unnamed foundation that had been started by a strange young woman, Adrianna Sable, several years prior. After the mysterious disappearance of her family, she started an obscure religious sect. It would seem that the extravagant home served as the headquarters for the group while she was alive. She was an apparent recluse, and few outside of her followers ever had contact with her. In 1994, Adrianna, like her family, disappeared and the house had remained unoccupied since, maintained by the trust she had established. Per the directions in the will, the home had recently been completely renovated and updated to make it palatable for the prospective new owners.

Meredith searched the county clerk's records and discovered that it was the first house built in the Mossy Hammock subdivision in 1986. It was built by Philip and Phyllis Seymour. They died together under mysterious circumstances, and the house was willed to their only daughter and her family. Apparently, the family had moved in shortly after that. Then the records became a bit more obscure. They indicated that in 1992, the new owner on record was Adrianna. The house was put into a trust with the unnamed religious organization as the beneficiary of its ultimate sale. After two hours on the computer, and following all the leads in the information provided by Mr. Haines, Meredith was convinced that it seemed completely legitimate.

"So, this Adrianna was a religious nut. Who cares? How can we walk away from this incredible deal?"

Thinking he would never answer on a Saturday, Meredith placed a call to the attorney on the card. To her surprise, he answered.

A raspy voice on the other end spoke, "Hello?"

"Yes, hello, is this Mr. Abaddonus?"

"Speaking."

"Good afternoon, sir. My name is Meredith Carson. I'm calling about the residence for sale in Mossy Hammock."

"Oh yes, Mrs. Carson. My associate Mr. Haines informed me that you'd probably be calling. Frankly, I was surprised you waited so long to call. From what I understand, you were quite excited about the house."

"Well, I definitely am interested, but of course I have my reservations. I want to tell you I know a thing or two about the law . . ."

"Oh yes, Mrs. Carson. I'm quite familiar with your reputation.

I've been in practice for what seems like an eternity now."

"Really? I'm not familiar with your work."

"Well, I do like to avoid the courtrooms. I do my best work behind the scenes. Being an estate attorney, I deal primarily with the affairs of the afterlife, as most of my clients are deceased."

"Well, I can understand desiring anonymity. Sometimes I wish I could exchange my life for a quieter life."

"Based on what I know, I can safely say your life is going to change drastically very soon, Mrs. Carson."

"That almost sounds foreboding, Mr. Abaddonus."

"Oh Mrs. Carson, don't read too much into it. I believe you were asking about the house?"

"Yes. Well anyway, I'm sure you can understand my reservations regarding the too good to be true appearance of this situation."

"I understand perfectly Mrs. Carson, but rest assured it is one hundred percent real. After my client, Ms. Sable, disappeared in 1994, her trust provided specific instructions that the house would not be sold until the year 2010, when one fortunate recipient would be chosen by a representative and myself to surrender the home for a well below market price. From everything I know about you and your husband, I have to agree with Mr. Haines' endorsement. I believe you are the perfect couple. I have no doubts that my client would be very happy."

"Thank you for taking time out of your day to talk to me, Mr.

Abaddonus. I look forward to speaking to you again soon."
"Anytime, day or night, Mrs. Carson. I never sleep," he quipped.

"I understand what you mean. I often feel that way myself—not enough time in a day."

"Especially true in my field of expertise. My work is neverending. We'll talk again soon."

"Good day, Mr. Abaddonus, and thank you again."

When Mike came home from the gym, Meredith had just finished her research. When he walked in the door, she rushed up and hugged him.

"Perfect timing as usual, Mr. Wonderful. Have I got a surprise for you! Today on my way home, I . . . "

Meredith went on to explain all that had happened, how she had toured the home and all the inquiries she had made.

Mike was understandably pessimistic and told her, "It sounds way too good to be true. I'll have to see it to believe it."

"I was the same way honey, but I've been on the computer and the phone the whole time you were gone, and so far, it all checks out. I even spoke to the attorney handling the estate, Mr. Abaddonus, and he verified my research."

That evening, Meredith enthusiastically called Mr. Haines.

"I'm sorry for calling at this time on the weekend Mr. Haines, but I've completed my research and I wanted to let you know that

my husband would like to take a look at the house."

Sam replied, "Of course, of course, I would expect nothing less. If you two are free tomorrow, I can meet you at the house. I'll let the guard know you're coming and to let you in. How does noon work for you? I like to sleep in on Sunday. Never been much of a churchgoer myself."

"Yes, noon works for us."

"Okay then, I'll see you tomorrow at noon."

"Thank you, Mr. Haines. We'll be there."

The next day at noon, as they approached the guard shack, Meredith recalled the incident that had happened the day before with the crotchety old guard. This time, however, as she approached, she saw a different guard who just waved her through the open gate without ever stopping to ask her who she was. She couldn't make out any of his features from behind the tinted window of the guard shack.

She said to Mike, "That's odd. I guess Sam must have given a good description of me."

Mike answered her and said, "That is odd. They would always stop me, even in my patrol car. I always liked this neighborhood. I never imagined we'd be looking at a house in here. I still say there's something off about this whole deal."

As they approached the house, Mike appeared to be taken aback by just what an impressive home it was.

"Are you sure this is the place? I expected something altogether different. This is completely changed from the house I remember years ago when I was patrolling the neighborhood. Very nice indeed."

Meredith gleefully responded, "My words couldn't do it justice. I'm starting to get a little excited again."

"Well, honey, we've had our hopes dashed several times already with every other house deal. Let's not let them get up too quickly.

Let's just take it one step at a time."

Meredith dejectedly answered, "I know. You're right, sweetheart."

They were greeted at the door by Sam, who introduced himself to Mike. "Sam Haines. Nice to meet you, Mr. Carson."

Mike shook his hand, "Mr. Haines."

"Sam. Please call me Sam."

"Okay, Sam. My wife has brought me up to speed on everything regarding this house. I must say, even after her confirmation, I'm

still very skeptical as to the validity of this scenario."

"Understandable, sir. Can I show you folks around?" Sam asked.

Without delay, Mike answered, "If it's all the same to you, can we just look around for a bit on our own?"

"Oh, by all means. I'll be down here should you have any questions."

Meredith said, "C'mon sweetheart, let's start upstairs."

As Mike and Meredith ascended the double winder staircase, he whispered, "That guy freaks me out. Could he be any more of a sleazy used car salesman? Maybe it's his leering eyes, his icy touch when we shook hands, or maybe the disingenuous tone of his voice, but it gave me the chills when he spoke. I haven't experienced anything like that since my investigation days, with those terrible investigations and those murdered babies."

Meredith could see Mike was slipping back into the nightmares of the past and quickly made light of the situation. "I bet ya a million bucks he couldn't tell you the color of my eyes."

Mike snapped out of it and remarked, "Yeah, but he probably knows the color, size and designer of your bra."

Meredith laughed, "Oh, stop it! He'll hear you!"

"And what's with all those rings? And that suit? And he smells like a cattle ranch covered by cheap cologne!"

The two laughed as Meredith slapped his arm, "You're too much." They continued their lighthearted banter up to the top of the stairs.

When they got to the top Meredith said, "Let's look at the baby's room. Wouldn't this be a perfect nursery? It's right next to the master bedroom."

"Yeah, this would be perfect." As they entered the room, Mike's blood ran cold when he felt an eerily familiar sensation of warm breath across the back of his neck, and a rushing sound like the haunting legion of voices from the past. "Mmmmiiichaellll." Mike froze.

Meredith asked, "Honey? Are you okay?"

He snapped to and replied, "Huh? Yeah, I'm good. Sorry, just another blast from the past. I'm okay now."

As Meredith continued the expedition through the vast estate home, she was more excited about this house than any of the other houses that they had previously looked at.

At the end of the tour, Sam asked, "Well, Mr. Carson? What do you think of our humble abode?"

"I think if it's legitimate, we just might have a deal."

Meredith squealed with glee, then hugged and kissed Mike. "I love you, love you, love you!!!"

Dr. Stark listened intently as Meredith then jumped ahead three months, to February 2011, when they were meeting at Mammon's office for the final signing of the paperwork.

Mammon said, "Congratulations. I knew everything was going to work out for you two."

Meredith proclaimed, "Oh Mr. Abaddonus, I can't thank you enough for all you've done for us."

"I just have a few documents I need to have you sign to finalize the deal."

"Of course, the paperwork," Mike stated. "Have to keep everything legal, right?"

"Especially in a room full of lawyers," Meredith touted.

Jokingly, Mike said, "All this paperwork! Feels like I'm signing my life away."

Smirking, Mammon avowed, "So it would seem, Mr. Carson. So, it would seem."

Mammon went on, "And one last document, I'll need each of you to sign concerning the final condition to the will. If at any time during the first five years, and if for any reason during this time you should abandon the property, there's a

*clause of first refusal which allows the estate to buy the house
back at the original sale price from the bank, regardless of the
home's current market value. Beyond that five years, your legal
obligations to this estate will cease and the home will be yours
to do with as you will."*

From across the room, Meredith heard a comforting voice
say, "Okay Meredith, I'm going to count backwards from ten,
and when I get to one, you'll awake, feeling refreshed and
better than before, with full recollection of everything that
happened. Ten . . . nine . . . eight . . . seven . . ."

When Meredith awoke, she had a contented smile on her
face.

"How do you feel, Meredith?"

"I feel good."

"That sounded like a very happy time in your life."

"Yes, that was a very happy time. We really love our
house. Mike's always telling me he can't believe how lucky we
were to have found it. It's so perfect. He always says it feels
like we must have made a deal with the devil."

"Well, I think we made some good headway today."

For the next hour, as they waited for Rebecca to return
from Mike's service, Yvonne kept the conversation light. She
had come to really care about Meredith and truly wanted a
positive outcome for her.

Rebecca arrived and Yvonne asked to speak with her alone.

"We made some good progress today. Try not to talk about
Mike unless she brings it up, and even if she does, don't go into
detail. She's still in denial and not ready to deal with the horror
of what she witnessed. We have a long way to go before she's
ready to confront his death, but she's stronger than she seems.

I'm sure we can help her. I scheduled her for a one o'clock appointment on Friday. Can you have her here then?"

Rebecca said, "I will, Doctor. Thank you."

"Rebecca, we've known each other long enough now. Please, call me Yvonne. I really do want what's best for Meredith."

"Thank you, Yvonne."

Yvonne turned to her patient. "Okay Meredith, I want you to go home and get some rest. I'll see you Friday."

THE TRUTH HURTS

That evening after dinner, Meredith was sitting in the living room with Henry and Rebecca.

Somberly, Meredith inquired, "So how was the service?"

Rebecca and Henry glanced at each other. Henry shrugged his shoulders and Rebecca told her, "It was respectful and in good taste."

"How is Nancy? I miss her."

Henry said, "She's doing as well as can be expected. She's worried about you, though. If you're up for it, maybe we can have her over tomorrow night for dinner."

Rebecca changed the topic and said, "Cynthia asked for you."

Meredith perked up. "Cynthia? Oh, my goodness, she made it to the service? How is she?"

"Yes, her younger brother brought her. Peter, isn't it?"

"Yes, Peter. He's so sweet."

"He certainly is. Anyhow, he brought her in that new van she got. I understand that after a little more therapy, she'll be able to drive it on her own with the hand controls. She misses you. She really wants to talk with you. You two have always been there for each other, and she feels sort of left out."

"Maybe I'll give her a call tonight."

Rebecca said, "I think that would be nice. I know she would love it, but only if you're up to it." Rebecca had forewarned Cynthia not to bring the subject of Mike up unless Meredith brought it up first.

Later that evening while upstairs in her old room, Meredith nervously called Cynthia on the phone.

On the other end of the line, a feeble yet familiar voice answered,

"Hello?"

"Cynthia? Hi, it's Meredith."

"Oh, hi Merry. How are you feeling? I'm so sorry I haven't been there for you through all you've been through."

Meredith expressed, "Don't you mean what we've been through?"

"Yes, what we've been through. I miss you, girl! You were there for me all along after the accident. I hope you know I'm here for you too, sweetheart."

"I know that, Cynthia. I'm sorry I haven't called you till now."

"Honey, you have no reason to apologize. I know what you're going through. I didn't want to talk right away either. When you're ready, we'll talk more. Just know I'm always here for you. I'm sorry I couldn't be there physically by your side, but I'm still trying to get used to this damn wheelchair."

"Ugh, I can't believe what we have been through this past year."

"We're gonna get through this together, Merry. I promise you we will."

"Thank you, Cynthia. I love you. I'll call you in the morning?"

"You call me anytime, day or night, just like I did to you. I love you too."

Meredith had trouble falling asleep. She went and talked to Henry, who gave her a sleeping pill to help her relax. She drifted into a deep sleep . . .

She suddenly found herself in her living room . . . Mike's there, too. The phone rings.

Mike answers the phone. From across the room, Meredith hears a thunderous voice from the phone yell out, "What's up, douche bag!?"

Mike is laughing and yells, "MOOSE!!"

Meredith laughs and listens to the conversation.

"Yeah, of course she's here . . . okay, hold on. I'll put her on. Honey,

Frank wants to talk to both of us. Grab the extension."

Meredith picks up the phone, "Hi, Frankie."

"Merry! How the hell are ya, sweetheart?"

"I'm good Frankie, how are you?"

"If I was any better, honey, I'd be in heaven! How's the new house?"

"We love it, Frankie. In fact, it feels like we're in heaven here."

Mike concurs, "I have to admit that despite all the early skepticism,

Meredith really pulled this one off. What a great house and neighborhood." Meredith asks, "How's Cynthia? I haven't been able to get hold of her in a few days."

"And what makes you think I would know anything about Cynthia?"

"Frank, did you forget she's my best friend? She tells me everything."

Frank laughs, "FYI, you're on speaker phone."

Suddenly, from the background they hear, "Not everything!"

"Oh my God, Cynthia? What are you guys up to?"

"We're coming down for a visit."

Frank chimes in, "Yeah, and we'd be making better time if I wasn't stuck behind this damn moving truck that's in my way."

Meredith asks, "Cynthia Sanders, why didn't you tell me you were coming?"

"Actually, it's Cynthia Peterson now."

"Huh? Wait, WHAT?! AAAAAAHHHHH, ARE YOU FREAKIN'

KIDDING ME?!"

Mike laughs and yells, "WHOA! MY BEST FRIEND IS MARRIED!?"

Meredith shouts, "I CAN'T BELIEVE IT, WHY DIDN'T YOU GUYS

SAY ANYTHING?"

Frank replies, "We wanted it to be a surprise. So, are you surprised?"

Mike says, "I think it's safe to say we're both blown away. We're so happy for you guys! This is indeed a great surprise."

Frank says, "The surprises aren't over, my buddies. I hope you're sitting down. Douche Bag, do you remember when I came down in

March?"

"Yeah, of course."

"Remember that house down the street that was for sale?"

"Yeah."

"Have you noticed that the 'for sale' sign is missing?"

Meredith shouts, "NO WAY!"

"Well, Cynthia and I are the new proud owners of 2450 Red Oak

Circle, at the end of your street."

Cynthia added, "Frankie bought it as a wedding present. He said I won't ever have to work again if I don't want, so we're on our way to Florida. Besides, he said if we're going to be godparents we need to be closer to the baby."

Meredith, now crying, replies, "I'm so excited. Our lives will go from dreamy to perfect with you two here with us. Now when you guys start your family, our kids can grow up together."

Frank starts to tell about their plans. "We're just about two hours away, just outside of Tampa now. We're going to take a cruise next week for our honeymoon. I know how much you guys enjoyed yours when you finally got to it. So we just wanted to say we . . . "

In the background, Mike and Meredith heard a scream. "FRANK, LOOK OUT! NOOOOO!" followed by a horrible crashing sound, then total silence. Over the open line, they hear the squealing of tires and other people's voices crying out, "Call 911!" Then, "He has no pulse. I can't get him out, he's trapped."

Mike cries out, "FRANK!"

Simultaneously, Meredith cries, "CYNTHIA!"

No response. After several minutes, the phone line becomes disconnected.

After repeated attempts at calling both Cynthia and Frank, they still get no answer.

Several hours pass by, and still no response from either of them. Mike and Meredith are consoling each other, fearing something terrible has happened to their closest friends. At six o'clock, Mike turns on the evening news.

"Topping tonight's headlines, I-75 just south of Tampa is completely shut down due to a major vehicle crash. Fox's own Joshua Billing is on the scene of this tragic accident. Joshua?"

"That's right Monty, the scene here is horrific. It would seem that a tractor trailer lost control and crossed over the median, striking several vehicles, including a large moving van . . . "

Stunned, Mike and Meredith are watching the television. Footage shows household items strewn all over the highway from the overturned moving van.

" . . . Also, before coming to a rest, the tractor trailer collided head-on with an SUV. It is confirmed that the driver of the SUV was killed on impact . . . "

Mike collapses to his knees, wailing bitterly; he recognizes Frank's SUV. The overhead shot from the hovering helicopter shows the remnants of a large black SUV. The impact with the enormous tractor trailer caused the front end of the vehicle to be pushed all the way into the passenger compartment. The wind causes the white and now red blanket hanging from the driver's door window to blow back. While the camera is unnecessarily zooming in for a close up of the tragedy, a large, bloody arm is revealed with a barely visible gold band on the ring finger glistening in the sunlight. On the ground is a large pool of blood mixed with vehicle fluids, metal and broken glass.

Meredith is hugging Mike and crying hysterically as they watch the horrifying images unfold before their eyes.

" . . . The passenger, a young woman, was airlifted to the trauma center after being ejected. The driver of the tractor trailer was transported to the hospital by ground.

"I spoke with the FHP trooper investigating the crash, who advised that they are waiting to contact family members before any more information would be released.

"With me now is Amir Micpani, driver of the moving van. Amir, what can you tell us about the crash? I understand you were moving for the couple in the SUV, is that correct?

"Yes, that is right. I feel so bad for them. They were newlyweds and after they moved into their new home, they were supposed to start their honeymoon. This is the worst thing I've ever seen. They were so nice. "

"So, very tragic news out here on the interstate. Back to the studio. " Meredith woke up screaming, "NO, NO, NO! FRANK, NO!"

Henry and Rebecca rushed in. Rebecca cradled the inconsolable

Meredith. "Shhh, it's okay sweetheart, it's okay."

Meredith cried, "I need to talk to Cynthia."

"Are you sure, honey? It's very late."

"Mom, please! I need to hear her voice!"

"Okay, let me get your phone honey, hold on."

Meredith called Cynthia, and they talked long into the wee hours of the morning.

The next afternoon, Rebecca was disclosing to Dr. Stark about the bad night Meredith had. She explained about the accident and the loss of Frank. Yvonne had not been aware of that until that moment.

"I see. I know I had her scheduled for next Friday, but can you get her here on Monday morning at nine?"

"Of course, Yvonne, thank you."

"I would love to address that today, but we're in West Palm. I hope this doesn't set her back. Okay, let me get started with her on Monday. I'm going to reschedule my ten o'clock to give us a little extra time."

"Thank you, Yvonne."

On Monday morning, Dr. Stark greeted Meredith warmly. "Well Meredith, I understand you had a rough night on Friday night. Can you tell me what happened?"

Meredith explained that she'd had a dream, but this dream was real, a living nightmare. She relived the terribly tragic event that had killed Mike's best friend Frank and paralyzed Cynthia from the waist down.

As she was reviewing the tragic events, Meredith became more upset. Yvonne decided it would be a good time to try hypnotherapy again.

"Okay Meredith, I want you to relax . . . "

Yvonne spent the rest of the session helping Meredith deal with the tragedy of Frank and Cynthia's accident that was upsetting her so.

"Okay Meredith, I'm going to count backwards from ten. When I get to one, you'll awake, feeling refreshed and better than before, with full recollection of everything that happened. Ten . . . nine . . . eight . . . sev . . . "

Meredith woke up and Yvonne asked, "How are you feeling, hon?"

"I'm feeling better."

"Do you recall everything?"

"Yes, Doctor."

"Okay. I want you to go home and relax. Doctor's orders!"

Meredith stated, "I believe my parents are going to have Cynthia and Nancy over for dinner. They were going to have them over on

Saturday, but decided that tonight would be better."

"How do you feel about that?"

"I'm scared, but glad at the same time."

"I believe that will be therapeutic for all of you. How is Cynthia handling her loss?"

"Better than I am. She's very strong."

"I'm glad you're reconnecting with Cynthia and Nancy. Don't be afraid to open up to them. Remember, everyone is feeling similar pain as well. You're not alone. It's okay to share your feelings with each other. They need you as much as you need them now."

"Thank you, doctor."

"Okay, then. I still want to see you on Friday. Is that good for you?"

"That would be fine. Thanks again for all your help."

"It's no problem. I'm glad we're making some progress. Have fun tonight."

Later that evening, Meredith was sitting on the couch when she heard a knock on the door.

Henry called out, "I got it!"

It was Nancy. Henry answered the door and the two hugged.

Nancy asked, "How's Meredith?"

"Doctor Stark says she's making good progress. How are you doing, pretty lady?"

"I'm still in shock. I can't believe my sweet Michael is gone." Nancy began to sob and Henry hugged her tightly, reassuring her that they were there for her as well.

He comforted her by saying, "We'll get through this together as a family, hon."

"Thank you, Henry. Can I see her?"

"Yes, yes of course. She's in the living room."

Nancy entered the living room carrying a small gift bag. Meredith jumped up and ran toward her. The two embraced and wept in each other's arms for several minutes.

Nancy declared, "Come, dear, let's sit down. I have something for you."

Nancy handed Meredith the gift bag.

"What's this?"

"Open it and see."

Inside, Meredith found a gold heart-shaped locket. Inside was a picture of Mike on one side and Meredith on the other.

"It's beautiful. Thank you, Nancy."

"It's very old. It belonged to my great grandmother. It has been passed down ever since. My mother gave it to me after Big Mike was taken from me, with a picture of him inside. It has helped me through the past several years. You can keep Mikey close to your heart. I want you to have it."

"I love you, Mom, and I love the locket, thank you. I'll cherish it forever."

"I know you will, sweetheart. I love you too."

Henry was listening in from the other room. Smiling, he then went into the kitchen with Rebecca.

"I think she's going to be okay. She and Nancy are having a nice talk."

"They both have been through so much," Rebecca said. "What time did you ask Cynthia to be here?"

"She'll be here in about an hour. I wanted Nancy and Meredith to have some time to catch up."

"Good idea. So, what's on the menu?"

"Honestly Henry, you and your stomach."

"Hey, a man's gotta eat."

In the living room, Nancy and Meredith continued their conversation.

"But Nancy, now I won't have a daughter to pass it on to."

"Then it's yours to do with as you wish. You're my daughter now, and it's yours. I pray it helps you as much as it has me." After about an hour, the doorbell rang.

Henry came rushing out, "Don't get up, I got it!" It was Cynthia. Her brother Peter had driven her over.

"Peter, won't you stay for dinner?"

"Thanks, but no, I have some things I have to do. Besides, I don't want to overwhelm Meredith. I'll talk to her tomorrow when I pick up Cynthia."

"Okay Pete, thank you for driving her."

"It's my pleasure. She's close to driving on her own. She's getting really good with those hand controls. Cindy, call me tomorrow when you want me to come get you."

"I will. Thank you, Pete."

Henry helped Cynthia inside. Their house was not exactly wheelchair friendly. Cynthia motored into the living room with her electric wheelchair. Meredith jumped up from the couch and ran over to her yelling, "Cynthia!" She hugged her best friend for several minutes.

Henry went up to Nancy, "Why don't we let these two catch up?

We'll keep Rebecca company and let those two talk." Smiling, Nancy answered, "Good idea." Henry and Rebecca left the room.

Cynthia asked, "Are you sure you don't mind me spending the night?"

"Oh Cynthia, no. I'm so happy to see you. Please forgive me for being so distant the past few weeks."

"Oh Merry, I love you. You don't owe me an apology. I'm here for you now, and for as long as you want me."

About thirty minutes passed, and from the other room Rebecca called out, "Who's hungry?"

Cynthia told Meredith, "I'm actually starving."

"Then let's go eat. Can't let my bestie starve."

That evening at the dinner table, Meredith seemed content for the first time since Mike's death. She was able to laugh and smile with her family surrounding her. Rebecca and Henry avoided the topic of Mike's passing and kept the conversation light.

After dinner, Henry and Rebecca talked to Nancy privately.

"So, Rebecca and I we were wondering, why don't you consider moving to Florida? We hate the idea of you being alone all the way up in Kentucky."

"I've been considering it for some time, but haven't given it any more thought since all this happened."

Rebecca said, "Well, we would love it if you moved down. The weather is great. It's a little hot in the summer, but beautiful in the winter."

"I do dread the snow."

"We would want you to stay with us until you found a place of your own."

"I couldn't impose."

Henry said, "We're family, sweetheart. It's no imposition. You could sell your house and pay cash for something down here. There are a few nice homes for sale in the neighborhood."

"I may do just that. But for now, I'm going back to the hotel and get some rest."

"We'll see you for lunch tomorrow then?"

"I'll be here."

Later that night in the downstairs guest room, Meredith and Cynthia were talking like old times.

"Merry, how are you doing? For real."

Seriously, Meredith answered, "I can't stop thinking about everything that's happened. Things were going so well, right up to the time we moved into that house. After that, strange things started occurring . . . "

It was quite late, and Meredith had taken one of the sleeping pills Henry had given her. As she talked, she drifted to sleep, and she started to dream about the time when she and Mike moved into the house.

She was transported back to the first day in the new house.

"Well, this is it, honey. We're home."

Mike picked her up and carried her across the threshold.

Meredith declared, "I love our life. Can things get any better than this?"

"As long as we're together, it can only get better, my love. Every day with you is better than the day before. I love you so much."

The two kissed, and suddenly the power went out. Mike laughed, "Seems someone doesn't agree. I'll go find the breaker panel and reset it."

Mike came back after a few minutes. "Huh, that's strange. The panel was fine."

He looked across the street and the power seemed to be on there. Shortly afterward, their power came back on.

Meredith said, "That's weird. I hope that doesn't keep happening."

"Probably a power surge or something."

That night, Meredith and Mike made love. It was a very special time for both of them. They could now start working on their long-awaited family.

Two weeks passed, and Meredith missed her period. Without saying anything to Mike, she bought a home pregnancy test. She couldn't wait to get home and went into the pharmacy's restroom. From inside the stall, a happy shout was heard. An elderly woman was washing her hands and asked, "Is everything okay, dear?"

Meredith responded, "Oh yes, ma'am. Everything is perfect!"

When Mike came home after working late at the office, he walked in and found the lights dimmed and candles lit throughout the house.

Meredith could hear Mike calling out, "Merry, honey? Where are you?" She left a note on the kitchen counter that read: Meet me upstairs. I'm waiting for you.

She could hear Mike running up the stairs. He burst through the double doors of the master bedroom. Meredith was waiting for him in bed, wearing a sleek, red negligée with lace along the bosom. Mike immediately started taking off his clothes. "Baby making time?"

Meredith smiled seductively. "You're too late for that, you horny little devil."

Mike was so excited that her words didn't register with him right away. He jumped onto the bed, and as he was kissing her he abruptly stopped. "Wait . . . what? Too late? How could I be too late?"

Meredith laughed. She reached under her pillow to reveal a white plastic stick. At the end of the stick was a window with a pink plus sign.

Meredith said, "Too late for baby making. You did that already. I thought that tonight we would celebrate."

Mike leapt from the bed and screamed, "WE DID IT!? MY BOYS DID THEIR JOB!? I'M GONNA BE A DADDY!"

"You're going to be a daddy, all right. But for right now, you're my daddy. Come here and help me celebrate, my gorgeous man!"

In her dream, Meredith then fast-forwarded four months and everything seemed to be going perfectly.

She was starting to show her belly and Mike was a proud, happy father-to-be. The nursery was already decorated in neutral colors. They had spent countless nights mulling over names for boys and girls. Meredith was happy with naming a boy Mike, and Michelle if it was a girl, but Mike said it was too common of a name. He wanted his son or daughter to have an uncommon name that would stand out. Eventually, they settled on the Nordic spelling for Mike, Mikael if it was a boy and Mikaela if it was a girl. It would be a good compromise for both of them.

One afternoon, they were at the obstetrician's office for an ultrasound. The technician applied the gel to Meredith's belly and probed around with the sensor until she got the best view.

"Well, have you folks decided if you want to know yet? Or do you want it to be a surprise?"

In unison, Mike and Meredith said, "Tell us!"

Mike was holding Meredith's hand when the technician asked, "Ready?"

Meredith squeezed her husband's hand tightly when they heard, "It's a boy!"

Mike shouted out, "Woohoo! A boy! Mikael it is, then." He was so excited.

Afterwards, Mike drove Meredith home and returned to the office to finish prepping for an upcoming case. When he returned home that evening, he surprised her with some blue flowers, blue balloons and a box of candy.

Meredith heard Mike call from downstairs, "Honey, I'm home!"

She ran out of the bedroom, and as she headed toward the stairs, she replied, "I'm here, darling. I'll be right down!"

As she neared the top of the stairs, she thought she heard an angry voice whisper from behind her, "He's mine, you whore!"

Suddenly, she felt a push from behind and tumbled down the stairs. Meredith let out a scream as she fell belly first, coming to a stop on the middle landing, lying face down. Mike hurried to her, "HONEY! OH MY GOD,

NO! HONEY, ARE YOU OKAY?!"

Confused, she said, "M-my belly hurts so bad."

Mike looked down and could see that her white pants were now saturated with blood.

"I'm calling 911. Just stay right there honey, don't move."

Mike got his cell phone and returned to her. "Yes, I need an ambulance sent to 2701 Red Oak Circle . . . yes, it's my wife. She fell down the stairs and now she's bleeding badly . . . I think from her vagina. She's also saying her belly hurts very badly. She's four months pregnant and she seems confused. PLEASE HURRY!"

Ten minutes later, an ambulance pulled up and Meredith was rushed to the hospital. Mike was by her side when the doctor came in and broke the bad news to them.

"It appears that you have suffered a mild concussion."

Mike said jokingly, "That's not so bad. I've had many concussions in my day."

"I'm afraid there's more. Please accept my condolences, but you have also lost the baby. I'll need you to stay overnight for observation."

Meredith looked up at Mike and cried, "I'm so sorry, honey. This is all my fault. Mikael . . . oh my God, honey, please forgive me!"

"This is not your fault." Mike hugged her tightly as he wept with her.

"Will she be okay, doctor?"

"I see no reason to expect anything less than a speedy recovery."

Meredith suddenly awoke from the dream. She had been crying in her sleep. She awoke to see Cynthia lying next to her in the queen-sized bed.

"Are you okay, Merry?"

"I'm sorry if I woke you, Cynthia. You've been through so much. I feel guilty for carrying on like this."

"My poor Merry, don't think twice about it. You were talking about Mike and fell asleep. I didn't want to wake you. You've listened to me go on and on after Frank died. I'm here for you, sweetheart. I'm confused about your fall. You were talking in your sleep and mentioned something about being pushed?"

"I did?"

"Yes, you did. You also said you heard a voice before you were pushed."

"I don't remember. I get these bizarre dreams lately. I don't recall them most of the time. I'm sure the fall was just an accident, my own stupidity. Oh Cindy, this is more than my heart can handle. Frankie, your accident, my precious husband and baby, all within a few months. I don't think I can take it!"

"Merry, you and I are going to make it. The boys would want us to. We'll do it for them."

"Thank you, Cynthia. I'm so glad you're here tonight."

"I'll always be here for you, hon."

"And I for you."

The rest of the night was spent reminiscing about old times. Cynthia kept the conversation lighthearted. Henry and Rebecca would occasionally hear giggling from downstairs.

"It's good to hear her laugh again. I'm glad you thought of having everyone over tonight. It was good for her. I guess mother does know best."

"Well, Dr. Know-It-All, you may know the body, but I know my little girl. My heart is still broken for her."

"Mine too, my love."

Eventually, everyone in the house fell asleep.

FACING THE PAIN

That Friday, Meredith met with Doctor Yvonne Stark again.

"Okay Meredith, today I think we're going to start addressing some tough issues. We've made a lot of progress. The last time we talked about the loss of Frank, and your friend Cynthia's terrible injuries. How did your dinner go the other night?"

"It was wonderful. You were right, doctor. Seeing Nancy and Cynthia again helped me a lot."

"I'm glad to hear that. Today, I want to start delving a little deeper into you and Mike. How do you feel about that?"

Meredith's eyes watered, and Yvonne decided it was best to utilize hypnosis once again to help her to relax.

Once Meredith was relaxed, Yvonne asked her to go back to a time after they had moved into the house.

"We were home in bed the first night after coming home from my accident, and I awoke to the sound of a baby crying...."

It sounded to Meredith like it was coming from the nursery. She got up to investigate. Her hands were trembling as she reached for the door knob. When she opened the door, she suddenly heard a woman screech, "He's mine now, bitch!!!" and the door slammed shut, hitting her hand in the process. Meredith screamed in horror.

Mike came running to her. "Honey, are you okay? What happened?"

Meredith was crying bitterly. "I heard our baby crying, then the woman..."

Bewildered, Mike said, "What woman?"

"I don't know, but she's in that room with our baby."

Mike stood up and opened the door. The room was empty. He turned on the light and showed Meredith. "Honey, the room is empty. I think maybe you were having a bad dream. C'mon, let's go back to bed." Meredith was still visibly shaken as they went back to bed.

She then recounted the tragedy with Frank and Cynthia. She also reviewed the incident when she fell down the stairs.

Yvonne made a special note as she again spoke of being pushed from behind.

Then Meredith went on to talk about other strange occurrences that happened after she got home from the hospital.

Meredith then recalled how the stress of losing Frank and the baby were starting to get to Mike. One night when she couldn't sleep, she was downstairs on the phone with Cynthia, when all of a sudden Mike came into the den.

"Who were you talking to?"

"Cynthia."

"Cynthia? Really? At this hour?"

"Yes Michael, Cynthia! I couldn't sleep. You know I always call her when I can't sleep. Why are you acting this way? I'm going back to bed." Mike just glared at her as she walked past him.

Meredith recalled that over the next several months, Mike's behavior had become more unpredictable. He would regularly accuse her of talking to another man. Meredith would always try to reassure him that there was no one else.

One night when they were arguing, Mike accused her again of cheating on him.

"Who is it? Who are you seeing?"

"What are you talking about, Mike?"

"I know you're seeing someone else. Don't deny it."

Yvonne felt that they were finally getting to the heart of the matter, and she interrupted. "Meredith, I want you to take me to the night Mike died. Remember, you are relaxed and calm. Nothing can harm you. You're safe here."

Meredith skipped ahead in time, recounting that disastrous evening. A couple of weeks had passed since the last fight they'd had, and Mike seemed to be more relaxed and coping with the stress of everything better. They were getting along again, and had not had an argument in quite some time.

Meredith cooked a nice dinner for them, and they watched a movie before going to bed. They had been working a big burglary case together where the evidence was strong against their client. They talked about the case in bed, and kissed before going to sleep. Mike was tossing and turning, and then he woke up, startled.

He turned over, got on top of and straddled Meredith, pushing down on her shoulders with both of his hands. He then started yelling, "WHY DO YOU WANT TO LEAVE ME!!? WHAT DID I DO? I LOVE YOU!! WHY ARE YOU DOING THIS TO ME!!?"

Meredith woke up, terrified. "What are you talking about, Mike? I love you! I'd never leave you!"

Mike had a distant look on his face; he seemed almost possessed. He began pushing down on her shoulders harder. "DON'T LIE TO ME!!!

I HEARD YOU! I HEARD YOU TALKING TO ANOTHER MAN!!!"

"MIKE, GET OFF! LET GO! YOU'RE HURTING ME!" Meredith pushed him off her, jumped out of bed and fled down the stairs. Mike pursued her and they continued fighting on the landing.

"I KNOW YOU'RE SEEING SOMEONE ELSE, BITCH! DON'T YOU FUCKING LIE TO ME!!! I'VE HEARD YOU LATE AT NIGHT TALKING TO HIM!!! I'M NOT STUPID!!!" Meredith grabbed her keys and ran outside.

"WHERE THE FUCK ARE YOU GOING, TO YOUR MAN!!?"

"I'M GOING TO MY PARENTS' HOUSE UNTIL YOU COME TO YOUR SENSES!"

"YOU'RE NOT GONG ANYWHERE, YOU FUCKING CUNT!!!"

Mike grabbed her, picked her up, carried her upstairs and threw her onto the bed.

The argument continued for several minutes, until they suddenly heard the doorbell ring downstairs.

Mike angrily whispered, "It's the fucking cops. You better not say a word. Keep your fucking mouth shut or I'll kill you!"

Meredith was terrified, and trembled in silence with his hand over her mouth.

After lying there for what seemed like an eternity in absolute silence, Mike got up and looked out the window. "They're leaving."

Mike looked at Meredith and could see that she was terrified. Then his countenance changed. "Oh my God, Merry. I'm so sorry. I don't know what's gotten into me."

Mike approached Meredith, and she recoiled in fear.

Mike started crying. "I'm so sorry, honey. I'm such an asshole. You deserve better!" He then left the room.

He closed the bedroom door as he left. Meredith heard the hallway linen closet door open and close, then heard nothing more. She assumed that he had grabbed a blanket to sleep on the sofa, the way he had done on other occasions lately. After spending the next several minutes reviewing Mike's terrifying and bizarre behavior, Meredith remembered his final words as he left the room, "You deserve better." Then she had a foreboding thought as she recalled the other item in the closet, his shotgun. Fearing the worst, Meredith quickly got up to look for Mike.

As she descended the stairs, she could hear Mike sobbing and saying, "I know, you're right. I don't deserve her. She'll be better off without me." Meredith was now running toward the living room, only to discover her worst fears unfolding before her eyes. She saw Mike on the couch silhouetted by the bright moonlight filtering through the large plate glass window, with the muzzle end of the short-barreled shotgun in his mouth and his finger on the trigger.

As she was running toward him to stop him, she simultaneously cried out, "I LOVE YOU! NO, DON'T! OH MY GOD! PLEASE, NO!!!!" as Mike pulled the trigger.

With a bright flash and a deafening explosion, suddenly her husband's headless torso was all that remained on the couch.

In shock, Meredith fell to the floor. Horrified, she got up and ran from the house wearing only her sheer nightie and screaming in terror, "OH MY GOD! OH MY GOD, HE'S DEAD! HE'S DEAD! HELP ME, HELP ME!!!"

From across the street, she heard, "Ma'am, come over to me! Quickly!"

Meredith could see it was a deputy. She instinctively ran toward him. When she got to where he was standing, he grabbed her and pulled her behind the cover of the tree.

Yvonne, quick to get control, snapped her fingers and said, "THREE!"

Meredith opened her eyes and looked at Yvonne. No longer in a trance state, she said, "He actually sat there with the muzzle end of a short-barreled shotgun in his mouth and pulled the trigger." Meredith's voice was flat now, tears streaming as she repeated the story, now fully aware. "It's funny, but my body was running toward him and it was as though I watched myself running to him. I was yelling, '*I love you! Please, please don't. . .*' but it had already happened. I was too late."

Meredith paused a moment, steeling herself as she mentally processed the finale.

"I'll never forget that explosion, or the bright flash in the darkness. When I got closer, I could see he had no head. No head, Yvonne."

Confident that she had heard enough, Yvonne stopped her and said, "Okay, Meredith. Your courage has astounded me. Do you feel amazed at your courage?"

Miserably, she answered, "I don't know, Doctor, but maybe someday I will."

"Meredith, do you understand that none of this was your fault? I believe that Mike had a psychotic break. His actions had nothing to do with you. The events of his life were more than he could handle. From the tragic loss of his father, the nightmarish murder scenes he witnessed, the loss of his best friend Frank, then the loss of the baby, I believe that it all contributed to his break. His delusions, paranoia and manic behavior were evident, as well as severe PTSD. I certainly wish I could have met him and helped him."

Meredith wept. She spoke more about that night and the deputy who was the first responder.

"It all seemed like a dream until now. I can't believe he's gone. Doctor, I would never have left him. I loved him so much."

"I have no doubt that he loved you, but he saw a lot, and unfortunately never properly dealt with it. I'm so sorry for your loss. The good news is I believe that you can begin the grieving process now. You were in denial prior to today. Remember to keep your friends and family close by and we'll continue our sessions for a little while longer, if you're okay with that."

"I am. Thank you so much for everything, Doctor Stark."

"The pleasure is all mine, Meredith. Call me anytime. I'll see you next week on Friday then?"

"Next week will be great."

Rebecca was in the waiting room waiting for Meredith. Rebecca could see that Meredith's countenance had changed and she seemed more aware of reality.

"You look better, honey."

"She's getting there," Yvonne said proudly. "Meredith, would you mind if I fill your mom in on our breakthrough?"

"No, that would be fine."

Yvonne proceeded to tell Rebecca that the grieving process could begin for Meredith now, and that it would actually be therapeutic if she could talk about it with family and friends, but warned that they shouldn't push her too hard.

Rebecca said, "Thank you, Doctor. My husband was right. Your reputation is well-deserved."

"Well, she's a strong young lady. She's seen a lot and has a long way to go for a full recovery, but she's well on her way." Meredith and Rebecca talked all the way home.

Later that afternoon around 5:30, Meredith asked Rebecca,

"Mom, would you mind driving me to the Sheriff's Office?"

"Of course not, honey. What do you need?"

"I want to find that deputy who helped me that night and thank him."

"That's a nice thing to do."

At the Sheriff's Office, Meredith asked, "Would you mind if I went in alone?"

"Not at all, sweetie. I'll be right here. Take your time."

Inside, Meredith went to the front desk and spoke to the clerk.

"Can I help you, ma'am?"

"Yes, I was hoping to speak to Deputy Mike Flaherty."

"I believe he just got here. He starts his shift in a few minutes.

Can I ask who wants to speak to him?"

"Can you please tell him it's Meredith Carson?"

"Of course, Mrs. Carson. You can have a seat. I'll page him."

A few minutes later, the secure lobby door opened, and there stood Mike Flaherty. "Mrs. Carson, how are you? Please come on back. We can talk somewhere private if you wish."

Meredith went back with Mike, and they spoke in the conference room.

"Please have a seat. Can I get you some terrible coffee or some water, perhaps?"

"No thank you, Deputy."

"Mike, just Mike."

"Thank you, Mike."

"So, Mrs. Carson, what brings you by? How can I help you?"

"I just wanted to take a moment to thank you for your kindness that night. My husband used to be a deputy, and I know you don't get to hear 'thank you' very often."

Mike laughed, "Well, that's true, but it was no problem, Mrs. Carson. I actually knew your husband. He was my primary FTO when I first got started. I truly admired him and I actually sort of modeled my career after him. He pushed me to get into better shape. I actually took his place on the SWAT team after he left the Sheriff's Office. He was a great man."

"He was. Thank you for saying so. He loved being a deputy."

"I understand he was quite a lawyer too."

Meredith smiled and said, "That he was."

"I'm sorry for your loss, Mrs. Carson. I was shocked when I found out it was him."

"Thank you, Mike. Please call me Meredith."

He smiled, "Okay, Meredith."

The two talked for over a half hour, reminiscing about Mike. Deputy Flaherty told her stories of things he watched Mike do, and she laughed, saying, "That was him."

"Well, I better let you get to work, Mike. Thank you again for everything and for taking the time to see me."

"No, thank *you* for taking the time to see me. I'm truly sorry for your loss. The entire office feels the loss. He will be sorely missed by

many. Anytime you want to talk, please come by."

Meredith returned to the car and said, "I'm sorry I kept you waiting so long, Mom."

"No problem, my darling. How did it go?"

"Better than I could have hoped. He was as nice as I remembered."

Three months passed. Cynthia had a proposal for Meredith. "Hey girlfriend, I was wondering if you were ready to move out of your parents' house yet."

Meredith said, "Why, what did you have in mind?"

"Well, I would love for my best friend to move in with me. Frank bought us that big house, and it's too much for me . . . plenty of room for one more. In fact, you could have the entire second floor to yourself. I have no use for it. It could be like old times, roomies again."

"Hmmm, that's an interesting proposal. It might be fun. I haven't been back to the neighborhood since all this went down."

"Oh Merry, I'm sorry. I wasn't even thinking about that."

"No, it's fine. I need to move on anyway. I think that would be great. Are you sure I won't be imposing on you?"

"Are you kidding me? This will be so much fun."

That evening, Meredith spoke with her parents about moving in with Cynthia. They both agreed it would be a great idea, but reminded her that her room at home was always there if she needed it.

That Saturday, Meredith was gathering up her belongings and getting ready to move to Cynthia's when Henry called her from downstairs.

"Meredith, you've got a certified letter here."

Meredith came downstairs. "Who's it from?"

"It's from a Mammon Abaddonus, Attorney at Law. Who's that?"

"Really? He's the attorney who handled the sale of the house."

Meredith opened the letter and silently read, "Dear Mrs. Carson, Per the contract that you signed prior to the sale of the home, should you abandon the property for any reason, the foundation, which I represent, has the first right of refusal to reacquire the property at the previous sale price. I have been notified by the bank that, in fact, they have not received any mortgage payments in four months and that they have begun the foreclosure process. This letter will serve notice of the Foundation's intention to reacquire the property. Please call

me if you have any questions. Mammon Abaddonus."

"As if I care!" Meredith crumpled up the paper and threw it to the ground.

Henry asked, "Is everything okay, sweetheart?"

"Yes, Daddy. The bank is foreclosing on the property."

"I'm sorry, dear. We can help get it back if you want."

"No, Daddy, I could never go back there again."

"I understand, but what about your credit?"

"I'll call Mr. Abaddonus tomorrow to discuss it with him."

"Well, I can borrow your uncle's pickup and we can go by the house to retrieve anything you need. One last trip and you'll never have to go there again. Your mom and I will go with you."

"Thank you, Daddy. That would be nice. There isn't much I want from there anyway."

When Meredith and her parents pulled up in front of the house, Henry said, "I'll go in first."

He came out a few minutes later. "It looks good. C'mon, let's get this over with."

A cleaning crew had been to the house months before and removed all evidence of the bloody massacre in the living room. The sofa was gone and the carpet had been replaced. The ceiling had been painted and it looked as if nothing had ever happened in there.

As Meredith entered, she said, "I don't know if I can do this."

"Come on dear," Rebecca said, "we'll take one quick sweep. You just point out anything you want and your father and I will get it for you."

As Rebecca and Meredith went upstairs to the master bedroom, they passed by the nursery. From inside the nursery she could hear the sound of a baby crying and a woman's voice shrieking "GET OUT, BITCH! GET OUT OF MY HOUSE!!!"

She cried, "No, No! I can't do this!" and ran downstairs.

Rebecca followed her. "Honey, what is it?"

"I heard the baby crying, and that woman telling me to get out!"

"I didn't hear anything, honey. We don't have to go back in. Was there anything you wanted from inside?"

"Just my wedding photo albums. Oh, and my wedding dress. I don't want anything else. The house can burn as far as I'm concerned!"

Henry asked, "Where are the albums honey? I'll get them for you."

"Thank you, Daddy. They're in the master bedroom, in the closet on the top shelf. My dress is hanging in there as well."

"Okay. Becca, you stay here with her and I'll go get that stuff." Henry went upstairs and found the photo albums in the closet. He looked inside. Every picture of Meredith and Mike had Meredith's

face scratched out. "What the hell? I can't bring this to her."

Then Henry looked for her wedding dress. He found it still hanging in the plastic preservation bag, but the dress was torn to shreds.

"She's gonna be devastated. I can't tell her about this."

Henry went downstairs, "Honey, I'm sorry. I can't find anything."

Rebecca piped in and said, "As far as the pictures, I have all the wedding photos at the house. We'll put together a new album for you. How does that sound?"

"That sounds good, Mom. Thank you."

"I'm sorry about the dress, honey."

"It's okay. Maybe one of the cleaning crew took it. I suppose it doesn't really matter."

The next day, Meredith moved in with Cynthia. For the two, it felt like their old college days. Meredith was happier than she had been in months.

On Monday, she called Mr. Abaddonus. "Mr. Abaddonus, Meredith Carson."

"Oh yes, Mrs. Carson, I see you received my letter. I was wondering if we could set up a time to have you sign some documents for me."

"What for? What difference does it make?"

"Mrs. Carson, as I explained to you some time ago, I deal with the affairs of the dead for a living. This is nothing new for me. I assure you I only have your best interest at heart. By signing over the house at this point, you can save your credit from ruination and we can avoid all this foreclosure nonsense. You'll walk away free and clear."

"Free and clear? Mr. Abaddonus, this house has cost me everything! But yes, I'll sign your documents if it means my ties to it are forever removed."

"Would this afternoon be too early for you?"

"This afternoon would be just fine."

Meredith met with Mr. Abaddonus in his office.

"And lastly Mrs. Carson, by signing this final document, the house will be transferred back into the Foundation's name and will remain part of the previous benefactor's estate."

Meredith signed the document. "I hope your benefactor will rest easy knowing she has her precious home back."

"I can assure you, she is quite at peace now. Everything has worked out for her."

Perplexed, Meredith responded, "Well, my husband is gone forever. Where's my peace, Mr. Abaddonus?"

With an unnerving smile, Mammon exclaimed, "Mrs. Carson, your peace will come in knowing he will forever be in a better place. Of that, I have no doubt."

Distraught, Meredith stormed out of the office. "Good day, Mr. Abaddonus!"

As she left the thirteenth-floor office, she looked back at the office door. There were no markings on the door except for a sign that read "Office Space for Lease."

An anxious feeling came across her as she scurried to the elevator, never looking back.

The house at 2701 Red Oak Circle would remain vacant for as long as anyone could remember. The house was always meticulously maintained, but no maintenance personnel were ever seen. Rumors would circulate among the neighbors about the house being haunted. Deputies would routinely be called out to investigate sightings of people in the windows and the screams of a man, however, nothing was ever found.

In time, Meredith was able to move forward with her life. She and Cynthia remained roommates and forever friends. The two had endured great tragedies together and had come out the other end fairly intact.

Nancy did finally move to Florida. She became very close to Meredith, Cynthia, Henry and Rebecca. She found a house less than a mile from Henry and Rebecca's, and the three were regularly seen gallivanting around town together.

Meredith never again allowed herself to go anywhere near the house.

THE HEART OF THE MATTER

November 1, 1989. The headlines of the Boca Gazette read:

ELDERLY COUPLE KILLED IN MYSTERIOUS HALLOWEEN CAR CRASH.

At approximately midnight on October 31ˢᵗ, Philip and Phyllis Seymour were on their way home from a charity Halloween ball at the civic center when their 1988 Cadillac appeared to have lost control and struck a tree. No other vehicles were involved. The driver, Philip Seymour, had no known health problems and alcohol is not suspected. Friends and neighbors were shocked and saddened at the news.

Authorities are still investigating.

At the reading of the will, Attorney Mammon Abaddonus was the executor of the Seymour's Estate.

"Mr. and Mrs. Schilling, you are the sole beneficiaries of the Seymour's estate. Mrs. Schilling, your parents were worth approximately five million dollars, not inclusive of their house in Mossy Hammock which is valued at well over one million dollars. The will stipulates that the estate will transfer to your daughter should anything happen to you and your husband."

In January 1990, a moving van pulled up in front of 2701 Red Oak Circle. A young woman and her family were moving in.

Thomas Schilling, his wife Felicia and their daughter moved into the house. They were an unassuming couple and the home was always quiet. They rarely spoke to the neighbors and tended to keep to themselves. The family lived there for approximately two years. Unexpectedly once again, the residents of the home made the local headlines.

October 6, 1992. The Boca Gazette headlines read:

LOCAL COUPLE FEARED AMONG THE DEAD IN FATAL NETHERLANDS PLANE CRASH

Unconfirmed reports that a local couple was visiting relatives in Amsterdam when on October 4th Israeli El Al 747 flight 1862, a cargo plane, crashed into the Bijlmermeer neighborhood of Amsterdam, killing 43 people. Three crew members and one passenger on the plane were killed. As many as 39 people on the ground were killed as well. It is feared that among those killed on the ground were two local residents, Thomas and Felicia Schilling. Dutch authorities are saying it may be impossible to positively identify all of the people on the ground.

November 1992. A troubled young woman received a phone call from Mr. Abaddonus.

"Well, Ms. Schilling . . . "

"My name is Adrianna. Adrianna Sable."

"Oh, forgive me, Priestess."

"How did you know about that, Mr. Abaddonus?"

"I know many things, Ms. Sable. But it would seem that your parents are assumed dead."

"They are, I know they are. They've been dead to me for quite some time now."

"I see. The fact remains that with their assumed demise, you are now to inherit the entire estate. For legal purposes, your name is Schilling, unless of course you would like me to legally change your name to Adrianna Sable."

"If you could do that Mr. Abaddonus, I will be forever in your debt. I want no affiliation with those people again."

"Forever in my debt, you say? You might not realize what you ask, Ms. Sable. Are you sure about that?"

"Mr. Abaddonus, I serve a higher power now. I fear no mortal man. Just make it happen, sir, and you will oversee all my affairs."

"Indeed Ms. Sable, you should fear no mortal man. Consider your request as if it was already done. It is as if it was foreordained. From this day forward, you will be known only as Adrianna Sable."

True to his word, Mr. Abaddonus made all the changes that she had requested. All records of her relation to the Schillings vanished. It was as though they had never existed.

Adrianna Sable, or Priestess Sable as she was known to her followers, began a religious sect called The Moloch Society. They worshipped an ancient God named Moloch. Moloch was worshipped by the ancient Phoenicians and Canaanites to whom they would sacrifice their children by burning them.

October 31st, 1989, Halloween night. It was shortly before midnight and Adrianna was alone in her room, playing with an Ouija Board. What started out as a game had become an obsession. Could she really summon spirits from another realm? She had read several books on summoning demons and had set her room up with a pentagram in the middle of the floor. She placed the Ouija Board on the floor in the center of the pentagram. She had written down a summoning spell from a book she had found on demonology, and recited it aloud while sitting cross-legged on the floor between two black candles.

With her hands on the planchette, she recited the spell. Her intentions were dark and her desire strong, but still she had some doubt as to whether it would work. To her surprise, after several minutes the planchette began to respond to her questions.

"Is there another present in the room with me?"

The planchette, or pointer, moved on its own to "Yes."

Nervously, Adrianna asked, "Do you wish to harm me?"

Again, the pointer moved on its own, this time to "No."

After several minutes, her nervousness changed to excitement. Adrianna asked, "What is your desire of me?"

Slowly, the pointer spelled out one letter at a time. "I"… "W"…"I"…"L"…"L"…"S"…"H"…"O"…"W"…"Y"…" O"…"U"…" M"…"Y"…"C"… "H"…"I"…"L"…"D."

Immediately, Adrianna was standing outside her body. She saw her cross-legged form sitting motionless in the center of the pentagram. Then an ominous voice surrounded her, "Come, witness the magnitude of my reign."

In a flash, Adrianna was standing at the top of a temple in ancient Canaan. She had been transported back thousands of years. At the head of the temple stood a statue of their deity. He towered above the city, with the head of a bull and the body of a man. In a cast metal bull, glowing red from the fire below, a door was opened. A priestess stood with an infant in her arms. She held the baby up to the god, and the crowd grew silent. After a prayer, the priestess dropped the child into the belly of the bull. A short-lived, distressing scream of an infant in torment came from the belly of the beast and the silent crowd of thousands of worshippers erupted into a raucous cheer. They had appeased their god once again. The soul of one innocent for the prosperity of their great city.

"See how the legions worshipped me! I was a powerful god to them. You, my child, will usher in a new epoch of my return to prominence. I am the one known as Moloch. In return for your devoted service, I will grant you your greatest desire."

"Oh, powerful Moloch, I am your humble servant. Do with me as you will. I only ask of you one thing. . ."

"My child, I already know that which you ask before you ask, for I am all powerful. Before this hallowed night ends, you will know that my power is great."

Instantly, Adrianna was once again in her room, standing outside her body. Moloch laid out his ominous plan for her. "You will be my new high priestess. You shall be known as Adrianna Sable."

"Adrianna Sable?"

"Yes child, a name fitting for a Priestess of the Dark."

In the end, she replied, "It is as you wish, oh mighty Moloch."

The next morning, Adrianna was awakened by her mother, Felicia, who was crying. "I have some terrible news, honey. Your grandparents were killed in a car accident in Florida last night just before midnight."

Adrianna sat motionless in her bed, with a slight smirk. She thought to herself, *Your will be done, oh mighty Moloch!*

In January, Adrianna moved into a new home in Florida. The plan had been set in motion. Adrianna would seek out the lost and the indigent to recruit them as followers. She would scour the malls and find wayward young people, many of them already dressed the part—Goths. Willing participants, looking for the social acceptance of their odd behavior and garb. Before long, Adrianna had hundreds of followers. They would meet at a secret location in the woods. They would perform rituals by sacrificing young animals, at first. But the bloodthirsty Moloch would demand a much more satisfying offering.

With her family on vacation out of the country, Adrianna was once again outside of her body in the center of the house.

Moloch spoke to her. "My child, you have done well. But my hunger grows. I must taste the flesh of a young child once again. Your followers are ready. The next phase of my resurrection requires a sacrifice. You will offer yourself to me, after appointing a new priestess. In death, you will rule at my side, more powerful than you could have ever dreamed. You will rule for eternity as my elder in the realm of death with your heart's desire completely fulfilled. Once again, by morning you will witness the power of my sovereignty."

The next day, the news reported a terrible plane crash in the Netherlands. Adrianna was assured in her spirit that her parents were among the dead. A month passed, and she received a phone call from Mr. Abaddonus confirming her parents' death.

Adrianna knew time was growing short. She would seek out and train a new priestess to assume her role. Following the instructions of Moloch, Adrianna retained the services of Mammon Abaddonus to transfer all of her holdings to an estate naming The Moloch Society as the sole beneficiary. The house at 2701 Mossy Hammock became the spiritual center for the cult.

October 30th, 1994. At their camp in the woods, Adrianna addressed her followers. "Tonight, dear ones, we celebrate. Tomorrow, Priestess Aveira Tenebrae will usher me into the dark realm of the netherworld. There, I will assume a position beside our powerful Moloch. I will live for eternity and will guide you from the other side. My physical home is to remain a sacred sanctuary where only the chosen few will enter. My blood will be shed upon the altar and will be forever consecrated as Moloch has willed."

The next night, October 31st. In the living room of the Mossy Hammock home, the new High Priestess and twenty of the most dedicated elders had been selected to gather for the ritual. Tonight would be the night Adrianna would be ushered into immortality.

A tarp lay spread on the living room floor. All the windows were covered with black cloth. A blood-orgy to symbolize the fertility of the priestess and to ensure the future growth of the cult ensued as part of the celebration. The blood of a consecrated bull that had been scarified the night before at the camp was poured upon their naked, writhing bodies as they indulged in every sexual pleasure imaginable, from the benign to the truly heinous. After two hours of the erotic feast, a final ceremony for Adrianna's conscious form took place.

The tarp was removed. With the blood that remained, a large pentagram faced downward was formed on the white tile floor. The time was now at hand. Adrianna, wearing a flowing black gown, willingly lay in the middle of the pentagram with her hands clasped together on her belly.

Priestess Tenebrae lit the black candles at each point of the bloody star. A large clock on the wall would indicate the precise time that Adrianna would be sacrificed. At exactly one second before midnight, the sacred bull horn-handled blade was plunged through her heart. All in attendance solemnly chanted an ancient prayer of sacrifice to Moloch.

A silver chalice collected the thick blood that oozed from Adrianna's chest, and all the cult members present drank of her blood. The thick, viscid lifeblood was sipped from the chalice, and Priestess Tenebrae glugged down the last drop. "It is finished. Our High Priestess is at his side. Moloch's will be done."

All attendees in unison echoed, "Moloch's will be done!"

Within an hour, all evidence of what had occurred in the living room had been removed from the house. The only remnant was the darkened stains where the plasma had impregnated the porous grout lines. If looked at from above, it would reveal the broken pattern shape of the room-sized pentagram.

Adrianna's body was then transported to the sect's camp. There, the remaining members joined the new High Priestess and twenty elders in a celebration to free any vestige of Adrianna's soul trapped in her mortal body by burning her corpse in a ritualistic bonfire. By dawn, there was no remaining evidence of Adrianna except for her ashes.

For the next seven years, the cult continued to grow. Members number in the thousands and are spread across several southern states. New chapters are being established regularly across the country. The members had gone from original outcast teenagers to housewives, college-educated professionals, and even government officials.

Their actual numbers are unknown, as they remain silent and undetected in their activities. No obvious affiliation is detected from one cult-cell to any other across various communities.

It is widely believed among the most devout cultists that Adrianna was Moloch's mother, revered by all as the true High Priestess. The Mossy Hammock home became a holy shrine to followers.

Priestess Tenebrae spent much of her time traveling abroad, spreading the dark gospel. Like Adrianna, Aveira would spend time in dialogue with Moloch and Adrianna while out of her body, receiving her orders.

After several years, Moloch revealed his growing impatience for the taste of an innocent's flesh. In January 2001, Priestess Tenebrae conscripted Jeremy Pickford, an eager young convert, to be the chosen one to abduct the first child for Moloch.

In a private ceremony one early Friday evening, Priestess Tenebrae blessed Jeremy. She baptized Jeremy by pouring the blood of a bull over Jeremy's head.

"Jeremy, you go forth now in the greatest service any mortal man could be asked to perform for his master. A child has been chosen . . . you also have been chosen. Go forth now with Moloch's blessing. Your reward will be great in the afterlife."

Jeremy then traveled two hours north to the home of the chosen child, Suzy Shinner. Though he had been blessed, all would not go as he had expected. The abduction initially was flawless, and while driving back with Suzy tied and gagged with duct tape in the trunk of his Camaro, he was careful to obey all traffic laws. His speed was just slightly above the posted limit, as it was common knowledge that doing the exact speed limit was usually a sign of someone doing something wrong.

Before he left, Jeremy went through his car with a fine-tooth comb. "Oil, check. Tires, check. Radiator level, check. Belts and hoses all look good."

Though he checked his lights, Jeremy could not have predicted that a headlight would burn out that evening. He was almost home. Suzy was still in the trunk. It had been an uneventful journey thus far. Then out of nowhere, "What the fuck? A cop? Why is he pulling me over? He has no reason to stop me."

Jeremy began to panic. He pulled over with the intention of cooperating. It must be something minor. He was fidgeting in his seat and looking back in his mirror. He could see the cop approaching, then stop and talk on his radio. "Where did he go?" He had his chrome .357 magnum in his lap, covered by his shirt.

Jeremy didn't see when the cop changed his approach to the passenger side. With the road noise now stopped and his radio turned down, he suddenly heard some rustling and crying from the trunk. Then Jeremy heard from behind him, "DRIVER! TURN OFF YOUR ENGINE AND SHOW ME YOUR HANDS! DO IT NOW!"

"SHIT, HE KNOWS!" Jeremy brought up his revolver and began pulling the trigger in the direction of the cop. He simultaneously mashed down on the accelerator and sped away as the cop started firing a volley of bullets at his vehicle, breaking out the rear window of his pristine classic muscle car. Jeremy realized that he had been struck in the left shoulder by the cop's bullet. He sensed that he was bleeding badly. Jeremy was driving his car as fast as it could go, but to his dismay the cop was quickly on his ass.

Jeremy thought, *I can't shake this guy! Damn, it's getting hard to breathe!*

He was getting lethargic, and as he attempted a high speed left turn onto Main Street, he lost control of his car. "OH, SHIT!"

Jeremy crashed into a large oak tree. Dazed, but still full of fight, Jeremy exited his destroyed, once classic Camaro and raised his revolver at the cop. The last thing he felt was the sting of multiple bullets entering his chest cavity. He collapsed dead to the ground.

Back at the camp, Priestess Tenebrae was anxiously awaiting Jeremy's return. "He's late. Everyone leave me. I must be alone."

The twenty original elders vacated the shanty and left Aveira alone to consult with their deity. An hour later, the sun was rising and Aveira exited the dilapidated shack.

"Moloch's will be done. Our master has informed me that this was a test of our loyalty. Jeremy is now with the master. We have passed the test and he will soon reveal the time of the consecrated child." The gathering then dispersed.

One year to the day, the second child, Amanda Rollins, was abducted. This time, Moloch's insatiable desire for an innocent's flesh would be fulfilled. Word of the successful sacrifice spread across the country through the cult's vast network of followers.

From that day forward, there have been reports of children being abducted on a regular basis. Most are never seen again. Then, reports of mothers sacrificing their own children began to surface. Moloch's influence was growing, despite the efforts of law enforcement officials to infiltrate the cult.

WHAT ABOUT ME YOU ASK?

As it turns out, what I thought or did had little bearing at all in the end. In your world, justice instills the idea of fairness, equality, impartiality and truth. In the netherworld, I see now it was all a huge lie. My life had been an orchestrated tapestry woven together for one purpose, which I'll get into momentarily.

I mistakenly believed that I was in control of my life. But death has shown me that my life's symphony was scored long ago, before my conception, and now I'm the captive. Don't get me wrong, I had a good life for the most part, better than most—full of the expected ups and downs. My lows, however, were very low, and collectively they became more than I could handle.

My best friend, Frank, was my most feared adversary in middle school, but he turned out to be one of the two best things to ever happen to me. If it wasn't for his taunting and tormenting, I may never have resolved to better myself. After he and I became best friends in high school, my life seemed to be perfect. I was happy, popular and athletic. Moose, as he was known, and I went to college together and played football. It seemed I had it all until that fateful day when my head got crushed by that brutal defense. That was the end of my football career. I never understood how one hit could change everything, until now.

As bad as that career-ending event was, the first real tragedy in my life came the day my mother, Nancy, called me with the horrible news that my father, Big Mike as we all called him, had been murdered by a man he had tried to help. But once again, in time, I came to believe that I was in control of my destiny and that all was working according to my timetable. I would do what I thought was right and not take any money from my mom. I would find a way to pay for school on my own.

Looking for a practical way to pay for college and eventually law school, I found a job as a cop. My search for a cop job led me to beautiful and seemingly quiet Boca Grande Shores in Dolphin County, Florida. Looking back, I should have listened to my instincts to run away and get the hell out of town when I had my first creepy encounter with the afterlife in that hotel room. But I was never one to believe in all that supernatural mumbo jumbo. I did eventually get the job. The pay wasn't great, but they did have tuition reimbursement, which at the time was my main purpose. Plus, they were the only agency hiring at the time. It was a long drive from the university, but with the advent of computers and online schooling, I was able to complete my education.

As it turned out, I really enjoyed being a cop. I excelled at the job and became a detective quicker than anyone else had ever done prior to me. My pride seemed to have gotten the better of me, and once again I felt confident that I was the master of my own destiny. But destiny would reveal the ugly truth in short order.

My firm unbelief in the supernatural would be shaken to the core almost immediately from the time I made detective. For the rest of my days, I would be haunted by all the horrific memories of those innocent children. My tenure as a detective would expose me to multiple horrendous murders. However, the memory of Amanda Rollins and how close I was to saving her, but failed, was especially disturbing to me. The final straw for me came the day I walked into the bedroom of little Miguel Lopez. His mother, Carmen, had sacrificed her own baby by plunging a nightmarish ritual blade into his tiny chest. That was my last day in Major Crimes.

As a younger man, I was not a fan of the death penalty. My father spent his entire career as a defense attorney keeping scum like Kearcy off of death row. But I believe it was in those moments by the fire that my outlook changed forever, when I looked into the charred, empty sockets that should have nestled two beautiful blue eyes belonging to Amanda Rollins. I never felt rage before like I felt that night. Even the death of my dad didn't elicit such anger. I sought justice that night and believed that justice had been served on a cold platter when that piece of shit, Mark Kearcy, met his demise. He had received the death penalty.

It took several years of appeals, but the day came for Kearcy to meet his fate. I drove all the way to the Florida State Prison in Raiford that day, and watched with gratification as behind the glass the needle was inserted into Kearcy's right arm. He didn't even flinch. That unrelenting twisted smirk was the only expression he showed. He slipped into unconsciousness after the barbiturates were administered. I gleaned great satisfaction after the paralytic was administered and I could see his breathing cease. But the heart monitor still showed a pulse. I couldn't help but feel angst waiting for the coveted flat line that would confirm his death. At long last, the final drug was administered; sweet, sweet potassium chloride. The heart-stopping elixir coursed through the villain's veins as my eyes were fixated on the heart monitor. Finally, it resulted in the desired effect and his heart stopped. At 5:32 a.m., the attending physician pronounced the monster dead.

Leaving the prison that morning, I had a false sense of satisfaction. With the monster now dead, I thought the images in my head would die with him, never realizing that those dreadful images would haunt me forever. All that would be bad enough on its own, but the dread that fate had in store for my future knew no bounds.

Now don't get me wrong, many good things happened to me during this time, as well. As you already know from what you've previously read, I met the love of my life, Meredith Porter during one of the darkest times of my life. Before Meredith, I had no shortage of girlfriends, but no one ever took my breath away like she did. From the moment our eyes met in that courtroom, I knew somehow that we would be together. I believed from our first date that she was my soul mate and that we would be together for eternity.

After we were married, our life was enchanted. Meredith helped make all the nightmares go away. She encouraged me and helped me to achieve my goal of becoming an attorney. When I finally went to work for the District Attorney's Office, I was convinced that nothing could make the happy times disappear. Together, we were on track for a life of real fairytale romance.

We started a law practice together, Carson & Associates. Of course, I was the only associate; she was twice the attorney I ever hoped to be, but it was wonderful to work together.

We determined that it was time to start our family after the practice was established. I suggested that we look for a home before having a baby. The first several house sales all fell through for one reason or another. I can still remember how beautiful Meredith looked when she came home that Saturday from the office. She was so excited. She started to tell me about a house she had found. I went on to the gym thinking to myself that it would just turn out to be another letdown.

I worked out hard that day. I recall being angry about the previous letdowns in our search for a home. I started to feel like a failure, like I was letting her down. I knew she wanted a baby, but I was insistent on having a home first. What a jerk I was. We could have had our baby anytime. I think somehow it all reverts back to my being in control—or thinking I was in control. By the end of my workout, I had spent most of my pent-up testosterone and was relaxed enough to be encouraging when I got home. I didn't want to discourage her anymore.

I can still hear her excitement when I walked in, as she ran up to me, hugging and kissing me and telling all about the research she had done regarding the house. I recall biting my tongue, but I allowed it to slip out that it sounded too good to be true. Undeterred by my pessimism, Meredith continued to ramble on about how everything checked out and she had a good feeling about this one. I agreed to meet with the realtor the next day.

I remembered patrolling that subdivision when I was a deputy, and from the moment we entered the guard gate, I had a queer feeling. The guard who usually stopped anything that moved just seemed to wave us through. I recall how we both thought that was odd.

When we pulled up in front of the house, I was convinced more than ever that this could not possibly be. As we approached the front doors, I reluctantly told her not to get her hopes up and I reminded her of all the previous disappointments. It broke my heart to see her beautiful, joyful visage become more subdued in appearance. I tried in vain to put on a happy façade as we entered the home.

I refused to tell let on that I had a bad feeling when we entered. She introduced me to the realtor, Sam Haines. I will never forget his shabby appearance and bogus smile. When he shook my hand, a chill ran up my spine. Both hands were full of rings; he was wearing that terrible plaid suit and gaudy gold chains. He reeked of Old Spice and cow dung, but Meredith was so excited...

We toured the house without the pleasure of Mr. Haines' company. The first uncanny event happened as we went in the room that was to be the baby's nursery. When we entered the room, I thought I heard a woman's voice that stood out among the throng of others that called out my name. I was immobilized momentarily, but that sort of thing had happened before. I instantly relived that moment in Amanda's room when a similar event had occurred. Meredith helped convince me that I was having a flashback. I convinced myself that it was the whole nursery scene that drew me back to that night.

I hate to admit that by the end of the tour, I did find the house very appealing. We spoke to Mr. Haines and agreed to meet the estate attorney, Mr. Abaddonus.

Now let me stop here for a minute. I know you must be thinking to yourself, how could he not see through the ruse? The truth is, I don't know. Maybe I was blinded by the appeal of the house, perhaps it was my desire to see Meredith happy, or maybe it was the foolish need to believe that all my good deeds were finally coming to a head and this great opportunity would be my reward. I suppose it would be easy to judge me from your perspective. If I had the luxury of reading about my life in a book, perhaps I could have avoided many of the nightmares that awaited me.

But I digress. The day came, and we moved into the house. For the next few months, everything went very well. I never let Meredith know about the bizarre things I experienced, or about the voices that I heard. I was on the landing that overlooked the tile floor in the living room one afternoon, and I noticed a pattern in the grout of the tile. When I looked at it at the right angle, I could see the pattern of what looked like a pentagram. I managed to convince myself that it was just a trick of the light, much like the carpet in Amanda's room. Needless to say, I bought a large area rug for the room that afternoon. Meredith believed I had done it to surprise her. Who was I to tell her otherwise?

I managed to get her pregnant within the first few weeks after we moved in. I, of course, believed that it was perfect timing, and it was, but it was not our timing, as I would soon learn. A prouder mother-to-be you have never seen, I can assure you. I couldn't help but fall more in love with her every day. She radiated excitement, and unlike other women, she was proud to show off her growing belly. I kept the voices in check, thinking all along that I must be suffering from PTSD or some other disorder.

We were home one Saturday afternoon and had just gotten out of the pool when our phone rang. It was Frank and Cynthia. They broke the most exciting news to us that they had just gotten married and had bought the house down the street from us. I won't go into all the grotesque details. It's too hard to recall, but you can go back and read that chapter again if you want.

Needless to say, this was a tragedy beyond what Meredith and I had ever experienced as a couple. That night, the voices were screaming at me. Neither of us talked to the other. We were each grieving in our own way, I suppose. But the voices convinced me that she didn't care what I was feeling. Of course, I know now that's absurd, but the voices were strong. After that night, the voices were clear, as if they were standing next to me whispering in my ears. I kept them suppressed and managed to hide the experiences from Meredith.

The day of our ultrasound was the first happy day we'd had since Frank was killed. I took Merry home and then returned to the office to finish prepping for a case. When I came home, I had bought her some flowers and candy. I remember calling her, and she called down that she was upstairs. I can remember how happy she still sounded. As she was coming down the stairs, she fell. Long story short, we lost the baby.

The first night home from the hospital, Meredith woke up to what she thought was a baby's cry from the nursery. She got out of bed without waking me and went to investigate. I woke up to hear her screaming. I'm not afraid to tell you it scared the hell out of me. I ran to her and managed to convince her that it was all just a bad dream. Boy, if I knew then what I know now, I would have scooped her up and ran out the front door never to return.

Well, I'm here to tell you that the voices were relentless after that. They would barrage me constantly with the idea that she was cheating on me. I know now that she loved me and would never have done anything like that. The first time I confronted her was when she woke up one night and called Cynthia. Of course, she was considerate enough to go downstairs so she wouldn't wake me up. But I awoke anyhow to the sound of a woman's voice telling me, "You fool. She's doing it again. She's talking to him, hiding from you downstairs, in the den."

I sprang out of bed, and to my dismay found a light coming from under the den's door. As I approached the door, I heard her say, "I love you sweetie, I'll always be here for you. I gotta get going now. I don't want Mike to wake up and not find me in bed." I barged into the room as she was getting up, and I started to confront her about who she was speaking to. She innocently told me she had been talking to Cynthia. I recall my blood boiling with rage as she looked at me, in disbelief at my behavior.

A few weeks passed. The voices continued to be relentless. I confronted her on several more occasions about why she was cheating on me and told her that I would eventually find out who it was.

Now friends, please bear with me. The next part is very difficult for me to share. Believe me, I take full responsibility for my actions and I don't look to blame anyone other than myself, but I do hope to clarify a few things for you.

One evening after she had prepared a nice dinner and we enjoyed a movie, we were sleeping in bed. Now, as clear as if you were to speak to me right now, that familiar woman's voice whispered into my slumbering ear, "She's fucking him behind your back. That dirty whore. She killed your baby and now she's fucking another man. You don't deserve that. You know who truly loves you."

My heart sank. I woke up angry and pounced on my innocent wife lying peacefully beside me. I pressed hard on her until she cried out in pain. She was always stronger than I gave her credit for, and she fought her way out from under me. I fell to the floor. You would think by then I would have come to my senses and realized how insane I was behaving, but no. Instead, my anger grew and I chased her down the stairs, where we continued to fight.

That night, we fought like we never had before. She became more scared and tried to leave, assuring me that she was going to her parents' house to allow me time to cool off. We were outside in the front yard, and when she insisted on leaving, I scolded her, grabbed her and forcibly threw her over my shoulder. I then carried her back up the stairs and threw her onto the bed.

Unexpectedly, the doorbell rang. I knew it had to be the cops. I myself had been on the other side of that door hundreds of times. I knew if they didn't hear anything, they would eventually go away. I cupped Meredith's mouth with my hand. My hand covered her face and she could barely breathe. I told her that if she said anything, I would kill her. I don't think I could have ever killed her, but it became apparent that she didn't believe that to be true, and even now I have no idea what was going through my mind.

Before that night, I had never physically harmed her. In fact, I had never touched her in any way other than affectionately. But that dreaded night, everything changed.

During my assault, I saw for the first time ever true terror in my wife's eyes. Her terror was not the result of a stranger's attack or a tragedy unfolding before her eyes. No, her terror was that of a woman betrayed by the man she loved, the very man who had promised to love and adore her for all time; the same man who vowed to always protect her at all cost. Yes, that very protector had turned against her and now was her accuser and attacker.

After it was quiet for several minutes, I knew the cops were leaving. I let go of her and looked out the window to confirm my suspicion. The two deputies were walking away.

I turned around and saw my beautiful wife curled up in a fetal position, crying. Instantly, all the rage escaped me and I was filled with regret for the actions I had taken against this sweet, innocent woman. I moved toward her to console her. However, instead of rushing to my open arms as she had always done before, she recoiled in terror whimpering, "Please don't hurt me!"

This was the lowest point of my life. All the bad and terrible things I had ever experienced culminated into this one moment. This one event was the absolute worst thing I had ever been part of. The loss of my father, the career-ending football injury, the grisly child murders, almost losing Meredith on our honeymoon, losing Frank, and Cynthia's life-altering injury—all were terrible things and any one of these tragedies might make someone snap. But none of those events came close to the heartbreak I felt seeing the terror in my wife's eyes at the sight of me. The precious love of my life, the woman I adored more than anything in this world, was repulsed and terrified of me.

I backed away while professing my sorrow for what I had done. I sincerely started to cry. I remember disconsolately saying, "I'm so sorry, honey. I'm such an asshole. You deserve better!" With that, I turned around and left the room.

As I left the room and closed the door behind me, the accusatory voices returned. "You know what you should do. There's no going
back now. She could never love you again. She hates you!"

I rationalized that the voices were right, and I went straightaway to the linen closet. There was where I kept my prized, short barrel pump shotgun with the pistol grip. I retrieved it and proceeded down the stairs.

Once downstairs, I went first to the bar, where I found an unopened bottle of scotch. I would partake in a few shots of liquid courage before shooting my final scene, no pun intended. Behind the bar, I also found a half empty box of cigarettes. I hadn't smoked since high school. These must have belonged to one of the workers who had come and gone from the house. I figured 'what the hell' and lit one of the cancer sticks, then smoked it on my way to the living room.

The living room was illuminated only by the glow from the bright moon outside. The room was a collage of shadows and reflected bluish moonlight. The tile floor was cold on my bare feet as I made my way to the sofa in front of the large plate glass window. I cracked open my scotch and chugged from the bottle, like a man finding an oasis in the middle of the desert. I paused for a moment to look outside. I could barely make out the silhouette of an old lady on the porch across the street, nosy Mrs. Johansen. Of course, it had been her who had called the cops, who else? I could see the deputy walking back to her, assumedly to tell her everything was fine.

I took up my position on the sofa with my back toward the window, took one last drag on the stale cigarette, then placed the still lit remains on the glass tabletop. One last swig of scotch, and I placed the bottle on the floor by my feet. I remember for a split-second questioning whether or not this was the right thing to do. But the whispering voices and the now half empty bottle of scotch reassured me, "This is the only way. Everything will be fine after this. Just end it, Michael. Come home now."

My thoughts were solely on Meredith. She didn't deserve any of what I had done to her. I loved her more than life itself, and now I would prove it.

I cradled the pistol grip between my legs; the moonlight was glistening off the well-oiled barrel. I leaned forward and inserted the business end into my mouth. The black steel was cold against my lips, and my teeth clanked against the metal. I can recall the taste of gun oil filling my mouth. It was bitter, but familiar. I had learned years before the importance of keeping my weapons cleaned and well lubed. I was quite proficient at keeping all my weapons in good working order. I had no doubt that this prized instrument of destruction would work flawlessly at its appointed time. I can still feel my tears running down my cheeks and into my mouth as the salty taste of the tears mixed with the gun oil.

This was my only chance to make everything right. She could now be free to find someone deserving of her. I was convinced she could never love me again.

My trembling thumb reached down and rested briefly on the trigger. With one last chance to change my mind, the voices whispered relentlessly in my ears, "Come, find the peace you desire . . . come home, Michael."

Five pounds of downward pressure on the trigger, and it would all be over.

The final decision made, my thumb depressed the resistant trigger, that five-pound trigger pull suddenly felt like a hundred pounds. My plan already set in motion, I suddenly heard Meredith cry out, "I LOVE YOU! NO . . . "

Everything slowed down. I could feel the trigger as it progressed halfway through its range of motion. Suddenly, I heard Meredith in the background. "I love you," she said. I immediately made the decision to stop; she couldn't witness this. But the deed was already in motion and the signal from the brain to the hand was not fast enough to stop the trigger traveling just past the point of no return. At that precise moment, I heard the click.

Milliseconds seemingly turned into hours. I can now recall the sensation of heat filling my mouth from the blast of the shell. I can still feel each one of the nine double ought buck pellets penetrating the roof my mouth and the back of my throat. I swear to you I could feel every .33 caliber lead pellet as it coursed its way through my shattering basal skull. Bone fragments and pellets were ripping my brain to shreds, vaporizing my dura, white and gray matter into ten thousand gelatinous projectiles that would paint the window, walls and ceiling of my once serene living room. Then silence.

Now I know what you're thinking— "That's all bullshit!" Well, friend, I challenge you to prove me wrong.

The next thing I remember, I was waking up on the couch. The room was still dimly lit by the moon. I was immediately relieved, convinced that I had been dreaming. I was sure everything I had experienced was just a nightmare and that Meredith was upstairs sleeping or perhaps wondering why I wasn't in bed next to her.

I was startled when he spoke to me. "Welcome home, Michael." From across the room in the maroon wing chair, against the wall opposite from the sofa, there he sat, Mammon Abaddonus, a well-groomed, handsome man who claimed to be old, but I swear didn't look any older than his early thirties. I first noticed his eyes. They were solid black; honestly, there was no sclera. He was wearing a meticulously pressed three-piece black suit with a custom tailored, white shirt. His diamond cufflinks sparkled through the ominous darkness. The red tie and the red rose in his lapel appeared purple in the blue-hued moonlight. His hair was slicked down and neatly parted. He smiled. His teeth were bright and glistened in the low light.

I immediately asked him what he was doing in my home.

"I was summoned here by the lady of the house, Michael. She called me here when she became concerned that you would not fulfill your end of the bargain. We were afraid that you had changed your mind about staying."

I asked him what he was talking about.

"Please don't let me keep you, Michael. She is waiting for you upstairs."

Immediately, I thought of Meredith. I rushed up the stairs calling out, "MEREDITH? MEREDITH!?"

There was no response.

Filled with hope that none of the nightmarish events had actually occurred, I made my way to the top of the stairs. "HONEY?" I called out. It was quiet.

From the baby's nursery, I saw a dim light coming from under the door. I could hear a woman's voice singing an ancient Gaelic lullaby,

"Hush Ye, My Bairnie." My mother would sing it to me as a young boy.

As I neared the room, I could hear,

"Hush ye, my bairnie
Bonny wee laddie
When you're a man you shall follow your daddie. Lift me a coo . . . "

Bewildered, I opened the door.

There she sat. Not my beautiful Meredith, but another woman. Next to her stood Mammon Abaddonus. I was swept back to that summer of 1985. I was looking out my window as a pretty young redheaded girl removed her top. A few weeks later, she was at the bus stop with me, Katie and Sheila, and for no reason started freaking out. I tried to console her and asked if she was all right. She yelled, "NO, YOU FUCKING JERK, I'M NOT OKAY! YOU'RE MY MAN! I GAVE MYSELF TO YOU AND THIS IS HOW YOU TREAT ME? WE WERE SUPPOSED TO BE TOGETHER FOREVER!"

The word "FOREVER" still echoes in my ear.

Now, back in the room, I started to yell, "Sarah? SARAH SHILLING!? WHAT THE HELL ARE YOU DOING HERE IN MY HOUSE?"

She smiled and told me, "Yes, Michael. That's who you remember me as. In my former life I was known by that name, but now you can call me Adrianna. I serve the Supreme One, the almighty and powerful Moloch."

Suddenly before my eyes, Mammon Abaddonus transformed from a well-dressed young attorney into a hideous beast. I recalled from my Greek mythology class that this was a Minotaur, with the body of a man and the head of a bull. I then remembered my research from working the Moloch Society cases that Moloch was a horrific god worshipped by the Phoenicians and Canaanites, a god who required the burning sacrifice of children. He couldn't be real, yet there he was standing before me.

Sarah smiled and said to me, "Welcome home, darling. Come and see your son." The redheaded freak was sitting in a rocking chair on the opposite side of the room, cuddling what appeared to be a blanket-wrapped infant.

Horrified, I began yelling, "NO, NO THIS CAN'T BE! THIS IS SOME KIND OF SICK JOKE!"

Time stood still. Sarah sat motionless. Mammon, or Moloch as he was now presenting himself, spoke up and assured me that this was no joke.

"I am known by many names, Michael. To some I am Satan, to others The Beast or The Serpent. To Sarah and her followers, I am Moloch. When you and I first met, you knew me as Nandi, but for you and Meredith I was Mammon. Through many ages and cultures, I have had many more names, but my favorite has always been The Deceiver."

In his hand was a document. He snorted, "Mr. Carson, as you can see in this document that you signed, you agreed to all the terms."

I cried out, "What the hell are you talking about? I never agreed to any of this. Where's my wife? Where's Meredith? This isn't funny! DEAR GOD, WAKE UP, MIKE! WAKE UP!!!!"

His countenance suddenly changed and he menacingly expressed in a growling voice, "Mr. Carson, this is no joke. I never understand why people don't take the time to read the fine print, especially when they're attorneys. Again, welcome home Mr. Carson." Suddenly he was gone, much the same way he had disappeared from the window of that motel.

I looked up again and Sarah was smiling at me. She said, "Come see your son. I brought him here for us. That bitch you married could never care for him like I can." She then held up a grotesquely undeveloped fetal form. His skin was translucent and I could see his organs. Two black undeveloped dots for eyes blinked blindly at me.

I covered my eyes and screamed out, "No, no, NO! Sarah, NO!

Please wake up, please wake up."

A piercing scream reverberated in my head. "MY NAME IS ADRIANNA!"

I backed up and screamed, "NO, NO, NOOOO!" As I exited the nightmarish room, I slammed the door.

So dear friend, this is to be my hell, trapped in this house with this psychotic evil woman and hellish baby for an eternity.

I can't imagine that I ever did anything to deserve this fate. I beseech anyone reading this, if you know of any way out, please help me. Please, dear God, help me . . . HELP ME! PLEASE HELP ME!!!! HELP ME, PLEASE!!!!

EPILOGUE

JULY 2014, LOUISVILLE, KENTUCKY. A chubby, shy, young loner stares out his window, on the second floor of his bedroom, at the moving van across the street. A new family is moving in. He sees a pretty, young redhead get out of the minivan. She looks across the street as she surveys her new surroundings, giggling at the sight of a cute, young man looking at her. She smiles at him innocently and waves 'hello'.

He swiftly closes his blinds and retreats to the sanctuary of his bedroom to daydream about the pretty, new girl. He thinks to himself, "She would never be interested in someone like me."

About the Author

A first-time author, M. Lee Mendelson and his wife Yvonne have six children between them, three boys and three girls. Yes–the Brady Bunch. He was inspired and encouraged by Yvonne to write his first book after he proposed the concept to her. M. Lee never dreamt of writing anything before his first book, but has now discovered he has a passion for writing, with one idea after another pouring out of him.

A rare native Floridian, M. Lee recently retired from a career as a full-time firefighter and part-time law enforcement officer. His twenty-six years of experience on the streets have given him a vast array of experiences; some good, some bad. He found retirement a bit boring after the first twenty minutes, and he has now embarked on his third career as a fire investigator.

His first book, Epistle of the Damned (adapted from first edition, *Letter from Hell*) is a complex horror/thriller novel with a little something for everyone. M. Lee's real-life experiences, coupled with an active and vivid imagination, allow his stories to come alive. Striving to paint pictures with words, he immerses the reader into his scenes. His ambition is that people will enjoy reading his work and deem it worthy to recommend to others.

MORE FROM CACTUS MOON PUBLICATIONS

What would you die for?

Samantha Danroe doesn't believe in magic. Her ex-husband cured her of happily-ever-after when he cheated on her three days after saying I-do. She doesn't believe in ghosts. Until her mother's ghost rises from a Halloween bonfire with a warning of death from beyond the grave. And she certainly doesn't believe in witchcraft. Until she becomes the prey in an ancient war waged between good and evil. A war whose rules she must scramble to learn to stay alive.

In need of protection, Samantha turns to the mysterious Nicholas Orenda, a sixth-generation witch on the trail of a creature who is systematically killing off his family. According to his family's prophecy, three will be sacrificed to the dark. His mother and grandmother are already dead, and Nicholas doesn't have time to play by the rules.

Samantha finds herself in the center of a deadly hunt for a mysterious foe. Can she find the strength to defeat a supernatural killer and prevent the third sacrifice? Or will she be the catalyst that opens the gates to the Underworld? *Song of the Ancients* is the debut book in the Ancient Magic series. Readers interested in witchcraft, shamanism--or just the dark side of the supernatural world around us--will enjoy this paranormal suspense, written by a real-life Wiccan High Priestess.

www.ingramcontent.com/pod-product-compliance
Lightning Source LLC
Chambersburg PA
CBHW051313250626
47155CB00007B/2298